IF

You're

NOT

the

ONE

Jemma Forte

 sourcebooks
landmark

Published by Sourcebooks Landmark, an imprint of Sourcebooks, Inc.
P.O. Box 4410, Naperville, Illinois 60567-4410
(630) 961-3900
Fax: (630) 961-2168
www.sourcebooks.com

Originally published in 2014 in the United Kingdom by Harlequin MIRA, an imprint of Harlequin Enterprises Ltd.

Library of Congress Cataloging-in-Publication Data

Forte, Jemma.
  If you're not the one / Jemma Forte.
      pages ; cm
  (softcover : acid-free paper) 1. Mate selection--Fiction. 2. Man-woman relationships--Fiction. 3. Chick lit. I. Title.
  PR6106.O7795I37 2015
  823'.92--dc23

2014044566

Printed and bound in the United States of America.
VP 10 9 8 7 6 5 4 3 2 1

For Ross

Prologue

Friday, May 18th

J ennifer Wright slammed the door and ran down the road as fast as her ill-fitting footwear would allow, tears blurring her vision. She didn't care how she looked. All she was conscious of was her need to get away from her husband and his ability to hurt her. Not that he was letting her get away that easily.

"Jen," Max yelled down the road, clearly in no mood to consider what the neighbors might think. "What the hell do you think you're doing? Come back. For goodness' sake, you've made your point."

Jennifer ignored him. If anything, she picked up the pace, wishing it was dark so her escape could go unnoticed. She'd always loved living in the suburbs of South West London, partly because everybody looked out for everybody else. Today, however, it would have suited her far better if she'd lived in a place where people didn't give a damn about their neighbors. That way, she could have wailed like a banshee and charged down the road without worrying she'd provide the man on the other side of the street (the dull husband of the quite nice woman at number forty-two) with a juicy bit of gossip.

She'd caught his look of alarm as he'd taken in her tearstained face and heavy coat, which was far too warm for this unusually warm May evening. Not that there was any way she was taking it off, for what Jennifer knew that the man from number forty-two didn't was that all she had on underneath was a bra, a G-string, garters, and stockings. The killer heels she'd originally teamed with the ensemble had been kicked off midargument, replaced by the footwear that happened to be nearest the front door—a revolting pair of sneakers, usually reserved for gardening purposes. Without woolly socks, her stockinged feet were slipping about inside them.

Panting with exertion, Jennifer came to the end of the street. She turned around to see what Max was doing. She could just about make him out, hanging out of their front door, obviously in two minds about what to do, given that their children were sleeping inside.

Screw him.

Karen. That's who she needed.

Fumbling in her pocket with shaky hands, Jennifer found her cell phone, which she'd had the sense to grab on her way out.

Half walking, half running, she rounded the corner onto the busy main road and scrolled through her phone, looking for her best friend's number. Wiping her face with the back of her hand, she managed to rub away some tears but was surprised by how persistently they kept coming. She acknowledged that there was a huge possibility she was having a nervous breakdown.

As she headed for the crosswalk, she listened to Karen's phone ringing and prayed she'd pick up. She did.

"Oh, Karen," Jennifer managed, speaking loudly against the traffic, choking on tears again.

"Oh my God, what is it? What's wrong?"

The concern in her voice almost floored Jennifer for a second. Thank God Karen's house was only ten minutes away. She couldn't get there soon enough. If only she'd chosen a less-hot coat.

"Oh, Karen, it's all gone wrong, and I just don't think I can do this anymore…" Jennifer broke off, stumbling over an uneven bit of pavement. Wretched shoes. Then a bus whizzed past as Karen answered, drowning out her response, which forced Jennifer to say, "Come again, Karen? I couldn't hear you."

"I said where are you? Do you want to come around?"

"Yes, please," Jennifer wailed, putting one foot out onto the road.

"Good," said Karen. "Well, come by straightaway, and I'll open a…"

But Jennifer never got to hear what her friend was going to open (though if forced to guess, she would have gone with a textbook bottle of dry white wine), because at this point, her phone was flying high up into the air and she was staring at it aghast, wondering why everything had suddenly gone into slow motion. At the same time, although she didn't exactly feel it, she was also aware of the most enormous impact, of a sickening crunching sound, and of the metallic taste of fear, dread, and regret coursing through her body, which was being flung skyward.

For a brief moment, as gravity was about to take command and begin Jennifer's terrifying and brutal descent toward the hood of a Ford Fiesta and the hard ground, she was filled with an illogical yet undeniable sense of embarrassment. For what entered her brain at that precise moment was that whoever came upon the scene was about to discover what she had on under her coat.

And that was the last conscious thought she was to have for a very long time to come...

J ennifer Wright hadn't been sure for a while if she really liked her husband anymore. As a result, she'd been suffering from a sort of creeping, low-lying anxiety for months. The thought of living out the remainder of her days in the suburbs with him terrified her, and she'd lost count of how many times she'd been struck by one solitary thought: *Is this it?*

To some degree, it was less a thought, more a feeling. She was only thirty-eight but felt like she was hurtling in slow motion toward middle age and decrepitude while swept up in an unstoppable snowball of routine, malaise, and domesticity. Lately, she could be in the middle of any number of mundane tasks when, from nowhere, she'd be hit by a strong urge to run barefoot through long grass, dance till dawn (preferably on some form of narcotic), sleep in a yurt, or, failing that, have the sort of passionate, filthy sex with a stranger that would leave her panting and covered in a film of sweat.

But Jennifer was a married mother of two with a slightly boring part-time job who was fully aware not only of how wildly inappropriate these yearnings were, but also how…impractical. There'd be consequences, ones she didn't have the heart to deal with, and besides, these days, if she danced till dawn, it would take her at least a week to recover, and, quite frankly, they couldn't afford the child care.

Is this it? whispered her subconscious again. That it might be freaked her out, to say the least, and often kept her awake at night as her mind swirled.

In a bid to make sense of what she was feeling, she'd even started seeing a therapist from time to time, but so far the sessions had only deepened her confusion. In the end, she'd decided that all she could do was wait things out, try to remain positive, keep taking the Prozac, and not jump out of a window.

Until one Friday evening in May, that is, when Jennifer decided it was time to take matters into her own hands.

All relationships go through patches, she thought determinedly, clipping on her garter belt and manhandling her breasts into her new black-and-red bra. She owed it to herself and to her children to try to make things better. Although she'd been hovering around the notion of what might happen were she and Max to split up, it was too terrifying a prospect to face head-on as an actual possibility. And besides, after eleven years together, she still *loved* Max. It was a shame it was such a familiar, unexciting version of love, which occasionally had the tendency to veer off into violent hatred territory. The fact that they hadn't had sex for over four months wasn't helping matters either.

Feeling surprisingly nervous, Jennifer pulled open her wardrobe door so she could appraise herself in the full-length mirror that hung behind it.

Wow. She hadn't looked this tarty in a long time. The evening sunlight poured through her bedroom window, bathing the entire room in a golden glow, highlighting her cellulite and the fact that they desperately needed a new rug.

At first, Jennifer felt incredibly self-conscious, standing there all trussed up. Eventually she grudgingly admitted that she kind of got away with it. She'd always had an hourglass figure, and these days it was covered by less flesh than it had been even prechildren. In her twenties, she'd taken her figure for granted. Postpartum, however, not only had she realized that she wasn't immortal, but she had also worked out that she was standing at a fairly major crossroads. One way led to elasticized waists, one-piece swimsuits, and never being able to reveal her upper arms again; the other, to still being able to look good in the odd bit from Top Shop, skinny jeans, and the vaguely hateful yet better than frumpy "yummy mummy" moniker. Terrified by the prospect of turning into her mother, Jennifer had jogged purposefully in one direction, started doing yoga, and stopped eating cake.

She peered at her face, wondering vaguely how old a complete stranger would guess she was. There was no denying she was in her fourth decade, yet it was hard to pinpoint exactly what was different about her face now from how it had been in her twenties. Yet that difference was there. She still had friendly, warm brown eyes, but nowadays, when she applied eye shadow, much of it disappeared into a crease she was pretty sure hadn't been there before. Due to her weight loss, she had good cheekbones and her thighs looked good, yet she had to make sure she didn't lose *too* much weight or her face might start to look gaunt. She had faint crow's feet around her eyes and a bit of a frown line that had deepened visibly around the time her babies had become toddlers, at which point there had suddenly been more to frown about. But she had a pretty face and, on a good day, could still scrub up well. She still had sex appeal, could turn a head and be whistled at by a builder, and her wide smile, good, orthodontically treated teeth (*thank you, Mum*), and long, thick head of (dyed) brown hair counted for a lot. But for how much longer was anyone's guess.

Turning around so she could glance back over her shoulder and examine what her bottom looked like in her new, very uncomfortable G-string, she decided that if she squinted, she didn't look *that* far off the girl she'd been when she'd first met Max. *Screw it*, she thought, fired up by a growing sense of confidence. She was old enough and wise enough to know that any normal red-blooded man wouldn't care anyway. Rather than scrutinizing her for imperfections, surely he'd only see the naughty underwear, the effort she was making, the invitation.

She drew the curtains. Better. Direct sunlight and partial nudity were best kept apart. Across the room, her phone was vibrating. She tottered over to it in her heels. The display showed it was Karen, likely phoning to check up on her.

"I feel like a call girl."

"Well," said Karen, "there are probably worse ways to feel when you're about to seduce your husband."

"Oh God," groaned Jennifer, returning to the mirror to examine herself from all angles again. "I'm not sure I can do this. I'm not sure I *want* to do it, truth be told. I've still got this week's episode of *The Apprentice* to watch."

"You have to," Karen said frankly. "Not see *The Apprentice*—though at some point do; it's hilarious—but have sex first. If you don't do it soon, he'll start looking elsewhere."

Jennifer wasn't so sure. Karen had been flabbergasted when she'd admitted how long their dry spell had been and was clearly working on the proviso that no man could live without sex, but then again, Karen was married to a man who woke her up most mornings with something hard jabbing into her back. Whereas these days, Max seemed to have lost his sex drive completely.

"Still on for a drink next Tuesday?" Jennifer asked, changing the subject. It felt weird making small talk while dressed like a sex worker.

"Definitely. I'll try to leave work a bit early, and I think Lucy's coming, but Esther still hasn't gotten a babysitter."

Just then, Jennifer heard the sound of Max's key in the lock. "Ooh, he's back. I'll call you tomorrow."

"Good luck."

Jennifer put her phone on silent, then raced over to the bed and got herself into position. As she did, it suddenly occurred to her that instead of being consumed by lust, Max might find the sight of her trying to seduce him wildly funny. *Oh my God, what if he laughs at me?*

She quickly swerved her mind back to the task ahead, acknowledging along the way that it was probably as much her fault as it was her husband's that they hadn't done it for so long. She was usually exhausted by the time he got home, busy trying to get the kids to bed and looking forward to nothing wilder than a glass of wine and watching some TV. Tonight, however, with the girls at a rare sleepover at their grandparents' house, there was no excuse. They *would* have sex. Being physically close was what was required to lessen the emotional distance between them. She felt quite militant about it.

She could hear Max taking his shoes off downstairs. She waited for him to call to her, but it sounded like he was heading straight for the kitchen. Still, he'd come looking for her soon enough.

Minutes passed. There was no sign of him. Then she heard him leave the kitchen and go into the den. Damn. This wasn't the plan. He was supposed to come upstairs and find her leaning back across the bed like a wanton sex goddess. Then, filled with raging desire caused by her wearing a bra that wasn't flesh-colored and underwear that wasn't from a Target pack of three, he was supposed to leap on her and ravish his way back into an intimate relationship.

Still nothing. Feeling irritated beyond belief, she felt like she had no choice other than to heave herself back up and reach for the house phone, the garter belt cutting into the crevice of her belly. She called his cell phone.

"Hello?"

"What are you doing?" she asked, making a monumental effort to sound less irritated than she felt.

"Nothing. Got myself a beer and I'm watching sports. Why, what are you doing? What are we having for dinner?"

As Jennifer was treated to a crystal clear image in her head of her husband in his usual position—lying on the sofa, caressing his nuts, "relaxing" with the TV on, while waiting for dinner to magically appear in front of him—any vague urge she might have had to sleep with him evaporated. She was a woman on a mission, though. The bra alone had cost forty pounds. She wasn't giving up that easily.

"Come upstairs."

"Do I have to?"

"Please, Max?" begged Jennifer, feeling the last vestiges of sex goddess slip away from her like smoke.

"Can't you come here?"

"Just come for a second, please? I'd really appreciate it."

"Bloody hell, Jen. I've had a long day, and I've only just sat down. Oof, great goal."

Jennifer quietly put the phone down and stared into the distance for a while before slowly peeling off her temptress outfit. Once she had, she shoved it all into the back of her drawer and replaced the expensive underwear with a pair of pajamas before heading downstairs to cook lamb chops, baked potatoes, and green beans, served on a bed of deep resentment.

Later, as she and Max sat chewing on their overcooked chops in front of *The Apprentice*, Jennifer wondered if Max would ever desire or appreciate her body again.

Is this it?

"Good day?" she inquired feebly.

"Er, would be if I could hear what was being said. Why would you speak right over the crucial bit?" He leaned over to get the remote so he could rewind.

Jennifer stared at her husband blankly, watching him ignore her.

In that moment, it hit her that she couldn't bear for things to continue as they were. She was physically and mentally frustrated, unfulfilled by her job, and sad, all of which she might have been able to accept. But she'd also been reduced to one half of a couple who sat next to each other on a sofa, bodies present but souls millions of miles away. And that she couldn't cope with.

Max continued to stare at the TV, oblivious to the maelstrom of potentially life-changing thoughts swirling around in his wife's head, unaware his other half was questioning how all the decisions she'd made in life had led to this bitterly disappointing moment in time.

Meanwhile, Jennifer began plundering the reserves of her memory, something else she'd been doing a lot lately, searching for feelings she longed to relive, for there was enormous comfort to be taken from the fact that, of course, things hadn't always been this way.

The Past

Summer 1994

Aidan

T he alarm beeped, penetrating the deepest of sleeps.

"Jen, wake up. It's already nine o'clock. We've got to get ready, and if you want a shower, you need to hurry. I said I'd meet Mark at the Pink Flamingo."

"Five minutes," Jennifer answered drowsily, idly scratching a mosquito bite on her leg. The whirring of the ceiling fan was in danger of lulling her back to sleep again, so she forced herself to open one eye, enjoying the gurgle of anticipation that was already building in her stomach, despite her groggy state.

They'd arrived on the island of Kos five nights ago after a fortnight of taking it relatively easy on the quieter Greek island of Santorini. Before that, they'd been to Mykonos and Rhodes. There had been the odd moment of tension, but overall, she and her friends had managed five weeks of traveling with no major disagreements and were having the time of their lives. They'd originally planned on visiting a few more islands before heading home, but Jennifer had a strong feeling they'd probably spend the remainder of their trip here, until either their money ran out or their livers packed up, whichever came first. Kos had proved too fun to leave, what with Bar Street (self-explanatory), the outdoor clubs that stayed open till the sun was starting to rise in the sky, the sandy beaches, and the biggest appeal of all—tons of gorgeous men.

They'd all slept with someone, but Jennifer rather regretted her liaison at the beach with a handsome Greek guy on their second night. She knew she'd lived up to the reputation English girls seemed to have, of being easy. By the same token, she'd decided not to lose any sleep over it. She wasn't proud of how little it had meant but still didn't see why girls should feel any worse than guys did about what amounted to nothing more than a consensual exchange of bodily fluids. The only thing that had been slightly awkward was bumping into him from time to time afterward. Neither of them could be bothered to keep up the pretense of interest once the act had been done.

"Can I borrow your red dress, Jen?" asked Esther, emerging from the bathroom in a towel, strawberry-blond hair hanging in damp tendrils around her face.

Since arriving on Kos, the four of them had eased into a routine that consisted of sleeping until midday, at which point they'd force themselves to get up, no matter how much their heads were splitting, for tanning purposes. Then, after an afternoon of roasting themselves at the beach, they'd return to the apartment, shower, slather themselves in more after-sun lotion than was probably necessary, and take a nap—making sure first, of course, that they'd set the alarm so there was no danger of missing out on another night of partying.

Without waiting for a response, Esther bent down to extract the dress, which was rolled in a ball and stuffed in Jennifer's rucksack. But the minute she did, the red dress became exactly what Jennifer wanted to wear that night. Esther borrowing her clothes was starting to get on her nerves, partly because with her long, freckled limbs, Esther looked amazing in all of them.

Esther was the rare sort of girl who actually looked better with no makeup on at all. She wasn't overtly sexy and yet was the most naturally pretty of the group. Back home in London, it was usually Jennifer's more obvious sex appeal or Karen's big breasts that guys noticed. However, while it might have taken their fellow students at college a few glances before they worked out how attractive Esther really was, on vacation, her tall physique and barefaced beauty made her the instant star of the beach.

"Um, sorry, babe, I think I'm going to wear it," Jennifer said sleepily.

Esther tutted. "Shit, what am I going to wear then?"

"Don't know, but hurry up," said Karen, who drew deeply on one of the two hundred Merit cigarettes she'd bought at Kos airport before adjusting her dress straps to heave her considerable cleavage up as much as possible. "I am so up for it tonight."

"Makes a change," teased Jennifer.

"Shut up," said Karen, grinning, teeth white against her brown face.

Normally her deep tan would have suited her, but on this trip, the browner she got, the more alarming she looked. Not for the first time, Jennifer visibly balked at the sight of Karen's hair. When they'd first arrived in Greece, Karen had announced her intentions to go blond with the help of a bottle of Sun-In. As usual, she'd ignored all her friends' protestations, despite that Sun-In was never designed to be used on dark hair. Her reward for being so pigheaded was patches of dodgy orange hair that looked like straw and were brittle and coarse to the touch. It looked horrendous.

Luckily for Karen, her attitude was in her favor. She'd always had incredibly thick skin, meaning it would take more than orange hair to ruin her vacation.

Tonight she'd tried to mitigate the hair disaster by gelling it all back off her face. It looked bizarre, but as ever preferring to concentrate on the positive, she was reeking of confidence due to how good her breasts looked in her minidress. Jennifer admired her for it.

As Jennifer looked at her friends, her best friends, getting ready for their night out, their biggest concern being what to wear, she was filled with the sense that this was a carefree time to be treasured. When they got home, test scores would be waiting for them, and the next stage of education would begin. But for now, they didn't have to worry about anything except getting a tan, a task the girls had applied themselves to with more zeal than they had their exams. Only Lucy, with her pale, almost-translucent skin and mousy blond hair, was still roughly the same color she'd started out, though not for want of trying.

"Do I look all right?" she asked, having slipped on a halter top and a pair of shorts.

"You look lovely," Jennifer said sincerely, lazily stretching one brown leg out over the white sheet she was entwined in. She loved having brown feet. "Those polka dot shorts are really cool."

"Come on," nagged Karen, who was dying to meet up with Mark. She'd met him four nights ago. He was twenty-four, from Liverpool, and worked as a carpet fitter, which had given rise to lots of predictable jokes about Karen getting laid.

"Right," said Jennifer, finally heading for the shower.

———

Two hours, a quick pizza, and one bar later, they were in the best spot on the island, Club Kahlua. The club was huge—and outrageously expensive to get into unless you struck it lucky and got a pass from one of the reps who scouted Bar Street looking for girls to lure inside. Jennifer and her friends hadn't paid to get in once so far, but poor Mark and his friends had had to pay up every night, much to their chagrin.

There was an inside section of the club, but the majority of it was outside, and in the middle was a massive pirate ship surrounded by palm trees. Walking in, having greeted the bouncers who they were on first-name terms with, the girls were met by a wall of house music and what felt like an electrical charge in the air, palpable anticipation. Then again, everything was always going to feel magical when there was a warm breeze, everyone had a tan, and people's biggest concern was who fancied them.

———

"You all right?" Lucy asked Jennifer, coming to join her in one of the outside seating areas where she had a good view of the ship and the main bar. She'd been sitting there for a while, on her own, enjoying the music and watching the world go by.

"Yeah, really happy. You?"

"Good. Bit sad, though. I don't want this to end."

"I know," said Jennifer. "It's been amazing. Still, I reckon uni's going to be a right laugh."

Lucy nodded. "Wish we were all going to the same one. You and Karen are so lucky."

"Look at Esther," interrupted Jennifer, nudging Lucy hard and laughing.

The two girls chuckled as they watched Mark's friend, who for some inexplicable reason was called "Bonehead," trying desperately to chat Esther up. Esther looked unimpressed as Bonehead advanced ever closer to her, shouting in her ear against the music. At the same time, she was backing away, partly because he had a terrible lisp so was spraying her with his enthusiasm.

"Mark's a lovely guy, but his friends are pretty annoying," said Lucy.

"I know," agreed Jennifer. "I feel like we've lost Karen to Mark too, which is a bit of a shame. She's bloody obsessed."

And then they saw him.

"Oh my God," said Lucy. "Are you looking where I am?"

Jennifer certainly was. He was absolutely gorgeous. She suddenly found herself sitting up and angling her entire body in his direction.

He was standing by the bar, to the left of the ship, and was nodding his head in time to the music, watching a group of girls who were dancing next to him. He stood out from the crowd. He was wearing a T-shirt and combat trousers, but his body was that of a demigod, and to Jennifer, he seemed to ooze testosterone, sex appeal, and something more dangerous. His arms were muscular yet lean and brown, and he put Mark and his friends to shame. They were mere boys compared to this prime specimen of manhood.

Just then, he turned and caught Jennifer's eye, and as he did, a number of things happened. First, Lucy realized in a nanosecond she was out of the running. Second, Jennifer sensed that the next few days were going to be very interesting. And third, he gave her such a confident grin that she suspected he was thinking along the same lines she was. It was as if he liked what he saw but, more thrillingly, knew he could have it.

"He's coming over," squealed Lucy, all flustered.

"Oh my God." Jennifer panicked, realizing her friend was right. "I shouldn't have had that slice with pepperoni on it. Quick, Luce, smell my breath."

"Fuck off, weirdo," complained Lucy, shoving her away. "And no, you're fine anyway."

Jennifer stopped breathing on Lucy, pulled her skirt down, and rearranged her legs to look as slim as possible. Then, as he continued his approach, she flicked her long brown hair over one shoulder, realizing as she did how obvious she was being. She flicked it back again but then worried she looked like she was having some kind of attack.

"All right, girls," he said, coming to a stop directly in front of Jennifer. His accent was broad and northern.

"All right," said Jennifer, looking him straight in the eye. This was going to be so much fun.

"Drink?"

Jennifer nodded, her eyes never leaving his. Nerves dissipating, she concentrated on letting him know she was more than a match for him and felt her stomach flip as he grinned again and looked her up and down in a way that could only be described as filthy. Every nerve ending fizzing, Jennifer watched as he returned to the bar, where the line for drinks was three people deep, while Lucy elbowed her excitedly in the ribs.

"Oh my God, oh my God, oh my God," squealed Jennifer, eyes still glued to him.

Unsurprisingly, the barmaid noticed him at once and served him straightaway. She obviously knew him, and the easy way in which he bantered with her made Jennifer wonder what she was getting herself into.

A minute later, he returned carrying three lethal-looking cocktails. Jennifer was pleased he'd gotten one for Lucy.

"Here you go. B52s."

"Thanks," said Jennifer, tossing her hair again and shoving her breasts out as far as she could until she realized Lucy was laughing at her, at which point she returned them to their normal vantage point.

"You're gorgeous," he said matter-of-factly.

"Not so bad yourself," she shot back, thrilled by his flirting.

"Thanks for the drink," said Lucy, giving her friend a large wink and slinking off to leave them to it and find some fun of her own.

During the next half hour, Jennifer learned his name was Aidan, that he'd been on Kos all summer, and that he was the most exciting person she'd ever met. He didn't seem to conform to any rules. He'd left home and was traveling the world, his only real plan being to escape his hometown of Carlisle and live in Australia. They'd already kissed, and it was so charged with sexual excitement, it had blown her mind.

He gently slid his hand up and down her thigh, which tickled in a gloriously shivery kind of way.

"Do you want one?" he asked, pulling a little bag of white pills out of his pocket. He took one out and offered it to her. It had a picture of a dove on it.

"Not sure."

"Your friends can have one too," he said. "I've got plenty and they're very clean."

Jennifer shrugged, determined not to display how much her mind was racing while she worked out what to do. She'd never had ecstasy before, but everyone she knew who had said it was amazing.

"If Karen's up for it, I will," she said, leaving Aidan behind to get her friend who was inside on the dance floor.

Once she knew she was out of his line of vision, Jennifer stopped trying to walk sexily and started galloping toward her friend, gesturing to Karen to meet her halfway. "Aidan's got some E," she shouted into her friend's ear over the deafeningly loud music. "Shall we have one?"

"Oh my God, so not only have you hooked up with the hottest person on the island, he's got pills as well?" Karen shouted back, out of breath from dancing, eyes shining. "You are such a bitch. Why didn't you say earlier? Make sure he gives one to Mark too."

Jennifer nodded and turned on her heel to find Aidan, hoping desperately he wouldn't have disappeared or met someone more interesting during the last forty seconds.

As she made her way back, she decided she should just go with the flow. Her father had always told her that it was better to regret something you'd done than something you hadn't, which sounded like good advice to her, even if he probably hadn't had illegal drugs in mind when he'd said it…

———

One hour later, Jennifer was standing in the middle of the club with her hands in the air, feeling happier than she ever had in her entire life. The music sounded amazing, and there was not one place on earth she'd rather be.

Suddenly she felt Aidan's hands on her shoulders. His touch was firm and felt so good that she staggered a little bit, almost losing her balance. She turned around.

"All right." He grinned, chewing gum, his eyes wide and pupils dilated.

"Yeah" was all Jennifer could manage to utter, but she grinned back at him and it didn't seem to matter in the slightest that she'd lost the power of speech. She couldn't care less. All that mattered was that she was with her best friends and with Aidan, who happened to be the most beautiful man she'd ever seen in her life. She looked over at Karen, who was dancing at one hundred miles per hour, as if someone had told her all human life depended on it, Mark watching adoringly from the side, a daft grin on his face. Meanwhile, Esther and Lucy had kicked their shoes off and were having a chat on the cushions, stopping from time to time to give each other a big hug. God, she loved them all.

"Good, isn't it?" said Aidan.

But Jennifer was too wasted to reply. Her jaw was trembling, and she could feel her eyes rolling back in her head, but she wasn't remotely bothered. Quite the opposite, in fact. Instead, she was relishing every minute of the warm, soupy sensations that were flooding over her.

"Hey, you, you okay? Come and sit down," instructed Aidan.

Happy to do as she was told, Jennifer let herself be led to the cushions where her friends were sitting.

"Jen!" they said as if they hadn't seen her for a week, eyes huge and shining.

"Come here, babe. Love you," said Esther.

"Love you too," she said softly before lying down on the cushions. "Don't you feel like rolling around on these?"

"What?" asked Esther, whose jaw was quivering slightly.

"I said," repeated Jennifer, suddenly desperate for some water, "don't you feel like rolling around on the cushions?"

Lucy nodded. "I do. I feel like stuffing them up my top too and pretending I'm pregnant."

"You girls are funny," said Aidan, head bouncing in time to the beat, and as they bathed in his compliment, it was like they'd known him for years. "Where did you all meet?"

"School," said Esther, looking really out of it.

Karen came whooping over. "Come on, you lot. Come and dance. Jen, on your feet now."

"Too wasted," she managed.

"But happy?" asked Aidan.

"Oh yeah," Jennifer said. "Can I have another one?"

"No, you cannot," said Aidan, stroking her leg as her friends looked on, not knowing whether to be impressed or worried by how well Jennifer had taken to the drug. "I can see I'm going to have my work cut out with you, you little minx."

And that was it. From that sentence forward, continuing in the vein of giving everything little or no real deliberation, choosing instead to be steered only by instinct and desire, as you do when you're young, Jennifer and Aidan were an item.

Present Day

Everything was very, very quiet, apart from the dull, ominous thudding in her head. Jennifer was aware that there was stuff going on around her—commotion, chaos even—but she could only vaguely decipher what any of it was. It all seemed so far away, and she wasn't sure she had the inclination to tune in properly anyway, for instinct told her that if she did, everything would really hurt. Instead, she let herself drift further toward a state of mental limbo, refusing to choose the path of either resistance or acceptance. Something terrible had happened—that was a certainty. Her entire body was like a piece of lead and somehow didn't feel like her own.

A scream pierced the warm, dense fog she was in. It was a guttural, horrifying sound.

"Jen!" yelled the same voice, its tone desperate and distressed.

Karen.

It was Karen.

And then came another voice, one she didn't recognize, telling Karen to stay back, not to touch.

She knew she should probably be feeling more than she was. Doing something perhaps, and yet doing anything was a complete and utter impossibility. She couldn't open her eyes and yet still managed to be dimly aware of flashing lights and, at one point, of someone manhandling her eyelids and asking her things. She wished they'd all go away and let the cloudy haziness enshrouding her to envelope her completely.

While Max went to collect the children from his parents, Jennifer raced around the house, trying to get it into a somewhat fit state. Fed up that her plan to seduce Max the night before had failed so dismally, she was aware she needed to cajole herself out of her despondent mood. Friends were coming for lunch and she was running behind. She wasn't feeling a huge amount of joy that they were coming. They'd had a lot of people over lately, and while it was nice to socialize, Saturdays were starting to feel as structured and routine as the rest of the week, what with the cooking, cleaning, and never-ending washing up and putting away. Still, in reality, if it had been Karen and Pete who were coming over, she'd be looking forward to it a whole lot more. Apart from anything else, Karen wouldn't care if the house was a mess or if Jennifer served up a bit of old spaghetti for lunch.

With Judith and Henry Gallagher, she felt obliged to try to achieve that "I've thrown this magnificent feast together effort- lessly, wearing an unstained silk dressing gown while simultane- ously raising two angelic children in a house liberally festooned with fairy lights" look, which actually requires lots of effort, perspiration, shouting at the children, and some swearing. But then, when it came to Judith and Henry, "friends" was a loose term, and therein lay the problem.

Judith was a work colleague of Max's who was all rightish, except she talked about work incessantly, in a way that tended to make Jennifer feel excluded from the proceedings. With Judith always hogging Max, Jennifer felt obliged to entertain Henry, who was hard work. A quiet, uninspiring, humorless bloke, Henry was one of those people who liked to exist under an umbrella of shyness, as if by labeling himself thus, he was excused from having to make any effort on the conversation front. As far as Jennifer was concerned, though, once past the age of twenty-one, no matter how bloody "shy" anyone was, she felt they should at least pepper a chat with the odd question, thus making it a two-way thing. As it was, whenever Jennifer was doing her bit by talking to Henry, she felt like she was interviewing him.

To add to the already nonenticing prospect of lunch with the Gallaghers, this was the third time in two years she and Max had invited them over for a meal and they'd never returned the invitation. Max insisted it was a good idea for him to "keep in" with Judith, for work reasons. But Jennifer was starting to think it was Judith's turn to spend tons of money at the supermarket on feeding *their* faces and that perhaps she didn't give a shit if they "kept in" with her or not.

Having finally finished tidying downstairs, even going so far as to squirt a bit of polish on the coffee table so at least the room *smelled* clean, she started on the children's bedrooms. By the time she'd gotten to her and Max's room, she'd lost steam and was over-whelmed by the prospect of still having to produce a meal for four adults, three children, and a baby. So after she'd stuffed everything that was on the floor into the laundry basket, she stopped for a second and sank onto the bed, taking advantage of the unusual silence. As she did, the disappointment from the previous evening washed over her once more, and she found herself wondering when and indeed *if* she should try her new underwear again. After all, Max wasn't psychic, so to be fair to him, how could he have known what she'd had in mind? If she'd been serious about having her wicked way with him, she probably should have gone downstairs and shown him what she was wearing, because if he'd had the visual stimulation, she suspected he would have gone for it. So why hadn't she done that?

She sighed. Marriage. It was such bloody hard work sometimes. "Make an effort" was all anybody said, and it *was* an effort. That was the problem. She missed the days when being with each other wasn't any effort at all, the days when *not* being together were the ones that felt like the effort.

Jennifer willed herself to get up and continue her attack on the house, but it wasn't happening, mainly because her thoughts had turned to a subject that had been occupying her mind a lot lately. Sex. Or rather, her lack of it. As soon as she allowed the thought in, she felt a lurch of possibility in her nether regions.

The next thing she knew, despite the potatoes desperately need-ing peeling if lunch had any hope of being served for one o'clock, her hand had slid into her underwear. Right, she needed to be quick, so who should she think about? Aware that time wasn't on her side, she turned to an old favorite, though part of her detested that she was still dining out on sex she'd had nearly twenty years ago. However, when it came to fantasy, Aidan was still guaranteed to get her going. And fast.

Once again, Jennifer returned to a hot, airless room, which had a bed with a squeaky mattress and a ceiling fan, and replayed the best sex she'd ever had. Images of brown limbs entwined and his strong, hard body pressing into hers, maneuvering her into positions she hadn't even known existed, swam into her head. An enjoyable three minutes later, her very old flame was on the brink of giving her an almighty orgasm when she became dimly aware of the key turning in the door downstairs. She couldn't believe it…

"We're back," called Max up the stairs.

"Muuuuummy," two little voices yelled in unison, feet charging up the stairs.

Jennifer gasped. "Shit," she said, withdrawing her hand and springing into an upright position, feeling utterly frustrated. Five seconds more and she'd have been there. "Hello-o," she called back with a slight screech. "Have you had a lovely, lovely time, kids?"

As she leaped up from the bed, she experienced a bit of a head rush. She quickly patted her hair down and did her jeans up, legs feeling a bit wobbly.

The children barreled in. "Mummy!"

"Hello, my little loves. How are you?" she warbled. "I've missed you. Were you good for Grandma?"

"Yes," said Eadie, sounding slightly lispy. She was seven and had recently lost four teeth in quick succession.

"What about you, Pol?"

"Yes," her youngest agreed, though she seemed more interested in trying to get her T-shirt off.

"What are you doing?"

"I need a wee."

"Okay, well, you don't need to take your top off to have a wee, do you? Come here."

"Jen," Max called up the stairs. "What the hell have you been doing? You haven't peeled the bloody potatoes. They're going to be here soon and nothing's ready. You haven't even set the table."

Jennifer rolled her eyes so vigorously they actually hurt. "Well, feel free to go for it."

"All right, there's no need to be sarcastic about it. It's just you said you'd get things under control while I got the girls, and nothing's done."

"All right," said Jennifer testily, stomping onto the landing and into the bathroom so she could plonk Polly on the toilet before heading downstairs.

She found Max in the kitchen, peeling potatoes angrily. Whole chunks were coming out.

"I'll do that," she said, trying to grab the peeler from him.

"No, it's fine. I'm doing it."

"What are you so grumpy about anyway? Is it that much of a big deal that little wifey hasn't done everything by the time you got back?"

"Little wifey hasn't done anything, let alone everything," muttered Max.

"Oh, rubbish," disagreed Jennifer. "The house was a complete state, if you must know, and besides, I'm getting a bit sick of having people over every single weekend when we don't even enjoy it."

"Yes, we do," said Max, shooting her a look of real disdain.

"No, we don't," she replied petulantly, simultaneously acknowledging that they were sounding like their children.

"We do," said Max, oblivious.

"Oh yeah, we're having a great time preparing for the arrival of smug, 'high-powered' Judith and dullard Henry. And it goes without saying I can't wait to spend the rest of the day washing up after them while you kiss her ass," huffed Jennifer.

Max wrinkled his nose at her choice of words, which made Jennifer giggle and broke the tension a little.

"Muuuuuuuuuuuum," yelled Polly from upstairs. "I've got wee wee on my sock."

"Yours," said Max.

Jennifer tutted before turning on her heel, wondering if she'd get away with quickly locking herself in the spare room so she could finish what she'd started earlier. Probably not.

Half an hour later, the doorbell rang. Taking a deep breath and summoning up a smile, Jennifer opened the door.

"Hello, everybody, come in, come in," she said, ushering them all into the house and down the hallway. "It's so lovely to see you all. Oh my, look at James. Hasn't he grown and doesn't he look *so* like you, Henry?"

"He's a chip off the old block all right," agreed Judith, immaculate as ever in tasteful navy, which she'd offset with funky "weekend" jewelry and ballet pumps. "No questioning who his dad is."

Jennifer agreed, because James really did look exactly like Henry, except given he was only ten years old, looking like a gone-to-seed, middle-aged man wasn't necessarily a good thing. "So how was your journey?" Jennifer inquired brightly, snapping out of her reverie before anyone noticed her staring.

"Fine," said Judith, kissing her on both cheeks and handing her a bottle of wine. "Sorry we're a bit late. Work's been sooooo manic I simply had to have a bit of a chill out this morning. I bet Max did too. We've been working like Trojans this week."

"I can imagine," Jennifer said, wanting to punch her.

———

An hour and a half later than planned, lunch was finally on the verge of being served.

The children were all starving despite having been fed various "just to keep you going" snacks and were getting fractious. Judith and Henry had polished off two entire bags of kettle chips and had already had an argument about who was driving home. Oscar, their eighteen-month-old baby, was sleeping upstairs, and they were well into a third bottle of wine. Meanwhile, Max was sucking up to Judith so much it was making Jennifer's skin crawl. She herself was worryingly tipsy given that she still had to get lunch on the table.

As Judith roared with laughter at yet another dull work anecdote of Max's, Jennifer flinched. The way Max was giving her his undivided attention was grounds for jealousy, only she couldn't be bothered to make a fuss. Instead, she felt saddened that every time she tried to join in with a vaguely witty remark, he barely looked in her direction. Perhaps she should get her tits out, she thought wryly, and run around the kitchen with them jiggling about.

With little enthusiasm, Jennifer replenished the chip bowl (this time with Doritos and Cheetos instead of fancy kettle chips—it was all she had left). As she did so, she smiled weakly at dull Henry, who sat on a stool by the island like a fat, useless turd. She was about to ask him yet another question about how his work was going when she realized she didn't care and couldn't be bothered. So, instead, she turned her back on him and bent down to open the oven to investigate what might be happening in there. As boiling-hot air blasted her in the face, she realized she was 100 percent, without a shadow of a doubt, drunk.

She was also glad, and a little bit smug, that for once she'd cut corners by picking up (on Karen's recommendation) some small stuffed chickens from the local deli. Not having to cook a meat dish of some description meant all she'd had to do in theory was make the roast potatoes and cobble together a salad. So why did it all feel as stressful as though she'd been preparing a banquet for eighty under the same conditions as the *Top Chef* final?

Seconds later, she emerged from the oven once more, red in the face, sweating and clutching the ludicrously heavy tray in an oven glove only to realize that the island needed clearing before she could put it down.

"Max," she called over to where he was deep in conversation with Judith about something tedious. "Max!"

"Hey, there's no need to yell. What is it?" he asked, trying to sound like he wasn't snapping when that was exactly what he was doing.

"Sorry," she said, not sorry at all. Her hands were practically on fire. "I was wondering if you could clear a space for this. It's very heavy." She grimaced.

"Oh, right," he said, finally realizing her plight.

Once she had dumped the tray on the island, Jennifer lifted the little chickens out and put them on the chopping board. They were less chickens, more parcels of poussin, tied up with string and stuffed with pork and herbs. Jennifer decided she wouldn't bother passing the meaty creations off as her own. After all, she'd never boned a piece of meat in her life and had certainly never been bothered to tie up anything you could eat with string.

"Ooh, those look wonderful, Jennifer," said Judith, gliding over to have a look at what she was about to stuff her self-satisfied face with. "Aren't you lucky, Max? That's what comes of having a wife at home who's got time to create things like this. Poor Henry is lucky if I remember to buy him a ready meal, aren't you?"

"I do work," Jennifer said a bit defensively.

"Do you?" Judith asked, looking first surprised and then apologetic, as if she'd just realized her error. "Oh God, of course you do, and it goes without saying that looking after children is probably the hardest job of all. I certainly wouldn't have had another if I'd had to stay at home and look after them," she exclaimed, and loud enough for her offspring to hear, which suggested to Jennifer that they'd likely need therapy in the future.

"No, I mean, I do work. I have a job," explained Jennifer. "*And* I look after the kids. I work at a real estate agency three days a week."

"Oh God, brilliant," said Judith lamely. "That must be really fun."

Jennifer picked up the carvers and tried not to look menacing. She really needed to eat.

"Those look good," said Henry, ambling over.

"Right, well, why don't you all sit down?" Jennifer said, wanting them out of her face while she plated up. "Judith, get the kids to sit down. We'll do their plates first."

"Oh, right," she said, looking startled at having been asked to do anything.

But Jennifer didn't care. She was too busy trying to figure out if the chickens were cooked through. To her alarm, they looked a bit pinky inside and, well, unappetizing.

"So, what's that then?" Max asked, also looking mildly alarmed by the color of the meat.

"Oh, that's just the pork they're stuffed with. Don't worry. It's supposed to look like that," Jennifer assured him, wondering if a night on the toilet lay ahead for them all.

"They don't carve very well, do they?" Max whispered.

Jennifer gazed hopelessly at the chickens, which had sort of collapsed in on themselves and were looking less and less appealing by the second. Sort of like gray and pink mush.

"Just get it on the plates," she muttered, feeling deeply stressed and too drunk and hot to handle the situation. She was pretty certain it was just the pork stuffing that was lending them that strange hue, but she was past caring, though she did add as an aside, "But make sure you give the kids the bits from around the outside."

Once the children had all been given their plates of food (which they unanimously declared they didn't like before having even tried it) and their drinks (one glass of juice being knocked over immediately, as tradition required), the adults got on with helping themselves to lots of salad and potatoes.

"You didn't make these yourself, did you?" Judith asked Jennifer, looking worried as she surveyed her plate of unidentifiable meat.

And here it was, crunch time, time for Jennifer to explain that no, of course she hadn't made them, and that yes, they did look a bit weird, didn't they? And this answer was on the tip of her tongue, but for some reason known only to the inner machinations of her befuddled brain, that isn't what came out.

Instead, what she experienced in that moment might well be what happens to mass murderers when they hear voices telling them to do things. To put it another way, the normal Jen, who usually prided herself on being down-to-earth and who hated making other women feel inadequate, temporarily disappeared. The new replacement version of Jen felt so belittled, she found herself battling with the desire to scream into Judith's smug face that she had a very good university degree and giving up her career to raise the kids had been a choice (albeit one she struggled with sometimes) so should not be sneered at. This, coupled with the fact that she was exhausted, in need of a vacation and sex, suffering from a monumental midlife crisis, and had been prescribed anti-depressants only a few weeks earlier, meant that when her reply eventually did come, it was very out of character.

"Yes, I did… I made them."

At the other end of the table, Max looked baffled and stared at his plate.

"Wow," said Judith tentatively. "They look really…complicated. How did you go about it?"

"Well," Jennifer said gingerly, suddenly feeling drowned by her own lie. "I...er...bought them, boned them...and then stuffed them with pork and herbs before...kind of tying them up."

"Right," said Judith, and in that moment, Jennifer knew Judith knew she was talking absolute nonsense.

"Mum," piped up Eadie, looking miserable.

"Yes, darling," said Jennifer, teeth gritted. "What is it?"

"I don't like my beef. It tastes like cat poo. Can I have some toast?"

"It's chicken, not beef, and it's *please may I have* some toast?" replied Jennifer.

"Please may I have some toast?"

"Yes." Jennifer sighed faintly. "Anyone else?"

For a second, Max looked sorely tempted but soon readjusted his expression when Jennifer glowered at him on her way to the toaster.

The rest of the meal was pretty torturous. Only Henry seemed blissfully unaware that he was eating something that resembled roadkill. Everyone else performed a sort of cutlery ballet around their plate, consuming lots of potatoes and salad and expertly leaving a pile of pinky-gray mush to one side with either their knife and fork or a napkin placed cunningly over the top.

After the meal, Jennifer cleared away, scraping tons of discarded meat into the food recycling bin. As she did so, she wondered at what point she'd become so sad and pathetic that she couldn't admit that she hadn't made the disgusting food herself and that none of them should have touched it in case they all got the chronic shits. When had she become the sort of person who cared what people like Judith and Henry thought, anyway? When had she transformed into such a middle-class stereotype, desperately trying to impress? When had she turned into Max's mother?

Much later that night, as she climbed gratefully between the sheets, head thumping with a same-day hangover, she said to Max, who was already half asleep, "The chicken was a bit weird, wasn't it?"

"It was all right," he said, his eyes shut and his body turned away from her. "It just looked a bit like cat food. Why did you say you'd made it?"

"Don't know," she replied truthfully, staring at the ceiling, hot with embarrassment just thinking about it.

"You did yourself a disservice anyway," he added. "Your cooking's far nicer, and I think Judith doesn't cook much, so it's not like you needed to compete. She works too hard to ever get around to doing any domestic stuff."

"Oh, so now you're having a go at me for not making something, are you?" she retorted defensively, gradually feeling more and more embarrassed that she'd passed off the stupid, dodgy-looking chickens as her own creations. Her tone wasn't helped by the fact that the mere mention of Judith's name was starting to send shivers up her spine.

"No." He sighed, clearly wishing she'd shut up and go to sleep. "I'm giving you a compliment on your cooking, but I'm also saying I think they knew you hadn't made it anyway."

"Really?" she asked. Despite that she'd figured this out on her own, having it confirmed was mortifying, to the point where yet another bad night's sleep was likely in the cards. "Why?"

"Because you went weird and replied really slowly, so it was obvious."

"Oh God, I'm so strange," she whimpered. "The thing is I'm very tired, you know."

"I know," he said, and with that he fell fast asleep, as he had an annoying habit of doing when he was tired, leaving his wife to ponder in the darkness that lying hadn't achieved anything. In fact, it was clear to her that the only thing she'd stuffed by doing so (and it certainly wasn't the chickens) was herself.

Perhaps the whole debacle was a sign that she needed to be more honest about a whole load of things.

Two hours later, bored of her insomnia, head whirring, Jennifer slipped out of bed and crept into the spare room. Able to spread out, she tried to relax and then decided to finish what she'd started much earlier in the day in the hope that a good, healthy orgasm might help her get to sleep. And so it was that she returned to that hot summer back in 1994 when, unlike now, food was of little or no consequence to her or her friends because they'd had far more interesting things to worry about.

The Past

Summer 1994

Aidan

"Come with me," said Aidan, the green eyes she'd gotten so used to boring into her, pleading with her. "I know we've only known each other five minutes, but what we've got doesn't come along every day. I'm telling you."

"How can I come with you?" repeated Jennifer, who was in complete turmoil. Something was pulling her, like a magnet, telling her to throw caution to the wind, to follow her heart, or, more accurately, her loins. She and Aidan had barely come up for air since they'd met, and Jennifer had never known anything remotely like it. She knew she was relatively inexperienced on the sex front, having only slept with three people (actually four—she kept forgetting the Greek guy on the beach), but Aidan had made her feel things she hadn't dreamed were possible. In bed, they made total sense together, and as far as she could tell, he was also an exciting person, someone who was creating his own path in life, one that wasn't constrained by parental pressure or some traditional idea of how things should be played out. That was the problem in a way. Jennifer had always *liked* knowing how things should map out. It had never occurred to her to stray even slightly from the plan she and her parents agreed was the right one for her. The right one for most people.

School, a part-time job, traveling. Next on the list was university, followed by career, marriage, babies. That was life. Wasn't it?

And yet here was someone asking her to go completely off the beaten track. And she was actually tempted. Sorely tempted. She was pretty sure she loved Aidan—or was on her way to falling in love with him—and knew if she let him go, she might regret it forever. The thought of never sleeping with him again, and therefore not experiencing that unbelievably exquisite pleasure, was unbearable too. She licked her lips and stared down at her green flip-flops.

"Look," said Aidan, "I'm not going to beg. That's not my style. And if you say no, I guess I'll understand, though I think you'd be making a massive mistake. Like I said, what we've got is special. I know it is, and besides, what's the worst that could happen? I'm asking you to come away with me, but I wouldn't be kidnapping you. If it didn't work out, you could just get on a plane home."

"But my university acceptance…?" questioned Jennifer, wondering if she could deny herself the opportunity to be with him when he'd turned her entire world upside down in a matter of days. University was something she'd always wanted to experience, but he was right. She could always change her mind, so maybe she needed to be more adventurous? But as this thought trailed away, it was replaced by the feeling of absolute certainty that her parents would be beyond livid with her for being so irresponsible and for not consulting them. Then again, it was her life. She was so torn.

"Look, the boat leaves in half an hour. I'm going to be on it," said Aidan. "If you're coming with me, you need to say good-bye to the girls and get your stuff. What's it going to be?"

"Oh God," said Jennifer. "I don't know."

And for the next ten minutes, she still didn't.

And then she had a chat with Karen, who looked at her with such horror that she was even contemplating the idea of going off with someone she'd known for a total of seventeen days that something took over. Something irritatingly sensible.

And so it was that the boat departed, taking Aidan off for adventure and ultimately Australia.

She may have made what she thought was the right decision, but that didn't prevent Jennifer from feeling utterly desolate and distraught. She wailed as the boat sailed into the distance and at one point contemplated throwing herself off the jetty and swimming after it. Anything to feel those arms around her once more. What had she done, and would she regret it for the rest of her life?

Present Day

*S*tay with us, Jennifer. Come on, love, you can do this. Hang in there."

Why was everyone yelling? She was so tired. All she wanted to do was sleep. She was so close to being able to slip away, yet wasn't being *allowed* to. She felt very muddled and had a vague sense of being bullied.

"Patient's suffering agonal respirations and has a CO_2 of eleven. Probably in anaphylactic shock. Let's commence CPR."

"Jen, please hang in there. I'm so, so sorry. I love you."

"Sorry, Mr. Wright. Can you stay out of the way? It's very important."

What is Max doing here? she wondered. For a second, she was tempted to open her eyes, but she wasn't able to because a burning sensation swept through her so violently, she would have done anything to make it stop. It was pain on a level she never would have thought possible. Every cell in her body was on fire, doused in hot, white agony. Then, as quickly as it showed itself, it subsided, and once again she reverted to her numb state of nothingness.

Then someone was applying pressure to her that hurt in a different way. She didn't want to be awake anymore. She craved peace and sensed a way she could achieve it. It would definitely remove the pain, and any further possibility of it.

But she wasn't sure she wanted to go that way either. She reflected for a second, as though she were suspended in time and space, floating almost. She wasn't ready for that, which meant there was only one option left. So, once more, she sank back into the gray fog, more cries of panic sounded around her.

As the paramedics went about their frenzied business of trying to save her life, the strangest things were happening in Jennifer's bruised brain.

None of us can really comprehend what the human brain is capable of doing, in the same way that Jennifer had no clue as to the true capabilities of her laptop. All she tended to use her PC for was to write emails, do a bit of shopping, or social networking, meaning its dual core processor was never fully taken advantage of. She was always stunned when Max, who was far more tech-savvy than her, did some simple task on her computer in a way that made her realize she was only ever utilizing around 10 percent of what it could do, if only she knew how to operate it properly.

It's the same with the human brain, only on a far grander and more mysterious scale, its true power being so tricky to tap. Most of its work and activity happens at a deeply subconscious level, and yet even beyond that, there are areas of it that we never unearth, even when dreaming.

Psychics do better than most. Whether you believe in them or not, they at least have more awareness of the various possibilities that we *could* utilize if only we tried.

Right at that second, within Jennifer's skull, a series of lightning-fast connections were being made, ones that she never would have been privy to if her head hadn't made contact with the ground quite as brutally as it had. Something extraordinary was happening.

As her synapses furiously connected and fused, three tunnels of white light suddenly showed themselves to her. There was one to the left, one straight ahead, and one to the right. *Is this what death looks like?* Instinct told her it was something different, and suddenly she knew, without needing to be told, that rather than leading her to the afterlife, instead, these tunnels represented different lives she could so easily have led.

What she was being given here was a gift. The gift of being able to see what life would have been like had she chosen another route at three different points in her life. And so it was that Jennifer allowed herself to fall into a deep and very informative coma. As her own private miracle started, she began to glide toward the first tunnel, the one to the left, which was swirling with clouds of light at its entrance. This was the one marked Aidan.

TUNNEL NUMBER ONE
What Could Have Been—Aidan

Jennifer slipped out of bed and padded across the room to pull the curtain back. Sunlight poured in, and though it was still early, she could feel the heat of the day penetrating the glass. She gazed out at the view, loving the way the sea glinted and twinkled through the gaps in the rooftops. Their little one-bedroom apartment in the bayside suburbs of Brisbane was very basic, very compact, but it was also only a twenty-minute walk from the beach.

She opened the window a fraction and breathed deeply. Then she tipped her face back and let the strong rays bathe her skin with their warmth.

It was strange getting up every day knowing it was going to be hot and that the sky would almost always be blue. She'd always considered herself a total sun worshipper, but having been away from home for so long, the sense of urgency to get out there and work on her tan had faded. Sometimes, she found the constancy of the temperature a little relentless, a tad monotonous, to the point where she'd recently found herself craving a bit of gray sky. This was ironic, given that she had always been the first to moan about the abysmal climate in England, and yet what she missed about the British weather was that subtle change of seasons. Nothing beat a glorious, breezy spring day or that first sniff in the air that told you autumn had arrived, when the light became more golden and the leaves were falling from the trees, crunchy and brown.

"Hey, sexy."

"Oh, you're awake," she said, turning around to see Aidan grinning at her from the bed. He was brown, toned, and fit from all the hours of running on the beach he was doing most days. She still felt a lurch of desire every time she set eyes on him.

"Yeah, funny that, given that you've pulled the curtains wide open. Now, seeing as you've woken me up, get your sexy bum over here," he said, eyeing her greedily in her small tank top and underwear.

"I know what you're after." She grinned back at him, knowing full well he'd have a raging hard-on. He woke up with one every morning. In that way, he was a bit like the Queensland weather—predictable.

"Just shut up and come here," he said, flinging back the sheets to reveal she was right.

Not needing to be persuaded, Jennifer approached the bed and succumbed to half an hour of intense passion. Before Aidan, she hadn't been aware of ever having such a voracious sexual appetite, but he'd awakened something inside of her that she supposed must have been lying dormant before.

After what was, as ever, mind-blowing, energetic sex, they both lay flat on their backs panting, sweating, sated.

"You're amazing," Aidan said, idly tweaking her left nipple.

"So are you," she replied. "Seriously amazing."

"Love you," he said, hugging her tight. As he did so, Jennifer marveled at how safe he made her feel. The chemistry between them was something she doubted could ever be replicated with anyone else, to the point that sometimes they were almost savagely passionate with each other. She didn't think there was anything she wouldn't be prepared to do with him physically, and as a result, she had never felt so confident in her own body or so empowered, knowing the effect she was capable of having on him.

"Are we going to the beach then?" asked Aidan.

"Not the building site?"

"Nah, that can wait. It's too much of a scorcher. Maybe tomorrow?"

"Okay," she agreed, flopping over onto her side so she could get up and start getting the beach bag ready.

And then the phone rang.

"Can you get that?" Jennifer asked lazily, then regretted it a second later when she remembered it would probably be the scheduled phone call she'd arranged with her parents before they retired to bed on the other side of the world.

"Yup, here she is," Aidan was saying in an unfriendly tone that confirmed it was them.

Jennifer sat up and reached over for her tank top, which she pulled over her head before taking the phone from him. It was such a small apartment that there wasn't anywhere for her to go where she could talk without Aidan listening in, so rather than standing up in the tiny kitchen, where he'd be able to hear every word anyway, she stayed where she was. Never having any privacy did get to her sometimes.

"Hi, Mum. How are you?"

"Oh, all right," said the familiar voice, made tinny from the distance.

Jennifer pictured her parents, sitting by the phone together, probably ready for bed in their dressing gowns, in the den with the radiators blasting.

"What have you been up to this week, Jen?"

"Oh, this and that," she replied. "Working, bit of beach action. You know. The usual, really."

"I thought you were going to that Surfers Paradise place."

"Oh yeah, we were, but we didn't in the end," said Jennifer, turning around so she had her back to Aidan. He looked grumpy, like he always did when she chatted with her parents. It was getting on her nerves.

Three months ago, at exactly the time her parents had been expecting her to be landing at Gatwick, back from her vacation with the girls, Jennifer had called them to break the news that she'd decided to throw caution to the wind and take an unplanned gap year. In Australia.

To say they'd been furious had been an understatement. Her father had shouted and her mother had wept, though it was less that she wasn't coming home and more that it was because of a man they hadn't met.

Their reaction had been *so* bad that Jennifer had considered giving up on her adventure altogether. She had thought it might be best to admit defeat and head home, tail between her legs. She'd been about to tell them she was sorry when her mother had interjected with, "One whiff of male attention, and you go and lose your head, Jennifer. It's pathetic, when you think about it."

That one comment changed everything. At that point, Jennifer's mood had switched from apologetic and shamefaced to resolute and determined. She'd been insulted by her mother's accusation and had said as much to Aidan when she'd gotten off the phone a few minutes later.

She'd left him drinking a beer and smoking a cigarette at a dusty roadside café in a busy square, and as she'd approached, it was obvious to her that despite trying to appear nonchalant, he was really nervous.

"What happened?" he'd shouted across the street to her as soon as she was in earshot.

"They went bloody mad," she called back. She jumped as a moped whizzed past, almost knocking her off her feet.

Gathering her wits and checking left and right, she finally reached his table, mind whirling as she tried to comprehend her conversation with her parents.

She'd always hated confrontation and had managed to avoid too many quarrels with her fairly conservative parents up until this point, which was partly why she was so livid. How dare her mother talk to her like that? Like she was some stupid, desperate tart who was so needy of male attention she'd do anything to get it. She'd never given them any cause for worry or upset in the past, and yet deviating off the path the slightest bit, they didn't have the patience to at least try to understand her reasons. Yes, Aidan had been a massive part of her decision not to go home, but that was life. You meet people and things happen. It seemed ridiculous for them to have formed an opinion of him already. It was so unfair. They gave her no credit whatsoever.

"So what's the score then?"

"I said I'd call back in ten minutes so we could all cool off," she'd replied, avoiding his stare.

"And?"

"Oh, I don't know," she'd replied truthfully, feeling unbelievably torn. "They're really mad at me, Aidan, and it was awful hearing them so pissed off. Plus, Mum's desperately worried that if I defer, I might lose my place altogether."

"Well, she would say that, wouldn't she?" suggested Aidan.

Jennifer shrugged, doubtful her mother was that manipulative. "I'm so thirsty, I almost feel faint. Have you got enough money for me to get a beer?"

"Yeah, go for it," said Aidan, pulling some ancient drachma notes out of his pocket and signaling to the waiter.

A few minutes later, once Jennifer had had the chance to glug back some of her cold lager, he inquired again. "So what's it to be then, babe? Sunshine, the land of opportunity, and some hot romance with me? Or back to Mummy and Daddy and the rain?"

"I don't know," Jennifer replied honestly. She felt conflicted and a bit stupid. She'd probably been deeply deluded, thinking her parents would accept her reasoning for ducking out. Plus, deep down, she didn't want to throw away her chance to go to university, even if it meant admitting she'd been rash. Their fury had really knocked her, though, and treating her like a child made it harder for her to decide what to do.

Realizing she needed time to think, Aidan dropped the subject, so they sat in tense silence, watching the world go by, until Jennifer got up. "Right, there's no point putting it off. I'd better go ring them back."

As she marched back across the busy road to the phone booth in the center of the square, her head was spinning. What should she do?

Her father answered. "I hope you're phoning to tell us you've seen sense."

This wasn't a good start in terms of making her feel like returning to the bosom of her family.

"I've phoned to discuss things like an adult," she responded.

"Well, that's a start," he said. "In that case, surely you can see that running off with some good-for-nothing beach bum, while ruining your life in the process, is entirely the wrong thing to do?"

It was a shame he'd taken that approach. It was a shame he hadn't simply asked her how she was, because he might have gotten a very different response, and the conversation may have played out another way.

As it was, three days later, Jennifer and Aidan boarded a plane to Australia, and although she experienced an underlying sense of panic, the fact that she was proving a point to her parents had become enough to prevent her from changing her mind.

If relations had been bad at that point, they'd taken a turn for the worse when she called them from Sydney, where she and Aidan stayed for the first few weeks before heading to Queensland, at which point her furious father had demanded to speak to her boyfriend. At first, Aidan had refused, which had made Jennifer feel very uneasy. Eventually, however, sensing that Jennifer was going to freak out, he'd acquiesced, albeit reluctantly. Her father had given him short shrift, venting all his frustrations and feelings of helplessness at the person he held responsible for his daughter's unfamiliar behavior.

Aidan hadn't appreciated being yelled at. Rather than taking the reprimanding on the chin, he'd retaliated with a few barbed insults of his own.

A few months on, things had calmed down a bit, but no matter how much Jennifer had tried to explain that Aidan had only been sticking up for her, her parents hadn't budged. Meanwhile, Aidan had refused to understand that they were only being protective and were worried about their daughter.

So here she was, having yet another awkward conversation with them while Aidan glowered and sulked next to her.

"So why didn't you go to Surfers Paradise then?" her mother asked in a way that sounded accusatory to Jennifer.

"Because we decided to go another time," she lied. In reality, they couldn't afford to rent a car—or go at all—but she certainly wasn't going to tell them.

"Hmm. Well, it seems a shame, since you're there, not to be seeing anything except Brisbane," her mother remarked pointedly.

Jennifer swallowed, determined not to have another fight. "How's Dad?"

"He's right here. Do you want a word?"

"Please."

"Hello, love," her father said. "You'll never guess what happened to Martin at work the other day."

Jennifer blinked back a tear at her father's endearment. And it was true, she never would guess, so Jennifer let her father chat away, filling her in on the day-to-day minutiae of his life in a way that made her feel closer to home.

Afterward, her mother came back on the phone. "I saw Karen's mum the other day."

"Oh yeah?" Jennifer asked, rolling her eyes and wishing Aidan would stop staring while simultaneously preparing herself for the next dig.

"Yes. Karen's loving university. She's got loads of new friends and is really enjoying her classes."

"Good for Karen," huffed Jennifer.

"Oh, don't be like that, Jen. I'm just saying. There's no need to be so defensive."

"You're not 'just saying,' though, are you? You're having another go at me for coming here, only I don't know how many times I have to tell you that I can go to university next year."

"*If* they agree to you deferring your place. We've still not heard yet, have we?"

"No, not yet," she agreed.

Minutes later, as she put down the phone, Jennifer swallowed hard.

"Hey, you okay?" Aidan asked. "Don't let them make you feel like shit."

But Jennifer's previous good mood had dissolved entirely. Every time she spoke to her parents, it was the same. It stirred up so many mixed emotions—doubt, fear, and anger at both their handling of the situation and her own.

"Listen, fuck 'em. Just forget about them, babe. Now, let's head to the beach."

"I don't know," she said flatly, wishing it were that simple. "Perhaps we shouldn't be going today. Perhaps it would be more sensible to head down to that building site to see if we can get you some work."

Aidan rolled his eyes. "You're such a killjoy. Don't let your parents ruin our day. Just because they want to be miserable buggers doesn't mean we have to be. I mean, look how gorgeous it is out there, and you want to sweat into town because some idiot from the café says there *might* be some work at the site? That's hardly making the best of the day, is it?"

Jennifer despaired. "I don't know, to be honest. I mean, yeah, it is a beautiful day, just like it was yesterday and the day before and the day before that. But it would also be good to be able to tell Mum and Dad that between the pair of us, we had a bit more money coming in. Besides, we're not in England now, you know? We don't have to drop everything just because the sun's out. I suspect it will be a beautiful day tomorrow too, only by then, if there is any work, it will have gone."

In her grumpy mood, Jennifer wished it would start raining. A bit of drizzle might force Aidan into doing something useful, and they could have a day off from the beach. She only had a couple waitressing shifts each week, and he was working as a bouncer every Friday, but that was the sum of their income. They were completely broke, and their lack of a plan bothered her, though every time she raised the subject, Aidan didn't seem to understand. As far as he was concerned, they were living in sunshine near a beach and having a lot of sex, so there wasn't anything to worry about. His needs were simple.

"Look, I'll go tomorrow when you're at work. There's no point wasting a day when we could be together, hanging out," he said.

"All right," she said, suddenly too hot and lethargic to protest. Besides, she was eager to get out of the stifling apartment. She decided to make an effort to snap out of the foul mood her conversation with her parents had put her in. She wished they would be more supportive.

Aidan came over and started to stroke her back in a way that made her shiver with pleasure.

"Hey, baby, it's okay," he soothed.

"I know," she said unconvincingly.

His hands carried on, traveling lightly up her back and around to her front, where he gently massaged her breasts. His touch was incredible and never failed to arouse her.

"Is that nice?"

"Mmm." She sighed, giving in to the sensations and reaching around to feel if he was getting excited. "Wow. We only had sex five minutes ago."

"That's what you do to me, baby," he whispered in her ear before pulling her around and kissing her passionately.

They fell into bed and her troubles faded away.

Present Day

Jennifer didn't exactly emerge from the tunnel. The sensation felt more like an expulsion—sudden, brutal, and delivered with no warning whatsoever. She was confused and depleted. Her brain needed time to process what she'd experienced. But she was nowhere near capable.

This was the most fascinating, terrifying, yet privileged gift she ever could have been given. She glanced around and noted that the three tunnels all still existed, though the first was shining less brightly. Somehow she knew she would have another opportunity to visit and felt relieved. She wanted to know more about how things would turn out with Aidan. For now, though, it was time to regain some strength, and with that final thought, she allowed herself to slip away.

Polly and Eadie need to get out and burn off a bit of energy," announced Jennifer.

"Take them to the park then," said Max, finishing the last bit of his toasted bacon sandwich and only narrowly saving himself from being swatted with a copy of the *Sunday Times* by winking to make sure his wife knew he was joking. "Come on, then. Let's take them to the swings now, and then perhaps we should go out for lunch, so you don't have to cook?"

Jennifer acknowledged that this was a kind thought but couldn't help but wonder what was preventing him from rustling anything up.

"Or, should I say, so you don't have to buy any revolting stuffed chickens that don't actually look or taste anything like chickens?" Another wink.

"Ha bloody ha," said Jennifer, laughing despite herself. "Okay, that sounds good. And there's a casserole in the fridge we can all have for early dinner, but there's not much more than that.

Hopefully it'll be quiet at work tomorrow, so I can go shopping on my lunch break. Otherwise, I'll have to do it later."

"Good," said Max. Jennifer knew he didn't care. Food was her department as far as he was concerned. "Right. Polly, Eadie, come and get your shoes on. We're going to the park," he yelled in the general direction of the kitchen door, getting up to put his plate in the sink.

"Let's aim to wear them out as much as possible," said Jennifer.

"Definitely," Max agreed. "Then we can plonk them in front of a DVD this afternoon, totally guilt-free."

"Sounds good to me," Jennifer said. She wondered if that meant he was thinking they might be able to sneak back to bed.

"I hope you don't mind," Max added, looking sheepish, "but there's a soccer game on that I really want to watch this afternoon, and I told Ted he could come and watch it here. He still doesn't have cable at his place."

"Oh…right," she said, feeling crestfallen and bored already.

"You don't mind, do you?"

"No," she lied.

———

Despite having been at the park all morning, Polly and Eadie were still full of energy. When Jennifer wasn't stopping them from killing each other over a broken Barbie, she was putting the laundry in, taking it out, or shoving it in the mountainous ironing pile. As she did so, she thought wistfully of prechildren days when Sundays meant lying in bed with a hangover, which would eventually be cured by a Bloody Mary and a roast dinner at the pub, followed perhaps by a movie and some sex. God, she was becoming obsessed. This must be how people felt when they came out of prison or the army.

"Come on, you two," she yelled when her daughters' whining had developed into full-blown wailing. "Eadie, bash your sister again and I'll bash you."

Of course she would never bash her kids in a million years, so the threat was rather empty.

Eadie eyeballed her mother through her brown bangs, as if weighing up how much trouble she'd be in if she ignored her. Then, having concluded that she could handle whatever was flung at her, she proceeded to whack Polly again.

"Right," Jennifer growled. "That's it. Up to your room."

Eadie burst into noisy sobs but headed for her room, stamping up the stairs as she went. Jennifer sighed heavily, sick of all the squabbling but partly blaming herself for it. No doubt her children had picked up on her unenthusiastic mood. Perhaps if she'd been perkier and more inventive in finding ways to entertain them, they'd have been fine, but she wanted to be able to leave them to their own devices for more than five minutes. She was tired and would like nothing more than to get into her pajamas and zone out to a bit of afternoon TV.

Max bounced into the kitchen. "Everything all right in here?" he asked, charging to the fridge to get a couple more beers. "Did I hear wailing?"

"Yes, you did," snapped Jennifer. "They're behaving like a couple of deranged chimps. I've sent Eadie to her room for bashing Polly."

"Yeah, Daddy, she hit me really hard," said Polly, rubbing her arm to demonstrate how much it hurt.

"Er, it was the other arm, Pol," said Jennifer wryly.

"How could you miss that, you bloody idiot?" Ted yelled from the front room. Max ran out of the kitchen, bottles of lager in both hands and one under his arm, skidding on the wooden floor of the hall in his socks. As he disappeared, he yelled over his shoulder, "Be good for your mother!"

"Come on, you, let's get some coloring stuff out," said Jennifer to her youngest, "but hurry up, because I need to make sure Eadie's okay. And don't think I'm happy with you either, madam," she added, noting Polly's smug expression.

A bit later, Jennifer went upstairs to check on Eadie, only to find that instead of quietly repenting for her sins, her eldest daughter had managed to work herself up into a terrible state, so outraged was she by what she considered to be unfair treatment from her mother. Too weary to argue further, or to point out that she wasn't the villain, Jennifer ended up stroking Eadie's hair and soothing her until she was calm enough to be left with her favorite DVD on. Once Eadie was happy, Jennifer decided to join the boys in the living room.

"Hello," Max said, looking distracted and surprised to see her standing in her own front room. He was on one sofa, Ted on the other. Both were sitting wide-legged on the edge, beers in hand. "You all right? Second half's just started. Why don't you see if there's a nice movie on upstairs? There might be a romcom or something."

"Because Eadie's watching *Tangled* on our bed, and as much as I enjoyed it the first time around, I can probably live without seeing it again," she replied, flopping onto the sofa Ted was sitting on. He shuffled over reluctantly to make room, his eyes never leaving the TV.

"All right, Ted?" she asked.

"Yeah, great, thanks," he said, reminding her of when Eadie's friends came around to play and answered her questions about school politely but with a tone suggesting they'd rather not be talking to her at all.

"How's Annabelle? Is she well?" she continued, not caring if Ted didn't want to talk. She did. She was bored.

"Not bad, thanks. Bit stressed. Callum has been out of school with tonsillitis, but other than that, okay."

"Good," she said, flicking through *Style* magazine.

"Hey, have you seen your ex's latest chart position in this year's Rich List?" Max asked, throwing the newspaper in her direction. The Rich List was printed annually by the *Sunday Times* and listed the country's top earners. It made Jennifer's mind boggle to see her ex-boyfriend featured on it year in and year out.

"Oh God." Jennifer rolled her eyes. "Go on then. Let's feel sick for a second."

"Stock for reUNIon went public this year," Max informed Ted almost proudly. "He's worth a billion now."

"You're kidding," said Jennifer, though soon she knew it to be true, for there it was in black and white, accompanied by a picture of him. Tim Purcell. The ex-boyfriend she'd dated for two and a half years, now a billionaire. She scrutinized his picture. His blond hair was slightly silver around the edges. He was a little more jowly but otherwise looked remarkably similar to how he had fifteen years before. He was good-looking in a Nordic sort of way and had always had incredibly nice skin, though his blue eyes were flinty and rather too deep set and his nose was a little too sharp. His face couldn't have been more different from the one of the man she'd eventually married. Max's friendly face may not have been anywhere near as chiseled, but overall she far preferred staring at it.

She wondered what it would be like to see Tim now, after all these years. Would they get along? They'd had a strange relationship. She'd always felt as if, more than anything, she'd *amused* him. She'd known he'd found her funny and sweet, but she'd never gotten the impression that he massively fancied her. Then again, for her, it hadn't necessarily been a relationship based on physical attraction either. She'd been so impressed by him and had liked being associated with someone who everyone on campus was aware of. If she did ever meet up with him again, she'd love to ask him what he'd seen in her. She doubted that would happen, though. They were hardly likely to bump into each other. They ran in different circles, and they'd never kept in touch because they'd broken up on such bad terms, which ironically was the one time he'd demonstrated that she had actually gotten under his skin. Or had it just been his ego making him so angry and upset when she'd told him she wanted to split up?

"What I'd do with a billion quid," mused Ted.

Buy yourself a cable subscription hopefully, Jennifer thought to herself, smiling blankly at him.

"Perhaps I should get in contact with Tim and ask him if I can have a thousand pounds that I could use to get the dryer fixed, pay some bills, and have a splurge at Macy's, eh? It would be pocket money to him," she joked.

"Bet you wish you'd stuck with him, eh, Jen? Instead of hooking up with this loser," said Ted.

Jennifer smiled and shook her head. "Not at all, Ted. He may be rich, but he was a bit of a cold shit."

"Bloody clever, though," said Max. "I mean, who hasn't been on reUNIon at some point or another? Apart from my parents, who are the only people I can think of."

It always struck Jennifer as strange when Max went on about how clever Tim was. It was almost as if he was proud that she'd gone out with him, but she'd have preferred it if he was a little bit jealous. As it was, she suspected he'd probably love to meet Tim, have dinner with him, be able to discuss his career with him. In fact, given the choice, it wouldn't have surprised her if Max chose going to dinner with him over her.

Jennifer's phone beeped. It was a text from Esther, saying she was around the corner at the park with Sophie and asking if she could pop by.

Jennifer phoned straightaway. "Please come around. Max and Ted are here watching soccer, and I would love to see you. Also, Sophie can sort my two out and give them something more interesting to do than killing each other."

Bored stiff of the swings, Esther was over in minutes.

"I am so glad to see you," said Jennifer, flinging her arms around her friend as soon as she'd opened the door. "Hi, Sophie. How are you, sweetie?" she asked her goddaughter.

"Good," said Sophie.

"Go on, then. Eadie's upstairs and, ah…here's Pol. Have you finished coloring?"

"Yes," said Polly, looking delighted to have a playmate who wasn't Eadie.

As the girls scampered upstairs, Jennifer ushered Esther into the kitchen.

"Am I glad to see you! What a dull weekend I've had. Bloody hell."

Esther giggled. "Why? What have you been up to?"

"Ugh," groaned Jennifer. "Well, we didn't have the kids Friday night, but we managed to totally waste that window of opportunity to have some fun by doing jack shit. Then on Saturday, we had Judith and boring Henry around for lunch."

"Oh God," said Esther, who had heard enough about them to imagine what that would have entailed.

"Quite, although I nearly gave them food poisoning, which added a very small frisson of excitement. Then today I thought we were going to have a nice family day, but it's ended up being a day of watching sports and drinking beer with good old Ted." This last bit she said in a hushed tone.

"All sounds joyous." Esther laughed, slipping off her jacket. She looked great as ever, but today she also looked tired. Under all those freckles, she was pale, though her naturally strawberry-blond hair was shiny and brushed, and no matter how tired she was, she always looked attractive. She'd aged well and always dressed in a way that made other women want to know where her clothes were from. She always added accessories and put outfits together so that you knew she hadn't just picked up whatever was on the floor and thrown it on. Today her printed scarf and gold bumblebee necklace were the items Jennifer was coveting.

"Sounds like you need a good night out with the girls."

"I do," agreed Jennifer. "You know we're going out on Tuesday, don't you? Only to the Hare and Hounds, but perhaps then we can get our calendars out and arrange something proper. Something that involves cocktails and dancing. Love that scarf, by the way."

"Thanks, and yeah, I do know about Tuesday, although I'm not 100 percent sure I can come yet. I still need to get a sitter sorted out."

Jennifer suspected at that point she wouldn't be coming. Such a shame, and it grated ever so slightly that Esther wasn't making it a priority.

"Tea?"

"Yes, please."

"Anyway, enough of my boring weekend. How's yours been?"

"Not bad, actually," Esther said, a sly grin lighting up her face.

"Go on," said Jennifer, getting mugs out of the cupboard, happy her friend had come. It had restored her equilibrium.

"Well, Jason and I are pretty broke at the moment, and we've been staying in a lot, but on Friday, my mum babysat so we went out and got hammered. I'm talking properly drunk, and when we got home and Mum had gone, we ended up"—Esther grinned and started shaking her head—"doing it in the hall. And then we did it"—again she had to stop while she snorted with laughter at the memory—"in the downstairs bathroom."

"You are kidding me," said Jennifer, full of mixed emotions. She was deeply impressed, terribly envious, and strangely proud to hear that people were still having wild sex with their husbands, even if she wasn't.

"I'm not," said Esther, giggling. "It was hilarious. You know the type of sex you have where afterward you're almost a bit embarrassed."

"You know, the last time I can remember feeling faintly embarrassed after sex was with Tim," said Jennifer, grabbing the milk out of the fridge.

"Really? Why? What did you do?"

Jennifer grimaced. "You don't want to know."

"Well, that's where you're completely wrong."

Jennifer wrinkled her nose. "Let's just say he was quite kinky and leave it there, shall we?"

"No way!" protested Esther. "I'm sorry, but you have to spill the beans now, missy. If you don't, I'll end up imagining all sorts of things that are probably far worse than the reality."

Jennifer sighed, knowing she was beaten. "Okay, but tell anyone this and you're a dead woman."

Esther pretended to pull a zipper across her mouth.

"Okay, so basically, toward the end of our relationship, Tim was only really up for it if I was…um…pretending to be someone else."

Esther's eyes widened. "You mean he liked role play?"

Jennifer nodded, went red, and chewed on a fingernail. "Liked" was an understatement.

Esther laughed heartily. "Oh God. I think I can vaguely remember you saying something about that at the time."

"Hmm," Jennifer said. "Anyway, maybe I should have just put up with his weird ways. Let me show you something." She hurried into the front room and returned with the Rich List.

"Bloody hell," said Esther, wide-eyed once she'd been shown the relevant bit. "That is a sick amount of money. God, I can't tell you how much we could do with even a little bit of that. Things are really tight at the moment, to the point where we're struggling some months to make the mortgage payment. I certainly shouldn't have treated myself to this scarf, I can tell you. I feel guilty every time I put it on. Can't you phone Tim and ask if we can have some?"

"I wish," said Jennifer.

"That could have been you," said Esther.

"Well, I don't know about that."

"It could. Don't you remember how gutted he was when you broke it off? You could be that rich."

"Ooh, listen to you, last of the feminists. I'd prefer not to be sponging off Tim Purcell, thank you very much. Though, having said that, I'm not sure what the difference would be to how my life is now. I hate being so bloody dependent on Max these days. In fact, I've been thinking recently about going back to school in an attempt to improve my pathetic earning potential."

"For what?"

"Haven't gotten that far yet," admitted Jennifer flatly. "Any ideas are very welcome."

Esther giggled. "So, hypothetically, if you had stayed with Tim, do you think you'd still be friends with us now?"

"Course I would," said Jennifer, insulted. "What do you take me for? Although I'm not sure Karen would be showing up at the mansion that often. She hated him, didn't she?"

"She did," confirmed Esther. "I always thought he was okay, though. He was so clever, had an answer for everything. Oh, and

I'll never forget that party he threw in your house that time. The one where Karen shagged Pete for the first time. It was awesome. Maybe even the best party I've ever been to."

"God, that party was fun, wasn't it?" agreed Jennifer. "Or are we looking back through rose-tinted glasses?"

As her mind returned to Tim, for once she allowed herself to be transported back to how life had been all those years ago. She always pretended she couldn't care less, but in truth, constantly being reminded by the business section of the papers that one of your exes was doing amazingly well in life was a little frustrating.

And deep down she knew it probably *could* have been her enjoying the fruits of his labors if she'd stuck with him. If she hadn't let her concerns that he didn't love her as he should overwhelm her. Or, more to the point, if she hadn't decided that, despite his protestations, he cared more about work than any living human being, and that in itself was a problem she'd never be able to overcome.

Still, that was all firmly in the past, and besides, she suspected that no amount of riches would ever have made up for the fact that she'd spent much of their time together dressed as a policewoman.

Tim

J ennifer was about to pour her powdered Cup-a-Soup into a mug when she made the mistake (or not, as the case may be) of glancing inside the empty vessel, at which point she gagged violently.

"Oh my God, that is so disgusting," she exclaimed, stomach heaving.

"What?" Karen asked, coming to join her in the small kitchen, opening the fridge, and peering in hopefully.

"This mug's got mold growing in it. I think I'm going to puke."

"Gross," said Karen, closing the fridge. She didn't fancy a stick of limp celery, a jar of Pond's Cold Cream, or some three-day-old noodles. "Shall we grab some fries before we get there?"

"Okay," Jennifer agreed, unable to bear the surrounding debris a moment longer.

As students, they expected to live in a certain amount of squalor, but the house they'd moved into for their last year of university veered dangerously into unsanitary territory. From the outside it was amazing: a huge Georgian terrace located smack in the middle of a square just off the Brighton seafront. The paint may have been peeling, but when you stood at the other side of the square, with your back to the sea, it looked exceedingly grand and still possessed the majesty of its era. Inside, however, it was a different story. The house had been adapted so it could be rented out with the student market in mind. On the first floor, there were three bedrooms and a bathroom, and the second floor had a vast communal lounge along with two additional bedrooms and a tiny kitchen. The third floor had three more bedrooms and another bathroom. Curiously, there was no dining table anywhere in the house, something all the parents who had visited found baffling and commented on, but none of the students cared. Meals tended to be consumed standing up or lying down.

Of course, eight bedrooms meant eight housemates, including Jennifer. Eight student human beings, whose priorities didn't involve anything like rubber gloves, cleaning solution, or tidying. As a result, the house constantly looked like it had just been burgled and the kitchen existed under a coating of grease. Dishes were done on a need-to-eat basis, and everything felt a bit sticky to the touch.

The only part of the house that wasn't completely grim to be in was Tim's room. It was on the top floor and was by far the largest in the house, a privilege for which he paid twenty pounds rent a week more than the others. Not only was his room the best in terms of size and view, but in startling contrast to the rest of the house, it was also kept clean and tidy. He paid fellow student Amber, a Chinese girl, six pounds an hour for three hours every week to come clean his room and wash and iron his clothes. This set him apart from his peers—but then Tim was a rare breed of student altogether. The most obvious thing that separated him from the rest of the student community was that he always had a bit of cash. Not just the odd tenner either, but wedges of the stuff he kept folded in a money clip. He'd gone to a very expensive school so undoubtedly had financial support from his family, but he also always had money-making schemes on the go, ones that actually tended to be successful. Tim had his own fridge, which was always well stocked with lagers and nice food, his own desktop computer complete with the latest operating system, and a two-seater sofa positioned against the window, meaning that when you lay on it, you could fully appreciate the sea view. He also had his own stereo and a kettle, making the room more like a self-contained studio apartment. Jennifer loved spending time in it. It certainly beat her tiny box room on the ground floor at the back of the house, with its view of an unsavory Mexican restaurant's backyard.

As Karen and Jennifer gave up the futile task of looking for anything that might be worth eating, they retreated to the lounge where Pete and Jim were playing video games and listening to music. Empty McDonald's bags littered the table, and with the curtains drawn, the only real light source other than a small side lamp came from the tropical fish tank that belonged to another of their housemates. Jim was only wearing his boxers, which wasn't a pleasant sight but one the girls were so used to that it didn't warrant a comment.

"Tim's not coming out tonight, is he?" asked Karen, collapsing onto the sofa, her short skirt riding up her firm but chunky legs. Her question sounded more like a hopeful statement and told Jennifer everything she needed to know.

"Don't know," she replied, immediately on edge. She wished Karen would get over her dislike of Tim once and for all. "Why?"

"No reason," said Karen. "I don't mind either way. I just assumed it wouldn't be his thing. Fun, that is. Joking!"

"You going to that karaoke thing?" inquired Pete, his eyes not leaving the screen.

"Yeah," Karen said.

"Do you want some weed?"

"Why not?" Karen replied.

"Okay, you figure out the weed, and I'll go find out if Tim's coming or not," said Jennifer, pointedly ignoring her friend's dig.

She thundered up the stairs to the third floor, taking them two at a time in the platform sandals she was wearing with a crop top that showed off her flat belly and a short A-line skirt. She banged on Tim's door and, after she was invited in, asked, "Are you coming out tonight or what?"

"I'm not, my precious," replied Tim, not looking up from his desk. "Sean's coming over to show me the code he's written. We're having a meeting."

"Ooh," she moaned. "Please come?"

Tim turned and gave her an approving look followed by a lop-sided grin so endearing it made her want to run over and kiss him. Not that she did. Tim's demeanor was generally one that encouraged people to keep their distance. But while they didn't tend to enjoy much spontaneous affection, what they did both relish was verbal sparring.

"Hmm, let me think about it. My options are (a) stay here and see all my ambitions and dreams come to fruition, or (b) go out in the rain to watch you and Karen murder what were perfectly decent songs to start with in a shitty karaoke gay bar on the seafront. No thanks."

"Vicky's coming," joked Jennifer, grabbing the life-size cardboard cutout of Posh Spice that Tim had pinched from Blockbuster Video the previous week when he was drunk. Posh Spice was wearing a white miniskirt and bra top, and Ginger Spice was downstairs in the lounge in her iconic Union Jack dress, but with an extra black mustache and glasses that someone had thoughtfully drawn on.

"Well, that's a different story then," said Tim. "If old lovely legs is going."

But he didn't mean it. His attentions were firmly back on his computer.

Jennifer tried not to feel disappointed. She'd been going out with him long enough to know he wouldn't change his mind and that there was no point grumbling, given that his drive, ambition, and clever brain were the things that had attracted her to him in the first place.

Half the time she didn't follow what he was talking about when it came to his plans to cash in on what he felt was going to be a huge surge in Internet usage, but his passion for the subject was infectious. His latest idea was to create some kind of platform on the World Wide Web for people to find old university, college, or school friends that then allowed you to find out how they'd done in terms of what jobs they'd gone on to, whether they were married, and if they'd had children. It would be called "reUNIon" and would work by allowing you to look up anyone and see their photo and who they were "friends" with. But in order to see their full page with more personal information on it, which would be formatted almost like a résumé, you'd need their permission first. The site would ask you to predict what you thought that person might be doing with his or her life. In other words, if you signed up for the site, you might receive an email from an old classmate, asking if you wanted to see what they had predicted about you. If you said yes, they were in and would be listed as a "friend." Tim was convinced that people's natural desire to know what others thought of them would be the key to its success.

"So what's Sean bringing around?"

"You wouldn't understand," said Tim bluntly.

"Try me."

"He's been developing some programs. I *told* you. He's written some code."

"For reUNIon?"

"Yes," Tim said, sounding exasperated, which in turn made Jennifer feel sad.

"Tim, someone here for you," Pete yelled up the stairs.

"Great," said Tim, bounding into action, brushing past her in his eagerness to get to Sean, practically flattening her as he did so.

Jennifer sighed. She'd lost him, so she might as well get on with her evening. Karen would be pleased, she thought as she picked her way across the landing, which had piles of dirty laundry strewn all over it.

Later that night, or rather in the early hours of the next day, Jennifer and Karen staggered home. After five minutes of taking turns stabbing the front door with their keys, they finally made it into the house. Giggling like schoolgirls, cross-legged and clutching each other in an attempt not to piss themselves laughing, it took them an age to get up the stairs. Once they had, they both raced to the bathroom and then reconvened in the lounge. They peeled their coats off, and Karen got out everything required for rolling a joint.

"I'm going to see if Tim's still up," said Jennifer, who couldn't be bothered with pretending she wasn't dying to see him.

"Fine," said Karen, a bit huffily. "No doubt he will be because he hasn't taken over the world yet."

As Jennifer bounded up the stairs, she decided it was time to have it out with Karen once and for all. Her constant jibes were getting on her nerves. It wasn't her fault Karen was single.

"Tim," she said, banging on his door, having seen light coming from beneath it. There was no reply, but there was music playing. She barged in.

Tim and Sean barely looked up, so engrossed were they, huddled over the wretched computer.

"Er...yoo-hoo, hello, earth calling my lame geek boyfriend."

"Oh, hello, you," said Tim, looking up. Despite looking exhausted and having the pallor of someone who hadn't had any fresh air all day, his eyes were shining and he looked thrilled. As he leaned back, his shirt rode up, exposing a glimpse of his lean, hairless stomach.

"How's it going?" Jennifer asked, suddenly feeling slightly

queasy. Running up the stairs probably hadn't been the wisest of moves given that she had liters of various spirits swooshing around in her belly. She swayed across the room and sank gratefully onto the bed. She reached down to pull off her shoes and chucked them across the room. They made a huge thudding sound as they made contact with the wall.

"Amazing," Tim said. "We're doing fucking amazing, thanks to Sean."

Jennifer smiled weakly in Sean's direction. Sean had the social skills of a jellyfish as far as she was concerned, and she was a bit jealous of him. Tim never looked this happy and satisfied after a night in with her.

"Come downstairs and have a drink with me and Karen," she said, trying not to sound petulant but not sure if she was succeeding due to being so drunk. Now that she wasn't breathing in lungfuls of sea air, the alcohol was making its effects known.

"Um…"

Jennifer got up, rolling her eyes heavenward, bracing herself for the inevitable no.

"Yes, why not, my little drunkard? I'd love to. And then you can tell me all about your evening."

Jennifer smiled. "I'll reenact it, if you like."

"Even better," Tim said, making a face. "Come on, Sean. We should have a break."

"Cool," muttered Sean, not moving.

Tim rubbed his face with both hands, then came over to where Jennifer was and regarded her with interest as she bent down to retrieve her clumpy shoes.

"I can see right up your skirt," he said, which gave Jennifer an immediate thrill. He lightly stroked her belly in a way that was quite nice yet also irritating. "You are wrecked, aren't you?" he asked, suddenly noticing how much she was frowning. Her brows were knitted together with the concentration required simply to stand up straight.

"I'm fine," she said defensively.

"Good," he said, running his hands up her back.

It was the affection she'd been craving for days, only being touched was making her feel more nauseous. She needed to eat. She needed toast.

"Can I have some of your bread?" she asked, pulling away and gesturing to his fridge. She lumbered over to it before he'd had the chance to answer.

"But of course," Tim said. "Eat an entire loaf if you like, my sweet. And if reUNIon takes off like I think it's going to, I shall buy you your very own bakery."

Jennifer wasn't listening. She was too intent on getting at the sliced white bread, which she had confidence would restore her sugar levels and make her feel less tipsy. She had planned on toasting it but in the end was so desperate for some starchy carbohydrates that she just ripped a slice in two and shoved one of the halves into her mouth.

As she chewed, it stuck to the roof of her mouth.

"Don't ever let anyone tell you you're not completely classy," Tim joked. "Third class, that is."

"Come on, let's go and have a drink then," she said, mouth full.

"Yes," said Tim. "Because you look like you need one."

Jennifer tried hard to think of a witty riposte, but it was too much effort so she gave up and staggered toward the door instead.

Tim followed her, but Sean couldn't be torn away from his computer for love, money, or vodka.

In the lounge, Karen was reclining on the main sofa, which was so threadbare and ancient, it had pretty much collapsed in on itself. Lying on it felt a lot like you were lying on the floor. She was doing some impressive recreational multitasking by rolling a joint, keeping one eye on the TV, and listening to music. "Don't Speak" by No Doubt was blasting.

"Evening, Karen," said Tim in a tone that suggested he was up for a bit of an argument.

Jennifer sighed inwardly as she realized she'd be in charge of keeping the peace.

"Right...booze," she said. "Shall I pour us all a vodka?"

"Yeah," Karen said. "Where's the bag? We didn't leave it, did we?"

"No, it's here by your feet," Jennifer said, extracting the plastic bag that had a half bottle of vodka and some orange juice in it from where it was wedged down the back of the sofa.

There were no clean glasses or mugs to be found in the kitchen, so she went downstairs to her room to fetch some paper cups she'd purchased the other week for times like this.

Due to being so utterly drunk, the effort of having charged downstairs at high speed left her swaying in the middle of the room for a few minutes while trying to remember what she'd come down for. Her mind had gone blank and she could hardly keep her eyes open. Finally it came back to her. Cups. Paper cups. Now she felt smug. Well done, her. She was conscious of needing to get back to the lounge quickly, so as soon as she'd retrieved them, she staggered back. It wouldn't do to leave Tim and Karen alone for too long. They'd only end up sniping at each other.

But it was already too late. As she approached the lounge, her heart sank.

"But wanting to know what people do is just blatant snobbery, isn't it?" Karen was arguing, albeit from a lying-down position that put Tim, who was sitting upright, at an immediate advantage.

"Oh, fuck off, Karen. You should hear yourself. What's snobby about being curious? About being interested?"

"Because you're suggesting that what we do defines us, like some middle-aged fart at a cocktail party saying, 'And what do you do?'" she said in a voice like Margaret Thatcher.

"Here are your drinks," Jennifer said brusquely, splashing liquid into the paper cups until they were pretty much two parts vodka, one part juice.

Tim took his and slugged it back. As he did, he winced. "Oof, that's strong."

"Wuss," Karen said unnecessarily, downing hers in one gulp and instantly looking like she regretted it.

"Anyhow," said Tim, "the point is, Karen, that if you think reUNIon is such a shit idea that you won't go on it, that is entirely your prerogative. And yet I'd bet good money that in five years' time, if you got an email telling you that Ed Fisher wanted to find out what you were up to, and not only that, that he'd predicted what he thought you were up to, you'd be intrigued. Don't try to tell me you wouldn't have a look at that point."

This was a bit below the belt. Up until five weeks ago, Ed Fisher had been Karen's boyfriend. Then he'd dumped her cruelly via text, telling her it was because he didn't really fancy her and saw her more as a friend. She'd cried for a week.

"If that asshole got in touch with me in five years' time, I'd be fucking livid!" she yelled.

Jennifer slugged back her drink nervously. "You two," she interjected. "Can we talk about something else for once?"

"Like what?" Tim asked sarcastically. "What do you want to enlighten us with, my angel?"

Jennifer gulped, and as she did so, she became aware of a terrible metallic taste in her mouth, swiftly followed by an ominous lurching sensation in her stomach. Horrified, she brought her hand up to her mouth.

"You okay?" asked Karen.

"Gonna puke," Jennifer managed, racing from the room as the cocktails she'd drunk earlier made an unscheduled reappearance.

"I am one hell of a lucky guy," said Tim.

"Yes, you are, actually," replied Karen loftily, though the sound of Jennifer puking violently into the kitchen sink wasn't really helping her case.

W hat's happening?" asked Max, leaping to his feet the second the doctor appeared through the door.

"Well, we're encouraged that she's made it through surgery. At one point, we were concerned about the buildup of blood around the skull, but it appears to have eased off. Having said that, she's not completely out of the woods yet, although her vital signs have stabilized."

A pause.

"Perhaps we should continue speaking in the corridor, Mr. Wright."

Good, thought Jennifer. She needed quiet and wanted to be left alone. In sterile silence. For a short while, though still unconscious, she'd been vaguely aware of what was happening on the surface. It was like a giant fist had gripped her, yanking her back from oblivion purely so she could address a thought that had been loitering on the periphery of her consciousness, tapping her brain, desperate for her attention.

Polly and Eadie. As maternal instinct took over and penetrated everything, her daughters were flung into sharp reality. Her babies, her girls. The stab of emotion she encountered in that moment as she thought of them was gut-wrenching, panic inducing. She didn't know if they were okay, and during this rare moment of lucidity, she understood she was powerless to find out. She couldn't be like this. They needed her. What was happening? She felt like a prisoner in her own body, helpless, petrified. If Max was here, wherever "here" was, then who was looking after them? Her mother? Karen? But as quickly as panic and fear welled up, it subsided again as confusion swamped her once more.

She battled to stay attached to the awareness of her daughters, but it proved too difficult. As quickly as their images had formed, they slipped away again until, within seconds, she couldn't remember anything. Instead, all that remained was the overriding sense that she was detached from whatever was happening and that she was being encouraged to drift further and further from it. Perhaps she should? At first, she'd been pleased to emerge from the fog, but it was enticing her back again. She succumbed once more, this time confident of what to expect. There they were, the tunnels of light, and for the second time, she was carried toward the still-open portal on the left.

TUNNEL NUMBER ONE
What Could Have Been—Aidan

Gasping, Jennifer jabbed Aidan in the ribs, signaling for him to roll off so she could lie back and enjoy the brief period of utter contentment that follows an epic orgasm.

"Wow."

"Wow indeed," agreed Aidan, reaching over for his rolling tobacco. She surveyed his back. Since he'd hurt his ankle, he hadn't been able to go swimming or running and he'd piled on the pounds.

He still had a lovely broad body, though, even if it was remarkably pasty and carrying a lot more fat than it had before. Still, his physique would always err on the side of good, for his frame was masculine, tall, and well proportioned. She surveyed the tattoo that spanned the width of his lower back. It was bizarre to think he'd had it done sixteen years ago, six months after they'd arrived in Australia—sun-drenched, heady, exciting days when it had still seemed like anything was possible. It was a Celtic pattern with a large sun in the middle, and recently Jennifer had started to hate the very sight of it. It represented the elusive sunshine that Aidan had been desiring ever since but that somehow always remained just out of his reach. As if to illustrate her point, a strong Carlisle rain started hammering against the windowpanes. Located on the border between Scotland and England, the miserable Carlisle climate could hardly be more of a contrast to the sunny warmth of Queensland.

"Typical," muttered Aidan.

"Why, what are you up to? Are you going to fetch that paint for Nathan's room?" Jennifer asked hopefully.

"No, I'm supposed to be signing on at three and I'm probably not going to have time to do that and get the paint, am I?"

"Guess not," said Jennifer flatly, hoping he wasn't trying to wriggle out of it. The feeling of peace she'd had from their physical exertions was as short-lived as ever. She'd finished work very late last night and was exhausted. Picking up the paint was the least he could do. She had no idea why he couldn't get around to it. It was as if he was deliberately not doing it to spite her. She was almost tempted to take the bus and collect it herself. That way they could make a start on Nathan's room like they'd been promising him they would since his birthday. But Aidan picking up the paint had become a point of principle because he hadn't worked for four months now. He'd had a good contract working for a local building firm but had fallen out with his boss when he'd yelled at him in front of the team for being late and a furious Aidan had yelled back. At the time, Aidan had tried to convince Jennifer that refusing to apologize and leaving made him a man of principle. She wasn't convinced. She thought it made him an idiot and very selfish. Now that he seemed to be in no hurry to find anything else, it pointed toward him being lazy too.

She inhaled deeply through her nose, as she'd been taught in yoga class, desperate to remain in a good frame of mind awhile longer.

Aidan sucked on his skinny cigarette.

"Did Olly say if he had any more decorating work?" she asked, knowing he'd hate her asking but unable to help herself.

"He didn't," Aidan replied tersely.

"All right, I was just asking," said Jennifer, getting up abruptly. She was so infused with intense frustration, she knew her mission to remain Zen was futile. She grabbed her old, frayed dressing gown from the hook on the back of the door and wrapped it around her thin body. Between working in the restaurant, Aidan's insatiable sexual appetite, and the stress of never having enough money, keeping the pounds off wasn't something she'd ever had to worry about.

"Well, don't. You know I'll tell you when he's got something. Why would I not?"

Jennifer didn't reply. There was no point. There'd only be a fight and she could do without one on her only day off. Instead, she left the bedroom and went into the tiny kitchen to make a cup of tea.

"Do you want a cup of tea?" she called, biting her lip in an attempt to quell the angry tears that were threatening to spill down her cheeks.

"Okay," called Aidan. "Seeing as I've got to go out in this rain, I may as well."

As Jennifer waited for the kettle to boil, she wished Aidan would go. Apart from anything else, her new book on reflexology had arrived, and she wanted to start reading it in peace. She was considering applying to a class. Emma, a friend of hers from yoga who was already a qualified practitioner, had told her a lot about it. The subject fascinated her. Becoming a certified reflexologist would not only provide a way to earn some more money, but could also be something she'd actually enjoy.

If only Aidan would find something to get enthused about, it would make life a lot easier. She was unable to prevent a solitary tear from rolling down her cheek and onto the laminate countertop, which, due to how old it was, never looked clean no matter how much she scrubbed it. She wiped her cheek impatiently, bored of feeling down. Bored of feeling bored.

She glanced at the cork bulletin board covered in bills, takeout menus, letters from Nate's school, and, in the middle, a photograph. An old, dog-eared photo of her mother and father, whom she hadn't seen for eighteen long years now. For what felt like the thousandth time, Jen's hand went to her dressing gown pocket to feel the letter she'd received from her mother the previous week. It had come to her work address, and she knew it pretty much by heart.

Her mother wanted to see her. Her father still hadn't come around, but her mother had decided it was finally time to let bygones be bygones. The only decision that needed to be made was where and when. Possibly the most surprising thing of all to Jennifer was that, rather than questioning the decision to contact her mother in order to hold out an olive branch, all she found herself debating was why she'd left it this long.

As she was stirring the tea, Aidan appeared behind her and wrapped his arms around her.

"All right, gorgeous?"

"Yeah," she said miserably, feeling anything but.

"You just rest up while I go out. Put your feet up," he said, as if he was bestowing some massive favor upon her.

Too right she'd be putting her feet up. She had a double shift tomorrow and one the day after that, and besides, "putting his feet up" was all Aidan seemed capable of doing these days, so why shouldn't she?

"Go back to bed, even. I know you've been dying to start reading that book. Then maybe me, you, and Nate can get takeout tonight?"

"All right," she agreed, slightly mollified. "Sounds good."

"Eh, what's up?" he asked, spinning her around to face him. "If you're still worried about my cell phone bill, don't be. Worse comes to worse, I'll get my old 'pay as you go' phone out, but knowing you, you'll rake the tips in tomorrow. I know my girl, and not only are you my sexy little minx, you're a bloody good waitress too."

In that instant, Jennifer figured she should just tell him. After all, given everything she'd given up for him over the years—friends, family, an education, prospects—surely he wouldn't begrudge her the chance to rekindle relationships that had been put on hold for so long. There wasn't so much water under the bridge as there was an entire river.

"Mum wrote to me," she said calmly, deciding to omit that she'd been the one to get in contact first.

Aidan's face froze.

"She wants to see me, and I think I'm going to go."

"Why?" he asked, looking totally flummoxed.

"Honestly? You need to ask why?"

"Of course I need to ask why," he exclaimed, looking thunderous. "After all these years of them being sanctimonious, judgmental assholes, I hardly think I'm weird for thinking you should give them a wide berth. They treated you like shit."

Jennifer shook her head. "No. That's the thing. I don't think they did. Not really," she said. "In fact, the older I get, the more I think I treated *them* like shit. I'm the one who disappeared off to the other side of the world. I'm the one who gave up going to university so I could go to Australia with a bloke they'd never even met. And I'm also the one who then had to break it to them that that particular pipe dream had been ruined due to you getting caught with drugs. I happen to think *most* parents would take a pretty dim view of that."

"This again," Aidan cried, outraged. "Are you ever going to get over it? It's not like I was dealing heroin or anything. It was just a little pot. Where's the harm in that? I was bloody unlucky to get caught, but I was hardly ruining lives."

"Except you were," Jennifer muttered, feeling on the brink of a very dangerous conversation.

"What's that supposed to mean?" he asked, his face stony.

"Nothing," she said, rolling her eyes in frustration. "It's just that…well, you have to remember that the whole point of me not going home was because we decided we wanted to live in the sunshine. Only it didn't quite work out like that, did it? Getting deported wasn't exactly the highlight of my life."

"Perhaps not, but then you forgetting to take your pill was hardly the plan either, was it?"

Jennifer shrugged. The memory of finding out that, on top of everything else, she was pregnant at the age of twenty-two was still more bitter than sweet.

"But I stood by you," retorted Aidan, indignant and hurt. "I stood by you when thousands of blokes might have left you to it or forced you to have an abortion. I was a free spirit, remember? Having a wife and kid wasn't exactly part of my master plan either, but I'm glad we did it. I wouldn't want to be without Nate, would you?"

"Of course not," said Jennifer sincerely. "Of course I wouldn't, but I'm not so sure I should have had to go without having my mum and dad in my life for all this time either. And perhaps if I'd been less upset with them, maybe even a bit apologetic about how things had turned out, I wouldn't have had to be."

She met his gaze. He looked defensive and huffy, knowing full well that her words were an accusation aimed firmly at him.

"Look at us," she said, gesturing around the small kitchen and apartment. "I'm thirty-eight, Aidan. Thirty-eight and living in a shithole. I work in a stinking restaurant I'm starting to hate, and for what? I've got no real friends here apart from Emma, and she's flaky at the best of times; no family, except you and Nate, of course, and I spend most of the time feeling..."

"Feeling what?" he replied, his voice hard.

"Feeling...a bit...embarrassed about how things have turned out," she admitted quietly, knowing that although it was a terrible thing to say, it was also true.

"Well, screw you," Aidan said, and as he did, the lurch in Jennifer's stomach told her she may have said too much. There were some things you couldn't take back, and as much as she resented him, he was still her man. For all their problems, he still held her tight, each and every night. They were still intimate all the time, and although things hadn't turned out like they did in the movies, their physical bond, the child they shared, and the years they'd been together were a pretty efficient type of glue.

"I'm sorry," she called after him as he walked away.

"Whatever, Jennifer. I don't want to hear it," he said, heading into the hall and pulling on his Doc Martens. Then he stormed out, presumably—hopefully—to go sign for that month's unemployment benefits.

Jennifer flinched as the door slammed. She stood still for a while, soaking up the silence and wondering what to do. Eventually she decided upon nothing. He'd be back later and they could talk then. In the meantime, she'd gotten a few things off her chest and she was still determined to meet with her mother—no matter what Aidan said. So nothing had changed.

TUNNEL NUMBER ONE
What Could Have Been—Aidan

Someone here to see you, love," said Lindsay, the manager of Red Peppers, the brasserie where Jennifer worked. The conspiratorial wink that accompanied this piece of information told Jennifer it was Aidan. She confided in Lindsay a lot. The older lady was kind, always had time to listen, and usually appreciated having a bit of gossip to think about other than what was happening at the restaurant. So last night, when things had quieted down around ten o'clock, Jennifer had told Lindsay how Aidan was sulking with her and had been ever since she'd announced her intention to see her mother. Lindsay's advice had been concise and to the point: "Tell him to bog off and to stop being such a baby."

"Go on, you can have a quick ten minutes," Lindsay said, grabbing an apron. "I'll cover for you. Has table nine had their wine?"

After she briefed Lindsay on her tables, Jennifer went to the front of the restaurant where Aidan stood waiting for her, incongruous in his huge, woolly cardigan and combat trousers. His hair had been slightly dreaded for a while, and not for the first time, Jennifer wished he'd smarten up his act a bit. If he stopped dressing like a vagrant, perhaps there'd be a sliver of a chance he could get himself some work. Funny enough, there wasn't a massive demand for middle-aged, pot-smoking surfer dudes in Carlisle.

"Is Nate at home?" she asked, exhausted to her very bones now that she'd stopped for a second.

"He's next door at the gas station buying a soda."

On cue, Nathan appeared, clutching a can of Fanta.

"All right, babe?" Jennifer asked, pleased to see him. He was still in his uniform. "Has your dad given you some dinner?"

Nathan nodded.

"What did you have?"

"We had some eggs, didn't we?" answered Aidan on his behalf.

"Shall I ask Lindsay if there's any spare banoffee pie?" asked Jennifer, knowing it was his favorite and wishing she had more time to cook for her son. He was looking so tall. His body, which at one point had been quite scrawny, all arms and legs, was starting to fill out. He was sixteen and growing before her very eyes. Her beautiful boy was on the verge of becoming a man.

"Banoffee would be great, if there is any," Nathan said, still boyish enough to get excited about his favorite dessert.

Jennifer gestured to Aidan to head out to the back of the restaurant while she got Nathan settled at one of the spare tables with his huge slab of banana, toffee, and cream pie.

"There you go, love. Get that in you. Right, I'd better go and see what your dad wants."

"Okay… Oh, hang on a minute, Mum. I've got something for you."

Jennifer watched as her son stood up briefly so he could get into the pocket of his trousers. He fished out a crumpled ten-pound note and five-pound coins and placed them on the table.

"What's that for?" she asked, bemused.

"It's for you," Nathan said, sitting down again and making a start on his dessert, eyes practically rolling to the back of his head as he enjoyed his first hit of thick cream and toffee.

"What's the money for, Nate?" repeated Jennifer.

"I earned it the other night when I babysat. I want you to have it."

"Don't be silly," she said immediately.

"I'm not. You're always working in here, and I know Dad hasn't done much lately. I just want to help out a bit."

Jennifer swallowed, touched by her son's gesture yet despairing that her boy was learning to be a man, not by example but as a result of his father's glaring uselessness. She was also deeply saddened that he'd picked up on how much they were struggling. She went to give him a hug across the table.

"Mum," he protested, embarrassed by her public display of affection.

"Sorry," she said, grinning. "It's just that I love you, my precious, generous boy. And I don't want you worrying about money. We're fine."

"Stop it," said Nathan, smiling.

"Right, I'd better go and see what Dad wants," she said, wishing it was the end of the night so she could go home with them. It had been a busy lunchtime shift, and the evening was shaping up to be the same, which was great in terms of tips, but not so good for her aching feet.

At the back of the restaurant, in the small courtyard, Jennifer breathed deeply. The fresh May evening air was good for the soul. Occasionally, when she could afford it, she liked to go to a yoga class in the church hall around the corner from the apartment. The teacher, Kerry, was amazing. She was fifty years old with a figure most thirty-year-olds would be proud of, which she attributed entirely to daily yoga. Kerry had once told Jennifer that everyone had a finite amount of breaths to take during their lives; hence, if you could slow down your breathing and therefore your stress levels, you could live longer.

Whenever Jennifer remembered this and made the effort to become "aware of her breath," she was dismayed to discover how sharp and quick her intake was. It was always a depressing reminder of the pace she was going. She often worried that if she didn't slow down, and if her teacher's theory was correct, she might keel over any minute.

"You all right?" asked Aidan, looking sheepish as she approached and flicking away the end of a cigarette, which he stamped out with his boot.

"Yeah. What did you want to talk about? Has this got anything to do with Nate? I'm worried about him, you know. He's not stupid. He can tell when things aren't right between us."

"Nate's fine. Come here, you," he said, drawing her tense body in for a hug.

Ordinarily she would have enjoyed the comforting sensation of being encircled in his arms, but she was too much in need of a shower to relax into it properly. Red Peppers was a lovely restaurant, but she'd be quite happy never to see a piece of deep fried Camembert again as long as she lived. It was their most popular starter, and the stench of fried cheese seemed to be ingrained into the fibers of every shirt she owned.

"So anyway, I came to say that if you really want to see your mum, it's fine by me."

"That's good of you," she said sarcastically.

"Look, you have to remember that, up until a week ago, I thought we were on the same page as far as your parents were concerned, you know? I mean, you're the one who used to get so fed up with their attitude and with how judgmental they were."

Jennifer shrugged. She couldn't agree or disagree, because she couldn't really remember how things had managed to get as bad as they had. She also wasn't sure she cared anymore. All she knew was that she had a family, and that, many moons ago, she also used to have good friends, better ones than she'd made since. Only the other day, she'd looked up Karen on reUNIon. It hadn't taken long to find her, at which point Jen had written her prediction of what she'd thought Karen would be up to now. She'd written that she thought she'd be happy, married, possibly with a couple of kids, and no doubt in some high-powered, impressive job, living the high life. She was still waiting to hear back, though, and if her old friend ever made the effort to respond, she wasn't sure she'd be brave enough to read what Karen had predicted for her.

After all this time, she still missed Karen. She missed all her old friends, in fact, but not as much as she missed the feeling of belonging. These days, she was starting to think she might need, or maybe just want, more in her life than she had at the moment. Hence the reflexology course. She'd given up a lot to be with Aidan and knew she was in danger of growing bitter if she didn't take charge of her own destiny, because she wasn't 100 percent sure he'd been worth it.

It hadn't mattered how many times she'd tried to stick up for him or explain that dabbling with a bit of marijuana hardly made him an evil drug baron; it had been a pointless task. Her parents were the kind of people who considered all drugs to be inherently dangerous and wrong. Worse still, what they really couldn't get their heads around was why he would have taken such a risk when he was responsible for their only daughter.

At the time, Jennifer had refused to consider that they may have had a point, for if she had, she also would have been admitting to herself and everybody else that she'd made a mistake. A huge, life-changing mistake.

She regarded Aidan. He was so bloody useless, and yet there was something about him that still, after all these years, she was drawn to, and whatever it was, it was a force to be reckoned with. She stepped toward him and held his face in her hands, looking up at him as she had a thousand times before.

"It's fine. Let's forget about it. I'm just glad you're cool about me seeing her."

They hugged, and as they did, Jennifer buried her face deep into Aidan's side. As ever, she drew comfort from the physical sensation of being held and used it as a balm to soothe her sad, troubled soul. This felt normal to her, but what she didn't realize was that she'd forgotten what it was to feel truly happy.

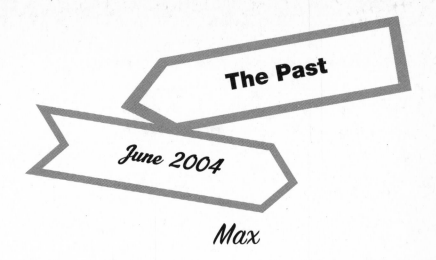

The Past

June 2004

Max

"I'm exhausted," declared Jennifer, flopping backward onto the huge bed and disappearing in a cloud of tulle, satin, and netting. The fabric at the bottom of the dress was no longer white but gray from where it had trailed along the ground all day.

"Tiring business, getting married," agreed Max from the other side of the room. "But did we have the best wedding or what?"

"By miles," said Jennifer contentedly, stretching her arms above her head and then swiping them up and down, enjoying the feel of the luxurious damask she was lying on.

"You look like a snow angel," said Max, swaying by the minibar as he tried to fix them both a drink.

"You look like a handsome movie star," said Jennifer, feeling totally drained yet exquisitely happy that after a long year of planning, it was all over, it had gone well, and they were finally alone. The two of them. Mr. and Mrs. Wright.

"You're my wife," Max stated.

"You're drunk. You're my drunk husband."

"You're sexy. Give us a flash of your panties."

Jennifer acquiesced.

"Ooh, that is sexy."

"Stop making drinks and come here, you big lug."

Max seemed more than happy to go along with that. Getting the tops off of various bottles was proving too much effort anyway. He weaved his way across the room and flopped down beside her on the bed, turning onto his side so he could stare into her eyes. "Is this the bit where I'm supposed to make mad, passionate love to you?"

Jennifer wrinkled her nose, not wanting to be unromantic but also not in the mood to pretend. "To be honest, I'm quite happy just lying here for a bit. This corset's bloody killing me and actually…"

"Go on…"

"I am absolutely starving. Do you think they're still doing room service?"

"Er, didn't we just pay for a three-course dinner and an evening buffet?" asked Max, twiddling a lock of her hair idly between two fingers.

"Yeah, and I hardly ate any of it," Jennifer admitted.

"Well, in that case, my beautiful bride must have some fries."

Max heaved himself into an upright position and reached for the phone.

"Yes," said Jennifer, punching the air. "Chuck a burger in while you're at it. Cheeseburger, please."

"And they say romance is dead," he quipped, shaking his head as he proceeded to place their order. Cheeseburgers and fries for two.

When he'd finished, they lay on the bed, both in their own world, quietly reliving parts of the day until Jennifer said, "I loved the part in your speech when you said you'd never met anyone who loved celebrating birthdays as much as me and that you'd see to it forevermore that mine would always be celebrated properly."

"I meant it. I've never forgotten that little speech you gave about birthdays when we met. It was sweet. Slightly weird, but mainly sweet. What other part was your favorite?"

"This is my favorite part." She laughed, reaching across to grab a certain bit of his anatomy.

Max grinned. "That's another reason why I love you. You're terrible. Ooh, hang on a minute. I just remembered I've got something for you."

"Oh no! You haven't, have you?" Jennifer sat up, looking worried. They'd made a pact not to buy each other presents, having gone way over budget on the wedding as it was. She had adhered to it so now felt dreadful.

"Don't panic. It's only something silly," said Max, who had gotten up and was scrabbling around in his suitcase. Eventually he found what he was looking for, a beautifully wrapped, rectangular-shaped present.

"Oh my God, thank you so much," Jennifer said.

"Open it."

Jennifer pulled off the velvet ribbon and the paper to reveal a smart blue box. She took off the lid. Inside was a photo frame, facedown. "Oh, baby, how lovely. A frame! We can put a wedding photo in it."

Max shook his head. "There's already a photo in it. Turn it over."

Jennifer pulled the frame from the box and turned it around. When she saw what picture he'd chosen, she felt sentimental but also a bit confused. "It's me."

"Certainly is."

"In my pink dress."

"Yup," said Max.

"On the night we met."

Max nodded.

"In a photo that was taken by my ex?"

This was the part Jennifer didn't really get.

"It is indeed."

She studied the photo for a while. She looked so carefree and, even she had to admit, quite sexy. Her younger self was gazing straight down the lens, her hair an unruly mane tumbling around her shoulders, her eyes full of promise and mischief. It was disconcerting to know that the person she was staring at in such an uninhibited way wasn't Max but Steve.

"So why this one? It's so dog-eared. Shouldn't we keep one of us together in it?"

"No."

"But..."

"No buts," said Max, sitting down next to her on the bed again. "I chose that one for a reason. I love that photo. Always have. Apart from anything else, it's a reminder that I should never take you for granted, because no matter how long we're together, how married we are, or how old we get, you will always be that incredible girl in the picture. That girl who I spied at the party, wearing that sexy pink dress, who made my stomach flip. And yes, someone else did take the picture, someone else who loved you because you're bloody easy to fall in love with, which is yet another reason for me to always look after and treat you as you deserve. Look at you.

You're so alive and beautiful, and sometimes I still can't believe you're with me. I never want to stop feeling as lucky as I did back then and as lucky as I do today that you're mine."

Jennifer had to look up to quell the tears that were threatening to glide down her cheeks. She thought her heart might burst with love, and she leaned forward and kissed him tenderly on the mouth. "That's so lovely. Thank you so much, baby. I love you so bloody much."

"I love you too."

"And I promise we'll have sex tomorrow."

"Come here, silly," said Max, signaling to her to lie down and snuggle in, at which point he wrapped his arms around her and held her tight. Minutes later, when his hold on her slackened, Jennifer realized he'd fallen asleep. *Oh well*, she thought. Two burgers for her then. Right on cue, there was a knock at the door.

———

Half an hour later, Jennifer was stuffed to the brim and Max was still passed out, fully clothed and snoring like a walrus. From time to time, she glanced back at the picture of herself, which she'd placed on the bedside table. She marveled at how happy she was and how loved she felt, and as Max continued to sleep beside her, her heart expanded with emotion. He was right, of course; she had chosen him and she was glad, for nobody who'd come before had ever suited her quite like he did and no one ever would. How amazing it was to feel so utterly sure.

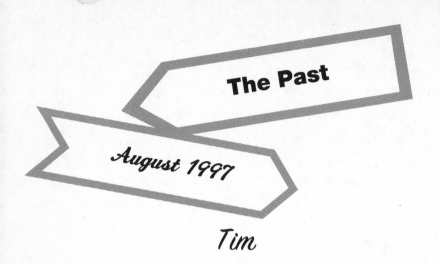

Tim

Things hadn't been particularly great between Jennifer and Tim for a while. Throughout their final year at Sussex, his obsession with reUNIon had overridden everything, including his studies, meaning that instead of doing brilliantly as predicted, he'd ended up with rather mediocre grades. Jennifer only truly realized the extent of his passion for reUNIon when he didn't seem bothered. She may have given up trying to compete ages ago, but that didn't mean she didn't feel jealous of the object of his obsession sometimes. If reUNIon were a woman, she'd merrily scratch her eyes out.

As for Jennifer, degree-wise, she'd done pretty well and was happy with what she'd achieved. But now, with university over, she was finding it hard to adjust and was worried that their student days may have been the glue holding her and Tim together.

Her mood was despondent, but then she was in a huge amount of debt, living back at home, and could only find a part-time job at a grocery store, whereas Tim had managed to rent an apartment that was ridiculously luxurious for someone of his age, companies were beginning to take an interest in his software designs, and he had lots of meetings lined up and a potential job at Apple. Being around him was enough to make Jennifer feel like one massive loser.

The pressure was on. That summer was the last bit of time she could get away with being directionless before people—her parents—started to lose patience. It was already the last day of August, summer was officially drawing to a close, and she was half expecting a PA announcement to go off, saying, "Jennifer, your time's up. You are now officially expected to get your shit together and be a responsible adult." It was terrifying, and yet the hardest thing was having to pretend she wasn't panicking inside and on the verge of a full-on meltdown.

She and Tim had gone out to a bar for drinks the previous night and had come back to his place after. Always preferable to hiding up in her small room at home, her mother banging on the door every five minutes, asking if they wanted a cup of tea when what she was really checking was whether they were having sex.

"Shall we go out for breakfast?" Tim asked, still typing away on his computer. He'd been up for a while, had showered, gotten dressed, and probably changed the world while Jennifer had been dozing and trying to figure out whether she wanted tea or coffee.

"I don't know," she said unhelpfully, staring into the distance.

Tim lived in Notting Hill in the most beautiful apartment Jennifer had ever been in. It had one spacious, light bedroom and a deluxe bathroom complete with walk-in shower. The living room, which was where they were sitting, had wooden floors, was big enough to include two large, gray sofas, and led onto a small eat-in kitchen that had been painted a startling but gorgeous shade of bright blue, the perfect contrast to the pale wood cupboards and stainless steel appliances. The living room walls were taupe and had two sets of floor-to-almost-ceiling glass doors, framed by wrought iron Juliet balconies. The doors were open and the morning breeze was blowing the calico curtains into the room.

"It's like a soft rock video in here," she joked absentmindedly, but Tim didn't reply. Instead, he shut down his computer and, almost without taking a pause between activities, leaped over to where she was sitting and made a lunge for her. With a look of intent and a mischievous, somewhat off-putting schoolboy grin on his face, he grabbed her, stuck his hand up her pajama top, and started massaging her left breast, though he wasn't particularly tender about it; if anything, it was slightly painful. However, mistaking her gasp of pain for one of passion, he upped the ante, and before she knew it, he was really going for it, twisting her nipple like he was trying to get an FM frequency.

Still, it seemed to be working for him because his breath grew short, and as he huffed and puffed in her ear, Jennifer decided she ought to try to get into it. However, when he suddenly stopped and looked at her with a pleading expression she'd come to know only too well, her heart sank.

"Real estate agent?"

"Really?"

"Yes. You should go out into the corridor and pretend you've arrived to do an evaluation."

Jennifer decided she couldn't pretend anymore. "Why can't I just be naked for once?"

"What?"

"Plain old me is never enough, is it? You always want me to be someone else these days. Honestly, I don't feel like putting on a suit and acting like I'm terribly excited by your apartment's potential." Her frustration was a long time coming. "For once, it would be nice if you wanted to have sex with me, Jennifer. Not Trixie the masseuse, Suzy the police officer, Laura the teacher, or now Jane the frigging real estate agent."

Tim pulled away, practically throwing her onto the other side of the sofa. "Oh well, that's charming. Talk about how to get rid of someone's erection, for Christ's sake."

"Well, I'm sorry," said Jennifer primly. "But perhaps you need to take into consideration what I want for a change, which is not always having to remember my lines and be in costume every time I want to have sex with my boyfriend."

"No, all you want is to whine at me," he said, though Jennifer noticed he'd had the decency to blush a pale pink.

"That's out of order," she snapped. "As if I whine?"

"It's true. Nag, nag, nag—that's all you do," he said.

"That's rubbish," she said, hurriedly pulling up her pajama bottoms. "What on earth could you say I nag you about?"

"Ooh, well, let me see now… My work, er… Seeing you, what I'm up to on a day-to-day basis, Sean, whether I'm coming out to whatever night of torture you and Karen have arranged…" He paused, letting his mean words sink in. He looked defensive, and Jennifer sensed he was only lashing out because he was embarrassed about his ridiculous addiction to role play.

"Frankly, what you should be focused on," he continued,

unable to look her in the eye, "is what you're doing with yourself and with your life."

"Oh well, it's all coming out now," said Jennifer, who was so angry she'd started contemplating what to throw out the window. On a braver day, she'd have gone for the computer but knew it would result in death, and not just hers if it landed on a passerby's head.

"I'm just saying that if you spent a little more energy deciding what it is you want to do rather than worrying about how much time I spend with Sean or how little time I spend with Pete and bloody Karen, you might be better off."

"Oh, will you get over yourself?" shouted Jennifer. "If I hear you mention Karen in an argument one more time, I'll lose it. What have you got against her? I mean, I know she can be prickly sometimes, but now that she's with Pete, she's calmed down and she's been so much more tolerant. Why can't you be the same?"

"Tolerant?" spat Tim. "If two people have to be tolerant of each other, then I would suggest they not bother going through the effort. Life's too short. And yes, that she's had a complete personality transplant since getting together with Pete hasn't escaped me, but why I should be a slave to her ridiculously volatile state, which seems solely dependent on if she's getting any sex, is anyone's guess."

"Well, at least she's not constantly trying to remember who she's supposed to be pretending to be that day because her boyfriend likes having sex with anyone but the real her," stormed Jennifer, livid beyond belief, springing up from the sofa and heading for the bedroom. Arguing while wearing pajamas was making her feel weird. She needed jeans and a sweater for this.

She had been so happy when Karen had gotten together with Pete at the end of university. Her friend was finally happy, and although nobody could have predicted that after a whole two years of living under the same roof, barely noticing each other, she and Pete would finally find each other (underneath a pile of coats in Jim's room, to be precise), it had taken the pressure off Jennifer. "At least Karen's got a personality, unlike the almost mute freak who is Sean," she yelled from the bedroom, where she had already yanked on some clean underwear and jeans and was in the process of hooking her bra.

"And at least he's got a brain and knows what he wants out of life," retorted Tim.

In that instant, Jennifer stopped feeling angry and went cold. A fraction of a second later, she realized she might be finished with this relationship. Because deep down, she knew that what he'd said earlier was probably right. With Tim, she *did* turn into a shrew, a nag. His success made her feel inadequate and yet didn't inspire her to do anything about her own situation. Instead, it fed her permanent sense of insecurity.

Did she love him? She didn't really know, so perhaps that answered that one. Did she like him? Sometimes. She loved the way he challenged and stimulated her intellectually. Did she admire him? Hugely. There was something about Tim that screamed, "I AM GOING PLACES." But did she want to go with him? She was no longer sure she had the energy or the desire to. If she thought about it, she might love his apartment more than him. It was a tough one, though. There would be plenty of girls lining up to take her place. No doubt they'd happily dress up like bloody Minnie Mouse if it made him happy. Was this something she'd regret down the line? Would she ever meet anyone else as eligible? Was the fear of ending up alone enough reason to stick with a relationship that didn't really make her happy?

Pulling a sweater over her head, she decided what to do, and as her decision was made, she was flooded with an eerie sense of calm.

"Tim," she said after she wandered back into the sitting room.

"What?"

"I can't do this anymore. We don't really make each other happy, so why are we bothering? I think we should call it a day."

"What?" he repeated, completely thrown. He sank down onto the nearest sofa, pulling his trousers at the thigh to achieve a bit of give, an action that reminded her of something her father would do.

"I just think we should admit defeat," she added more gently. "You're right. I do spend far too much time complaining, mainly because I get jealous of how much attention you pay to your work all the time."

There, she'd said it.

Tim sighed. "And I only get frustrated because I know how much potential you have, and it irritates me to see you procrastinating all the time and never actually…doing anything."

"Which just goes to show how different we are as people and that we'd probably be better off without each other," she said flatly, knowing she was right and wishing she'd had the balls to say it two years earlier.

Tim got up and paced the room. "You're wrong," he said.

"Am I?" asked Jennifer.

110

"Totally wrong," he said firmly. "You're right for me, Miss Drew."

Jennifer flinched. She'd always hated how he used her last name as a term of endearment.

"Opposites attract and I don't really mind your inertia. I only worry because I know not having any direction gets to *you*. Personally I wouldn't care if you never did anything, because I'm more than happy to take care of you. You know I am. You know I'm an old-fashioned bloke at heart, and I have no problem with men taking care of the finances and women looking after the home."

"We're not living in the Dark Ages," she spluttered. "I don't want looking after, thank you, and I don't necessarily want to be a damn housewife either." Jennifer was surprised by her own use of the word *necessarily*. It was as though she was hedging her bets, which, disappointingly, meant Tim was probably right: she didn't know what she wanted out of life.

"Oh well, that really is a load of crap, if you don't mind me saying," said Tim. "Of course you do. I've been looking out for you ever since we met, but I'm saying that I don't mind. I like it."

Jennifer was completely on the back foot. Was that really how he'd seen it all these years? Like she'd been some pathetic, free-loading sap he'd had to look out for? And what exactly had he done for her? Even as this last thought was formulated, she was already thinking back to university and of all the times Tim had bailed her out. Of all the times he'd "taken care of" a phone bill she couldn't afford. Of how much food she used to squirrel out of his fridge, realizing each time that she was saving herself a bit of money. She hardly ever paid when they went out, and when she did, she used to make a thing of it, making sure he got the message. Ultimately, however, if she had occasionally taken advantage of his deep pockets, it had only been because she knew he could more than afford it and because he never minded. She felt ashamed. It was time to get a backbone.

"Well, I do mind you saying," she said. "I don't want to be taken care of, and I wasn't really aware that I had been or that you'd noticed. I mean, you've always been very generous, but I wasn't aware I was riding on some Tim Purcell gravy train."

"Oh, come on, Drew," he said. "Don't give me that bullshit. And don't make some big issue out of it. I like that you're a bit scatterbrained, that you're quirky. I need that. It's a good foil for me. You're funny and sweet. I like your little eccentricities."

Jennifer gulped. How sad that in two and a half years, this was the first time he'd been able to articulate what it was he liked about her. She'd always wondered. "You make me sound a bit...simple."

"Well, I have to say, Drew, at times, I wonder."

"My name's Jennifer," she said firmly. "Not Drew. Just Jennifer. I am not a private school boy."

Tim's face was grim, his eyes flinty and confused. She could see his mind racing, so desperate was he to regain control of the situation. For a split second, she felt really angry with him, because he was quite controlling in a passive-aggressive kind of way, and perhaps if he hadn't put her down as much as he had, she might have had a bit more confidence in herself.

"So what are you saying? Do you want a break?"

"No," she said quietly. "I think we should split up. I'm saying that while we've had some great times, we've forgotten how to have fun, and we're still young, so that's not right. I'm saying that we don't bring out the best in each other and that I don't want to compete with reUNIon anymore. I'm really sorry."

Tim gazed at her in shock from across the room, and if she'd had any lingering doubts as to whether she was doing the right thing, they all disappeared, because there wasn't just a physical distance between them but a whole aching chasm of wrongness. If she ended up lonely and depressed for the rest of her life, so be it. Surely it was better to be single than in a vaguely dysfunctional relationship.

She waited patiently, expecting Tim to digest what she had said, to think logically about it before analyzing the facts, and then to interpret and manage them dispassionately. To her surprise, he did something very out of character, something she never would have expected.

He cried.

"Don't do this, Jen," he pleaded, his blue eyes brimming with tears.

For a while, she didn't reply. She was too surprised by his...surprise.

"I just don't think we bring out the best in each other," she repeated, feeling a definite and very welcome sense of relief about having reached her decision. It was then that she realized just how many doubts she must have had. "I'm sorry."

"I can't believe you're being such a bitch," said Tim.

"Don't get nasty," she warned.

"I have done nothing but love you," he ranted. "And this is how you repay me. How could you?"

She sighed and, not wanting to continue the scene, went to get her stuff from the bedroom, though she'd probably leave the policewoman outfit where it was.

"Just think about it for a few days, Drew…um…Jen. Don't do this on a whim. You'll regret it."

"I'm sorry," she repeated. "I've made up my mind."

She gathered all her stuff into her bag and switched on her phone. How odd. She had eight new text messages and the voice mail symbol was flashing. The first message read: Have you seen the news?

"Weird," Jennifer said.

"What?" Tim asked, looking fairly pitiful. His tears were terribly disconcerting. So out of character. They didn't suit him.

"Turn on the TV for a second," she instructed, and when he ignored her, she went back into the living room and did it herself.

Within seconds, the reason she had so many messages, five from her devastated mother, became clear. Princess Diana had died.

For the next three hours, what had passed between Jennifer and Tim became irrelevant, unimportant, and completely secondary to the story unfolding on the news. They sat gazing at the footage in shock, feeling desperately sad. Jennifer was in tears and Tim was pretty choked up, which was unexpected given that he was completely antiroyalist. It took a while before Jennifer finally felt able to wrench herself away from the TV to make her journey back to her parents'. As she said good-bye, she suspected it was the last time she would see Tim. Deep down, she doubted they'd remain friends.

She was partially right. It was the last time Jennifer would see Tim in the flesh, and yet a mere twelve months later, there was no escaping his face, and she saw him practically every day. For when reUNIon finally, possibly inevitably, took off, it was everywhere, and so was Tim, including, on one occasion, on the ten o'clock news.

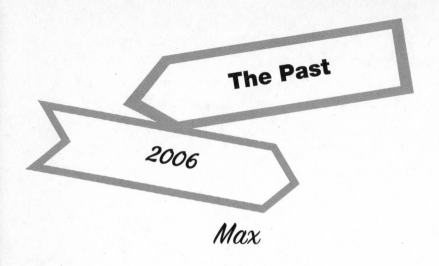

The Past

2006

Max

"Going out somewhere?" Jennifer's boss, Janine, yelled after her departing back.

"Er, family dinner, but I'll be in early tomorrow."

"No problem," replied Janine, waving her hand in an airy manner designed to suggest that she was cool either way when clearly she wasn't. She seemed flabbergasted that Jennifer was doing the unthinkable and committing a huge office offense by... wait for it...*leaving on time*.

It annoyed Jennifer. Her hours were nine thirty to six, but her colleagues were miserably competitive. Staying at their desks later than was required had practically become a professional sport, meaning anyone wishing to attempt some sort of a life during the week appeared to be slacking.

Still, she wasn't going to fret about that. She had bigger things to think about.

Half an hour later, she emerged from Clapham North subway station, and as she headed home, she ended up breaking into a trot, unable to prevent a wide grin from spreading across her face. She wondered if passersby could tell that she was a spectacularly useful and clever creature just by looking at her.

Jennifer was happy to see that Max had obeyed orders and arrived home as promptly as she had.

As soon as she walked in the door, he looked up and raised an eyebrow, not wanting to preempt what she was about to say but unable to hide his anticipation.

By way of reply, she simply nodded, eyes shining. To prove it, she pulled out the stick she'd peed on eight long hours before. She loved what that stick had told her so much, she'd allowed it to remain alongside the luxury lining of her beloved Coach handbag.

"I knew it," said Max, punching the air and leaping up to hug her. "Oh, Jen, you clever, clever thing. That's amazing. When did you find out?"

"This morning," she said, so relieved to finally be able to talk about it. "I just had a feeling. My boobs were really aching and I had this odd crampy feeling, so I thought, right, no point putting it off."

Max hugged her tightly.

"But we're not allowed to get excited yet," Jennifer instructed pointlessly, "and I don't want to tell anyone until we've had the scan. Except my mum. Obviously."

"Agreed," said Max solemnly. "Oh my God, Jen, I can't believe it."

Later, as they ate dinner in front of the TV, grinning like idiots at each other, it was impossible to ignore the fact that, all being well, in around thirty-four weeks' time, their lives would change forever.

In the end, it was Jennifer who gave in. "I guess we'll need to move then."

"Guess so," agreed Max. "God, suburbs, here I come. I'm going to need a shed, obviously, and to start getting excited about stuff like mowing the lawn."

"Janine's going to be gutted, you know," Jennifer replied distractedly. "She won't want anyone else handling the Lancing project. Perhaps she'll make Ed and Sue share my workload till I get back, rather than get a freelancer in?"

Jennifer was part of a small marketing team at an ad agency and had played an integral part in winning Lancing's business. Lancing was a recruitment firm in need of a total image overhaul and with a big enough budget to pay for both print and radio advertising. Jennifer had a great relationship with them so Janine had put her in charge of the project. She'd been looking forward to the challenge of overseeing everything and having some creative input for the first time too. It would be strange handing the responsibility over to someone else. There was so much to consider; it was quite overwhelming.

"What do you mean?" Max asked. "I thought you said you don't want to be one of those women whose nanny knows more about her child than she does."

Jennifer finished her mouthful before replying. "I don't. And

I'm not sure if I will be going back yet, but I might, and either way, it's going to affect things massively for all my colleagues. And besides, what I said didn't necessarily mean I don't want to work."

"Oh, right."

Jennifer twirled her spaghetti. She wanted to change the subject, but it proved impossible. Perhaps it was her heightened hormones, but his question had made her feel uneasy, like they weren't quite on the same page.

"But seeing as you've brought it up, the last time we spoke about it, I *told* you I wasn't decided either way. Don't you remember me saying I might go part-time? You seemed completely cool about it."

"I am cool about it," Max said. "Whatever you decide to do, I'll be right behind you."

"Okay. Good."

"Course I will be. Though what I will say is that knowing Janine, if you go part-time, she'll want her pound of flesh, only for less money than you're getting now, which might be more stress than it would be worth."

Jennifer had to concede that he might have a point. Janine could be a taskmaster.

"So if you work, great, the money will be handy and I'm sure we'll make it work somehow, but be prepared to hand the majority of your wages over to a nanny."

Jennifer had assumed they'd both pay for a nanny if they both worked. She wasn't sure what to say.

"And if you don't, then that's great too and you'll be doing the most important job in the world."

Jennifer wished he'd stop addressing the television.

"But whatever you do is great by me and we shouldn't be having this discussion now anyway," he added, reaching over to give her foot a squeeze. "Tonight we should just be enjoying the fact that after all these months, I no longer have to shag you on command or constantly be aware of what your eggs are up to at any given moment."

Jennifer smiled and concentrated on feeling reassured, determined not to let anything ruin the evening. This was what they'd both wanted for a long time. So why did what Max wanted seem so apparent? *The most important job in the world.*

Later, Jennifer phoned her mother. She'd been dying to make the call for so long. Her mother was predictably thrilled, so it was a very special moment, marred only by the cogs that persisted on whirring in her brain to the point where she ended up broaching the subject again, keen to get another point of view.

"What do *you* think, Mum?"

"I think it's a bit early to be worrying about all of this, but I agree with Max. It's up to you, love. Though, for what it's worth, I would think very carefully before giving up your financial independence."

Jennifer was surprised. Her mother had been a housewife all her life, so she'd have bet heavily on her having the opposite view.

"Why?"

"Oh, I don't know. I just think times have changed. You young women have so many more choices than my generation did and that freedom has been fought for, so you should be careful with it."

"Okay," Jennifer said. "I will be, and I haven't decided either way yet anyway. I like my job, but I want to be the best mum in the world too, and I'm not sure if I'll be able to pull both things off at once."

"True." Her mother chuckled. "Well, listen, either way, we're very proud of you. Proudest day of my life was the day you graduated from university, and I'm sure the next one will be when I see you being a wonderful mother. But don't forget you've got a clever brain in there. Working isn't just about money; it's about your identity as well. And you're very lucky to have the choice."

"I know," Jennifer said ruefully. "Although sometimes I think having no choice is almost easier because then you just have to get on with it, whereas having choices means I have to make a decision that could turn out to be the wrong one."

"Well, that's life, isn't it? A series of decisions, some bigger than others, of course, and some that we don't even realize will affect our lives but do. Should I turn left or right? Get the bus or the train? Stay in or go out? But enough of this gloomy talk. We've got a lot to be thankful for and I've got booties to knit, so let's speak tomorrow, shall we?"

"Thanks, Mum," said Jennifer sincerely, grateful that her mother didn't seem to have any agenda and was happy to be objective and let her come to her own conclusion.

———

Later that night, Max snuggled in for a hug. "You asleep?"

"Nearly," Jennifer murmured. "Why?"

"Nothing. It can wait. Night night."

"No, go on. You've got to say it now," she said, irritated. This whole hormone thing wasn't boding well so far.

"I was just going to say that I really don't want you worrying about work during this pregnancy. I know you love your job, but you're growing our baby now, and I will always look after and provide for you both."

"I know," said Jennifer, wondering if her husband was going to go the whole nine yards and put her in an actual cave and perhaps start venturing out to hunt for their food. "Now go to sleep. I'm tired."

For three days a week, Jennifer worked at Hayes and Ludlow, one of the many real estate agencies on the High Street. She was amazed how any of them managed to stay in business. So many shop fronts had changed in recent years, hit by the recession, but it seemed that in this enclave of South West London, if you were a hairdresser, an Indian restaurant, or a real estate agent, you could weather any financial shit storm.

Sometimes, when she thought wistfully of her old job, it felt more like an old life. A life where she'd worn a suit and used to go for after-work drinks with colleagues. A life where, once a year, they'd all travel by bus to Swindon and have an uproarious few days, which made all the long hours, tricky clients, and ever-decreasing budgets they endured the rest of the time seem worthwhile. Still, after having children, the cost of child care meant it hadn't made much financial sense for her to continue working. Plus, nothing could have prepared her for the demands of motherhood or how intensely she'd love her baby. With Max growing more and more resistant to the idea of her going back, it hadn't seemed worth the battle. Going back would have compromised everybody's setup and would only have benefited her, in terms of retaining her sense of who she was and continuing to utilize her brain. And life wasn't all about her anymore. So the suits she could no longer fit into properly had been put away, as had any shoes with a vague heel. She'd gradually come to terms with the fact that the hours between six and eight were no longer nice ones for a drink, unless you counted a quick swig of wine gulped directly from the bottle in order to get through bath time, and on the whole, she'd been happy with this arrangement. When considering leaving her offspring in a nursery or with a babysitter when she didn't really have to, she'd experienced so much guilt that she hadn't known whether she'd have coped with the separation anyway. So it was fortunate that Max's wage was enough for them to survive on. Just about. Although their monthly expenditures became something that had to be planned down to the last penny.

However, when five-year-old Polly had started school, working had become a sensible option again. The money would be extremely useful, and it certainly beat feeling obliged to clean the bathroom on a daily basis. Of course, having been out of the rat race for so long and with jobs so scarce, Jennifer had known she was unlikely to get anything even vaguely resembling her old career in marketing. She did take Janine out for a hopeful coffee at one point but soon realized that, as far as her old boss was concerned, she was already from a different era in terms of how much the business and their practices had changed. So although being a real estate agent hadn't exactly been her burning ambition in life, when she was offered the job, she'd decided it was far better than nothing. She got to poke around people's houses, it got her out of her own house, and there was the added bonus that she got to chat to Lee all day.

Lee was lovely. He was young and really quiet, or at least he was until you got to know him. He had a kind face and a shaved head, usually two things that don't go hand in hand and yet possibly should, for as it turned out, they were a remarkably good combination. Jennifer liked hearing about his exploits, mainly because they didn't resemble her own life in any way at all. That day, he was filling her in on what he'd been up to on the weekend.

"So then where did you go?"

"So after that, we ended up going on to this amazing club in Shoreditch. Have you heard of East Village?" he asked, at which point Jennifer decided she might love him for assuming there was the possibility she'd know where the hell he was talking about.

"Um." She turned her head to one side in what she hoped was an attractive fashion. "I've definitely heard of it," she lied. "But I don't think I've been there."

"Oh, right. Well, you should. It's brilliant. There was this one DJ who I'd definitely go see again. He was amazing. He played, like, really good dubstep mixed up with more commercial tunes."

"Cool," said Jennifer, wondering what dubstep was and deciding to google it and find out the minute she could. God, she'd love a night out clubbing. She hadn't had a proper dance since... well, probably New Year's Eve, and that was in someone's kitchen, surrounded by balding men who were wearing cords or chinos.

"What did you do?" Lee asked.

"Oh...well, the kids had a sleepover on Friday so we just had a night in," she said, blushing as she did so, hating how that mere sentence sounded so full of innuendo. Wasted innuendo. "Then, on Saturday, we had some friends around for lunch, which was really fun," she fibbed.

"Oh cool, that sounds nice," he said politely.

"How old are you?" she asked suddenly, changing the subject.

"Me?" asked Lee, looking surprised.

"Well, there's no one else in here right now."

"Twenty-one."

"Ooh, lucky bastard," she replied flatly.

He shrugged, conveying that of course there was nothing lucky about it at all. Twenty-one years was simply the amount of time he'd been on the planet.

"I'll be twenty-two in October," he offered almost apologetically. "Why? How old are you then? You're not that old."

"How old do you think I am?" she asked, noting the word *that* and not liking it. She knew full well asking him to guess was a horrible thing to do to him, but she didn't care enough to stop herself.

"Um..."

She could see Lee concentrating, desperate not to mess up his answer, thus offending her. She knew then that whatever age he thought she was, he would undoubtedly shave a few years off to be polite.

"Thirty, thirty-one?"

"Thirty-eight," she said, surmising that he must have thought she was about thirty-four, which wasn't bad at all. She'd take that.

To her immense pleasure, Lee looked genuinely surprised. "Oh, right. Well, you definitely look younger than that. You're a proper..."

"What?" Jennifer laughed.

"Nothing." Lee blushed, looking mortified. "I was about to say something really awful. Something that would have made me sound like such an idiot."

"Oh, go on; you've got to say it now," Jennifer urged. This was more fun than she'd had in ages, but just then, Patrick Ludlow, one of the partners, came in, putting a stop to any more inappropriate, nonwork-based, vaguely flirtatious chat.

Jennifer reluctantly picked up a set of keys on her desk and went to meet her two thirty viewing, the last one she'd do before picking up the children from school.

In that moment, she hated herself a bit because deep down, she'd been hoping that Lee had been about to call her a MILF. A word that was tasteless at best and offensively sexist at worst, that would ordinarily have her feminist hackles up. Yet had Lee thought she was one, she would have felt rather pleased. Oh God, she was going through some kind of "phase." There was no doubt about it.

As she showed a couple around a rather pokey, overpriced two-bedroom apartment, she recalled her conversation with Lee and wondered how she seemed from his perspective. Like a boring housewife? Or like a sophisticated older woman? She prayed it was the latter.

Twenty-one. That had been a fairly devastating moment. She'd had him down as at least twenty-five. *What was I up to at twenty-one*, she wondered once she'd said good-bye to the disillusioned and thoroughly depressed couple who'd just realized they could probably never afford to get on the housing ladder unless they bought a Dumpster for a house.

At twenty-one, she'd been in her last year at university and was going out with Tim, of course. Tim, who was busy planning the empire he was going to build and rule. God, it all felt like a million years ago.

———

That night, Jennifer cooked an especially nice dinner for herself and Max, insisting that they eat it at the table over a bottle of wine.

"So, how was your day?" Jennifer asked.

"Good, thanks. Judith and I had to give a presentation this morning, which went really well. She certainly knows how to communicate, that one. I'll give her that."

"Did she ever 'communicate' anything about last weekend, by the way? Like, for instance, did she have chronic diarrhea on Saturday night, or was she okay?"

Max grinned. "I think she was fine, although I had to come clean about the chickens."

"What do you mean?" Jennifer asked, frozen in horror.

"It's not a big deal. I just told her they were from a deli and that we'd been a bit worried that we might have poisoned everyone."

"Oh God." Jennifer cringed, wishing he hadn't and feeling furious that he was always being so fucking chummy with Judith.

"She was fine," Max added. "We laughed over it. We also laughed about the fact that Henry just shoveled it all in without even a second look while we sat there not saying anything but all privately worrying for our guts."

"So you were laughing at me," Jennifer mumbled.

Max tutted. "No, we weren't. Funny enough, Judith and I don't spend our time being mean about you."

"Oh, well, what do you and Judith spend 'your time' doing then?" Jennifer spluttered, shaking Parmesan vigorously over her spaghetti Bolognese.

Max sighed but said nothing.

"What?" Jennifer snapped.

"Nothing."

"No, seriously, what? Don't just sigh like that. I'm not stupid. I can tell you've got something to say."

"I'm a bit fed up with you being so…angry all the time. I don't know what's gotten into you lately. You're so aggressive about everything."

Jennifer put the cheese down and regarded her husband before exhaling hard. He had a point. Yet what she wanted to articulate—but couldn't—was that she was only acting aggressively because lately the way he was being made her feel so defensive. "I know. You're right. I don't know what's gotten into me lately either."

"Not me, that's for sure," Max quipped, which did at least raise a smile, albeit a sad one.

"I just…"

"What is it?" he asked, and for the first time in a long time, Jennifer felt like he really wanted to know.

"I don't know," she said truthfully. "It's just lately I've been questioning everything, you know?"

"Like what?"

"Like what the hell I'm doing with my life. I mean, I'm thirty-eight. I work three days a week in a real estate agency, which is perfectly fine, only I earn less money than our weekly food bills, which is ironic, because if I'd stuck at my old job, I wouldn't be paying for much child care now that the girls are at school."

This was a familiar, well-trodden theme that she tried to gloss over, not wanting to annoy Max so much that she lost his attention.

"You and I seem to be in a bit of a rut. Plus I seem to irritate you more than I used to, and I know we've got everything and that I should be bloody grateful for that...but I just feel so sad at the moment. And...frustrated... And, if I'm being totally honest, I'm getting a bit fed up with hearing about flipping Judith every five seconds."

Max looked at her for a while, then shoveled more spaghetti in his mouth, seemingly unmoved by her outburst.

"You," he said, pointing at her with his fork, "are having an MLC."

"A what?" Jennifer asked, irritated that he had already come up with some crap acronym for what she felt was a pretty life-changing and difficult phase. Was that the best he could do?

"An MLC," he repeated. "Mid. Life. Crisis. You've always been a bit impatient, so instead of waiting to get to forty, you're bringing it forward to thirty-eight."

"I'm not sure it's as simple as that," Jennifer said, feeling flustered. "I mean, I'm sure there is a bit of that in the mix. I hate being our age sometimes. I hate that we never go out dancing and that a lot of people my age wear boot-cut jeans, but it's more than that, Max. I don't think the doctor just hands out antidepressants to anyone."

"I know," he said, not looking totally convinced. "And I know you've been really down, but you've got to remember that you're doing great. You're busy with the kids, and you've got a job, which helps bring in a bit of spending money."

"Patronizing."

"Sorry."

"How about a vacation?" Jennifer suggested, suddenly desperate not to be anxious and confused all the time. "I know we said we weren't going to have one this year, but you know what? I think it might be just what we need, as a family and, more to the point, as a couple."

"No," said Max. "You were the one who wanted to paint the front of the house last year, so let's just stick to the plan. We can go to my parents' during the summer for a while."

"Oh, well, that'll be a stress buster," Jennifer said sarcastically before taking a deep breath and trying again. "Okay, look, I know money's a bit tight, but how about if I take on some extra days at the agency? Then I can pay for us to go away."

"Er...where?" Max laughed in a way that made her want to grab the cheese grater and use it on his face.

"I don't know. Perhaps we could get a good deal somewhere last minute in Spain or wherever. I just think I've been feeling so down lately that a change of scene might sort me out, give me something to look forward to. I don't care if it's somewhere cheap and cheery."

"I think it's a bad idea," Max said. "I would rather not go anywhere than go somewhere shit and depressing just because it's the only thing we can afford. If my contract gets extended, we'll go on vacation next year, but this year we're in the middle of a massive recession, in case you hadn't noticed, so we have to go without and that's that."

"Again, patronizing," Jennifer said.

Later, as they sat in silence watching TV, Jennifer thought despairingly of their earlier exchange. She wasn't naive or stupid. She knew they were in a recession but sometimes wished Max would be a little less cautious. Yes, they would have to scrimp a bit to go away, but wouldn't it be worth it? Wasn't getting things back on track between them worth splurging on? *A divorce would be far more damaging to our finances than a vacation*, she thought bitterly, deciding against voicing this out loud.

For some reason, Tim popped into her head. *There is no chance he's going without a vacation this year*, she thought wryly. His wife was probably on one long holiday, like a leathered lizard bedecked in jewels. In fact, they probably owned a frigging island somewhere.

"Do you want to watch another episode?" Max asked with a yawn.

"No, that's all right," she said. "I think I might take a bath."

Ten minutes later, as she slid into water hot enough to cause serious problems with her veins, Max gave her a terrible shock by poking his head around the bathroom door on his way to bed.

"By the way," he said, "if you start wearing miniskirts with knee-high boots, we can definitely confirm the MLC."

Jennifer summoned her most sarcastic face possible and casually flipped him the bird, thinking as she did so, *And I can confirm that you are well and truly getting on my nerves.*

H ow did it go?" Karen asked as Jennifer barreled toward her friends in the pub, looking flustered.

"Fine," she said dismissively, not wanting to discuss the disaster that had been Friday night and her failure to lure her own husband into bed.

"You all right? You look stressed."

"Oh, it's just Max," she said. "He knew I wanted to get out tonight and promised he'd get back early but of course ended up *having* to stay later at work. He's being really weird at the moment."

"Well, it's not his fault if he has to work late, I guess," Karen said mildly, holding her handbag on her lap. Having come straight from work herself, she was wearing a rather staid black skirt suit, and not for the first time, Jennifer thought it a shame her friend refused to ever do any exercise. She was still carrying an awful lot of the extra weight that she'd put on when pregnant with Suzy. It didn't really matter, of course, and yet being a bit tubby and having such a huge bust made her look rather matronly, which in turn aged her considerably. She didn't resemble the feisty, big-breasted sex bomb she'd been in her youth.

In stark contrast, Lucy was looking better than ever. Having been the ugly duckling of the group when they were younger, she'd taken firm control of her appearance. She was gym- and yoga-honed, spent a considerable part of her wages on good haircuts and highlights, and had worked out that what suited her most were slim-fitting clothes in shades that complemented her English complexion.

"Anyway, enough of all that," said Jennifer, not wanting to sound like all she did was moan yet still not able to quash the uneasy niggle she'd had for ages that all was not right with her husband. "How are you both, and where's Esther?"

"Couldn't get a sitter," said Lucy. "Or wouldn't get a sitter, not sure which. I think money's a bit tight for them at the moment."

"Ah, fair enough then," said Jennifer, thinking what a shame it was and how pathetic that it was seemingly impossible for their foursome to be exactly that. It always proved so difficult to find a time when they could all abandon the responsibilities of work and child care for a few paltry hours. "I'm going to the bar. Are you both drinking wine? If so, I'll get a bottle."

When Jennifer returned from the bar, Karen seemed determined to get to the bottom of things. "Come on, Jen, you're obviously fed up. Why don't you tell us what's really wrong? It can't just be Max getting home late. Surely that's not such a big deal?"

"Oh, I don't know," replied Jennifer, smiling wryly at how well Karen knew her. "It's no biggie really. I'm just generally feeling a bit down. Bit depressed about being so unemployable and unsure how to fix it. Plus, things aren't that brilliant between me and Max at the moment, which he keeps blaming squarely on the fact that I'm having some sort of midlife crisis, which, to be fair, I probably am."

"Aren't we all?" asked Lucy with a laugh.

"I expect so," Jennifer agreed. "It's a weird stage of life. I keep reminding myself that I've 'got it all'—two lovely children, a husband, and a nice roof over my head, etc. Yet if you'd told me when I was twenty-one that by the time I was thirty-eight I'd be completely exhausted, work part-time in a real estate agency, and my marriage would be a bit stale, I'd have been horrified. Still, I'm not the only one feeling like this, am I?"

"Course not," agreed Karen vehemently. "Take last week, for instance. I got told by my bitch boss that I can't have a pay raise *yet again*, then five minutes later found out my male equivalent is earning ten grand more a year than me, so believe me when I say I know that 'how did it come to this?' feeling."

"Well, there you go then," Jennifer said. "But because I don't have any hope of resurrecting a decent career for myself, I should probably focus more on how drab things are between me and Max."

"Oh, you and Max are solid as a rock," protested Lucy, but Jennifer couldn't agree. It was her relationship, after all. She was the only one of them in it, so surely she was the one with the right to make sweeping statements about the state of it. "Christ, if you two are in trouble, what hope is there for the rest of us?"

Jennifer shrugged, not wanting her and Max to be held up as an example of the perfect couple all the time, a symptom of having married someone who got along well with her friends. She figured it was time to inject some positivity into the conversation before they all got the urge to smash their wineglasses and communally slash their wrists. "Well, I think there is hope, and it comes in the form of Esther and Jim, because although they've been together since the dawn of time, I don't think *they* have any problems in terms of staleness. I know they have problems financially, but the other day she told me that after a recent night out, they ended up doing it in their downstairs bathroom! I couldn't believe it."

Lucy gasped. "You're kidding me. They're like rabbits. How do they manage to keep things so fresh? I'd genuinely love to know."

"Why? Aren't you and Dave getting along?" Jennifer asked.

"Oh, we're all right," Lucy said flatly. "You know, we're fine, though recently I've wanted to murder him on pretty much a daily basis. It doesn't help that I've got a terrible crush on this guy who works in the deli around the corner from my work and I've developed a complete fantasy about him. I know it's because my sex life is so nonexistent at home, but I've been going there fully made-up most days. We've never had so many olives in the fridge. The kids actually know what a pimento is."

"I had no idea you and Dave didn't have a great sex life," said Jennifer, genuinely shocked.

"It's not really the sort of thing you broadcast, is it?" Lucy shrugged. "And it goes without saying I would appreciate it if you kept it firmly under your hat, please."

"Of course," Karen said. Jennifer could tell Karen was dying for a cigarette and was surprised she hadn't stepped outside for one yet. Jennifer figured Karen didn't want to miss any of the conversation.

"Oh, Luce, I know how you feel," Jennifer said, full of empathy. "I know Max loves me, but sometimes I feel like he hasn't looked at me properly for years. It sucks, doesn't it?"

"It's awful," agreed Lucy, leaning in and lowering her voice. "I mean, you know you've hit rock bottom when you go to the clinic for a vaginal probe to check you haven't got fibroids...and you actually enjoy it."

Karen recoiled, her face a shocked picture, turning this way and that to check no one near them had heard. "That's one of the funniest and most disgusting things I've ever heard in my life."

"I know," Lucy said. "Or the most depressing, I'm still not sure which. I even told Dave about it, to demonstrate how truly desperate I am for him to get his mojo back, but he just grunted and called me a weirdo. Now, come on, Jen. Max can't be that bad."

"Mmm...you say that, but I can't remember the last time he told me he loved me. Every time I try to reach out to him, he's either too tired or can't be bothered. He's so...casual about me, so complacent that sometimes I really wish..." Jennifer stared down at her glass, and for a worrying moment, she thought she might be about to cry. "Sometimes I wish I could have that feeling again. You know, the one you get when you first meet someone and everything's amazing and he's madly in love with you and can't keep his hands off you." She stopped, needing to express herself fully but slightly embarrassed by the next bit. "I suppose I want to be...grabbed. I want to be...desired, loved."

"But Max does love you," insisted Lucy, seemingly determined not to hear what Jennifer was saying. Maybe Jennifer's woes held a mirror up to her own marriage. "Any fool can see that."

"Oh, I don't doubt he loves me, like he loves his slippers or his iPad, but I don't think he *fancies* me anymore. He never wants to throw me on the bed or stroke my face or stare into my eyes."

"Oh, for God's sake!" Karen giggled despite herself. "You've got two children; of course he doesn't. That sort of passion never lasts, but it doesn't mean he doesn't find you attractive anymore."

"Then how come we haven't had sex in months?"

"How many months is 'months'?" asked Lucy.

"Four...no, actually, five now."

Already privy to this information, Karen simply looked on, though her face demonstrated exactly how dire she thought this was.

"I'm not kidding," Jennifer said in case anyone thought she was.

"Well, I don't think that's that bad," Lucy admitted, looking miserable.

That shut them up.

"You are joking?" Karen asked. "Why? How many have you gone without for?"

"Sixish?" she said quietly.

"That's awful, Lucy," Karen stated.

Jennifer agreed. She was dumbfounded and wondered if there was an actual complacency virus going around.

"Well, it's probably not *that* out of the ordinary," Lucy said defensively. "I mean, we have two children who never sleep. Honestly, it's like I've given birth to vampires, and Dave's been so stressed since losing his job, he's lost all his confidence. Sex is the last thing on his mind right now."

"Fair enough," agreed Jennifer. Dave's sense of self-worth had diminished before their very eyes after he got laid off. "And

I suppose with me and Max, we were never the sort of people who liked doing it in the evening. We always used to like doing it on the weekends, you know, when you could be leisurely about it in the mornings, so when you have children, there's never really an opportunity."

"Blimey," said Karen, still looking like her friends were talking another language. "I think Pete would prefer doing it in *front* of the children, no matter how scarred it would leave them, rather than go without."

Jennifer sighed. "It's not really sex I miss. It's excitement. Sometimes I find myself worrying that I could be on my deathbed, thinking, 'Why didn't you get your kicks when you could, you silly woman? Before you were too old and ugly to do anything about it.' The other day, I found myself remembering the time we went to Greece."

Her friend's faces immediately lit up at the memory.

Karen grinned. "Oh my God, what were we like? Do you remember that awful carpet fitter I was seeing?"

"Mark," Lucy said.

"Yeah, Mark. Did I tell you he sent me a Facebook friend request?"

"No way," said Lucy.

"Yup," said Karen proudly. "He sent me a prediction via reUNIon too. Sorry, Jen."

"Do you remember sexy Aidan?" asked Jennifer, ignoring the reference to reUNIon. She was used to it.

"God yes," said Lucy. "I was so jealous of you. He was beautiful."

"I know. I'd love to know what he is up to now."

"Drug dealing in Australia?" suggested Karen drily.

"No," tutted Jennifer. "He's probably in Oz, but I don't think he'd be doing that. Don't you remember he wanted to start up a scuba diving school? He's probably living the good life, on the beach, brown as a berry, healthy and happy."

"Do you remember how close you came to running off with him?" asked Karen. "I still get palpitations thinking about that now. I remember standing on that jetty thinking, 'Oh my God, I'm going to have to explain to her mum when she comes to pick us up at the airport: "Ah, hello, Mrs. Drew. No, Jennifer isn't with us. She's decided to stay with a sex god named Aidan and his nice big bag of white pills, which are the other thing she's taken quite a fancy to."'"

They all laughed.

"I seriously considered going with him, you know," Jennifer said.

"I know you did," Karen said. "Don't you remember me crying about it?"

Jennifer nodded. She could remember only too clearly the details of that scorching hot afternoon. But she'd hate her friends to know quite how often she'd found herself recalling them lately.

"You were always lucky on the man front. Do you remember Steve?" Karen added.

"Ah, lovely Steve," cooed Lucy, looking positively drippy. "He was such a dear, wasn't he? I always had a bit of a soft spot for him, and in terms of someone adoring you, my God, Jen, you couldn't have asked for anything more. He used to look at you like a puppy dog. Now there's an example of a man who would have walked on hot coals for you and was always complimenting you, but if you remember, it used to drive you mad," she said, practically wagging her finger. "To the point where it was the precise fact that Max was a bit cooler with you that made you feel like you'd met your match. You loved that he wouldn't let you get away with stuff like Steve did."

"True," Jennifer said. "I did love Steve, though, and I always appreciated how sweet he was to me. Finishing with him wasn't an easy decision by any stretch of the imagination. I got rid of a good man there, and we all know they don't grow on trees, don't we?"

"We do," said Karen, "which is why you're so bloody lucky to have bagged another one. Babe, I reckon you need to stop thinking there's something better for you out there. Stick with what you've got. It works. You've got a lovely house and two happy, secure children, and if you upended all of that, who knows how difficult life would be?"

"Who said anything about upending it?" Jennifer asked, unnerved by Karen's ability not only to hit the nail on the head, but then also to smash it hard with a mallet to illustrate her point. Karen had never been one to mince her words, but Jennifer didn't like how close to the bone she'd gotten this time.

Present Day

How is she today? Any change? Sorry we're late. We would have been here earlier but we wanted to check on the girls first."

"Thank you," said Max, bursting into tears, which surprised him more than it did anyone else. He had thought he was bearing up well, but the sight of Jennifer's parents looking so flooded with anxiety for their daughter was too much and brought home the severity of the situation once again. The guilt was eating him alive.

"Oh, you poor man," said Lesley, his mother-in-law, drawing him in for a hug. It was the first time she'd done so during all the time they'd known each other, but he went with it and was surprised by how comforting it was to be drawn into her ample bust.

"How are the kids?" Max eventually managed to ask. "They don't know anything yet, do they?"

"They're fine; don't you worry about them. They've still no idea, which I think is for the best at this stage. Till we've got a better idea of what's going on. Anyway, we left them with Karen, happy as pie, playing dress up. She's been a star."

"When's the doctor coming around?" asked Jen's father, Nigel.

"I didn't know he was unconscious," joked Max weakly.

Lesley and Nigel looked baffled.

"Sorry. That wasn't even funny, was it? In fact, it's the sort of feeble joke Jen would usually crack at a time like this," Max babbled. "Out of nerves. Completely inappropriate. I haven't slept much lately. I think I might be going a bit crazy."

"It's all right, love," said Lesley, eyeing him with such a mixture of concern and pity, it was obvious she concurred with the analysis of his mental state. "Do you remember when Uncle Ken died and Jennifer got the giggles at the funeral because the vicar's toupee was blowing around in the wind, then started to slip off his head at the graveside?"

"Oh gosh, yes," Max said, smiling sadly at the memory, grateful to Lesley for bearing with him.

"Thinking about it now, it probably was quite a comical sight, but at the time, I was furious with Jen for not having more decorum," she added.

They all fell silent for a second, lost in memories. Max hated it. The atmosphere they were creating was too similar to how people reflected about the deceased, yet his wife was still alive, sort of.

"Anyway, the doctor should be here by now," he said, determined to change the mood despite still being pretty choked up and having to use every ounce of bravery to stay composed. "You don't like to make too much of a fuss, because the staff have all been amazing so far, but at the same time, they never come when they say they're going to."

"Oh, but you're right, you mustn't make a fuss," agreed Lesley, clearly horrified at the mere thought.

What her mother said was one of the few things to penetrate Jennifer's consciousness.

It was a typical comment for her mother to make. She was the type of woman who'd rather eat a dish she hadn't ordered in a restaurant, even if she hated it, rather than "make a fuss." The familiarity of this personality trait was, in itself, a comfort. It was also a comfort to be aware of the presence of people, ones she knew cared about her, only she was still very confused about why she required comfort. Something terrible had happened. But what?

Hearing her mother's voice made her desperate to find out whether she would have rekindled her relationship with her had she stayed with Aidan. She hoped so. It wouldn't say much for either of them if they couldn't have found it within themselves to have salvaged something.

The next thing Jennifer knew, she was tumbling through space once more, a sensation she was becoming accustomed to. Hovering outside the portal, she was reluctant to go, *scared* to go.

It would be beyond devastating to discover that her relationship with her mother hadn't been able to survive one lousy decision. She waited, floating, like a fish suspended in a bowl, wondering what was going to happen. There were, after all, two other portals to visit. She wanted to discover what would have happened between her and her parents eventually, but perhaps that wasn't supposed to happen, for she found herself being pulled in another direction. It was time to explore the second portal. The one marked Tim.

TUNNEL NUMBER TWO
What Could Have Been—Tim

So you can't come?"

"I'm so sorry, Karen. I would love to, but I'm meeting Tim. He's taking me to some event. In fact, I'm in a bit of a mad rush. I couldn't get out of work as early as I wanted to and I've still got to get ready."

Jennifer could practically hear Karen's irritation crackling down the phone, but there was no way she was going to cancel her plans just to placate her. She was getting fed up with always feeling like she had to choose between her best friend and her boyfriend.

"What's it tonight, then?" asked Karen reluctantly, and Jennifer could picture how Karen would roll her eyes with disdain.

"Tim's got tickets to the Serpentine party in Hyde Park. It's supposed to be pretty amazing. There'll be lots of people from the art world but also loads of celebs and cocktails and canapés and all of that malarkey. Tickets are a few hundred quid a pop."

Jennifer winced. Had that sounded like she was showing off? She hadn't meant it to. She just wanted to demonstrate to Karen that her plans weren't all that easy to break.

"Oh well, having a curry with me and Pete can't compete with that," Karen said.

Jennifer despaired and not for the first time wished she'd never told Karen about the argument she'd had with Tim the day Princess Diana had died. It was nearly a year ago, but ever since she'd confided in her that for an insecure moment, she'd briefly considered finishing it with him, Karen had acted like she had carte blanche to be as scathing as she liked about their relationship.

Jennifer felt a constant need to justify her decision to stay with him. Yet it didn't seem to matter how many times she explained that she'd decided not to dump him because he had so much to offer, in many different ways—her friend refused to listen.

She was sick of it. It was her life, and it wound her up that Karen acted as though her and Pete's relationship was so perfect by comparison, to the point where the more Jennifer thought about it, the more she was starting to think that perhaps Karen might be a tiny bit jealous. After all, Karen and Pete struggled to make ends meet most months, whereas she'd gotten herself a nice job in marketing and Tim had made it. He'd done what he had always set out to do. He'd invented something and it was all coming to fruition. He was rich. reUNIon was taking off, and that was entirely down to his hard work, vision, drive, and dedication to making it happen. She was *proud* to be with him. He was so clever, a genius to some extent, and yes, he may appear distracted much of the time, but then of course he was. He had a growing company to manage. He had the attention of many major captains of industry, politicians, and the media, and not just in Britain but globally.

"Well, have a great time," Karen said flatly.

"I will," said Jennifer, sad that, once again, Karen had rained on her parade. She sighed but, eager to keep the peace, attempted to make sure their conversation ended on good terms. "Can I come around next week instead?"

"Course," said Karen. "Why don't you come around next Tuesday or Wednesday?"

"It's a date," Jennifer said. "Though Tuesday probably works better for me and it's sooner, so stick it in the calendar."

After they'd gotten off the phone, Jennifer allowed herself five minutes to sit on the bed and gaze dolefully at the wall until she realized that unless she got a move on, she'd be horribly late.

Forty minutes later, Jennifer was dressed and ready to go. Tim had bought her a beautiful wrap dress from a very expensive shop in Notting Hill. It was silk and the colors were vibrant, fiery oranges and reds. The style was slightly too conservative for Jennifer's taste, but she appreciated how lucky she was to have it and wanted to please Tim by wearing it, even if she did think it would be better on a woman in her forties. He'd suggested she go to the hairdresser and have a blow-dry, but she preferred her hair more natural. All the moneyed women around Notting Hill looked like clones of one another as far as she was concerned, with their coiffured, crash helmet, blond-highlighted hairstyles.

As she applied a final slick of lip gloss, the doorbell rang, so she picked up her clutch bag and clacked to the door in her high heels.

Tim's driver was standing on the front step.

"Oh. Hi, Ray. Is Tim not with you?"

"He got held up but said to say he'll meet you there."

Jennifer's smile slipped slightly, but there was no point saying anything to Ray. In fact, there was no point saying anything to anyone. Her boyfriend would be there when he could be, and if she had to sit outside the Serpentine in the car for a while, that's what she'd do. There was no way she was going into that party on her own.

Twenty minutes later, Jennifer was idly staring out the window when the car glided up to the pavement.

"Hang on a minute. We're not here yet, are we?" Jennifer asked. Why were they stopping in Knightsbridge?

Ray turned around from the front seat. "Mr. Purcell requested we make a quick pit stop here, if you don't mind."

"Oh, right… Er… Shall I wait in the car then?"

"No, miss. If you would be so kind, there's someone waiting for you inside, so you should come with me."

Thoroughly confused, Jennifer looked out the window again. They were outside the Mandarin Oriental Hotel, and Ray had already come around her side of the car to open her door. Wondering what on earth was going on, Jennifer got out, hoping this wasn't going to take too long. She'd be annoyed if Tim was still doing business. She hadn't seen him properly all week, and he'd promised her that tonight he'd finish at a decent time so they could enjoy the party. As she followed Ray up the steps of the hotel, she got the strangest sense that the hotel doormen were expecting her.

"What's going on, Ray? Where are we meeting Tim?"

"Don't you worry," he said mysteriously. "But I'd best leave you to it, Jen. I can't leave the car here, I'm afraid. I'll get a ticket."

"Oh, really…" she began, but he'd already turned and gone and was hurrying back to his waiting car.

Feeling rather self-conscious and a tad irritated, she resigned herself to the fact that she had no other choice but to go into the hotel and find out what was going on. So she let the enthusiastic doorman usher her through to the main reception, where the first thing she noticed within the opulent surroundings was a uniformed member of the hotel staff clutching an enormous bouquet of white flowers. There were lilies, roses, and white delphiniums so large, they pretty much covered the woman's entire face. They were absolutely beautiful, and Jennifer wondered who they were for. And then the legs beneath the flowers started walking toward her.

"These are for you, Miss Drew," said the woman once she was only a few feet away, almost teetering underneath the weight of the blooms and handing them over to Jennifer.

She gasped, overwhelmed and enjoying the incredible perfume that was coming from them. "Oh my gosh. They're amazing. Thank you so much. Are you sure they're for me? Are they from Tim?"

"Indeed they are, miss. Now, I'd like you to follow me, only perhaps let's leave the flowers with reception to look after and we can collect them again later. They're a bit too big to carry around, aren't they?" she said, smiling.

At that point, all the irritation and confusion Jennifer had been experiencing dissolved, and she started to get excited. There had been so many times over the years when she'd had to put up with broken arrangements or had to wait around for Tim for hours on end while he finished up his business, but never had any of those times involved being handed a massive bouquet. She felt like Julia Roberts in *Pretty Woman*. It was pretty intoxicating, and it was also obvious that Tim must have planned something. She was touched. It had been a long time since he'd done anything romantic for her. For a brief moment, she wondered if he was going to propose, but as quickly as the notion came to her, she dismissed it again. No, he wouldn't. Would he? Maybe it was dinner before the party? Once they'd disposed of the flowers, she followed the woman through the hotel toward the elevators. Jennifer watched as she pressed a button for one of the top floors. As the elevator made its ascent, the two of them stood in awkward silence, grinning inanely at each other.

When the elevator doors opened, Jennifer stepped out and found herself in a spacious corridor, decorated in decadent red.

"This way, please," the woman said with a polite smile.

Jennifer followed, full of nerves. They walked to the end of the plush, thickly carpeted corridor, at which point the woman took a key card out of her pocket. After she unlocked the door, she stood aside to push it open so the room was revealed.

Jennifer gasped. The room, which must have been the hotel's most luxurious suite, was carpeted with candles, save for a path through the middle that led to a terrified-looking Tim.

"What's this?" Jennifer squawked. "What are you doing?" Not the most romantic or profound thing to say, but her nerves were getting the better of her.

"Well, come in then," said Tim.

Jennifer made her way toward him, walking the path between the flickering candles. Once she'd reached him, she watched incredulously—and for a second, it was as if life had gone into slow motion—as Tim got down on one knee, producing a blue box from his pocket and saying, "Jennifer Drew, I know I'm not perfect, but I hope I'm perfect for you. Please, will you marry me?"

Tears filled her eyes. She couldn't believe it. Couldn't believe she was being asked, for starters, but also couldn't believe how much effort Tim had gone to and that he had it in him to be so romantic. He opened the box, and the sight of the ring distracted her from his question. It was amazing. Not the kind of ring she ever would have imagined a girl like her to wear. It was from Tiffany's, a ring for a rich person, a statement ring. The kind of ring that would need insuring and to be locked in a safe when on vacation. The sort of ring you couldn't in all seriousness contemplate wearing if you planned on doing any cleaning, gardening, or swimming. The diamond was enormous, a proper rock, which glinted and twinkled in the candlelight and was set off by a traditional platinum band.

Her mind was swirling this way and that. She looked up at Tim. He looked nervous. Did she want to be his wife? Did she want to spend the rest of her life with him?

She gulped. She may not have expected it then, but deep down she must have known this moment was a possibility. And she wouldn't have stayed with him all this time if it wasn't what she wanted. Would she?

"Well?" Tim asked, looking positively pained.

She laughed. Poor man. He was waiting. He was on one knee. She did love him. Of course she did.

"Yes."

"Thank goodness for that," Tim exclaimed. "And thank goodness I can get back up—my knee's killing me."

Getting to his feet, he shook out his cramped leg, then came toward her. They both smiled at each other.

"So, Mrs. Purcell, are you happy?"

"Yes," Jennifer said, eyes shining, wondering who to call first. Probably not Karen. She batted that depressing thought out of her head, determined not to give any head space to anything as gloomy as her friend's disapproval at this special time.

"I suppose I should kiss you then," Tim said.

"Yes, you should," Jennifer agreed, laughing at how deeply unspontaneous he was. God forbid he ever just grabbed her and kissed her because he was overwhelmed by the desire to do so.

Tim came toward her and, bending forward slightly, met her mouth with his. It wasn't the best kiss in the world, but it was a happy one that firmly sealed the deal, and she hugged him with real affection.

So that was that. She was going to marry Tim, her boyfriend of four years. She would be Mrs. Tim Purcell, wife of the founder of reUNIon. She could hardly believe it. Her mother would be ecstatic. Karen, not so much…

Present Day

Max tore through the hospital, searching for a doctor, frantic in his pursuit. Finally, after running up and down corridors, he spotted a nurse.

"Hello." He panted, relieved beyond belief. It was so frustrating when you desperately needed but couldn't find someone medical. It made him feel so helpless. "I need you to come to Jennifer Wright's room right away, please."

"Everything okay, Mr. Wright?" she inquired calmly.

"Yes, I think so. Well, I'm not sure really, but unless I'm hallucinating, and I'm afraid there's a chance I could be because I can't remember the last time I had a proper night's sleep, I think my wife just smiled."

"Okay..." said the nurse, looking grave but not as excited as Max thought she should be.

"Seriously, her face definitely changed, which is amazing, because surely that must mean she's thinking about something, or dreaming, or hearing, which in turn must mean her brain is functioning on some level."

"I'll see if I can find Mrs. Wright's consultant, and if he's here, I'll ask him to come see you in your wife's room. But please try to stay calm. I'm afraid that sometimes, when a patient is in a coma, their body can make involuntary reflex movements. It can be very distressing for relatives because this can give what usually turns out to be false hope."

Max stared blankly at her. He knew his wife better than anyone and would stake his life on the fact that she had smiled. Voluntarily. He was convinced of it.

"Hmm, well, thank you, and if you could find someone, that would be great, please," he said, on the verge of tears. Not just any old tears either, but violent sobbing he was determined to hold back until he was alone. He headed away from the nurse and back to Jennifer's room. When he got there, he closed the door behind him and allowed the inevitable tears of frustration to pour down his face. Collapsing into the chair he'd spent an unreasonable amount of time sitting in lately, he wept noisily until some of his grief and helplessness had worked its way out of his stressed-out system.

When he'd finished, he felt calmer. He also felt exhausted, drained, and very sad. He stared at his wife. His silent, slightly waxy-looking shell of a wife. Was she still in there? Could she hear him? Would there be a day when they'd be cuddled up in bed, feet entwined, talking about how lucky they were to have gotten through this nightmare and still be together? If she did wake up, would she ever forgive him? He'd give anything for the opportunity to tell her how much he loved and missed her, how much he'd taken her for granted and that he was sorry. He reached over for her hand. It was warm but disconcertingly limp. Was he being punished? It felt like it. He was a pathetic cliché. When Judith had showed him some attention, it had flattered his ego so much. Only now that this had happened, any "feelings" he may have had for Judith had vanished without a trace, completely annihilated by the horror and realization of the heartache he'd caused. He remembered being fifteen and his mother walking in on him and Sarah Fisher in his bedroom. He'd had his hand in her underwear at the time and had been about as excited as only a fifteen-year-old boy could be in the same position. Yet the minute his mother had appeared, his ardor had been instantly extinguished by embarrassment and shame. This situation felt similar somehow, which only made him feel more foolish. Every time he recalled the night of the accident, he experienced a fresh stab of mortification. And now...

Why had this happened? Why?

Not wanting to go down that particular path, which only led to more frustration, he thought back instead to the smile on Jennifer's face, which had brought with it such an incredibly soothing rush of hope, it had almost bowled him over.

He'd been dozing off at the time, and although the memory was a bit hazy, he was pretty sure it had been the slight rustling sound of a sheet that had made him look up. Rustling was probably too strong a word, for it had been a minute sound, barely discernible, but there nonetheless.

As he'd glanced up, instantly alert, it had seemed like Jennifer's hand might have been in a slightly different position than it had been before. Then, without question, her face flickered. Her mouth seemed to curl in an upward motion, and it looked to Max like his wife was smiling.

———

Later, as the weary consultant and even wearier Max discussed what he'd seen (or as the consultant preferred to put it, "what he *may* have seen"), deep inside Jennifer's psyche, a different type of debate was going on.

She'd emerged from the portal marked *Tim* and was still mulling over the fact that if she'd stayed with him, they would have ended up engaged. Who'd have thought? She wondered what she should do. Previously, after a trip to her alternative life with Aidan, she was so depleted, her body took time out in the gray ether to recover and recharge. But this time, she felt fine. She was intrigued, fascinated, in fact, to find out more. It seemed her brain agreed, for she found herself floating toward the tunnel again, where no doubt she would discover how things would have gone. Would she have been blissfully content, living out many people's version of a fairy tale? It certainly seemed like a possibility.

TUNNEL NUMBER TWO
What Could Have Been — Tim

You look nice, Mummy."

"Thank you, Hattie. Come here, darling," Jennifer said, beckoning to her youngest daughter for a hug.

Hattie padded across the vast dressing room to where her mother sat at her dressing table, putting the finishing touches on her makeup and spritzing her neck, wrists, and hair with perfume. Eau d'Hadrien by Annick Goutal, the one she always wore. Years ago, Tim had told her it was really attractive for a woman to have a signature scent, so she'd stuck with the one she'd had at the time, and it had become the smell her children would always associate with her.

She drew Hattie toward her. The little girl was already in her gingham pajamas and had obviously had her hair washed, as it was still damp and drying into natural ringlets.

"Are you okay, sweetheart? Where's Deck?"

Hattie shrugged, looking fed up. "Putting Jasper to bed, but I want *you* to read my story today."

"I can't tonight. You know Daddy's got all his work people coming and Mummy's got to be there."

"But you haven't read stories for ages."

"Yes, I have," said Jennifer, refusing to be put on a guilt trip, something Hattie was very good at. "Who read *The Selfish Crocodile* to you yesterday?"

Hattie tried to continue looking sad but ruined the effect by allowing a small grin to escape. "But before that you hadn't."

Jennifer paused. Her daughter's cut-glass accent still took her by surprise sometimes. She was starting to sound more and more like the queen, a result of the very expensive school she'd started at last September. Jennifer wasn't sure it sat well with her. She worried that later on in life, if her daughter sounded too posh, she might be bullied. She wondered what she could do to combat the problem. Force her to watch box sets of blue-collar shows perhaps? Get her a job in a garage? Get Aunty Karen to give her antielocution lessons?

"Look, I know it's been a busy time, sweetie, but Daddy goes to Hong Kong next week, and then I won't have so much going on in the evenings. So I promise I'll make up for it on the stories front then. But right now, I've got to get downstairs or the first guest will arrive and I won't be there, so go back to your floor and find Deck, will you?"

Hattie turned around and padded out of the room, an air of weary resignation about her, which made her look even more adorable. It was her little shoulders that got to Jennifer. She sighed, wishing she didn't have to go downstairs and play the corporate wife. Deep down, she was only too aware that she constantly seemed to be telling all four of her offspring that she didn't have time for anything that mattered to them. Still, Tim had never been so busy, so she didn't have much choice.

If only she could convey to Hattie that, given the chance, she'd do anything rather than have to entertain the bunch of stiffs who were on their way. Gouge her eyeballs out with a spoon. Anything.

———

Forty minutes later and the evening was well underway. Nearly all of the twenty guests had arrived and were being plied with drinks and canapés. As ever, Jennifer had done her homework, so she knew not only everyone's names, but also what they did, what their other halves' names were, and how important to Tim they were in terms of business, on a scale of one to ten. She would allocate time to making sure they were being looked after accordingly.

———

"Darling, will you make sure there's some more claret for Jeremy?" Tim asked. He didn't even look her in the eye, just gave her elbow a discreet nudge before turning his attention back to the man who had a redder nose than Rudolph. However, it appeared Jeremy's attention had been stolen away by a woman with impressive cleavage that he was practically dribbling into.

"And try to look a bit happier," added Tim, seeing as he wasn't being listened to anymore. "You look like you're here under duress."

Jennifer gave him a withering look. "Ten out of ten for accuracy," she shot back.

"Don't fuck this up for me, Jen," he said resolutely, a fake smile plastered across his face. "I need all of these people on my side if there's going to be a merger. And if it's so much of a chore for you to be here, try thinking of it as your job."

"All right," she agreed between gritted teeth, nodding politely at someone who'd just arrived. "But stop lecturing me, will you?"

Tim looked at her with enormous disdain, but she couldn't take him seriously. "You've got canapé on your nose. It looks ridiculous."

Tim looked chastened and patted his suit jacket, searching for a hanky. "You could have told me earlier," he snapped.

"Terribly sorry. I didn't realize I was supposed to be monitoring your face," added Jennifer primly, her own face a mask of composure. "Though if I had, I would have told you that you've also got what looks like a piece of duck stuck between your teeth. I'll get that claret."

Over the years, Jennifer and Tim had gotten saying one thing while looking like they were saying another down to a fine art. Anyone observing would probably have thought the couple had just shared an affectionate private joke as opposed to a series of scathing put-downs. But then, as the wife of someone as powerful as Tim, Jennifer had learned how to play the game and how to cope with tedious evenings spent entertaining his dull clients and associates. Not that it was exactly hard. All she had to do was look groomed, make polite conversation, and give instructions.

Come to think of it, that was pretty much all she did these days. She gave instructions to the chef about what everyone would eat, and then, when it was served, everyone complimented her on how amazing the food had been, which always felt weird when she hadn't even shopped for it, let alone prepared it. She gave instructions to the agencies she hired when they needed extra help on top of the help they already had. On this occasion, she'd instructed that they needed an experienced cocktail maker to work behind the bar, plus three waitstaff who could pour drinks and serve dinner. That afternoon, she'd instructed her hairdresser and her personal yoga instructor on when she wanted her next appointments to be. On Monday, she would give instructions to their full-time housekeeper; the gardener; and their two Filipino nannies who, between them, worked every day. Otherwise, Jennifer never had to "do" anything.

A few weeks ago, on a rare night out with her friends, she'd said as much but hadn't received much sympathy from Karen. "Oh, my heart bleeds," she'd said. "Well, how about instructing them all to fuck off for the day and doing your own cooking and cleaning for a change? Or maybe, and call me crazy for suggesting it, try looking after your own kids for a whole twenty-four hours? You never know. You might enjoy it."

Karen had been particularly brutal because she was drunk, but Jennifer was glad she hadn't sugarcoated what she really thought. It was just so difficult to explain to her friends that doing everything herself actually sounded unbelievably appealing, liberating even, yet at the same time, the idea of it frightened her half to death. Having so much help all the time had gradually made her feel superfluous to anyone's needs, especially when it came to the kids.

Tim had paid for maternity nurses to be there from day one. When their eldest, Edward, had been born, Jen had never forgotten the feeling of elation she'd had. She'd produced a human being, a breathing little person, and furthermore, despite having him at the Portland, the private hospital where only the rich and famous could afford to give birth, she had managed to buck the trend and have a natural delivery. It had been painful, brutal, bloody. She was a total hero! It was the first time in a long time she'd felt worthwhile, clever almost. And then the maternity nurse had arrived and taken her little bundle away. Never had anything felt so utterly wrong.

Despite her protestations, Tim had insisted. She need never have uninterrupted sleep, he'd said. She could remain in the marital bed at night and concentrate on getting her figure back by day.

This "luxury" was the saddest thing she'd ever experienced. To this day, she was certain it had contributed to her postpartum depression. Only the worse the depression got, the more it was deemed a good idea for her to have more help.

Sometimes she couldn't believe that she and Tim had gone on to have three more children. Or, more accurately, she couldn't understand why they'd bothered. Edward was thirteen and on his way to becoming a moody teenager, Tilly was ten, Hattie was six, and Jasper was four. They were four children with vastly different personalities, interests, and needs. She loved all of them, of course, yet there was no getting away from the fact that neither she nor Tim had played much of a role in actually raising them. In fact, sometimes she felt that, as far he was concerned, they'd been churned out like status symbols. The only thing that made her feel better about her mothering skills was that no matter how dubious they were, they were hundreds of times better than Tim's fathering ones. At least she'd changed the odd diaper herself, when she'd been allowed. Plus, much of her time was spent torturing herself with maternal guilt, whereas she was pretty sure that, for Tim, the way he was as a parent wasn't something that ever pricked his conscience. He paid for everything and was old-fashioned enough that he felt that was all that was required.

She slipped away from the drawing room, leaving her guests, not one of whom she considered to be a friend, to mingle, drink champagne, and eat their canapés.

She was grateful for an excuse to leave for a minute. Prior to Tim's request/order, she'd been struggling to make small talk with the wife of his financial adviser. At one point, things had gotten so desperate that they'd discussed *for twenty-five minutes* whether children should be allowed to give up piano lessons.

Jennifer made her way through the corridors and into the spacious hallway, stopping only to check her appearance in a huge gilt-edged mirror that hung on one wall.

She looked immaculate. Her hair had been blow-dried that afternoon. It was smooth but with a wave at the bottom. Very Kate Middleton. She was wearing a new silk shift by Stella McCartney, which probably wasn't quite conservative enough for Tim's tastes but that she loved, with some gorgeous Marc Jacobs heels. Her skin was looking far younger than her thirty-eight years, due mainly to some expertly injected Botox and aided by monthly facials. She looked rested, slim, toned, and totally dead behind the eyes.

Her phone vibrated in her pocket. It was a text, one that improved her mood beyond measure. It was the fix she needed and she responded quickly before continuing on her way to the staircase that led down to her vast kitchen. So vast, in fact, it took up the entire basement floor of the house and was larger than most people's apartments.

Downstairs, their chef, Joe, and two of the waitstaff were milling around, engaged in one activity or another.

"Hello, Jennifer. Everything all right?" Joe asked, treating her to a big, friendly grin. He'd been with the family for four and a half years.

"Fabulous, thanks. The quail eggs are disappearing as soon as they're brought out, as are those homemade cheese straws."

"Oh good, that's what I like to hear."

"I'm here to ask if you'd mind going to the cellar and grabbing another bottle of the Montrachet for Jeremy? You know Jeremy—the one who's got a face like a side of beef."

Joe laughed. "I do indeed."

"I can get it if you want," one of the young waiters offered.

"No, don't you worry," Joe insisted. "The starter's all plated up, so I'm fine to go. Besides, it's best to make sure we open the right one, eh? Some of those bottles are worth more than you'll earn in a year, young man."

"Thanks, Joe," Jennifer said, leaving them all to it and clip-clopping out of the kitchen.

Upstairs, back in the hallway, she hesitated for a fraction of a second, checking to make sure no one was around. Then, certain she was alone, instead of making her way back to the party, she turned left, heading to the rear of the house and the largest of their three sitting rooms. She closed the door quietly behind her and picked her way across the room to the French doors that led out onto the garden, one of the largest in London. The striped, immaculate lawns went on for almost as far as the eye could see, and the rest of the garden had lots of topiaries and neat, color-coordinated beds. Despite having four children in the house, there wasn't a plastic slide in sight.

Jennifer ventured out onto the flagstones and tiptoed along the side of the house until she came to another door that was ajar. As soon as she reached it, a hand appeared and yanked her inside.

She giggled and felt a lurch of happiness and desire as those same hands drew her in to him and then started to explore every inch of her body.

"Oh my God, you feel so good in this dress."

"Do I?"

"Yeah, you look amazing in it too. Absolutely gorgeous."

"Oh, I do love you," she whispered, her heart full to the brim with love and lust. How was it even possible to feel this turned on so quickly?

"I love you too, gorgeous girl," said Joe, his hands everywhere, his mouth in her hair, kissing her face, her neck. "What's the situation later?"

"I don't know," she said doubtfully. "You know how he gets at these things. He'll probably be up till five, talking utter shit, but if I can come see you, I will. I'll have to play it by ear."

Joe groaned, pulling her into him. "Please try. I've missed you so much it's ridiculous. It's been far too long since I've had my lovely girl lying next to me."

"I know, you don't need to tell me," Jennifer said, wide-eyed. "I've been pining for you the whole time."

"But if you can't get away, no worries, my love. I don't want it to be a stress."

"Okay. Speaking of which, how long have I been?"

"Don't know," Joe said, pulling away. He stroked her face tenderly, and her heart contracted. His expression looked hurt, par for the course these days. Their affair was getting harder and harder the deeper they fell.

"I love you," she said passionately.

"I love you too, little squidger," said Joe, his Yorkshire accent such a contrast to Tim's clipped, private-school tones. Then again, everything about him was.

"Don't forget the wine," she whispered, tearing herself reluctantly away and back outside.

"I won't," he said, disappearing back toward the cellar.

———

"Where've you been?" Tim asked ten minutes later, having spotted her as soon as she'd reappeared in the drawing room. "I asked you to get more wine, not drive to France and stomp on the grapes yourself."

"Sorry," she replied. "I was just making sure everything's under control for dinner. I think we should start getting everyone into the dining room. Otherwise, we won't be eating till ten."

"Right you are."

As the evening progressed, Jennifer's mood took a serious nosedive.

She did her best to be engaging, to be the perfect hostess, but her heart wasn't in it. It wasn't even in the same room. It was languishing downstairs in the kitchen. She played with her food. Joe had cooked the most incredible rib of beef, which he'd served with creamy artichoke mash, perfectly cooked vegetables, and a fricassee of mushrooms that was out of this world. But she had no appetite. The latest antidepressant she'd been prescribed made her feel a bit wired, and not for the first time, she wondered if they were a waste of time. Was she really clinically depressed? She was starting to doubt it, because she never felt even remotely miserable when she was alone with Joe. Quite the opposite. And yet for years, doctors had told her she had depression when there was a distinct possibility she'd just been fed up, bored, or in a bad mood.

For what felt like the thousandth time that hour, her thoughts returned to the man who had been her best friend for two years and her lover for seven months—seven amazing, painful, confusing, sad, yet unbelievably golden months. Since she and Joe had become lovers, she'd reassessed everything. She was constantly saturated in intense stress and guilt—not surprising given that she was committing adultery—and yet also felt more *herself* than she had in a long while.

Joe, it seemed, was her soul mate, her rightful other half, but while that bit was clear, the situation was so complicated. For both of them.

Joe was a good man for whom sleeping with someone else's wife had never been the plan. He'd fallen hard and was never going to be satisfied with being Jennifer's bit on the side. The two of them were smitten, utterly and hopelessly in love to the point of obsession. Every meeting was tinged with tragedy, worry about the future, and deep frustration. Whenever they had sex, the strength of her feeling meant she always ended up in tears at the end because she was in a painful quandary. If she were to leave Tim, she'd be breaking up her family, turning her back on a man who may have been flawed but had always stuck by her. She'd be doing the wrong thing no matter how right it felt and would be losing everything familiar to her. If she stayed, however, she'd ultimately lose Joe, and that was too unbearable to contemplate.

The situation was starting to make her feel ill. Having to decide whether to leave the father of her children was excruciatingly hard. She'd been with Tim since university, and people constantly told her how ridiculously lucky she was to have landed him. As if she were a consolation prize by comparison. Then, of course, there was the lifestyle she enjoyed, the money. Tim had made her sign a prenup, and being the romantic idiot she was, she'd agreed happily, wanting to prove she wasn't with him for his cash.

As much as Joe told her there were more important things in life than money, she had her children to think of and was unable to comprehend how she would cope, having been dependent on Tim for so long. Was she crazy for even considering leaving him? Look what she'd be giving up. She glanced around the opulent dining room, the work of an overenthusiastic interior designer desperate to justify his grotesque fee, and the bunch of corpses who sat around the Louis XVII table. On second thought…

"So tell me, Jennifer, what are your plans for the summer?" asked Maurice Fellowes, one of the largest shareholders of reUNIon who Tim had cruelly placed next to her.

Maurice was the short straw from what was already an unbearably tedious crowd. In fairness, not all the entertaining they did was quite this bad. Sometimes they had uproarious dinner parties with clever, creative people. People who had helped make reUNIon what it was or others they simply knew for social reasons. However, these days, reUNIon was only a fraction of the business Tim was involved with, and it seemed to Jennifer the more money you accrued, the more you were obliged to socialize with people to whom you wouldn't ordinarily give the time of day.

"Well, we're going to our place in the South of France as soon as the children finish school for the summer. Then, at the end of August, Tim and I leave them there and we go to the Earl of Bradwick's boat. You know Bradwick, I'm sure?"

"Oh yes, frightfully nice chap."

Jennifer smiled pleasantly, wishing she could think of a reason to go see Joe in the kitchen. The thought of being separated from him for a whole summer was unbearable. She was already determined to concoct some story so she could return to the UK for at least a week in August. He'd asked her to come to Yorkshire with him, and there was nothing she would rather do than spend time hidden away in a little cottage with him. It would be heaven. By contrast, the prospect of spending weeks in luxury with Tim filled her with nothing but a sense of dread and foreboding.

She sighed heavily.

"What are you and Margaret doing for the summer, Maurice?" she asked, trying to be polite.

"We're braving Cornwall and just praying it doesn't rain like it did last year."

How brave, thought Jennifer wryly, aware that the house they owned there was more like a castle and was fully staffed. She was pretty sure they'd survive.

"And then we'll be going on to Tuscany, where we shall stay until the end of September, which is always the nicest month there, I find. This is excellent meat, by the way. Wonderful food, and you're a marvelous hostess, Jennifer."

"Thank you," she said. Every time someone complimented Joe's meat, it made her laugh inside. She wondered if that made her a very sordid individual.

Ugh, what she wouldn't give for a normal night out. With normal people. Thank God she still had Karen, Lucy, and Esther in her life, although even with her old friends, having so much money sometimes created problems, no matter how hard they all tried to pretend it didn't. Not for her. She couldn't care less about it and would gladly have given them all as much as they wanted. Writing checks meant nothing to her, and if paying meant they all got to do things together, she was more than happy to facilitate that. But her friends had their pride, and how much generosity it was appropriate to accept was one of the things Karen found particularly tricky to handle. As a result, it was often them, as opposed to her, who were guilty of making an issue out of her wealth. Sometimes they didn't include her in things because they assumed she'd turn her nose up at it when she would have loved to have been invited. At other times, when she invited *them* to events or to come abroad with her and Tim, they couldn't always afford the flights or the spending money that was required but didn't know how to tell her without it sounding like they wanted her to cover it. The one saving grace was that every April, without fail, they allowed her to pay for the four of them to go on a girls' skiing trip. It was always the best week of her entire year.

Her phone vibrated in her pocket. She expertly managed to slip it out and onto her lap, her gaze never leaving Maurice's rheumy eyes as he blathered on about restaurants in Tuscany and how much he loved peasant food.

As soon as she thought she could get away with it, for a mere second, her eyes flickered onto her lap. The text read: Hello, sexy. Hope you're not bored rigid. Have put something special in Tim's dessert. Hopefully see you later xxx

Why does everything in life have to arrive needing to be assembled?" swore Max, who was struggling to make sense of the instructions he was holding. Not surprising given he was staring at the section written in Swedish.

"It can't be that hard," Jennifer said.

"Ugh," Max replied, expressing how hungover he was. The night before, Ted had come around to keep him company—to watch sports—while Jennifer was out with the girls, and between them they'd managed to get through more beer and red wine than was necessary. The fact that Jennifer had predicted this would happen only made matters worse.

Meanwhile, Polly and Eadie were watching, thrilled because they knew full well that while bedtime might be imminent, it would also be impossible due to the chaos in Polly's room. There were bits of wardrobe everywhere, plus the contents of Max's toolbox all over the floor.

"Yeah, come on, Daddy," Polly joined in. "It can't be that hard."

"When I need your opinion…" he said, frowning at her. "Christ,

Jennifer. In future, perhaps we should pay a bit more for furniture so it doesn't need to be made from scratch."

Jennifer was livid. "Hang on a minute. The reason I went out of my way to drive all the way to flipping Brent Cross to get this was because you moaned so much when the last credit card bill came in. I thought you wanted us to cut back!"

"If I moaned, it was only because you spent fifty pounds on your mother's birthday present," Max muttered, refusing to catch her eye. He knew how inflammatory this comment would be.

Jennifer seethed. "You're out of order."

Max just shrugged.

"Why shouldn't I treat my mum on her birthday? And why should I be made to feel guilty every single time I buy something from our joint account?"

"And why haven't I gotten any new furniture for my room?" piped up Eadie, looking miffed.

"Because you don't need it," Jennifer said, taking a deep breath to bring her temper down. "You've got a great wardrobe in your room, and poor old Pol has had to make do with no hanging space at all until now."

"Hold on a minute, Jen," Max said, still looking flummoxed. "I think this screw needs to go in there."

"Are you sure?"

"No, but at this point, I can't stare at these stupid, indecipherable things anymore, and you never know, it just might be worth a go, so humor me."

Jennifer rolled her eyes.

"What?" Max snapped.

"Okay," said Jennifer, growing tired of his grumpy tone of voice. "First, I'm wondering why you have to do this now, when the girls need to get to bed, when it could easily wait until the weekend. Second, I'm still furious that you're making me feel bad for spending fifty quid on my mum when she's helped us out so much lately. And third, I was just thinking how quickly Steve would have had these up."

This last comment was a reference to her ex, which she was confident her husband would find amusing. She'd made her point so now hoped to cajole him out of his mood with a private joke.

She couldn't have been more wrong. At first, he gave her a look and a faint smile, but seconds later, once he'd had the chance to fully digest what she'd said, he retaliated in a way that seemed uncalled for.

"As it happens, I'd rather get this out of the way as opposed to spending my day off on Saturday doing it, and with regard to Steve, we can't all be good at everything," he said, looking pissed off. "Just as you aren't a breadwinner like Judith, for example, I'm not good at sodding DIY. Though if you would rather be with someone who is, perhaps you should look Steve up and tell him you're on the market. I'm sure he'd leap at the chance to meet up."

"All right," Jennifer said, stung by his hurtful words. "There's no need to jump down my throat. I was only joking. Usually you're up for a laugh about Steve. And there's no need to bring up frigging Judith's name or to pit me against that silly witch. Or to point out I'm not a 'breadwinner.' That's just nasty. And if that's what *you* want, then perhaps you shouldn't have made me feel so guilty about wanting to have a career."

"Oh, get over yourself," Max said.

By this point, Jennifer was fuming.

"Stop arguing," Eadie barked fiercely. Both children had been very quiet up to that point.

"Sorry, love," Max said. "We're not arguing, just having a debate."

That's rich, Jennifer thought, who was itching to say as much but didn't for the girls' sakes. They didn't need to hear them squabbling anymore. Not for the first time, she despaired over Max's recent attitude toward her. Why was he speaking to her so dismissively? And how dare he put her down for not being an equal breadwinner. That part was unforgivable, especially because she had a job that paid for all sorts of bits and pieces. He was an asshole. The thing she had treasured most about their relationship was that he was her best friend and that, together, they usually saw the funny side in everything. She missed that and realized their relationship was heading for a slow, painful death unless they did something about it, and fast. The saddest thing of all was that it wouldn't take much to get things back on track. They just needed to be nice to each other, to treat each other like friends. It was something they'd managed to do even when the children were babies and life was much harder than it was now. Familiarity breeds contempt—it was the biggest cliché of them all.

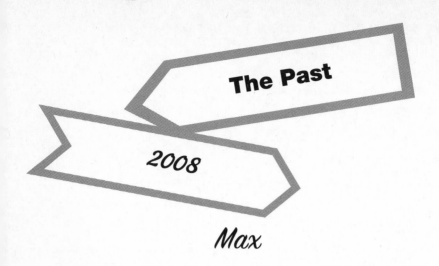

Max

Max and Jennifer were on a mission. A mission to leave the house, something Jennifer hadn't done for ten whole days, ever since she'd arrived home from the hospital with her second baby girl.

Of course, when you're recovering from a cesarean section, there's really no point attempting much. She had been opened up like a can of peaches to produce her own fruit. The hours leading up to major surgery hadn't exactly been restful either. She'd endured an intense thirty-six hours of pointless contracting because, as it turned out, Polly's noggin was in the wrong position to allow a natural delivery. Still, as Max had kept reminding her, it could be worse. If she were a Tudor or medieval woman, she'd be dead. Not that this had come as a massive comfort at the time.

Physically, she'd been through an awful lot, but at thirteen days after the birth, she was getting better in small increments. She was capable of mild shuffling and of getting in and out of oversize tracksuits and Ugg boots all by herself. Bending down to put tights on still couldn't be contemplated, and other small tasks had become huge mountains to climb. With a newborn and a toddler to cope with, simply finding the time to have a shower, for example, was a huge deal, and her first post-op bowel movement was worthy of a phone call to her mother. So the whole family attempting to leave the house en masse, dressed and with everything they needed to go shopping, was going to be a drama of epic proportions.

In the kitchen, as she and Max packed bags, cajoled two-year-old Eadie into getting dressed, changed diapers, and generally tried to make it all happen, Jennifer couldn't help wondering what she was going to do when her husband had to return to work the week after. How would she ever cope?

"I'll never manage," she whimpered.

"Nonsense," said Max, trying in vain to collapse the new, so far unused double stroller so he could get it into the trunk of the car.

"You can't leave me. Ever. You'll have to resign and go on unemployment."

"You'll be fine," he reassured her, albeit absentmindedly. "How on earth does this frigging thing work? Eadie, darling, get out of the way, please. Daddy's trying not to freak out here."

Eadie looked militant, as she had ever since Polly had arrived, clearly not sure how she felt about this young upstart, this pretender to her throne, turning up and taking her mother's attention away. Polly was a hungry baby and pretty much never off the breast, so it was hard for Jennifer to give her eldest the attention she required.

Jennifer winced as Polly sucked away. The idea was to stuff her to the brim to give them more shopping time. Her nipples were on fire, and her exhaustion wasn't helping her pain threshold. She'd probably averaged around four hours of sleep a night for over a fortnight. Not that Max was faring much better. Polly was sleeping—or not, as the case may be—in their room, and Jennifer insisted he help out with the odd bottle during the night. Although, in reality, whenever she missed a feeding, her breasts would swell to such gigantic, milky proportions, she'd end up itching to ram them back into the baby's mouth again to relieve the pain.

Still, they were muddling through, helped by enormous amounts of hormones and the wondrous feeling that they'd pulled off some sort of miracle by producing an actual, real-life person. And love. That they loved each other and their offspring helped immensely.

But as Max struggled with the stroller, she suspected their love was about to be sorely tested.

"Look, just try to cast your mind back to how they did it," said Max, looking at his wife in despair. "You must have some idea, surely?"

"Don't call me Shirley," she retorted, easing Polly off her breast. Gingerly, she stood up and placed the baby over her shoulder to burp her. "I told you. I think you pull that lever thing and then sort of bend it backward."

Max sighed. "I'm not being funny, but you must have thought it worth finding out how to use it when you bought the bloody thing."

"Obviously," Jennifer said, feeling defensive. She collapsed back onto a kitchen chair. She had been shown numerous times how to do it but for the life of her couldn't remember. "I was eight months pregnant," she said huffily. "So it's not like I had a proper working brain. Besides, you need a degree in physics to work it out. Why can't they just make these things simple?"

Almost by way of reply, Polly gave an enormous belch and puked down her mother's back.

"Oh God," Jennifer said with a defeated sigh.

"Okay," Max said, throwing the double stroller to the ground in disgust. "Unless we can collapse it, we can't get it into the car, so we're going to have to think again. What if we take the sling and Eadie walks?"

"Can you get me a tissue or something? I'm covered in spit-up."

Max raced to the sink and chucked a damp cloth at Jennifer, which she caught with her free hand.

"It's not going to work," she said, sponging herself down with one hand and trying not to drop the baby with the other. "Eadie will go a few yards and start whining, and if it's going to take ages, we can't go anyway. We need to leave now so we've got enough time to get there and back before Polly needs another feeding. Especially seeing as her tummy's basically empty again and I'm not pulling these udders out in any old place. I'm also not going out only to end up sitting in the car feeding."

"Right," Max said. "Well, I don't know why you got rid of the old stroller."

"Not helpful."

"No, it wasn't."

"I meant your comment wasn't helpful. I got rid of the bloody thing because there wasn't room in the hall for two massive wheeled contraptions."

"Okay. Look, I'll just put Eadie on my shoulders then or carry her. Let's just go, though. Otherwise we'll never get out."

"Okay," Jennifer said. "Except next week when I've got to get her to day care on my own, what am I going to do? My scar still hurts. I won't be able to carry her then. I need a stroller, Max."

Max looked horror-stricken when Jennifer succumbed to a huge rush of hormones and started to weep.

"Right, you stay here with the baby," Max said, realizing how much he needed to take charge of the situation, "and I'll take Eadie with me. Where's the video camera?"

"Why? What are you doing?" asked Jennifer, who wasn't sure what she was crying about, though being covered in spit-up might have had something to do with it. Still, by the sound of it at least, she didn't have to go out anymore, and for that she was grateful. She wasn't fit for public consumption, and there was nothing she wanted to buy anyway, unless you could buy sleep.

An hour and a half later, Max was back, having filmed a slightly bemused and self-conscious sales assistant demonstrating slowly and methodically exactly how the new stroller folded and collapsed.

"You're brilliant," Jennifer said as she watched the footage over and over again. She hadn't been as impressed by anything for ages. "A proper evil genius."

"No, you're brilliant," Max said, handling the stroller like an expert, unfolding and folding it repeatedly. "There's no way on earth I would have remembered how to do it either. Stupid machine."

Later that night, Jennifer was sitting in the kitchen feeding Polly, Eadie was fast asleep, and Max was washing and sterilizing bottles and tidying up.

Jennifer was so exhausted, her eyes were almost rolling back in her head. Still, as she looked down at her little bundle with her soft, downy cheeks and tiny, wrinkled foot poking out the end of the blanket she was wrapped in, she felt a huge pang of love.

God, her back ached, an aftereffect of the epidural. And she still felt very strange in her undercarriage. As for her breasts, they felt like they were burning.

Just then, Max discarded his dish towel and came to sit next to his wife. "Are you okay? You look like you're in pain."

"I'm a bit sore," she admitted.

"Oh, Jen, I'm so in awe of you. You've been so brave and so bloody amazing."

"Have I?" she asked, feeling choked.

"Oh my God, yes. I mean, look. Look what you've done," he said, gesturing to Polly, who had fallen asleep on her mother's breast. He bent down to take his daughter, still handling her like she was the most fragile thing in the world, and kissed the top of her head. Then he kissed his wife tenderly on the cheek. "And you did it with no fuss."

"Apart from when I called you the *C* word and threatened to kill you."

"Apart from when you called me the *C* word and threatened to kill me," he agreed, regarding her with real affection. "I think you're amazing. Jen, you're my hero. I love you so bloody much. And I know sometimes you find it hard being stuck at home and get frustrated, but I want you to know that you are doing the most incredible job."

"But will you ever fancy me again?" she asked. "Look at me. I'm a big, fat, lactating cow, and I look so pale and tired and ugly."

"Oh, shut up, you silly moo. I love you to bits, and to me you're the most beautiful woman in the world. I don't care what you're wearing or how tired you are; to me you'll always be my girl in the pink dress."

"Really?" squeaked Jennifer.

"Really," Max said. "You're still the love of my life. Admittedly, I've seen you look better than you do this precise second and you might want to wash your hair at some point, though I've got nothing against dreadlocks per se…"

Jennifer laughed and then gasped as her scar twinged again.

"Painkiller?"

"Please."

"And then shall we go to bed? Not that there's much point, of course"—Max, who had quite impressive black rings under his eyes, yawned—"given that this little one will be up in a few hours. But we could give sleep a go, I guess. And we can also have a cuddle."

"That would be nice. But no hanky-panky."

"What do you take me for?" Max winked. "Besides, that tracksuit's good birth control for now. It stinks of spit-up."

R ight, come on then, you two," Jennifer said firmly. "It's time for bed and your father clearly isn't going to be finished for hours. Polly, go in our bed and I'll move you later."

"Ooh," Eadie whined. "That's not fair."

"Tough."

Once the girls were finally asleep, Jennifer got the chance to tell her husband exactly what she thought of how he'd behaved earlier.

"Every chance you get, you compare me to that bloody woman. Why do you do it?"

"I don't," Max said.

"You do," Jennifer said, despairing. "You bring her name up all the time to the point where at one stage, I thought you might be having an affair with her. Though, in reality, I think you'd be more discreet about it if you were. As it is, you're constantly going on about her or comparing me to her. It's not bloody right."

"You're being paranoid," Max said a tad too defensively.

Jennifer leaped on her instinct.

"What? What is it, Max? What aren't you telling me? Do you have feelings for her or something?"

"No," he said, outraged.

"Promise," she said faintly, terrified in case she was about to discover something she didn't want to confront.

"Will you stop going on?" Max asked, looking monumentally pissed off.

"It's just that you're being so snappy with me."

"Not this again!" he shouted. "Will you stop going on and on about how I've changed? It's driving me mad."

Jennifer blinked and wondered whether to press the issue further. After all, he'd kind of illustrated her point. Plus, she still wasn't wholly convinced there wasn't something to get to the bottom of, and yet if there was, did she even want to know?

Max let out a huge sigh. "Look, Jen, I'm sorry. I'm tired and grumpy and bored of having the same conversation over and over again."

Jennifer's eyes filled with tears, and she sniffed hard in an attempt to keep them at bay.

"Look how keyed up you are. Relax these shoulders," Max said, coming over and kneading her shoulders with his hands. They were so rigid it hurt but in a pleasurable kind of way.

"Hmm." She closed her eyes. "That's nice," she mumbled, giving in to the sensation.

"Good," Max said. "Maybe that should be your birthday present. A nice massage somewhere."

"Okay." A solitary tear escaped and ran down her cheek. She quickly wiped it away.

"Or perhaps call Steve and ask him to do it, seeing as he was so brilliant with his hands."

Jennifer pulled away, ready to retaliate, but to her relief, she could see Max was joking.

"Idiot," she said softly, playfully hitting him on the chest.

"Ah, Steve," Max mused, a smug grin on his face. "Do you remember the party?"

"Course I do," Jennifer said.

How could she forget? It was the day she'd met her future husband and the day poor old Steve had dimmed by comparison. She still felt mildly guilty, even after all these years. Steve had been nothing but lovely to her, and if Max hadn't turned up, she'd probably still be with him. But Max *had* turned up and she'd gone for it because she'd recognized a twinkle that was extremely attractive.

She looked at Max, hating how detached she felt from him almost as much as she hated that she'd had doubts about him. She'd always trusted her husband, but lately it was almost as if she didn't trust herself. It wasn't that she'd ever do anything, but she felt at a bit of a crossroads in general. Recently she'd found herself thinking about the past all the time, about how things had turned out and how things might have been. So perhaps she was projecting her own rubbish onto Max? In which case she needed to stop, because it wasn't fair. She sighed. When was she going to shake this miserable feeling?

The Past

January 2000

Steve

At long last, the most anticipated New Year's Eve in recent history was finally out of the way and Jennifer couldn't have been happier. It was comforting to know she'd never be required to suffer the question "What are you doing for the millennium?" ever again. Well, not unless she planned on living for another thousand years. And in the unlikely event she did, at least by that point, she'd be perfectly within her rights to answer, "Nothing. I'm not doing anything. I don't get out much these days because I should really be *dead*."

The pressure to do something "amazing" had bored the pants off her, and to make matters worse, she knew Tim would be doing something incredible, for he was now a millionaire, a fact that seemed to be rammed down her throat wherever she went. She hadn't met anybody else even remotely worth seeing since they'd split up, so she couldn't help but wonder if perhaps she should have stuck with him. At least she would have had exciting plans for the millennium.

There was no escape at work either. What everyone was going

to do for the big night had been all anyone could talk about for months. Inevitably, of course, there had been a handful of smug people with bigger paychecks than her who had been able to say things like "We're off to the Pyrenees" or "I'm going dolphin watching in San Diego" and even "We're just going to a small bash for five thousand, in Paris, with fireworks." It goes without saying that these people didn't just earn more than her, but also must have been stupidly organized. She and Karen hadn't been able to find even a local restaurant for them and their friends to go to that wasn't either fully booked or extortionate, so as far as they could work out, these people must have booked these "experience of a lifetime" events when they were toddlers.

In the end, Pete and Karen had hosted the night at their place. Dinner for twelve with lots of music, and if that had been that, it might have been a pretty enjoyable evening. As it was, however...

Karen had invited Pete's cousin David to the dinner, purely so she could try to match him with Jennifer. David was relatively good-looking but excruciatingly dull. At a certain point, due to the huge quantities of red wine he was drinking, his mouth had become incredibly dry, unlike his sense of humor, to the extent that his tongue kept getting stuck to the roof of his mouth as he talked. But to Jennifer's horrified fascination, instead of deciding that talking wasn't worth the effort, he'd battled on regardless, waffling away, trying to combat his dry mouth by glugging back yet more wine. This did nothing to solve the problem but everything to ensure that over time, his teeth were stained red and his breath became vile. Jennifer would rather have slept with a member of her immediate family than have sex with David.

The final nail in that coffin was delivered when he proceeded to talk at length about how reUNIon was such a great invention and how his sister had reunited with her now fiancée on it.

By this stage, Jennifer was seriously considering getting a cab home, despite not being midnight yet.

———

The next morning, she woke up to the first day of the new millennium feeling not only hungover and rancid, but also horribly anxious.

Deep down she knew she'd done the right thing because she didn't really miss Tim. But what if no one else came along?

On the upside, the millennium New Year was over, and for that, she was both grateful and relieved.

So the grayness and general frugality of January were very welcome, until January 7, when her boiler broke down. And then it was just shit.

———

"Coming," called Jennifer, rushing to answer the door, wishing she had slippers on as the floor tiles were so cold underfoot, even with tights on. Her tiny one-bedroom apartment in Tooting, which was hers and hers alone and therefore a space she usually adored, was freezing. She'd slept in a tracksuit and a coat, but when she'd woken up, her nose, one of the only things that hadn't been submerged under the covers, had been nearly frozen. Unable to have a hot shower, her greasy hair resembled a bird's nest. Getting ready for work, she'd tried to solve this dilemma by scraping it all back into a ponytail and had compensated with extra makeup, which, on her pale, winter-worn face, made her look a bit like a drag queen. She was cold to the bone and couldn't warm up.

"Hi," said the affable-looking plumber standing on her doorstep, who she hoped was going to be the answer to her prayers.

"Oh my gosh, thank you so much for coming. I'm desperate," she said, pulling her coat tighter around her. Underneath she was wearing a suit, ready for the day ahead. "I don't suppose there's any chance you could have it fixed sooner rather than later? I've got a massive day at work and should really be there right now but didn't think I could cope with returning to this ice block again."

"Er, well, give me a chance to have a look at what's happening and I'll let you know. But if I can, I shall get it sorted for you ASAP."

He had an Essex accent.

"I'm so sorry. You must think I'm insane. I think the cold may have frozen my brain," said Jennifer, standing back to let him in, a good start in terms of him being able to fix anything. "Then again, I may have just gotten confused because I think it might be warmer outside than it is in here."

"No worries," said the plumber politely.

"Sorry, I'm Jennifer," she said, starting again.

"Pleased to meet you. I'm Steve."

———

Forty-five minutes later, the boiler had clunked into action, hot water was swooshing around the pipes and the radiators, and

Jennifer was free to escape to work, unwashed but confident that when she returned, she wouldn't have to sleep in a coat.

"Thank you so much," she gushed.

"No worries," said Steve. "Glad I could get it sorted, and thanks for the tea."

She was struck by what a nice face he had. During all the time they'd been chatting away, he'd been on his knees, half inside the closet where the water heater lived, so all she'd been able to examine so far had been his backside. It was a nice backside, but it was rather heartwarming to discover that he had a face to match. It was an open face that wasn't dazzlingly good-looking but was really pleasant. He had a good, even smile and blue eyes. He smiled back at her. "So, you off to work then? You said you're in marketing, but what does that actually involve?"

"Well, basically, it's all about identifying who your customers are, then creating value for them and making sure you keep them," Jennifer said. She really did have to get going, so she went to get her bag so she could write Steve a check and leave.

"Yeah, I know that," he said, rolling his eyes. "What do you take me for? What I mean is, who do you do marketing for? Or, if you like, who's your market?"

"Oh, right," she said, surprised. She grinned at him, though as she did, her teeth chattered together. She felt like she might never be warm again. "Big questions," she said, deflecting because she was in a rush and her mind was focused on the meeting she desperately needed to get to.

"Sorry. You've got to go, haven't you?" he asked, taking the hint.

"I do, I'm afraid," she replied, rooting around in her bag

until she finally came across a pen at the bottom. "How much is that then?"

"Eighty," said Steve.

"Okay," said Jennifer, trying to mask her disappointment as she scribbled down the amount. There was no way she'd be getting the shoes she'd been lusting after this month. She should have been a plumber. She ripped the check out and handed it over.

"Thanks a lot. So anyway, sorry, because I know you're in a rush, but I don't suppose, and I promise I never usually do this, but do you fancy going for a drink one night?" Steve asked. As Jennifer looked up to check she'd heard right, his cheeks flamed red. "And I promise, no more dull questions about work."

"Er... I don't know," Jennifer replied.

"Okay, no worries. I shouldn't have put you on the spot," Steve said, turning away and bending back down to rummage in his tool bag as if he suddenly needed to find something.

Jennifer regarded him. He seemed like a perfectly decent guy, and he had just fixed her water heater. Plus, who else did she think she had lined up exactly? Pete's cousin David? Her last meaningful relationship had been with Tim and that had ended over two years ago. She'd had a couple of terrible dates, thanks to being forced by Karen to give online dating a go, and a one-night stand she could hardly bear to think about it had been so unbearably clunky.

So why would she turn down a date with a man who had four limbs, seemed nice, and had just saved her, definitely from frostbite if not death by hypothermia? Was she insane?

"Actually...I'd love to go for a drink," she said shyly.

"Really?" He looked delighted and flashed her a wide grin.

"Yeah." She grinned back. His smile was infectious. He had lovely teeth.

"Great. That's really good then," he said. "Okay, well, I've got your number. I'll give you a call and perhaps we could go for dinner after or something?"

"That would be very nice," she said. They both stood there, still grinning but also feeling mildly awkward.

"So…anyway…" she said, trying to walk out the front door at the exact same time he did.

"Oh, sorry," he said.

"No, no, after you," she said as he went to grab his tool bag, realizing they were going to have to cope with leaving the apartment at the same time and therefore continuing the conversation even though it was clearly time for it to end.

Jennifer felt gauche as they shuffled out the door together.

"Okay, well, I'll see you soon then," said Steve once they were both outside and Jennifer had locked the door behind her. "I'm going this way, to the van."

"Oh…er, right," said Jennifer, wondering whether to pretend she was headed the other way but knowing it would only make her later. "Um…I'm going that way too, actually, toward the tube."

"Oh cool," he said, his face coloring a little.

They ended up strolling down the road, together but not, both smiling despite the awkwardness of the situation. Eventually Jennifer decided to do them both a favor by saying something. "So where do you live then, Steve?" she asked at the precise moment he decided to say, "Well, this is me. My van's parked here."

"Oh, right… Well, not to worry then." Jennifer cringed, feeling unbelievably self-conscious, yet also hopeful he would call her. There was something about him that appealed to her more and more by the second.

"At the moment, I'm staying with a mate in Mitcham, though..."

"Oh, great. Not too far then, I suppose," she said. "Okay... Well, see you. Give me a call."

"Will do," he said.

Jennifer grinned as she walked away. It hadn't been the smoothest of meetings, but she had a funny feeling that their date would be a good one.

Present Day

J en, I don't know if you can hear me, but it's me, Max…"

Jennifer waited for him to continue, but when silence followed, she assumed she'd imagined what she'd heard. But then he spoke again.

"Anyway, the doctors think it's worth a go. Talking to you, that is, so I'm going to sit and chat, just in case."

It was strange. She kind of understood what he was saying and yet it was like he was speaking a foreign language. She suspected her brain couldn't cope with the task of listening and understanding at the same time. Instead, the words were just noise.

"We all really miss you. It's very quiet at home without you. The girls are fine. They know Mummy's having a long sleep, and they say a little prayer for you every night. I'm keeping close tabs on them, and the school has been brilliant, especially Miss Kelly, who's been keeping an eye on Pol. So that's all okay. Think they might be getting a bit fed up with my cooking, though…"

Max's voice cracked and he stopped talking for a moment. He cleared his throat.

"For that matter, I am too. Anyway, I've brought a paper with me, so I thought I might read some of it out to you."

But Jennifer had tuned out again, had slipped back to where she'd come from, with intent, for the last time she'd emerged from a portal, she'd noticed that the one to the left, the one marked Aidan, was growing faint. She'd had a strong inkling at the time that if she wanted to find out anything else from that parallel universe, she'd have to do it quickly, while it still existed. She'd even considered what might happen if it closed while she was inside. Would she be trapped? Would she remain Jennifer from that life forever? She hoped that wasn't a possibility. There was nothing about that life that made her feel particularly proud or happy. Had she gone with Aidan, it seemed she'd have had a forlorn existence compared to the one she enjoyed with Max. In her real life, she'd gotten her education, stayed in touch with her friends and family, and gone on to create a safe, secure, and largely happy family unit of her own. In the world of Aidan, she felt sorry for Nathan. Sorry for her own son. The son she might have had…

As she slid back into the tunnel, she became desperate to know that there was some form of resolution, if not for her, then for the boy. He needed his extended family, she decided. Not just a worn-out mother and a lazy, work-shy father.

The portal was weaker than ever, and as she glided toward it, she felt more nervous than she had been about anything in the whole of her thirty-eight years.

TUNNEL NUMBER ONE
What Could Have Been—Aidan

J ennifer sat in the café, drumming the fingers of one hand on the Formica table while decimating yet another packet of sugar with the other. She wished she hadn't ordered coffee. She felt jittery enough as it was, and the caffeine she'd consumed wasn't making life any easier.

Where was her mother? Why wasn't she here yet?

For the hundredth time, she glanced at the black-and-white clock on the wall. Three thirty-two. Her mother was officially two minutes late for their meeting. Still, it wasn't like she was coming from around the corner. She had a long train journey from the suburbs of London up to the very north of England and then a cab ride to contend with. The wait was unbearable, and Jennifer needed the bathroom again. Stupid coffee.

Jennifer stood up and, for the second time since she'd arrived, headed for the tiny restroom at the back of the café. Once she'd finished, she checked her reflection in the cracked mirror above the small basin.

She didn't usually wear a great deal of makeup, but today she'd taken extra care with her appearance. In the days leading up to this, she'd agonized about what to wear. She didn't want to appear dowdy or plain in her standard jeans and same old T-shirts that she wore day in, day out. But she only had them or a couple of dresses she reserved for special occasions. She'd decided that what she needed was a happy medium, because as much as she wanted to look nice, she also wanted to avoid looking like she'd tried too hard. In the end, she'd splurged on a new shirt. It had been so long since she'd treated herself to anything, she'd decided the occasion merited it. Besides, it had been on the sale rack so had only cost her twenty-eight pounds as opposed to forty-two. It made her feel like a million dollars. Well, maybe a thousand…

Anyway, the point was it was *new*, which was thrilling.

She sighed at her reflection. No matter how many layers of blusher she added, she knew her mother would detect the tired aura that constantly existed around her. Would it also be noticeable that she dyed her own hair and that she looked a few years older than the thirty-eight she'd lived?

It suddenly occurred to her that if her mother had arrived, she might think Jennifer hadn't turned up. With a start, she hurried out of the bathroom, only to spot her mother sitting at a table, looking as nervous and anxious as she felt.

Her mother was so much older.

Of course this was going to be the case, and yet no matter how much common sense told her to expect someone she hadn't seen for years to have aged, it didn't stop it from being a shock. Her mother looked far more like a grandmother these days. It was the strangest thing.

Tears pricked Jennifer's eyes. It was so good to see her, but perhaps it wasn't until that very second that she realized not only how much she'd missed her, but also how much she'd missed out on.

Unsure how to behave, she felt nervous as she approached the table.

"Mum," she said, completely choked.

"Oh, Jennifer," said her mother, leaping to her feet, her nerves clearly frayed by the stress of the situation. "You're here. I can't believe it."

"Neither can I," said Jennifer, and the two women stared at each other, both too moved to speak.

"Oh, come here," her mother said eventually, gesturing to her daughter to give her a hug.

As they embraced, Jennifer couldn't help it—she sobbed noisily into her mother's shoulder. Eighteen years was a long time.

"I'm sorry," she repeated, that being all she could manage.

"Me too," her mother said. She broke their embrace and motioned for Jennifer to sit down opposite her. "Now," she said briskly, apparently determined not to let her emotions overwhelm the moment. "Come on, we'd better pull ourselves together or they'll be sending in the men in white coats for us. Shall we order some tea and cake?"

Jennifer nodded as she sat down, grabbing a white paper napkin out of the stainless steel holder to blow her nose. "Oh gosh, I'm so sorry about weeping. I really didn't want to be like this."

She looked up to see that her mother was staring at her, and for a few seconds, she stared back.

"Do I look awful?" Jennifer asked feebly.

"No, love," her mother said, her whole face crumpling. "You look absolutely wonderful, a sight for sore eyes." And with that, she burst into tears.

"Oh, Mum," said Jennifer, feeling stricken and standing up to reach across the table. "Come here."

Her mother gladly accepted a second hug, and they stood like that for some time, in a very awkward position that neither of them wished to change. What anyone else in the café might have been thinking was unimportant.

When they finally let go again and sat down, Jennifer absorbed every detail of her mother's face. She was so lined, so gray. She'd put on weight and looked quite tubby around her middle. She also looked like home.

"So, have you been happy?" her mother asked, getting straight to the heart of things.

Of all the questions her mother could have started with, Jennifer wished it hadn't been that.

"Um…yes," she replied after a lengthy pause, which kind of said it all.

"And Aidan, has he been good to you?"

"Yeah, Mum, Aidan's fine. I know you have this idea that he's some kind of monster, but he honestly isn't."

"And Nathan?"

"He's amazing. It's just so sad you've never been able to find that out for yourself."

"There's still time," her mother said, pulling a hanky from her handbag and gripping it so tightly that the blood drained from her knuckles. "If he'd see me, I'd love to take him out. I don't know. I mean, what do you think?"

Jennifer's heart ached as she took in her mother's pained expression. How much time had they wasted?

"I'm sure he'd love that," Jennifer said. "He's a real sweetie. Tries to pretend he's all cool in front of his friends, but it's all a front. Underneath he's soft as butter."

"You've got a northern accent, you know."

"No, have I?"

"Oh, definitely," her mother replied.

"So what do you want to do now? Shall I get you this tea and cake? Or we could take a walk around town?" Jennifer was not particularly relishing the idea of showing her the drab apartment where she lived, which was what they'd originally arranged to do. Ideally she'd postpone that a while longer.

"Do you know what? I think I might have changed my mind. I'm not sure I could eat cake after all, which is not like me... Shall we have a little walk instead?" her mother suggested. "That train journey was a long time sitting down. It would be nice to stretch my legs."

"Good idea," Jennifer agreed, motioning to the waitress that she'd like to pay for her coffee.

They gathered their bags and left the warmth of the steamy café for the cooler streets of Carlisle.

"It's so good to see you, Mum," she said.

By way of reply, her mother extended a hand and reached for Jennifer's to give it a little squeeze.

In that small moment, it appeared that things were going to be okay.

Jennifer left work at six o'clock on the dot after what had been a relatively successful day. That afternoon, she'd managed to secure a deal on a three-bedroom house that had been lingering unsold for far too long. The manager had been so happy to finally get rid of it that he'd been particularly complimentary to Jennifer about her selling skills. Although, deep down, Jennifer wondered if anything she said when showing people around properties actually made the slightest difference to whether they ended up deciding to buy them. She sometimes caught herself solemnly saying things like, "And this is the bathroom," as if she were enlightening them with knowledge they'd otherwise not have been able to figure out themselves. Still, she wasn't about to let her boss know that she'd been pretty much superfluous to the buyer's decision-making process and allowed him to believe instead that without her, the agency would still be burdened with a house most people in their right minds would never purchase because the ground floor was so dark it felt like a dungeon.

Feeling chirpier than she had in a while, as she wandered home, she contemplated the upcoming weekend. Tomorrow was Friday, and once the children were in bed, she planned on reprising her original plan of putting on some tarty underwear and seducing her husband. And this time it *would* work and they *would* have sex and they would reconnect on lots of levels and all would be well. After all, there was a huge possibility that a lot of this angst she'd been experiencing lately was because she simply needed a good shag.

Then, on Saturday, the girls both had parties to go to, and she and Max were going out in the evening for dinner with friends she actually liked.

Yes, she'd definitely been worrying far too much about stuff that, in the grand scheme of things, was probably all fairly manageable and not too disastrous. No one was dying. Everyone had their health. She was a lucky girl and needed to keep reminding herself of that.

Toward the bottom of her road, she realized her phone was vibrating in her handbag. Scrabbling around for it, she caught it just before it went to voice mail.

It was their nanny, Ivana.

"Hello," she said, wondering what she wanted and betting they'd run out of something.

"Jennifer…"

Oh God, thought Jennifer at once, for Ivana sounded very distraught. Her heart skipped a beat and hundreds of thoughts flashed through her mind in a nanosecond before Ivana finally managed to utter, "I'm so sorry. I think Eadie's broken her arm."

Later, around the time Jennifer had originally been hoping to be sliding into a nice, relaxing bath, she and Max were sitting at Kingston Hospital, feeling traumatized and looking almost as white in the face as the cast that was now wrapped around their eldest daughter's arm.

Jennifer felt like a shadow of her former self, having experienced the most stressful few hours of her life. The image of Eadie's arm sticking out at such a bizarre angle was burned into her retinas and would undoubtedly never leave her.

Upon racing into the house, she'd found her daughter in a state of shock, lying on the couch in a daze, white as a sheet with her arm at a disgusting angle, which Jennifer had struggled with even being able to look at. She'd stroked her brow and told her everything would be all right, grateful that Eadie was so still and calm because the arm thing made her feel very nauseous. Ivana had already called the ambulance, but she was racked with guilt and worry and was wringing her hands, pleading with Jennifer for forgiveness. Not that it sounded like she could have done anything to prevent the accident. Eadie had simply been bouncing on the trampoline in the yard, just as she did most days after school. She'd slipped and landed awkwardly, and that had been that. Jennifer knew this was the case, and despite maternal instinct wanting someone or something to blame, she knew this wouldn't be fair so kept quiet.

The minute the ambulance arrived, Jennifer burst into tears with relief that someone with medical training had arrived.

"Is she going to be all right?" she wailed.

"She'll be fine, but let's get her to the hospital as soon as we can," the paramedic said calmly.

The shock was starting to wear off, meaning Eadie was far more aware of the pain she was in. She started crying and repeatedly yelling "ow ow ow" until she'd wound herself up into a terrible state. She didn't want the paramedics to move her, so getting her into the ambulance was a bit of an ordeal.

Jennifer hated seeing her daughter so distressed but knew she had to remain strong, at least till Max could join them. Thankfully, she'd gotten through to him on his cell phone straightaway, and between them, they'd decided that the best plan would be to meet at the hospital while Ivana stayed at the house to look after Polly, the only one in the family who seemed perfectly oblivious to the drama going on around her.

In the ambulance, the paramedics were able to administer some heavy-duty pain relief to Eadie, which they assured Jennifer would calm her down. Jennifer spent the rest of the journey wondering if it would cast her in a bad light if she were to ask if she could have some too.

Once they'd finally arrived, they had to wait for ages in the emergency room. When Eadie was wheeled into a room to have her arm x-rayed and set in a cast, Jennifer was still without her husband and had to continue being stoic while ignoring the desire to retch every time her gaze fell upon her little girl's bent arm. When Max arrived at the hospital, having jogged all the way from the train station, he was a sweaty, stressed mess. He was waiting for them as they emerged from the treatment room, and Jennifer realized she had never been so happy to see anyone in her life.

Eadie was on a gurney, pale and whimpering, and he immediately gave his daughter an enormous, reassuring hug.

"Are you okay, Eadie Beadie?" he soothed, stroking his daughter's hair and kissing her puffy face tenderly.

"It still hurts," Eadie moaned, holding out her rigid, plaster-casted arm. Remembering what lay beneath and the process that had occurred to get it back into a normal position, Jennifer's stomach turned. She'd have made a lousy nurse. Doctors and nurses were saints, as far as she was concerned.

"You are so brave," Max told his daughter. "And you know what brave people get?"

"Presents?" Eadie tried hopefully, her tearstained face looking something other than pained and distressed for the first time in hours.

"Too blooming right they do," Max said. "Sackfuls of them. Maybe even a Wii?"

"Yay!" squealed Eadie, her face a picture of disbelief.

Seeing her little girl look vaguely comforted meant Jennifer didn't get annoyed by Max's slightly dubious parental approach. Screw it—if Eadie wanted a Wii, she could have one. She was just grateful that Max was there. For the first time in a long while, she recalled how much she loved him, why she'd married him, and the security and comfort that doing so had brought into her life.

But it was amazing how things could turn on a dime.

As soon as they'd gotten Eadie into a room where she could wait comfortably for the doctor to come check on her, Max turned to his wife and asked, "Can I have a word?" This struck

Jennifer as a bit odd. He was her husband. He could say what he liked. He hardly needed to make an appointment.

"Course you can. Eadie, darling, you try to close your eyes now and have a little rest."

Eadie must have been exhausted because she didn't put up any resistance to her mother's suggestion and merely closed her eyes. Jennifer and Max pulled the curtain shut around her bed and walked quietly out into the corridor.

"Who was keeping an eye on her when it happened?" Max demanded to know as soon as they were out of earshot. His voice was full of rage.

"What do you mean?" Jennifer asked, who was so tired she could only think about getting home and to bed. "You know who was—Ivana."

"Well, how could she allow this to happen? I know the kids like her, but after this, I think we have to ask ourselves if we can trust the care of our children to her."

"Oh, for goodness' sake, Max. It could so easily have been one of us. It was an accident. It's not like Ivana went up to her and snapped her arm in two."

"But that's the thing," Max retaliated. "It wasn't one of us. It was Ivana, who's a very nice girl, but is she responsible enough to be in charge of our kids? Given that we're standing in a hospital, I'd suggest the answer might be no."

"Why are you sounding annoyed with me?" Jennifer asked. "What the hell have I done? Our daughter's broken her arm, and you're standing here yelling at me."

"I'm not yelling," Max yelled, "but, to be honest, I do resent the way you've always made me feel like a bastard for preferring my kids to be looked after by one of us rather than a stranger. And then this happens."

"Well then, why don't you bloody well resign and look after them yourself?" retorted Jennifer, who had never been angrier in her entire life. "Because what you're suggesting is that I'm a terrible mother and that somehow this is all my fault because I had the audacity to be at work today. Well, fuck you, Max."

Max flinched, but his expression remained stony. "Don't make a scene. People are watching."

"I don't give a shit," she said, lowering her tone slightly. "And don't you dare make Ivana feel bad when we get back either, because if you do, I will be absolutely livid. No one feels worse about what's happened than she does right now. She loves the girls to pieces, and all my friends comment on how wonderful she is when they see her out and about with them. Now, before I lose it completely, we need to find out when we can get out of here. Eadie's exhausted."

"She's not the only one," said Max, looking shifty, and Jennifer could tell that he knew he'd been out of order.

She suddenly didn't feel so cross anymore, just tired to the marrow of her bones.

"I'm sorry," Max mumbled.

"Whatever," Jennifer said, past caring.

"I'm sorry," he repeated. "It's just stressful, that's all. On the way here, I kept thinking how I was in and out of the emergency room as a kid and I was fine, but you still can't help panicking."

"I know," Jennifer said. "And I was here and had to deal with it.

But we have to keep it in perspective. It's a broken arm, and it'll mend. What we should probably be more worried about is the fact that our youngest might be a sociopath. I've never seen anyone so unbothered by witnessing someone in horrific pain."

"Right, I'll go and see if we can get out of here," Max said, looking sheepish. "I know they said we should wait to have the cast checked again, but I'm tempted to say that we'll bring her back in the morning and get it looked at then."

"Okay," Jennifer agreed, equally keen to get home. As Max went off in search of a doctor, Jennifer returned to Eadie, who was fast asleep, worn-out by her stressful experience.

When Max came back ten minutes later, he gave her a thumbs-up. "We can go. We just need to sign a form on the way out."

"Great," Jennifer said. "Though it almost seems a shame we'll have to wake her up now."

"Well, when our cab's here, I'll carry her. That way, with a bit of luck she might stay asleep. Then, when we get home, I might eBay that bloody trampoline."

"Do it."

"And perhaps I'll take the day off work tomorrow," he suggested. "That way we can bring Eadie back here to get checked together."

"If you want," said Jennifer, who could tell he was trying to make amends.

"Plus we're both exhausted, so it would give us a chance to relax."

"I suppose... Oh shit."

"What?"

"I'm supposed to be seeing my therapist tomorrow. My appointment's at eleven. I'll have to cancel if Eadie's not at school."

"You didn't tell me you had an appointment," said Max, regarding his wife quizzically.

"It's no big deal," Jennifer said.

"Well, you shouldn't cancel. Doesn't she charge for missed appointments?"

"Yeah."

"You go then, and I'll bring Eadie on my own," said Max, obviously still trying to make up for what he'd said earlier.

"Fine."

"Great."

Inside, Jennifer still felt murderous toward him, but teetering on the verge of wanting a divorce was so terrifying it galvanized her into making more of an effort than she normally would. "And then tomorrow night," she found herself saying, "we should, you know, have a bit of a romantic night in. If you know what I mean?"

"Sounds good to me," Max said hesitantly. "And impressive that despite the strip lighting, smell of antiseptic, and our bandaged child being only feet away, you've still got sex on your brain whereas here I am, thinking how I might finish putting together that wardrobe properly."

"Yes, well, it would be nice not to have it lying on the floor anymore," Jennifer replied, faintly embarrassed and fed up beyond belief.

"I'll get you lying on the floor," said Max, assuming he'd been forgiven and pinching her bum.

"Maybe," Jennifer said primly.

"And after your Steve jokes the other day, I'd better get my act together and show you that I can actually be quite useful to have around. Otherwise, you might run off with the plumber."

"I doubt it," Jennifer said. "You saw the last plumber we had around. Mick, with no front teeth."

"True," Max said. "He hardly lived up to sweet Steve's standards, did he?"

Jennifer didn't reply. Steve had been sweet. Really sweet, and there was no harm in that. He'd been her "one before the one" who could have been "the one" if fate hadn't stepped in and brought Max to her. Perhaps she should have stayed with him after all. He never would have spoken to her like Max had.

"Anyway, you sit down, and I'll go sign this form and come back for you both."

"Okay," Jennifer agreed.

She sank into the plastic chair next to Eadie's bed and wondered how it would feel to deal with incidents like this as a single parent. Horrible, no doubt. Terrifying, in fact. Still, thankfully, she didn't have to worry about that. Max had offered to take the day off tomorrow. It was a start, and with a bit of luck, she wouldn't have to set foot in a hospital again until the cast needed taking off, which suited her fine.

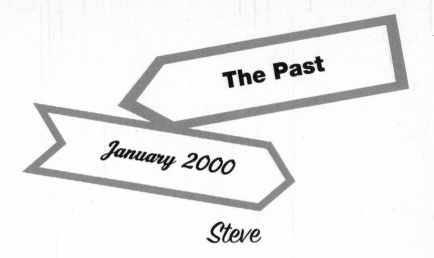

The Past

January 2000

Steve

J ennifer had been looking forward to her date with Steve all day, which was a good sign. First dates were usually nerve-racking events, but she wasn't dreading this one at all. They'd had a couple of fairly long chats on the phone already, which helped. Both times, the conversation had flowed easily and had given her an indication that the date would be enjoyable as opposed to a terrible ordeal.

She'd taken all the first-date precautions, of course. She'd washed her hair the night before, and when she'd gotten home from work to shower and change, she'd also shaved her armpits, sorted out her bikini line and legs, and put on a sexy, matching bra and underwear set. She certainly wasn't planning on sleeping with him tonight but would be prepared nonetheless. Just in case.

They'd agreed to meet at a pizza place. Not very imaginative, but at least she knew the food would be nice and that she could dress casually. She was wearing jeans with a flowy top and high-heeled ankle boots. Despite feeling relatively confident, she still had butterflies as she approached the restaurant at seven minutes past eight.

As soon as she walked in, she spotted him. Good. She would have hated to have arrived first. She was quite taken aback by how good he looked. She'd remembered him as having a nice face, but actually, on second sighting, she realized he was far better looking than she remembered and had the sort of face most women would notice in a crowd. His eyes were really blue, and you could tell that although he wore his hair short, it wasn't because he was going bald but because he had a lovely shaped head and good bone structure, and it simply suited him that way.

He waved at her as soon as he spotted her and got up from his seat, which she thought was chivalrous. He'd obviously made an effort. He was wearing a nice white shirt and smelled of some herby aftershave.

"You look nice," he said, leaning in to give her a kiss on the cheek.

"Thanks," she said shyly, sitting down in the chair he'd pulled out for her. His manners were impeccable.

"Did you come straight from work?" he asked.

"No," Jennifer replied. "I popped home, actually, as I tend to have to wear suits and stuff to work. You know, really 'officey' clothes."

She decided it probably wasn't necessary to add, *I also needed to sort out my pubic sideburns*, especially since a waitress had come by to take their drink orders.

"Do you want a drink?" Steve asked.

"Yes, definitely. I'll have a glass of white wine, please."

"And I'll have a Coke, please," Steve said.

Jennifer cringed as the waitress wrote the order down. *Soda for dinner? Really?*

"Are you not a big drinker then?" she asked, wondering what

kind of person she was that she'd rather he was than wasn't. At university, being able to drink huge amounts had almost been a badge of honor.

"Not really. I like beer," said Steve. "But I'm not really into wine."

"Fair enough," Jennifer said.

"So, tell me about yourself," Steve started. "How come a gorgeous girl like you is single?"

Pretty smooth, thought Jennifer. She grinned, flattered. "Well, I was in quite a long-term relationship at university. Two and a half years, to be precise."

"Okay, so what happened—if you don't mind me asking, that is?"

"No, not at all. Um… Well, I'm not sure, really. I guess it wasn't so much a case of anything specific happening to end it but more realizing we just weren't compatible. He was a really clever guy and interesting to hang out with, but he was a bit of a cold fish at times. He was incapable of expressing his feelings, so I spent the whole time wondering if he actually fancied me or whether he was with me for the sake of it."

"Really?" asked Steve. "If I was your boyfriend, I wouldn't be able to stop telling you how pretty you are."

Jennifer didn't know how to react. It was a lovely thing to say. He sounded so sincere too. Not creepy or disingenuous at all.

"Thanks," she managed in the end, once she'd gotten over the shock of being complimented. "Um, anyway, I guess it didn't feel like he loved me in the right way, which probably sounds a bit weird, but by the end, as far as I was concerned, it felt more like we were friends than boyfriend and girlfriend. I don't know."

"Fizzled out?"

"Yeah," Jennifer said a bit doubtfully. She was revealing more than she had intended but was unsure how to stop the information from coming out of her mouth. "Though, to be fair, it wasn't ever really sizzling, even at the beginning, so there wasn't a great deal of sizzle to fizzle. Besides, he had a wife, of sorts."

"What do you mean?" said Steve, looking a bit taken aback.

"He was married to his work," said Jennifer, teetering on the verge of telling him about Tim, only partly wondering if she should so early on. Still, she'd gone this far. Perhaps she'd just get it out of the way. "Have you heard of reUNIon?"

"Of course, yeah."

"Okay, well, he kind of invented it."

"You're kidding! He isn't that Purcell bloke, is he?"

Jennifer nodded.

"Wow," Steve said, seemingly trying to recover from having been emasculated within the first few minutes of the date. "Okay, so very clever bloke then, although if you don't mind me saying…"

"Go on," Jennifer encouraged. "Say what you like."

"I always think he comes across as a bit arrogant in interviews."

"I agree."

"And he can't be *that* intelligent if he let you slip through his fingers," he added, going red as he did.

Jennifer grinned. He'd already paid her more compliments than Tim had in their whole first year of being together. It was nice.

"Well, that's very kind of you to say. And what about you? How long have you been single? Not long, I bet."

Jennifer cringed. She'd been trying to match his kindness by saying something nice too, but in the process had managed to make herself sound like a cheesy old lothario.

"Oh, let's see now…about six months."

"Okay, and who was your last girlfriend?"

"Lauren," replied Steve, and as he said her name, Jennifer could tell that Lauren had meant a great deal to him. "We went out for about three years."

"Right, so a long time then," she said, suddenly unsure of how they'd gotten onto the subject of their exes so quickly. Surely this was more of a third or fourth date kind of topic? "So was it a difficult breakup?"

"Yeah, I guess."

"So…what happened then?"

For the second time, Steve's face colored, and he seemed unsure about replying.

"What?" Jennifer asked, his reluctance to answer making her far keener to find out more details.

"Well, it'll probably sound a bit heavy and I don't want to scare you off. We haven't even ordered yet," he joked, looking more than a little uncomfortable.

"I know." Jennifer grinned. "I was thinking the same thing myself when I told you about Tim, but you've *got* to tell me now, and I promise I won't get scared," she said, despite not being 100 percent sure she meant it. If Lauren had found out he was a cross-dresser or that he had a penchant for sleeping with goats, Jennifer couldn't be sure she wouldn't be leaving before she'd even ordered.

215

"Thanks," she said to the waitress who had arrived with their drinks.

Steve seemed grateful for the distraction and said they'd like to order their food. So they did, though Jennifer wasn't letting him off the hook that easily.

"So," she prompted as soon as the waitress had left, "what happened?"

"Okay, well, before I say, just bear in mind that we were together for a pretty long time. So I guess you consider lots of things that don't even enter your brain when you first start going out with someone."

"Good disclaimer. Now tell me," she insisted.

"Right," said Steve, who'd accepted that he wasn't going to be able to wriggle out of an explanation. "Basically, what happened was, I realized we weren't on the same page as far as what we both wanted out of life."

"In what way?"

"She didn't want to have children. Ever."

"Ah," Jennifer said, feeling mildly relieved. That was a good answer, one that didn't have her running for the hills. "Okay, well, fair enough then. I would say that's a pretty sensible reason to have ended things, if you know you definitely want them."

"I do," Steve said with feeling. "I love kids. Ideally I'd like three, I think. Not that I said that to Lauren. I mean, if she'd agreed to trying just for one at some point, I probably would have stayed with her, but she point-blank refused to even consider it."

"Was she a real career girl then?"

"Er, no, not really," Steve said, shaking his head. "She's a beautician. She just doesn't like being around kids. It's weird.

Her sister's got a couple, you see, and she kept saying that her sister had lost her life. That she was always tired, that she was fat and never had any money. Only whenever I went around there, I always thought her sister looked fulfilled and like she wouldn't change her life for anything. Besides, I think not wanting to lose your figure is a pretty lame reason for not wanting to have a child."

"Was the sister fat?"

"Hardly the point."

Jennifer blushed. She'd heard a story on the news the other day about a man who had murdered his wife after cooking dinner for her, and all she'd been able to wonder, apart from how awful it was, was what he'd cooked her. It was just the way her brain worked. The details seemed important.

"I know it's not the point," she agreed. "And I know I'm terrible, but I still have to know. Was she?"

"Um, yeah, a bit," said Steve, rolling his eyes in mock disapproval but clearly amused.

Jennifer nodded while considering everything he'd said in the last few minutes. It was endearing hearing a man speak that way. In her experience, it was usually women who dreamed and talked of motherhood in the future and men who appeared to go along with it when the time was right. She tried to think if she and Tim had ever discussed if they'd want to have children one day but she couldn't remember. She didn't think he'd have been against it, but she couldn't remember him ever stating that he wanted to. Besides, being a father would take some of his attention away from reUNIon, and that would never do.

There followed a bit of an awkward silence, only because given what had just been said, Jennifer felt obliged to announce her own views on procreation. After all, if she didn't want to have children one day, there was almost no point in her being there. No point in him treating her to a casual pizza. Steve was right, of course. Only insane people would think about such things when they'd just met someone, and yet the stark reality was that once you plowed deeper into your twenties, you only really embarked on a relationship if you thought it might end up leading somewhere. Otherwise, what was the point?

"Well, for what it's worth then," she said in a voice that she hoped sounded lighthearted, "I'd like at least a couple of kids one day."

"Okay," said Steve, raising his glass of Coke to her. "Well, good for you, and don't worry. I'm not planning on impregnating anyone in the near future."

He smiled cheekily, acknowledging that he fully comprehended how crazy the conversation was; they hadn't even slept together yet. At the thought, her stomach flipped in a very good way.

"Anyway," he continued, "that was a bit awkward, wasn't it? Sorry about that. I honestly didn't mean to extract your personal views on whether you'd like to be a parent within the first ten minutes of the date."

"It's okay," said Jennifer, who thought he'd managed to break the ice quite successfully. At least he could laugh at himself. It was sweet.

"Right, so what shall we talk about now?" he asked.

"Ooh, why don't we go straight for another contentious and deeply personal subject?" Jennifer suggested. "Maybe who we'd vote for in the next election? Or how much we earn? Something nice and delicate like that."

"Good idea, or perhaps you could just tell me how your day's been. Might be less controversial?"

"Okay," Jennifer agreed, and from that point onward, the evening veered into more standard first-date territory but with the edge of nerves completely extinguished.

———

Later, after they'd had their meal, they left the restaurant and stood out on the pavement, both reluctant for the date to end but unsure as to whether the other person felt the same. In the end, Steve broached the subject.

"Well, I've had a lovely time, but if I'm honest, I'd like the evening to continue a bit longer. It's only nine thirty, after all. But if you're tired…"

"No, I'm fine," Jennifer said. "Why? What were you thinking?"

"We could go for a drink in a pub?" he suggested. "Or, and I hope you don't think this sounds forward, perhaps we could go back to your place for a cup of tea and just hang out for a bit or something?"

"Sure," said Jennifer, who quite fancied doing that. She really wanted to kiss him. "Or we could go to yours? Mitcham isn't far."

"Ah," said Steve. "Actually, I'm not based in Mitcham anymore."

"Oh, right," Jennifer said, wondering why he suddenly looked so sheepish. "Where are you then?"

"I've, er, moved back home, for the short term," he said, and Jennifer realized at this point that he blushed incredibly easily.

"You mean, with your parents?"

"Just with my mum, actually. My dad died a few years ago, so Mum's on her own. Well, strictly speaking, that's not true. She's got a boyfriend named Derek, but they don't live together."

"Where's your mum's place then?"

"Leytonstone."

"Leytonstone?" she exclaimed. "That's miles away, isn't it?"

"It's not close," he agreed. "But it's not that bad. When I'm working, I drive a motorbike to get down to these parts and just leave the van parked somewhere overnight. I biked here tonight, actually."

"Right," said Jennifer, trying not to feel so downcast that he lived so far away. With his mother! He was twenty-eight years old, for Christ's sake.

Her expression must have given her away because Steve piped up with, "Like I said, it's only temporary. I was spending so much on rent that it was getting really difficult to save. Living at home for a few months means I can save for a down payment for my own place. And besides, living with Mum isn't so bad. We get along really well. Plus, I get a great dinner every night. She even does my laundry and ironing."

"Ah, that's nice," said Jennifer, though she would have been more impressed if he'd said he did his own laundry. If he wasn't paying rent, surely it was the least he could do? There was nothing sexy about imagining his mother washing his underpants for him.

"So, can we go to your place, or would you prefer the pub?"

"Let's go to my apartment," said Jennifer, her mind racing as she tried to remember what sort of state she'd left it in. She prayed she'd put away the hair removal cream. Otherwise, that disgusting fishy odor would be lingering in the air. She'd have to get him in the living room so she could straighten up quickly.

———

An hour later, Jennifer was on the verge of her first kiss with Steve. They'd had cliché cups of coffee and had sat on the sofa together, chatting away about this and that, both keen to get to the point where they could go in for a kiss, wondering who was going to initiate it. Finally, just as he had all evening, Steve took the lead. He reached over gently and turned her cheek so she was facing him fully. Then, staring at her with real tenderness, he pulled her toward him and kissed her in a way that made her feel like the most beautiful girl in the world. Then he slowly opened his mouth a bit and kissed her more expertly than anyone had since Aidan all those years ago.

It was absolutely amazing, and when his hand started stroking her leg, she almost melted with pleasure. It wasn't long before their breathing got heavier and the kissing became more urgent. God, she'd forgotten how much she loved kissing, and it appeared he did too, because instead of trying to move things on, he kissed her for ages, taking his time over it and seemingly enjoying it as much as she did. It was incredible. So sexy and so sensual. By the time he started touching her breasts, she was desperate for it and was hinting for him to do so by pushing herself against him. He knew exactly what he was doing and seemed only too aware that, in itself, the wait was one of the hottest things about the whole experience.

Every time his hand made contact with any part of her, it felt insanely good, so when his hand slid to the top of her jeans, she couldn't resist letting him undo the fly. He touched her through her underwear in the most sensual way imaginable. He stroked her gently yet firmly and left her panting for more. However, remembering this was a first date, she pulled away, breathless, knowing that despite him living with his mother and drinking soda with his dinner, she definitely wanted to see him again.

"Are you okay?" he whispered into her ear, his voice thick with desire.

"Yeah," she said. "You're an amazing kisser."

"So are you," he said. "I am so turned on."

Her gaze went to his trousers, where she could see for herself exactly how turned on he was. She clearly wasn't going to be disappointed in that department either.

"I think perhaps we should stop, though," she said. "I mean, I don't want to, but it's probably for the best, don't you think? It being our first date and everything."

"Whatever you say, beautiful."

It was the "beautiful" that did it. It almost made her cry. She had longed for Tim to say nice things to her for years. Had yearned for a bit of attention to the point where, at times, she'd almost been reduced to begging for compliments, like a dog sniffing around a table for crumbs. And here was Steve, who she hardly knew but who had been so lovely all evening, telling her she was beautiful, and it was so lovely to hear. It was like pouring water on a dried up old plant.

"Perhaps we can do some more kissing," she suggested.

Steve was more than happy to go along with that plan, although it didn't quite end there. Half an hour later, unable to resist, Jennifer ended up having sex with him. On her sofa. And it was bloody great.

W hat Jennifer couldn't have known was that she had been in a coma for three weeks. Three long weeks, during which her friends and family had had to come to terms with the fact that she may not return to them. No matter how many times they asked the doctor for his opinion, he could only offer them vague replies. The fact was that no one knew what was going to happen to Jennifer, whether she'd live, die, or remain in no-man's-land until someone else made the heartrending decision for her.

Of course, this was far harder for them than it was for Jennifer, for she was oblivious, cocooned in her own little world. A gray, foggy world that she drifted around in, sometimes aware of her anchorless state, occasionally surfacing to hear snippets from the real world before descending back to the place she was better able to handle.

Meanwhile, her body was doing its very best to recover from the shock it had endured, and her brain was scrambling to repair itself.

Her consciousness was buzzing, yearning to make another journey, desperate to find out more about how life could have been.

She started her descent.

It took a while, but when she reached the tunnels, as she'd suspected it would have, the first portal had disappeared completely. Instead of a gray, swirling, cloudy mist, there was now just a black nothingness in its place. Tunnel number one was shut for good, so she would just have to accept that and be thankful for what she had learned from it. However, the second portal, the one marked *Tim*, was still very much available, though it was a few shades weaker than it had been before. The third, which she had yet to explore at all, was still as bright as anything.

Tim or Steve?

So far she'd learned that by staying with Tim, she would have turned into the kind of woman she'd probably detest if she was to meet her at a party. Groomed, pampered, and not really serving much purpose other than being a wife. She also appeared to be miserable, unsure, and too hung up on her "lifestyle" to do much about it.

There didn't seem any point checking out life with Steve yet. He could wait. She could visualize it so well anyway, whereas she couldn't even begin to guess what would happen to her in the second portal. Would she leave Tim? Would she break Joe's and, indeed, her own heart for the sake of her children—or out of fear?

TUNNEL NUMBER TWO
What Could Have Been—Tim

B ut what I don't understand is why you can't just fly Karen out here?" repeated Tim, regarding Jennifer in a way that told her to tread carefully.

He was perched on the edge of their enormous seven-foot bed, which was still rumpled from where he'd had his post-lunchtime nap. Their housekeeper, Jacqueline, ensured that more often than not, lunches were the sort that needed to be slept off. She lived locally in Antibes and brought all their meals to the villa every morning on huge earthenware platters or in brightly painted dishes that were typical of the region, along with fresh baguettes and croissants for breakfast and copious bottles of wine. Life in France was one long, blissful blur of eating, drinking, swimming, fending off cheese and rosé refills, and playing with the children. This year, however, as far as Jennifer was concerned, there was nothing blissful about it. She was in her own private hell, missing Joe while feeling stressed and confused about the decision she needed to make.

After his nap, Tim had showered and changed into olive-green linen trousers, a white shirt, and Hermès dark brown suede loafers with no socks. His helicopter was due to meet him at the helipad, but he seemed reluctant to go, preferring instead to watch his wife pack while seemingly trying to get to the bottom of what her last-minute trip to the UK was really all about.

Jennifer wished with every fiber of her being that he'd just leave so she could have some space, stop being questioned, and concentrate on what she wanted to take. She was excited by the prospect of her escape and nervous that something would happen to prevent her from going. She also felt guilty as hell and was aware that no matter what, it was vital she appeared nonchalant and normal. She was being scrutinized. She could sense it. It was all so exhausting.

The large terra-cotta floor tiles were cool under her bare feet. She was wearing a bikini with a flimsy Melissa Odabash caftan over the top yet still felt hot and flustered. It was ninety-seven degrees outside, and although they had a very sophisticated air-conditioning system installed throughout the villa, in the daytime, she preferred the windows open. Their house was situated high up in the mountains of Antibes, in between Nice and Cannes, and the view of the twinkling Mediterranean was phenomenal. She also liked the windows open so that she could hear her children's squeals from the infinity pool down below, where they played for hours every day under the supervision of Annie and Deck and a lifeguard. The grounds were so vast, there was enough distance to render their boisterous screams of excitement and all the splashing into a soothing sound.

"Do I look all right?" asked Tim, who seemed to have grown tired of waiting for his wife to give him a straight answer.

"Yes," she replied, not giving him so much as a glance to at least pretend she was interested. If she had, she would have thought he looked smart, older than his years, and conspicuously wealthy. Joe would never wear such a stuffy outfit.

Joe.

Would there ever be a minute, a whole sixty seconds, when he didn't pop into her brain? He consumed her thoughts. She was so in love and, for the first time in her life, finally understood why people spoke of being "crazily" or "madly" in love, for what she was experiencing felt like madness.

Distracted, what Jennifer didn't pick up on was that had she given Tim just a second or two of attention, it might have appeased him greatly and made her getaway far easier.

Tim's eyes narrowed, seeming to recognize that her mind was elsewhere. She hoped he wouldn't consider canceling his trip to Monaco, which he'd announced a fortnight ago he wanted to look into making their primary residence.

"When's your flight again?" he asked.

"First thing in the morning. Early."

"So what are you doing this evening?"

"This evening?" she repeated, going to the closet to find socks, which were almost an alien concept when you'd been barefoot for weeks.

"Yes, this evening. What are you doing? Are you eating here? Do you have dinner plans with anyone?"

"No," she said, irritated. "Of course not. I'm just going to be here. I want to spend time with the children before I leave. And besides, I've had enough dinners out recently to last me a lifetime."

"Right," Tim said. "I didn't realize it had all been such a chore for you."

Jennifer rolled her eyes.

"It's just I thought you might have arranged to see Gail and James or something."

"God no! Why would I want to do that?" she replied, a little too vehemently. Gail and James were two of their oldest friends, but on this trip, Jennifer had had her fill of Gail, who had become increasingly materialistic and superficial as the years had rolled by. These days, Gail wouldn't contemplate eating at a restaurant unless she thought it was one worth being seen in, which made the vacation not feel like a vacation at all. Gail had also really over-done it on the fillers and cosmetic-surgery front, so she constantly looked like she was trapped in a wind tunnel.

"What about you? Are you going out this evening?" she asked, realizing too late how sharp her tone had been and changing the subject to avoid a fight, which would only delay his departure further.

"Not sure," Tim answered. "Pierre's having something on his boat tonight, so I may go to that. It depends on these viewings and how long they go on for."

"You don't really want to live there, do you?" Jennifer asked wearily.

"I wouldn't be looking if I didn't want to," said Tim, sounding irritated. "Why would I waste my time?"

"Well, it would have been nice to have had a discussion about it," she replied, wondering idly which jeans suited her best from the pile she'd selected.

"Well, when *you're* earning billions of pounds and the government wants to fleece you for half of it, despite that you've done more for their economy than the rest of the population put together plus contributed to endless charities, then you can have your say, can't you?"

Jennifer clenched her fists so tightly, her nails made indentations on her palms.

She stayed silent, although if Tim had bothered to ask whether she wanted to uproot the children to live in Monaco, she would have told him she had no desire to live there whatsoever. She would also have added that she found the whole idea repugnant. They had so much wealth, they could easily give away far more than 50 percent and still never have to work another day in their lives.

"Anyway, Monaco aside, which we can discuss when you're back, I have to say, I still don't get why you're going to Karen. Or why you're avoiding giving me an answer. I mean, if she's prepared to take days off work just to hang out with you, then surely she'd rather do that here in the sunshine than there in the pissing rain?"

Jennifer glanced at the clock on her dressing table. His helicopter was due at four. It was five to. She was so tense, she would have done anything to make those five minutes pass more quickly. Only once Tim had gone would she relax, and then their paths wouldn't need to cross again until she returned from her trip.

She sighed heavily, hoping that would be enough to shut him up. Apart from anything else, she wasn't getting very far with her packing. This was another perfect example of where less would be more. She had such a stupid amount of clothes to choose from that trying to condense what she'd laid out on the bed was more stress than if she only owned a few pairs of jeans in the first place. Next month, she was going to have a huge clear-out and give loads away to charity.

Right, she needed to stop wasting time. Joe wouldn't care what she was wearing, as long as her underwear was nice, of course, and she should be ruthless, because ideally she'd take hand luggage, a luxury she could never enjoy when traveling with four children plus staff.

She glanced up. Tim was still staring at her and not in a sentimental way. He was watching her like a hawk. The clock said two minutes to and they could both very clearly hear the chopper arriving. She felt horribly uneasy.

"So Karen calls and you just go running. Again, it just seems a bit odd to me that she would expect you to leave your children in the middle of your family vacation to go listen to her problems."

"Oh, for goodness' sake." Jennifer huffed, finally realizing she needed to say something. She continued to avoid his eyes by going to search for some ankle boots in the walk-in closet. "I've told you thousands of times now. She's got a lot of stuff going on in her personal life and she's asked me to come and see her so we can talk it through and spend a bit of time with each other. That's it. She wants me to go there, and I don't want to insist that she comes here. Why should she?"

"Because it's a damn sight nicer here than it is in shitty Wandsworth," he said, gesturing outside to the stunning panoramic view that lay before them.

"Look," said Jennifer, feeling unbelievably claustrophobic despite the never-ending vista. "I'm not saying it again. *Me* leaving the children is easy. They're happy here and have endless people to look after them. You're not even going to be around for the next week, so it's not like we'd be spending any time together, whereas Karen simply hasn't got the funds to uproot herself and Suzy to fly over here because I've told her to. So I'm going to her and that's final."

"But I could pay for—"

"I know you could pay," said Jennifer, her anger growing. God, if she really had been going to see her friend, he was being very awkward about it. Pretty hypocritical given that he'd been known on occasion to casually announce in the morning that he was off to another continent for a few days, having failed to remember to tell his assistant to tell her. "But I don't *want* you to pay for her, and Karen doesn't want you to either. So that's that. Come on, Tim. How often do I ever go away and do anything for myself? Once a year with my friends and that's it. Other than that, I'm at your beck and call or with the kids, but I really want to do this. I want to be there for Karen when she needs me, and it might help build a few bridges at the same time. You know how she thinks I'm too busy for my old friends these days."

"So what exactly is going on with her anyway?" asked Tim, who *still* didn't look totally convinced. He was irritatingly sharp.

"Her marriage," said Jennifer a tad too quickly.

Tim pondered this for a while before saying, "Well, that doesn't surprise me, I suppose. If I were Pete, I'd have left her years ago."

"Ha bloody ha," retorted Jennifer. "Now, does that mean you're going to stop nagging me and let me go with your blessing? Because apart from anything else, the helicopter's here."

"Fine," said Tim.

Jennifer breathed a sigh of relief. But the feeling that she'd gotten away with it may have been hasty, because just as she was about to head for the en suite bathroom to sort out her toiletries, Tim came up behind her and grabbed her arm. As she spun around to face him, his expression made her gulp. It was flinty and cold, his smile had faded away, and his eyes had a warning in them as he said, "But if I ever find out you've lied to me, I'll kill you."

Jennifer felt petrified, so she regarded him for a while as she tried to work out the best way to respond. Eventually she decided to go on the offensive. How dare he threaten her like that? She hated him. The sooner she got away, the better.

"And if you ever speak to me like that again, I'll divorce you," she replied icily, at which point Tim looked thoroughly thrown.

"I was only joking," he said lamely.

"Well, don't. Because it's not funny, and what you've said is a pretty disgusting thing to say to your wife," she said, blinking away angry tears. She shoved Tim away. He was blocking her path, and she didn't want to be near him a second longer.

"Well, I apologize then," he said flatly, unsmiling. "And I'll leave you to pack now. My chopper's here, so I might as well say good-bye."

"I'll see you in eight days," Jennifer said grimly.

"You will. Oh, and, Jennifer?"

"Yes."

"Make sure you don't forget to pack these. They're vital for a trip to see Karen, I'm sure."

With her heart in her mouth, Jennifer turned around slowly to see Tim clutching a very sexy, very flimsy pair of underwear. She felt sick.

"Oh," she said lightly, snatching them away from him and stuffing them back into a drawer. "I won't be needing those, that's for sure."

"Right," he said, his face impossible to read. "I'll be off then. I'll just go say good-bye to the children."

"Bye. Have a great week in Monaco."

"Thanks," he said and left without so much as pecking her on the cheek.

TUNNEL NUMBER TWO
What Could Have Been—Tim

Joe had been dozing on and off for an hour, his face a picture of pure contentment, his huge body heavy with sleep. All Jennifer had done during this time was stare at him, for his was a face she could quite happily gaze at for hours on end. In fact, she reckoned she could do it for at least a month without getting bored.

She'd felt the same way when each of her newborns had first arrived in the world. She'd spent hours examining their faces, drinking them in, marveling at their very presence and at how miraculous it felt to have them in her life. But she'd never felt anything remotely similar for an adult before. For someone who had facial hair and size twelve feet. And yet the comparisons between her feelings for Joe and the unconditional love she felt as a parent didn't end there. During one of her long, angst-filled telephone discussions with Karen (which she'd come to rely on increasingly as she tried to work out how to untangle the extraordinary mess her life was in), she'd told her friend that Joe was the only person alive, other than her kids, whom she could say with any certainty she'd take a bullet for. Not needlessly, of course. She wouldn't do it just to prove a point or anything. That would be ridiculous. Yet, if it was a case of saving either herself or him, she'd sacrifice herself every time, just as she would with each of her offspring. However, if the choice were between saving herself or Tim, she'd scamper out of the line of fire quicker than you could say "Sorry, love!"

Karen had laughed heartily at this (perhaps with slightly too much relish) before adding, "If you think about it, it would probably be worth shoving Tim in front of a bullet. You'd get the life insurance, for starters. Plus that way, everyone would feel sorry for you for being widowed, so when you 'suddenly' took up with Joe, they'd all be happy for you. Perfect."

At that point, Jennifer had checked herself. Reaching the point where you started fantasizing about the untimely death of your husband wasn't healthy, even if her best friend had clearly been doing it for years.

Joe's eyes slowly opened. When he realized she was watching him, a leisurely grin sprawled across his face. "Hello, you. Have I been asleep?"

"Yeah," Jennifer said, laughing.

"What you laughing at?" he asked, still half asleep.

"You've been out for an hour."

"An hour? Have I?" he asked, yawning and stretching out his huge arms before pulling her in for a hug. Jennifer had noticed that his Yorkshire accent had become more pronounced as soon as he'd arrived back in his home county. "And what have you been up to while I've been resting my eyeballs?"

"Staring at you," she admitted, totally unashamed. They were both far too smitten with each other to bother trying to be cool.

"Stalker," Joe said.

"Creepy," Jennifer agreed, nuzzling herself right into him.

"Ah, this is such heaven," he said, his eyes still squinting while he continued to wake up. "You realize we've done nothing for forty-eight hours now," he added, one hand squeezing her bum appreciatively. "God, I love this bottom, you know."

"I wouldn't say we've done nothing," said Jennifer, thoroughly enjoying the sensation of having her bum stroked and stretching out one smooth, brown leg from beneath the sheets in order to wrap it around one of his large, hairy ones.

"We've hardly left this room since we got here," laughed Joe.

"Yes, we have. You even made a roast yesterday. And we went to the pub."

"For about half an hour," he said, turning around in the bed but pulling her arms around with him so that she was hugging him from behind. Jennifer loved the way Joe was in bed. Not just when they were having sex (they'd both agreed that the phrase *making love* was repellent—just one of the hundreds of silly yet important things they were in total agreement on), but when they weren't too. He was unbelievably affectionate, and last night she'd woken up briefly a couple of times to find that they were completely entwined with each other.

She nestled into his broad back, inhaling his smell and feeling more secure and happy than she had for ages. For them, the prospect of being able to spend one entire night together was stupidly exciting, so the fact that they were spending seven whole nights in a row together was almost too much to comprehend. It was ridiculous, but two days in and they'd already discussed how depressed they were about their little slice of heaven coming to an end.

"Are you complaining? Do you wish we were sightseeing?"

"No," he said. "Just being with you is bloody bliss. I don't need anything else. Not even a TV."

"Wow, now that is love. A proper declaration if ever I heard one."

"It is. Now could you give my back a scratch, please, my little angel? I've got an itch."

Happy to oblige, Jennifer removed one hand from his and scratched his back.

"Ooh, that's better. Thank you."

"Pleasure. Now how about anywhere else? Have you got an itch around the front?" she teased, sliding her hand around him, reaching for his cock, which was already at half-mast. "Ooh, that's a surprise."

"You can't blame me. I'm lying next to you," he said, turning around again so their faces were only centimeters apart.

"I love you," she said for the five hundredth time that day.

"I love you too," he replied sincerely, his eyes searching her face. "So, so much. Never leave me, will you?"

She shook her head, her eyes filling with tears.

He stroked her cheek. "Hey, little squidger. Don't cry. It'll all be okay."

She nodded but the tears kept on coming. She was so stressed all the time. No matter how hard she tried to keep it at bay, her anxiety about their situation was never far from the surface.

"You only get one life, you know," he said, and his eyes were so sad and full of concern that she'd probably never loved him more than she had at that precise second.

"Do you want to go for a walk?" She sniffed, wiping her face with the back of her hand. She didn't want these precious few days together to be marred by her constant angst. She wanted to relish every second they had together and enjoy the present. "The sun's out."

He shook his head and grinned. "I want to kiss you."

A lazy, passion-filled, self-indulgent hour or so later, Joe emerged from the bathroom, still wet from the shower. "Come on," he said, drying himself vigorously. Although Jennifer was completely sated, she experienced a fresh lurch of potent desire just looking at him. "Let's get out and get some fresh air so at least we can say we've done something today. Time to leave our pit of passion."

Jennifer loved every minute of their walk through the Yorkshire dales. The countryside was gorgeous, rugged and hilly, strewn with purple heather, and patchworked with green velvety fields. It was a lovely warm day, but not boiling hot like it had been in France. There was a strong wind, and the clouds scudded across the sky as if in a race.

"It's so beautiful here," she exclaimed as they came to the crest of a hill. She was completely breathless, as was Joe, who flung himself down onto the grass.

"Come and share this view with me."

She reached out and let him pull her toward him until she was sitting between his legs, his arms wrapped tightly around her. Joe was a large man, six foot five with the stature to match. She loved this about him. It made her feel small, feminine, protected.

"I'm so happy to be here with you," said Joe, nuzzling her neck with his nose. "I've dreamed of this, and here we are."

They both stared at the majestic countryside that was spread out before them. It was seven thirty, the sun was starting to sink in the sky, and the light was incredible. Jennifer wondered why anyone in their right mind would want to inhabit a city. "Do you hate living in town sometimes?" she asked, a little terrified of what his reply would be.

"Er...I'm definitely a country boy at heart," he said eventually. "Always will be, but there are things about living in London I appreciate. It's a very beautiful city and full of so many different cultures. I've learned a lot. Having said that, I do prefer the pace out here, and I crave this feeling of space at times. I'd be more than happy to move back out again, even if it meant working in a nice pub that served really excellent food. Nice hearty stuff that was done properly."

Jennifer digested this. Could she picture herself living in the country? She couldn't see Tim letting her take the children out of the schools they were in.

"But listen, what have we always said the meaning of life is?"

Jennifer smiled, her fears dissipating already.

"Sofa," she whispered.

"Sofa," he repeated. "Home is where your heart is and with the person you want to be sitting next to on the sofa, and for me, Jen, that is you. So if that means I have to live out my days in the most overpriced part of London, surrounded by snobby assholes, where I can't afford to buy a beer, let alone an apartment, then that is what I'll do so that your kids can keep going to those disgusting schools where they're forced to wear boaters and speak Latin for no sane reason."

His tone was far less harsh than the words he was saying. Jennifer loved it when he told her how it was.

"Sofa," she repeated, laughing, her heart contracting with its usual mix of love, fear, and dread of what she was facing.

"Now, let's take a picture on my phone of you and me with our view behind us."

They both wriggled around and Jennifer snuggled in as Joe extended his arm around them both so that the lens of his phone was pointing toward them. She smiled into the camera, desperate to milk every second of the time she had with him. Would there ever be a time when they could just be together without constantly pondering the situation they were in?

"Look at that little face," said Joe, his deep Yorkshire voice laden with affection as he regarded the snap he'd just taken. "You are a beauty, Jennifer. Look at those eyes."

"Don't be silly," she said. She thought she looked terrible in the photo, what with hardly any makeup on and her hair a mess.

"You've got no idea, have you? Hey, what's up with you now? Why are you looking sad all of a sudden? Do we need to have a chat?"

Jennifer blinked, loving him for being so intuitive but hating herself for being so miserable.

"Well, if you could bear it," she said finally.

"Come on then, sulky," said Joe amiably. "Let's be having it, squidger. What's on that mind of yours now?"

"It's just… I just…"

"What?"

Jennifer struggled to find the words to convey what had been gnawing at her. "I know it's difficult because we've not had the chance to experience being with each other under normal circumstances but…but, what I'm trying to say is, if I leave him, then we *have* to work out, Joe. I need us to make it. I don't think I could bear to have two failed relationships behind me, and I don't want to go through all the pain and upheaval and nastiness of a divorce only to find that when I'm out the other side, you've…changed your mind."

She looked tentatively at Joe to gauge his reaction and was dismayed to see that she'd done exactly what she'd worried she might do by displaying a lack of faith. She'd pissed him off.

"Don't be cross. I'm only being honest. You know all I want is to be with you but…well, the whole thing is just so…it's so bloody big. I'd be lying if I said it didn't scare me, and I suppose I need to be reassured that you really feel the same way as me and that this isn't just about the chase of someone who's not available."

Joe looked deeply offended.

"Not that I think you'd ever do that consciously," she rattled on, knowing that whatever she said was only going to make matters worse. "But Karen did ask me once if perhaps the depth of feeling we have for each other might be heightened by the situation we're in, and perhaps it is?"

Joe lay back on the earthy ground and stared at the sky.

"Talk to me," urged Jennifer.

"I don't know what you want me to say," he mumbled, unable to look at her. Her stomach flipped as she realized how upset he was.

"Well, just say what's in your head."

Joe's whole face had darkened, and when he still didn't say anything, her heart sank. She could also feel herself getting irritated. Shutting down like this was a waste of time. She knew she was being needy and no doubt annoying, but she couldn't help what she felt, so what was the point of punishing her? She was on the brink of leaving her husband. It didn't get much bigger than that, and she didn't mind admitting she was beyond terrified. Why couldn't he just humor her and give her the reassurance she so obviously needed?

"Please, Joe, just talk to me."

"I've got nothing to say."

At a loss about what to do, she lay next to him for a while in silence, wishing she'd kept quiet and ignored her own pathetic insecurity. She prayed this wasn't going to ruin an entire night or more. What a waste that would be.

However, to her surprise, as they lay side by side, she felt a hand reach for hers, at which point her stomach flipped back to normal, for she knew this was Joe's way of telling her it was all right.

"I'm sorry," she said, tears racing down her face. She really did have to address how much she was crying all the time.

He pulled her toward him so she was lying on his chest.

"You're such an idiot," he said quietly, his voice full of nothing but despair and love.

"I know," she blubbered.

Joe turned to face her, and for a while they just stared at each other, saying nothing. Then he held her face in his strong, warm hands and said, "After some of the things you've said, I don't think there's anyone else on the planet I would do this for, but as it's you, I'm going to say it. Again. And then I'll say it again after that if I have to. I love you, Jennifer. I love you more than any other human being in this world. I want to be with you. And that's that. And I'm not Tim, so please don't act as if I'd ever be as complacent or thoughtless as him, because it makes me feel like a pile of shit."

"I'm sorry," she said truthfully.

"And accusing me of only being interested in the chase is about one of the most insulting things you've ever said to me. I hate that you're married. I hate that in order to be with me, you have to break up your family. In fact, the only thing that enables me to cope with it is that I can see how unhappy he makes you. You once said to me that the two issues were almost separate and that you'd probably have left him anyway. So why make me feel dreadful by implying that you wouldn't?"

Jennifer felt wretched. How could she explain that, if it wasn't for Joe, there was probably no way she'd leave, despite the awful state of the marriage? She simply wouldn't have the guts. Staying put would be easier.

"I'm sorry," she repeated.

Joe shook his head despairingly. "Look, I know you'll be sacrificing a lot if you leave Tim, but are they really the things that matter? I can't offer you five-star luxury and a designer wardrobe, but you wouldn't be the woman I love if that was all you were interested in. I will always look after you, and I am here to support you as much as I can in every way. I will take on those kiddies as my own and am prepared to sacrifice having ones of my own if it means being with you. But I am not going to sit here and beg you to leave. That has to be your decision. And if ultimately it comes to that and you tell me you don't want to or that you can't, then I will understand. And I won't hate you. I will still love you, but I will let you get on with your life. I'll move back here and spend the rest of my days trying and failing to forget about you. But I will say this, and it's not a threat, Jen, but I can't do this forever."

"Do what forever?" she asked, her heart pounding with fear. What was he saying?

"Be in this state of limbo," he replied simply. "Because it's not easy not knowing if you're going to lose your world from one day to the next. I know it's hard for you and I don't want to rush you, but at the same time, I'm not sure how much more I can take."

Jennifer gulped and nodded. She had to make a decision soon. For all their sakes.

A couple of hours later, they were back at the cottage. Joe had opened a bottle of red wine that they were getting through nicely, and he'd also cooked a delicious risotto with mushrooms and chicken and tons of Parmesan cheese. Ensconced together, away from the rest of the world, they couldn't have been any happier.

They ate in front of the TV so that they could keep half an eye on an episode of *Don't Tell the Bride*. It was a particularly funny one because the groom was getting everything slightly wrong. By the time they'd gotten to the bit where the bride was about to discover which dress had been chosen for her, which they both suspected she'd hate, Jennifer and Joe had tears of mirth rolling down their faces. The two of them had been making a stream of sarcastic running commentary throughout the show, and at this point, snorting with laughter, Jennifer managed to say, "Hey, if we were on this show, what kind of dress would you pick for me?"

Joe gave her a very strange sidelong glance, gathering the last bits of risotto onto his fork. "What do you mean?"

"What kind of dress would you go for?"

"I'm not marrying you," he said, not unkindly but firmly, certainly as though he'd given the matter some thought. It wasn't the lighthearted response she'd been expecting.

Jennifer's face fell. She felt quite thrown. She'd only been joking. She wasn't proposing or anything. She was married, for Christ's sake, so getting married again was hardly something she was thinking about at this stage.

"Okay," she said, trying not to look offended. She was surprised by how disappointed she felt that he didn't want to marry her.

Joe regarded her for a while, clearly weighing up whether to say anything else to go along with his very bald statement.

"It's just that you've done it all before," he explained. "With him, so I don't see the point."

Jennifer could be pretty astute when she wanted to be. Sitting on the sofa, feet curled under her, she nodded but dropped the subject. Instead, she turned her attention back to the TV. Then, a little later, once what he'd said had melted away into the atmosphere a bit, she got up and went to give him a cuddle that he was more than happy to receive. Inevitably the cuddle turned into kissing, which turned into groping and eventually resulted in full-blown passionate sex on the floor.

All the while they were having sex, touching each other with a real urgency, kissing, rubbing, licking, and sucking each other into an emotion-fueled frenzy, it was as if Jennifer had had an epiphany. When Joe had told her he wouldn't marry her, strangely it had been the most revealing sign of how much he truly loved her. She would never forget how sad his face had looked and, although on paper his words didn't seem romantic, knowing him as she did, she had found it to be the most meaningful and heartbreakingly beautiful gesture ever. What it demonstrated was that he had thought about having her as his wife despite that she was still married to someone else. He'd thought about it at length and it clearly pained him that she'd done it before with someone who wasn't him. Of course, he didn't know that first time around had been more of a stressful experience than anything else. The wedding had been so huge, it had totally swamped the reasons behind doing it. She'd not really enjoyed it, had felt pressured throughout, and had had tiny doubts even as she'd walked down the aisle, which she'd valiantly dismissed as jitters.

But he didn't know that, and who could tell what ran through that head of his when he thought about these things? It must have been incredibly difficult, and she didn't give him enough credit.

Joe loved her.

He really, truly loved her, and it was that moment that marked a change for Jennifer, because whereas he might not be sure about whether he wanted to marry her, she was. She should be antimarriage altogether. She'd broken her vows. She'd failed at the whole thing miserably, but then again, was it any surprise? Ultimately, she'd married the wrong person, and yet here was the right person, inside her now, loving her to within an inch of her life, and there was no way she was going to lose him. So that was that. Her decision had finally been made.

"What?" He panted, breathless after an enormous orgasm. He rolled off her and lay flat on his back. "Why are you grinning?"

"No reason," she said. "I just love you. And I've made my decision. I know what I've got to do."

TUNNEL NUMBER TWO
What Could Have Been—Tim

The day Jennifer chose as the one she would finally tell her husband she was leaving him began pleasantly enough.

Tim had originally been due back from Monaco the day before but had called to say he'd been delayed. On the one hand, Jennifer was delighted to have another day's grace from seeing him. On the other, she could hardly bear the suspense. Still, she'd decided to make the most of her rare time alone with the kids. Aware of how hard the nannies had been working lately, what with her having been away, she'd instructed them to take the day off. It was so rare that she was in sole charge of her own children, it was practically a novelty, and at lunchtime, she'd thoroughly enjoyed the simple tasks of fetching the food out of the fridge, cutting up the younger one's food, pouring their drinks, and setting the table. Thanks to one of her many discussions with Joe, she insisted that the children help her with all of this. Joe had pointed out in Yorkshire that if they didn't start helping out with normal domestic tasks, they'd leave home pampered to the point where they wouldn't be equipped to look after themselves. Jennifer totally agreed.

Unused to seeing their mother whirling around the kitchen, enthused and for once not looking distracted and worried, the children were responding eagerly and enthusiastically. For the umpteenth time, Jennifer resolved to be a better parent and to ensure that, from this point on, she took more control of their upbringing. It wasn't too late for them to benefit from more of her influence and less of Tim's. It wasn't too late for her to be the woman she knew she could be.

At one point, Tilly started singing a One Direction song, so although they were still eating, Jennifer went to get her Mac so they could all listen to it and have a bit of a dance, something their father would never approve of and that therefore would never happen when the nannies were on duty. As a result, Jennifer and the children were all so busy singing at the top of their lungs that none of them heard the distant sound of the helicopter landing on the grounds.

So they had no idea that Tim had arrived back at the house, meaning that when he entered the kitchen, he found them all dancing around screaming, *"You don't know you're beautiful,"* while using various kitchen implements as microphones.

It was only when Hattie yelled "Daddy!" that Jennifer realized he was there, at which point she immediately switched off the music.

"What on earth are you all doing?" Tim asked, and his look chilled her to the very bone. The happy atmosphere in the kitchen vanished instantly.

Tim looked disproportionately pissed off, and Jennifer's heart lurched with dread. Did he know? He looked so angry.

"Oh, come on, we were only playing around," said Jennifer,

motioning to the children to sit down at the table, which they did with no fuss. They never challenged Tim, although recently she got the distinct feeling that Edward, their eldest, wanted to and probably would in the not-too-distant future. At that moment, still out of breath, he was watching his father from beneath his bangs. His expression broke Jennifer's heart.

"Hmm, well, I suggest you sit down when you eat in the future or you'll get indigestion. Where are Annie and Deck?"

"Gone into town. They needed some time off." Jennifer's tone was defiant.

Tim didn't say anything for so long that Jennifer felt like she needed to fill the gap.

"How was your trip?"

"Enlightening" was all he would say, and again her heart somersaulted with what could only be described as terror. The vibe she was getting from him was not good at all.

But then he turned everything on its head once again, making Jennifer wonder if perhaps she was just paranoid.

"I got you a present," he said, reaching into his pocket and pulling out a small jewelry box.

"You shouldn't have done that," Jen replied. She noticed that Jasper was looking a bit anxious, obviously having picked up on the tension in the room. She went to ruffle his hair reassuringly.

Meanwhile, Tilly was staring down at her bread and cheese and almost seemed to have turned to stone, a stark contrast to the happy little girl who had been bounding about only minutes before, acting her age in the most carefree way. Only Hattie seemed completely oblivious to the strained atmosphere. But then, that was Hattie. She was the most robust out of all of them. Jennifer's heart ached with love and guilt on behalf of her children. Living like this wasn't good for any of them.

"I probably shouldn't have," said Tim, a crooked smile on his face. "But I have, so open it."

Jennifer was left with no choice other than to cross the kitchen and take the box from his hand.

"Open it," he insisted again when she hesitated.

Finally she opened the box to find an exquisite pair of emerald-and-diamond earrings nestled on navy silk. They probably cost thousands. They also would have required precisely no thought on Tim's part. She didn't want them.

"Thank you," she said robotically. "They're beautiful."

"Good. Right, I'm off to take a shower. Feel free to pick up where you all left off, if you really want. I don't want to be a spoilsport. Besides, if you insist on leaping around like chimps, it's probably best you do it when we don't have any houseguests."

"Can we put it on again, please, Mummy?" begged Hattie instantly.

"Um, I don't think so," muttered Jennifer, and all four children instantly knew that the window during which their mother had been liberated enough to have some fun had shut. They didn't bother protesting and picked at their lunches until they were allowed to get back to the pool.

For the rest of the day, Jennifer felt like she was treading on eggshells and avoided Tim as much as possible. She spent much of it on a lounge chair under an umbrella, her youngest boy, Jasper, cuddled into her, wrapped in a towel because he'd developed an earache so needed some serious TLC. As she stroked his hair and watched the others splashing about in the pool, she'd felt overwhelmed with conviction that bringing Joe into their lives would be a positive thing for her children too. Of course it would. He would be an amazing stepfather. After all, she'd seen him interact with them on countless occasions, and while it would obviously take some time for them to adapt to the fact that their parents had separated and that their old chef was now her partner, they'd get there eventually.

She was so desperate to speak to Joe, but it was ages before she got an opportunity to call him. Finally, once the kids had come in from swimming and had showered and been fed, and the nannies were back on duty, she managed to sneak away. Checking first that Tim was safely ensconced in his study, she went upstairs, figuring that the safest place to call from was her walk-in closet. When his phone went straight to voice mail, it was a terrible anticlimax, and she tried three more times before eventually admitting defeat and leaving a brief but urgent message for him to call her.

She put the phone back in her pocket, willing it to vibrate, and sighed. She hadn't spoken to Joe since first thing that morning. It felt like years. Probably due to a certain amount of nerves on both parts, their conversation had ended rather tense, which only made the fact that she couldn't get ahold of him now all the more frustrating. At the same time, she knew it was unfair to expect him to hold her hand through this. To say it wasn't the easiest of times for either of them was an understatement.

In Yorkshire, when she'd informed Joe of her decision to leave Tim, she'd expected him to be jubilant and ecstatic that she'd finally made up her mind.

However, while he was clearly pleased, he'd also been disheart-eningly cautious. "You can still change your mind, you know," he'd said at one point.

"But I don't want to," she'd retorted indignantly. "I'm telling you I've decided, and I know it's taken me a while to get here, but I know myself and now that's it. I thought you'd be pleased. I thought it was what you wanted."

"Oh, it is," Joe said sincerely. "It's everything I've ever wanted, but I'm worried for you. I know what this means and the shit you're going to have to go through now. It might be what I want, but it doesn't feel like cause for celebration. I'll reserve that for when everything's sorted out and we can be happy and start the rest of our lives together."

A few hours later, once all the children were fast asleep, Jennifer regarded herself in the floor-to-ceiling mirrors that covered an entire wall of her dressing room. She looked fine. In fact, she looked good. She was tanned and had gained a few pounds during her time in Yorkshire with Joe, which probably wasn't a bad thing. She had lost a lot of weight due to stress and had been starting to look too thin. But now she just looked slim, enviably as opposed to worryingly. She smoothed down her Marc Jacobs sundress and applied a quick slick of lip gloss before promptly wiping it off again. What was she doing? What precisely did she need to look good for, anyway? She supposed it was her version of putting on armor.

Right.

She was ready, or at least as ready as she was ever going to be. She was also ridiculously scared and nervous, and there were a million things she'd prefer to be doing at that precise moment. Like eating cat food, wrenching off her fingernails with a rusty screw, or running a marathon in nothing but a pair of clown shoes, in the rain. Only none of these things were on the agenda. Telling her husband she was leaving him was.

Since that pivotal moment in Yorkshire, Jennifer had known what she had to do. Her feelings for Joe had become an unstoppable force. She simply had to be with him, and no matter how sad it made everybody short term, she fully believed they would all be better off in the long run.

Jennifer took a deep breath, left the sanctuary that was her dressing room, and went downstairs to find Tim, who was outside on the terrace, looking at some papers.

"You okay?" Jennifer asked, taking a seat opposite Tim. The moonlight was bouncing off the pool. Everything looked so beautiful. *Will I miss it?* she wondered.

"What do you want?" Tim asked, looking up briefly.

The look in his eyes made her recoil.

"Um, I wondered if we could talk."

Tim picked up the crystal tumbler next to him and took a slow, deliberate sip of his gin and tonic. "Go for it."

"Right, well, I don't think I need to tell you that we haven't been getting along well lately."

"No, you're right. You don't. You're not even wearing the earrings I bought you, which is pretty ungrateful."

Jennifer immediately felt on the back foot. She'd always known Tim was her superior intellectually. He could spar verbally with the best of them and would always have an answer, a riposte, or a quick-witted put-down. But today she wasn't looking for a discussion. She was telling him something, and that was what she had to keep reminding herself.

"Look, Tim, I know you don't want to hear this, but I have to say it anyway."

He continued to read his papers, which seemed so rude. In a way, it helped.

Jennifer cleared her throat and ran her palms down her dress again. She was sweating. "I think it might be time we went our separate ways, Tim. I've not been happy for a long time now, and I doubt you are either. So while we're still both young enough to rebuild our lives, I think we should call it a day and try to do so as amicably as possible for the sake of the children."

Tim swirled the ice around in his glass, making a chinking sound. For a second, Jennifer wondered if he'd heard what she'd said. She felt a sudden wave of nausea and an intense flash of frustration that Joe hadn't been on the other end of the phone earlier. She needed him so much. Where was he?

She opened her mouth to reiterate, but Tim cut her off.

"So you have the audacity to sit there and calmly tell me that you've decided we should 'call it a day.' As if ending our marriage is as important an issue as changing your mind about what dress to wear or what color paint you're going to decorate a room with."

"No, of course not," Jennifer began. "It's not like that at all. In fact, for what it's worth, it's taken months of turmoil for me to arrive at this conclusion. There is absolutely nothing about this decision that has been light or easy, and I am so bloody sorry, Tim."

"So how many months exactly have you been thinking about this then?"

Jennifer gulped, steeling herself for the onslaught she knew was around the corner, mind whirring as she tried to second-guess why he was asking. "Look, you can't pretend you haven't noticed," she said, trying to avoid answering. "We've barely been speaking for months. We've been in separate bedrooms the vast majority of the time for years now, and I can't remember when we last had sex. This isn't a marriage, Tim, and I know I'm the one saying it out loud, but come on. You've never got anything good to say about me. You're always putting me down and acting as if I irritate you, so, honestly, I'm surprised you're not pleased."

"'Pleased,'" Tim repeated. "Mmm, interesting choice of vocabulary there. You're surprised I'm not pleased that you've taken it upon yourself to be such a selfish bitch that you would actually consider breaking up this family, destroying the children's lives and everything I've been working hard to build for the last God knows how many years with zero consultation or regard for my reputation."

Jennifer blinked. Was that all he cared about? She was amazed she'd lasted as long as she had in this sham of a relationship.

"But that's just it," she said. "Your reputation has nothing to do with our marriage. A marriage is a relationship between two people. Everything else just surrounds it. But our connection has died, Tim. You don't love me. You don't even like me."

"Ah, finally you're speaking some sense, because you're right there," he said coolly, putting down his papers and drink and leaning in to fix her with a stare that turned her stomach. "I loathe you, and do you know why?"

She shook her head, sure he was going to fill her in anyway.

"I loathe you because without me, you'd be absolutely nothing. I have carried you since university, and you know it. You're a spineless, directionless, useless individual, but for some reason, I took pity on you and have let you ride on my coattails for all these years."

"I've given you four beautiful children," Jennifer said quietly, her eyes pricked with tears. What he was saying was so hurtful. So cruel. So disgusting.

"Yes, you've *had* four children. Well done, you, for being fertile. You haven't given me anything. You're not even a good mother."

"That's not fair," she said. He may as well have slapped her. It would have hurt less.

"Maybe not, but it's true. You do the bare minimum."

"Only because you've always controlled me so much that that's all I've been allowed to do. My only crime is that I've been weak. I've let you steal all my confidence to the point where I've lost control of my own kids." Even as Jennifer said it, the truth in what she was saying finally caught up with her, and she vowed then and there that she would change, starting by playing a proper part in how her children were going to turn out. She wasn't going to be dictated to any longer.

Tim stood up and paced the terrace.

Jennifer felt incredibly vulnerable. Perhaps this had been a mistake. Perhaps she should have waited till they were back in London.

"You're a lying whore," Tim said icily, almost from nowhere.

"I beg your pardon?" asked Jennifer, who was shaking.

"When were you going to tell me about your revolting little secret, eh? Or were you not going to bother? Because we both know what this is really about, don't we?"

He knows, thought Jennifer. *Of course he does.* How could she ever have thought she could keep anything secret from the omnipotent Tim?

She analyzed how she felt. Numb, really, but underneath, there was also a definite sense of relief. She didn't want to lie anymore. She was sick of living like this. To hell with it.

"I love him," she said calmly.

Tim threw his head back, and only then did Jennifer see for the first time a glimpse of how he wasn't just angry but also hurt. She'd damaged him with what she'd done. Of course she had, and what could she have expected his reaction to be?

No matter how unpleasant he'd been to her, he still had the moral high ground. She was the one who had been unfaithful.

"You stupid, stupid bitch," he said, the cool tone having disappeared altogether. "And how long has it been going on then? Because naively I had hoped you'd only decided to be a disgusting whore a short time ago, only now that you've told me you've been debating whether to leave me for months, I start to wonder. You see, I'm not stupid, Jennifer, so it doesn't take a great deal to figure out that this is all about your selfishness and desire to fuck someone."

Jennifer swallowed, aware that without knowing exactly what he knew, she should be treading extremely carefully.

"It's not. They're two separate issues. That never would have happened if I wasn't deeply unhappy. I'm not justifying anything, but you have to know that wanting to split up with you is because I honestly can't see a way to make our marriage work."

"I had you followed when you went to 'Karen's,'" he said, using his fingers to make quote marks around her friend's name. "A love nest in Yorkshire with my now ex-chef. I've never known anything so pathetic in all my life. But I tell you what; if that's what you think you want, then you're very welcome. Only I'll tell you this for nothing, my dear."

His use of the words *my dear* made her feel faintly sick.

"You've chosen the wrong person to pick a fight with, because I am going to make sure you end up with nothing. And when I say nothing, I mean no money, nowhere to live, no friends, and no children."

"You can't take my children away. You're being ridiculous," said Jennifer, and though her tone was designed to sound throwaway, she couldn't disguise the very real sense of panic that was rising up inside her. He was insane. "I'm their mother. The law would never allow you to take them from me," she added more confidently than she felt.

"We'll see about that," threatened Tim, taking a step toward her, eyes blazing with fury and contempt.

She swallowed. "Well, there's probably not much point in talking further tonight, so why don't we sleep on it and try to have another chat in the morning?"

"There's nothing to discuss," said Tim, stepping back again and picking up the sheaf of papers he'd been looking at. He sat down and returned his attention to them.

She'd been dismissed.

Happy to get away from him, she turned to enter the house, desperate to get ahold of Joe and tell him what had happened. Surely he'd be answering his phone by this point?

"No doubt you're off to phone lover boy to fill him in on the latest."

She stopped in her tracks. "Don't be ridiculous," she shot back, unnerved by his accuracy. Shit, maybe she should wait until tomorrow to contact Joe? Knowing Tim, he might come and listen at the door and there could be the most horrific scene.

"Still, if you really want to speak to him, maybe try him. After all, it's been hours since you spoke to each other, hasn't it?"

How could he possibly know that? Jennifer's eyes widened with fear. Was Tim toying with her, or did he really know something?

She turned. "What are you doing?" she asked, no longer bothering to try to sound nonchalant. She didn't care if he knew she was frightened. She needed to know what was going on.

"Me? Oh, I'm not doing anything. It's our ex-chef who's been very busy. And on that note, I want to make it very clear that he is not to come within a mile of any of my properties ever again. He also won't be working anywhere in London again, which is a shame for you."

"What are you talking about?" Jennifer asked, her entire body trembling as she tried to digest what was happening. She'd lost control of the situation completely. How could she ever have imagined she could take Tim on?

"Well, think about it," he said, tapping his temple. "If he can't work in London, then he can hardly stay in the city where your children will be remaining, which means you'll have some decisions to make. And in case you still don't get it," he said patronizingly, "it means you'll have to choose between your children or an out-of-work, out-of-shape chef. So how are you going to negotiate that one, eh, wifey?"

"Where's Joe?" she asked flatly, heart pounding.

"Oh, don't you worry about him," Tim said with a smirk.

"Tell me what you've done!" screamed Jennifer, who had officially lost it. She hated him with every bit of her being. He was a cruel bastard. "If you've done anything to hurt him, I will call the police."

"Oh, will you, now?" asked Tim mildly. "Interesting that even after all these years, you still insist on thinking I'm stupid. Ironic, really. Jennifer, do you really think I'd get my hands dirty over this?"

Jennifer was in floods of tears. He clearly knew where Joe was and she didn't, and the sense of helplessness was so intense she could hardly remain standing up.

"Please, tell me where he is." She wept.

Tim regarded his sobbing wife with contempt. "Why should I?"

"Because no matter what I've done to you, you can't do this. It's not right and you will damage your reputation if you do something stupid."

"But I've already explained. *I'm* not doing anything. Look at you. You're a sniveling wreck. It's pathetic."

Hearing this, Jennifer forced herself to stop crying. Her tears were only aggravating him further, and for Joe's sake, she had to play this right. The situation was too serious for her to fuck it up by letting her emotions get the better of her.

"Okay, listen," she said, changing gear completely. "I promise that if you tell me what you know, because I can tell there's something going on, then we can work things out and make sure that no one ever knows about any of it. So come on, Tim, tell me."

Her tone was calm and measured and a bit like she was talking to somebody who was standing on the edge of a cliff, about to throw himself off. But it seemed to work. The madness Jennifer had recognized in Tim's eyes seemed to be abating slightly.

"Joe's not far from here."

"What do you mean?"

"He's in France."

"Here? In France?"

"That's what I said."

Jennifer paused. She was confused. What the hell would Joe be doing in France? Could he really be only a few miles away from here?

"Why? Who's he with?"

Tim regarded her coolly before replying. "One of my men."

"What do you mean, 'one of your men,' Tim?" Jennifer demanded. Once again, fear had gotten the better of her and had turned her tone shrill and hysterical.

"I'm not going to talk to you while you're in this state," said Tim, marching brusquely past her.

But there was no way Jennifer was standing for that, not if he really did know anything about where Joe was. Without considering what she was doing, fueled by rage and frustration, she launched at him like a woman possessed. "No, you don't," she screeched, grabbing at the back of his pale pink shirt.

It was an attack Tim hadn't been expecting, and his loafers slipped on the terrace tiles, causing him to stagger sideways before falling to the ground, at which point his wife climbed on him and started pounding his chest with her fist.

"Tell me what you know or I'm calling the police!" she screamed.

"Get off me! You're crazy!" Tim yelled, trying to protect his face from the punches that were raining down on him.

"Where's Joe?" she repeated as Tim finally found the where-withal to fight back. Grabbing her wrists, he heaved her away from him.

"You're insane," he yelled, flinging her to one side with considerable force. "Get off me, you fucking lunatic."

Finally Jennifer's adrenaline started to subside. Panting, she reached over to pick up one of her sandals that had come off and slid it back onto her foot. She also got up from where she was sprawled on the ground and smoothed down her hair.

"Just tell me," she repeated. Her legs felt like jelly.

Tim regarded her for what felt like an age, clearly trying to decide what to tell her. For the first time, Jennifer sensed that he was floundering a bit.

"There's nothing to tell," he admitted finally, his tone weary.

"What?"

"I wanted to spook you, make you feel as dire as I do. I have been having him watched, though, and I wasn't lying about one thing: he caught a plane this afternoon."

"Why?"

"Why what?"

"Are you having him followed?"

"Why do you think?" Tim spat. "Because the minute he started sleeping with my wife, what he was up to became my business.

And besides, at some stage, I may pay the asshole a visit and explain that shagging your boss's wife doesn't exactly bode well when it comes to getting a reference."

"And you haven't done anything else?"

"What do you take me for?"

"Okay then," said Jennifer, whose breathing was returning to normal. "Okay," she repeated, walking away.

"Where are you going?"

Jennifer turned around and was hit by a fresh, overwhelming sense of guilt and betrayal. Now that she knew Joe was safe, her focus returned to the fact that she'd just imparted the biggest of body blows to her husband. "To find Joe. I'm so sorry," she said.

"You will be," he replied, his face sour with regret and contempt, but this time Jennifer could tell his heart wasn't in it. It was over.

———

The second she was out of earshot, she pulled her phone out of her pocket and dialed Joe's number. To her immense relief, this time it was ringing, and sure enough, the ringtone was foreign. She was desperate to find out what he was doing in France. She hoped he was okay.

"Hello, babe, is that you?"

"Joe!" she exclaimed, flooded with relief. "Where are you?"

"France. I've come to be near you. I've just gotten through passport control and was about to call you, but you beat me to it."

"And you're okay?"

"Fine, yeah, of course. Are you? I was worried you might be mad with me for flying over, but I couldn't sit around at home wondering what was going on. I've been a wreck. I know there's not a lot I can do, but at least I'll be nearby if you need me."

"Oh my God, I love you so much." Jennifer gulped. "Listen, I've got loads to tell you. I'll come and meet you. Give me forty minutes or so, and I'll be there. You're at Nice airport, right?"

"Yeah, but listen, if it's tricky to get away—"

"It's not. I'm on my way. Just stay put till I get there. Promise?"

"Promise," he said.

And with that, Jennifer grabbed a set of car keys and, without looking back, slammed the front door behind her and raced across the gravel driveway to where the Jeep was parked. Once in the car, she turned on the ignition and sped toward the electric gates, the only barrier that lay between her and freedom. Rolling down the window, she punched in the code. The wait for the gates to open was agonizing, but finally they did, and once there was enough space to squeeze the Jeep through, she took off at such a pace that the tires screeched underneath her.

She'd been coming to France for years now, so she knew the mountain roads like the back of her hand. Joe. She and Joe were going to be together. She couldn't believe it, and though it had been horrific having to tell Tim, it was done. She put her foot down a little harder. She just needed to get to him.

Heart racing and adrenaline pumping through her system, Jennifer didn't take a moment to gather herself. If only she'd stopped for a second and taken a long deep breath. If only she'd realized that once she reached Joe, they'd have the rest of their lives together and that getting to him a few minutes earlier wouldn't make any difference. The physical desire to be with him was so immense that common sense took a backseat. The relief of telling Tim after the most painful year of her life was so enormous it propelled her down the twisty mountain roads in a reckless fashion that she wouldn't normally have contemplated. She flew around the corners and bends perfectly, driving with accurate precision—but what she couldn't have known was that a moped was approaching around the next bend. A young man was coming back from the bars in Nice. Earlier on that day, he'd gotten a promotion, so he'd stopped after work for a beer or two. Now he was veering unwisely into the middle of the road. As Jennifer turned the corner, she saw him far too late and was traveling at such a speed that she didn't have enough time to react. The shock of seeing his headlight in her line of vision was so great that she lost control of the wheel and the Jeep hurtled toward the edge of the cliff. Meanwhile, the brakes she'd slammed on didn't have time to bring the vehicle to a stop. The man on the moped, who had managed to steer himself to safety, watched in horror as Jennifer's Jeep smashed through the low metal barrier at the side of the cliff top and, although her death would be instant once she made contact with the rocks at the bottom, the drop down toward them wasn't. That fall took five long seconds, and the thoughts that flashed through Jennifer's mind and the feelings she experienced in those last few terrifying moments were even darker than the ones Joe would have to live with for the rest of his life.

Present Day

Max had hit a wall. His own health had taken a battering due to stress and lack of sleep, and he was starting to feel quite unhinged. Only yesterday he'd been swamped by a worrying desire to grab Jennifer's inert body and start shaking it in the hope it might wake her up, jolt her out of her coma. It was at that point that he finally admitted defeat and called Karen. Up until then, he'd refused to let her take over, worried that the one night he didn't keep vigil would be the night something happened. As Karen arrived, she could tell Max was on the brink of collapse. He couldn't be bothered to put up any resistance, as he had been doing for weeks. Instead, he waved good-bye sadly and ambled away.

Once he'd gone, Karen went to sit next to the woman who'd been her best friend since middle school, who she'd shared a quarter of a century of friendship with, a friendship she simply couldn't comprehend not having as part of her life going forward. Karen chose not to think like that. As far as she was concerned, Jennifer was going to get better and that was that.

"Hello, you," Karen said. Unlike Max, she didn't feel at all self-conscious talking to someone who was in a coma. If anything, it was a similar experience to talking to Pete when he was watching his soccer team on TV. "Do me a favor and get better, will you? I miss you, you big goof."

———

Max had been right, of course. The one night he wasn't at the hospital, something was bound to happen.

It was around two thirty a.m. Karen was asleep on the pullout bed, which was next to Jennifer's. She didn't know how Max had suffered it for all these weeks and now fully understood why he'd been complaining of a sore back. The bed was profoundly uncomfortable, the springs having given up the ghost years ago, and it had taken Karen ages to drop off. However, she was finally asleep when the machines around Jennifer started beeping urgently.

At first, Karen wondered if an alarm had gone off. Was it time to get up for work? It was only when a nurse burst into the room that she remembered where she was, at which point she sprang up, eyes wide with fear.

"Oh my God, what's happening?" she asked frantically.

"Just a second, please," said the nurse as two other nurses joined her in the room.

The sound of the machines was distressing but not as much as what Karen saw next, which was that Jennifer's face was contorted into the most frighteningly strange expression while her body was jerking in a disturbingly unnatural way.

"Is she in pain?" screamed Karen, wondering what the hell she should do. "Why does she look like that? Is she waking up?"

But no one would answer her. The room was filling with more and more medical staff, all far too busy tending to the patient to give any clue as to what might be happening to her friend. They were all shouting at one another, mainly medical jargon Karen had no chance of understanding. They injected something into Jennifer's arm, they checked her pulse and changed her drip, there was more frantic shouting, and then finally the machines calmed down.

Karen was completely traumatized.

"What happened?" she begged to know, tears rolling down her frightened face.

"Don't worry, she's stabilized now," said one of the remaining nurses. "She was having some sort of seizure. She seemed very distressed, but she's fine now. You should try to get some sleep and we'll get the specialist to come talk to you tomorrow."

"Okay," Karen said, her voice a whisper.

Once everyone had left the room, Karen went to sit next to Jennifer. She took her limp hand. "Hey, you. You gave us a bit of a shock there, lovely..."

Karen trailed off, blinking. She switched on the bedside lamp to make sure she was seeing what she thought she was.

When the light from the lamp illuminated Jennifer's face, she knew she wasn't hallucinating. There was indeed one very real tear rolling down her friend's still face. It was quite possibly the saddest thing Karen had ever witnessed. What was going on in that brain of hers? And how could Karen have missed how unhappy she was? If she pulled through this (and after what had just happened, Karen was finally admitting to herself that it was *if* as opposed to *when*), she vowed to do everything in her power to make her friend happy again.

The next morning, a vaguely refreshed Max arrived back at the hospital, only to be told that his wife had suffered some kind of seizure during the night.

As Karen filled him in on what had happened, any benefit he'd been feeling from his short break from the hospital was totally erased.

"Max, look. I don't know whether I should be telling you this because it's a bit upsetting, but at the same time, the doctors thought it was a very encouraging sign."

"Tell me."

"Okay…" Karen knew she had to fill him in but wondered how to broach the second half of her news. "Well, the first thing is, she cried. At least, I saw a tear roll down her face."

"Really?" asked Max. Karen could tell he was a mix of emotions, which were leaving him unsteady.

"Yes, which is pretty amazing. It shows more or less that there's no way she's brain-dead. I mean, she can't be."

"What's the other thing?"

"She said a word, Max."

"What? When?" he asked, looking appalled to have missed it. His wife had done nothing but lay there for weeks, and the one night he chose to be away, she'd practically put on a show.

"At about three in the morning, just after I noticed the tear rolling down her face."

"And what was it?" Max practically yelled.

Karen gulped and then she made a decision. Sometimes, she decided, there was such a thing in life as a good lie. A bloody necessary lie.

"The word she said was…Max."

"Was it?" asked Max, his whole face lighting up and tears springing into his eyes. "I can't believe it. Oh, Jen," he said, rushing over to the bed and taking his wife's limp hand and rubbing it with his. "Oh, Jen, I love you. Thank you so much. I needed a sign, I really did, and now you've given me one."

Karen watched nervously, a weak smile on her face. What was going on between Jennifer and Max? Not for the first time, she berated herself for not having paid more attention to her friend when she'd tried to tell her she wasn't happy. It had been easier to assume her friends were just having a rough patch. Looking at Max, she could tell their problems had scratched far deeper than the surface. In the meantime, she didn't have the heart to tell Max what her friend had really said, and more than ever she prayed that Jennifer would wake up soon. Apart from anything else, she needed to ask her: "Who on earth is Joe?"

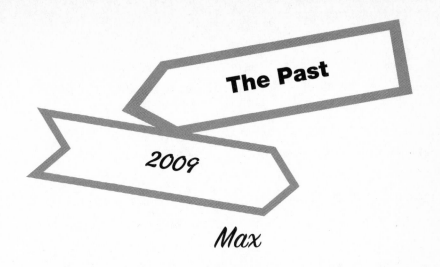

The Past

2009

Max

Thirty-three, thought Jennifer, studying her gray complexion in the harsh light of the bathroom and slapping on yet more pink blusher. She felt more like eighty-three. Eadie was two and a half and Polly was six months and teething badly, so sleep was a thing of the past. Jennifer had never been so desperately in need of a break from the crying, the diapers, the demands. A romantic dinner out would be just the recharge she required.

Of course, in some ways it was tempting not to bother and to become one with the sofa like they did most nights, but she'd always said that birthdays were to be celebrated and she was determined that this one would be no exception. So Max had booked a table at a local restaurant, fancy enough that it warranted her wearing something that wasn't yoga pants but not so fancy that the fact she hadn't been to the hairdresser for months was a problem.

It would be such a treat to spend some proper time with Max and sheer luxury to be able to abandon her babies for a few hours of precious, uninterrupted adult time.

She sighed now as she opened the bathroom door and the sound of Polly screaming from her crib hit her in a wave. "Coming, baba, coming."

Half an hour later, having plonked Eadie downstairs in front of the TV and strapped a still-fussy Polly into her bouncy chair, she called Max's cell phone. It went straight to voice mail. This was a good sign. He was probably already on the subway heading home.

She left a message: "Hi, it's me, birthday girl. I'm so excited! Eadie's bathed and fed and Polly's bathed but not fed, because her gums are pretty much on fire. She's basically been screaming all day, but anyway," she said in a singsong voice, trying not to lose her mind, "I can't wait to hand them over to Mum, and more importantly, I can't wait to see you. I can't believe I'm going to be getting out of the house and eating with someone who doesn't need their food cut up or blended. So please hurry. Wahoo. Better go and grab Pol. See you soon. Call me."

One hour later, there was still no sign of Max. Jennifer's mother had arrived and had taken over looking after the girls, leaving Jennifer wondering what to do. She felt trapped. She was desperate to escape the confines of the house but didn't particularly fancy sitting in a restaurant on her own. Where was he? Of all the days to be late.

She phoned his cell phone for the fourth time. Finally he picked up, but as quickly as her heart leaped with joy, it sunk again like a stone when she recognized the sounds of a bar in the background.

"Where are you?" she asked, instantly cross. Had he not even started the commute home yet? She'd kill him. At that moment, she was swamped by a really bad feeling about how the night was going to pan out.

"I'm just having a quick pint with a few people from the office. I won't be long."

"But we're going out. It's my birthday and I'm ready. You said you were going to take me for a drink beforehand."

"Well, sorry, but I couldn't really say no. They all wanted me to come for one. You know what it's like. You have a nice bath or something, and I'll leave as soon as I've finished this one."

"But I'm ready and I can't believe you haven't left. Why do you need to have a drink with them? Why couldn't you just say that it was your wife's birthday? You see them every bloody day, and meanwhile I'm sitting here dressed up to go out, with makeup on, for the first time in what feels like far too long, waiting for you!"

"All right," said Max. "Calm down. Bloody hell, all I've done is come for one pint. It's only seven. I'll be home by eight."

"Only if you leave right now," said Jennifer, hot tears pricking her eyes. She was unbelievably upset. "I told you Mum was coming early, and how often do I get the opportunity to go out before the girls are asleep? Never. Whereas you get to go out all the time."

"All right," Max said moodily.

Jennifer could tell he was slightly drunk. The situation was getting worse by the minute.

"I'll come now then," he huffed.

Jennifer felt like bursting into tears. "Well, that's very good of you, given that it's my birthday. Or perhaps you'd forgotten?"

"Hardly, as if you'd bloody let me, going on and on about it like a ten-year-old. Every frigging year."

Jennifer was stunned. She gulped, waiting for him to realize how cruel he'd been and to say sorry.

"I'll see you soon" was the only thing he said before putting down the phone.

Jennifer felt like he'd taken a chisel to her heart and chipped a tiny little piece of it out.

Y ou haven't been in for a while. It's good to see you."

"Good to see you too," said Jennifer, though she wasn't entirely sure it was. She'd taken a break from therapy to reflect on whether it was actually working for her. On balance, she'd decided that it was. She wasn't a very patient person, never had been, but it had become clear that achieving anything from the process would take time. There were no overnight answers. Instead, she tended to go away after a session, ponder what had been discussed, and understand more about *why* she felt the way she did but not necessarily what to do about it.

She was also very wary of the constant need to analyze her childhood. It felt a bit pointless. Her parents had done their best. They were good people. The past was done. What she was after was some help with the present. Still, she had decided to persevere.

"So what brings you back today, Jennifer?" asked Susan, a petite woman in her sixties with a cropped hairstyle and disarmingly deep voice, which wasn't the only clue to her voracious smoking habit. Susan's face was considerably lined for her age and there were deep grooves running down toward her top lip. She always insisted Jennifer take her shoes off when entering her house, which was where she held her sessions.

"It's been a bit of a mad week, I suppose," admitted Jennifer. "Yesterday, Eadie, my eldest, broke her arm. It was horrific."

"Oh my goodness. How terrible! Is she okay?"

"Yes, she's fine."

"And are you okay?"

Jennifer paused. Why was it the minute she got into this room, she always wanted to blub like a baby?

"Um..." She blinked rapidly. Thankfully, Susan realized she needed helping out.

"Tell me about you and Max. Last time I saw you, you had some concerns about your relationship. How are things now?"

"Not great," said Jennifer dolefully. "I don't know really. Yesterday, at the hospital, I was so desperate to see him, but when he finally arrived, all he did was lay into me about what had happened. Like it was my fault. It was so strange. I'd been expecting a hug and for him to ask me if I was all right. How he reacted just highlighted that there's a big gulf between us at the moment."

"Why do you think that is?"

Jennifer exhaled noisily, already despairing at what she was about to say. "He keeps banging on about how wonderful this woman at work named Judith is and it really upsets me. And she's a career woman, obviously, who barely knows what her children's names are."

"And how does that make you feel?"

"Inadequate, lacking by comparison, and also annoyed at myself for not having focused more on what I want to do."

Susan nodded.

"I get a bit jealous too. There was a time when Max thought I was the best thing since sliced bread. Now I just seem to annoy him. Though perhaps I'm being ultrasensitive."

"Going back to what you said earlier. Why are you annoyed with yourself? Do you regret your decision to stay at home?"

"I think that's the problem. I didn't really know what decision to make so I just went with the flow and tried to do the easiest thing for everyone. And in many ways, I'm glad I did. I've been able to be there for the girls and it's been incredibly rewarding. But now that they're getting bigger, I suppose I worry about being so financially dependent. Especially with our marriage on shaky ground."

Susan's gaze never left Jennifer's face.

Jennifer was filled with the familiar urge she often got when she came here to punch Susan square in the jaw. It was nothing personal. Just a response to the situation, the fight-or-flight reflex kicking in.

"Have you told Max any of this? Have you discussed your fears?"

"I've tried to, but we never seem to get any proper time together, and half the time, he doesn't listen anyway."

She sighed heavily and it occurred to her then how odd it was that she was sitting in someone's spare bedroom, on a sun lounger that had been covered in a throw to disguise it, pouring her heart out to a stranger. A stranger who she occasionally spotted doing her shopping at the supermarket, no doubt spending the money she'd earned listening to people like Jennifer moaning about their lives.

Silence filled the room, but Susan's expression didn't change, which made Jennifer want to say something purely for shock value, just to see if it would.

After what felt like an endless pause, Susan finally spoke. "Do you think there's any chance at all that you're having a midlife crisis?"

Jennifer couldn't help it. She rolled her eyes.

"What?"

"I'm sorry; it's just you're not the first person to suggest that that's what all this is about."

"And are you?"

"No."

"No, you aren't having one?"

"No. I mean, yes, I am. I mean… What I mean is, there's not a chance I'm having one. I'm definitely having one."

For once, Susan looked mildly taken aback. This was pleasing to Jennifer.

"Okay, so do you want to tell me about that?"

"Well, I think that what I'm trying to say is that I know I am definitely, without a shadow of a doubt, having the biggest midlife crisis ever."

"Okay."

"But I don't think that should be taken lightly."

"Right."

"Look, I really hope you don't think I'm being rude. It's just that even when *you* asked me that question, it was almost as if you were dismissing having a midlife crisis as something I should be able to face up to and get over."

Jennifer paused to give Susan a chance to defend herself, but her silence appeared to indicate that she'd prefer Jennifer continue instead. So she did.

"Admittedly, I used to hear the phrase myself and think it was a tired old cliché that applied purely to people who were desperate to regain their youth or who wanted an excuse to wear leather pants. Only now I'm having one myself, I realize it's a far more complex stage. There's a reason it's been given the label 'crisis,' and I think people should focus more on that word. You know, Susan…"

Jennifer paused for a moment, trying to find the right words.

"Go on…tell me what you're thinking."

"Well…I don't think what I'm feeling is as straightforward as simply not wanting to be middle-aged. I think what I'm going through is something I really need help with, and I suspect it's the same for everyone who goes through it. I know for some people it may manifest itself in dressing like an idiot, or having sex with someone just to feel they're still vaguely desirable, but those are just symptoms that stem from suddenly wondering what the hell has happened to you. To me, a midlife crisis is more about waking up one morning and wondering how on earth you've ended up doing what you're doing. It's the sudden, awful realization that so much of your life is behind you and yet you haven't achieved what you wanted to, and it's likely that you never will. It's about assessing where you're at and mourning your hopes and dreams and that sort of fizzy sense of confidence you have in your youth when it feels like anything's still possible. Then, once all that's caught up with you, you start to examine other areas in your life, at which point if you realize anything is lacking, the crisis just gets worse."

Jennifer tucked her hair behind her ears. "Look, if I'm being totally honest, Susan, which I know is the whole point of coming here, I suppose, at the moment, I'm wondering if I can stand to be with my husband for the rest of my life, because I'm not sure he really loves me anymore. Meanwhile, it's also dawned on me that my earning prospects are dismal and that I'll probably never fall in love again, which somehow feels like a monumental disaster. Is it wrong of me to want to experience feeling giddy with love again before I die? Is it weird that not knowing how I'm going to fill my time for the rest of my days terrifies me? Because despite not being young anymore, I'm also a long way from dead, and with a bit of luck, I've still got a lot of life to live. Only now I'm finally wise enough to understand how quickly it's all going to fly by."

Susan nodded.

Jennifer swallowed hard. "Sometimes I lie awake at night, listening to Max snore, and I start to feel panic rising, start wondering if I should be grabbing my life with two hands and giving it an almighty shake, because I can't think of anything worse than looking in the mirror in another ten years' time and thinking, 'Well, you've had it now. You've lost the opportunity to make yourself truly happy.' I don't want to die wondering what could have been." Jennifer blinked, determined not to cry.

Susan looked terribly sympathetic. "And what else?"

"I think it's a stage that shouldn't be mocked, because it's actually terribly hard and I can't bear what I'm turning into. I've spent most of this week daydreaming about my past, wondering what life might have been like if I'd made different decisions or perhaps stayed with other men I've loved. And it's scary, because I *should* be happy, but I'm not, so then that makes me feel selfish and guilty, which is even more depressing. I can't even eat. I've lost fifteen pounds in a year. I just want to be happy, Susan. I want to get out of this mire. I want to know that I've led my life in a positive way and that I haven't missed out, and most of all, when I ask the question 'Is this it?' I want to feel like if it is, then that's okay."

Once she'd finished, Jennifer wasn't entirely sure where her outburst had come from but she felt better for it, if a little embarrassed. She watched motes of dust swirling in the shaft of light pouring through the window.

Thirty more seconds of silence passed, and Jennifer could feel her face going red. She sat on her hands as she waited for Susan's response and hoped that when it came, it wouldn't be one that would belittle everything she'd just expressed. She hoped Susan had been listening properly. If she had been, then she'd know she wouldn't want to be patronized with something along the lines of "Well, how does that all make you feel?"

It took an age, but finally Susan's response did come, and when it did, it couldn't have been more unpredictable.

"Well, at least you're thin."

Jennifer turned in amazement, wondering if her therapist was being sarcastic. However, when she caught Susan's eye, she was rewarded with a reassuring, wholly understanding wink.

"There is that," she replied, acknowledging Susan's joke with a smile. "Being a size eight again is pretty good."

"On a serious note, I want you to know that I for one respect everything you're feeling. This is a really tough chapter in your life. I also want you to think this week about what the root cause of your unhappiness might be. I can tell that your soul is yearning for some change at the moment, but have you ever considered that by changing what you've already got that you might simply be swapping one set of problems for another?"

Jennifer cocked her head to one side as she thought about this. This was more like it. This was what she came to therapy and paid forty pounds a time for. What Susan had said was very interesting.

"And do you not think that while you and Max certainly have some work to do on aspects of your relationship, rather than this being all about him, this is really about you? It's about you working out what you want, about figuring out who you are and what makes you happy. Because until you can be happy in yourself, I don't think anybody else can fill that gap for you."

"Susan?"

"Yes?"

"Do you ever think that perhaps life should be full of change?"

"What do you mean exactly?"

"Well, why does convention dictate that we should expect to find a relationship that will last forever? Maybe every relationship has a different life span. Perhaps we're supposed to be with different people for certain periods of our lives, and as we change and our needs develop, the person we should be with should change too. I think people who find one person who makes them happy their entire life just got lucky."

Susan pondered this for a while. "Are you trying to tell me there's someone specific you're considering a change with?"

"No," said Jennifer hurriedly. "I'm not. There isn't anyone in my life except Max. In fact, lately, I've spent more time harking back to the past as opposed to thinking about anyone in the present."

"Give me an example."

"Well, I've been thinking a lot recently about the boyfriend I went out with before Max. His name was Steve. I actually met Max at a party we were at together and was convinced Max and I were far more suited. Yet I'm pretty sure that Max has never loved me as much as Steve did. Perhaps if I'd stayed with him, I wouldn't be feeling like this right now. Perhaps if I *hadn't* given Max my number at that party, I would still be with Steve and living very happily."

"Or perhaps you'd be with Steve and wondering if you should have gone off with Max while you had the chance. It's impossible to say," mused Susan, "and it's also very difficult to reflect on the past and remember how we truly felt at the time when our perception is so colored by the present."

"Mmm," agreed Jennifer, who was pretty sure this would be one of those comments she'd need to go away and think about before making up her mind.

"Perhaps for next week, you should concentrate on trying to reconnect with Max again. Try telling him how you're feeling. I think you could be surprised by the results."

"Really?"

"Really," Susan said kindly, and it occurred to Jennifer that she hadn't wanted to punch her in the face for a whole twenty minutes. Progress. This was a pretty good session.

"I tried to seduce him last week, but it failed miserably," Jennifer admitted for no other reason than the memory had just popped into her head.

"How do you mean 'failed'? Could he not perform?"

Jennifer wrinkled her nose, embarrassed. "No, nothing like that. I just got all dressed up in a bid to make an effort, but he didn't even come upstairs to see me when he got home from work, so I gave up."

"Okay," said Susan. "So Max wasn't actually aware that you were trying to seduce him?"

"No."

"So what you were really upset about wasn't being rejected but the fact that when he got home from work, he didn't seek you out?"

Jennifer sighed. "I suppose so."

"Well, perhaps you need to tell him what your needs are. He may be totally unaware of how you're feeling, and he at least deserves the chance to put things right. No?"

Jennifer shrugged. She almost preferred it when Susan remained impartial.

"How are the antidepressants going?"

"I've stopped taking them," Jennifer admitted.

"Why?"

Another shrug.

"Okay, well, it's not for me to tell you what to do, but I strongly recommend you go back to your doctor and discuss that with him. If you are suffering from depression, you need to give them a chance to work."

"I don't think I need them," Jennifer said.

"What do you think you need?" Susan asked softly.

"I think, after having talked to you today, that I need to talk to Max properly and to try to set aside some time for us to perhaps go away and attempt to sort things out."

"That sounds like a very positive idea."

———

A while later, Jennifer left Susan's house feeling considerably better than she had when she'd first arrived. There was clearly not going to be an overnight solution to how she was feeling. She still had a lot of thinking to do and it would take time, but one thing she could take control of was trying to save her marriage. It felt like a step in the right direction.

Present Day

Jennifer's brain was beginning to recover from the accident. Most of the time, she was still existing in her otherworldly state. However, these periods were interspersed with short spells during which her consciousness allowed her to connect properly with the here and now.

After tunnel number two had shut behind her for the last time, Jennifer had been beside herself with distress. She'd experienced a level of love she hadn't previously known was possible and then she'd died. It was all so incredibly painful.

She'd been so distraught and grief-stricken that it had been too much to cope with, causing her to suffer a seizure. The machines bleeping had signified the second when her brain had truly engaged with the enormity of what would have happened in France had she chosen that path in life.

Ever since, she'd felt like a wounded animal. But her body was getting stronger and refused to give up its battle for recovery. This, coupled with willpower and emotional resilience she never previously would have given herself credit for, meant that eventually

Jennifer was ready to consider her next move. It was either that or give up, but her instinct to survive was stronger. So she'd decided that she had to hold on to the fact that the painful outcome in France hadn't been her true fate or the one she'd really chosen. It was utterly tragic, but thank God none of it had come to pass. Those children didn't lose a mother, because they didn't really exist. Joe didn't lose the love of his life. But when it occurred to her that he might actually exist in the real world…the idea was too mind-boggling to contemplate. And yet it also wouldn't go away.

Steve

§ teve whistled appreciatively. "You look stunning, babe. Absolutely stunning. Let me take a picture."

Jennifer struck a pose. Hands on hips, she stared suggestively down the lens of his digital camera.

"Flipping heck," said Steve, looking at the result. "Check you out."

Jennifer came over to have a look and had to admit it was a good one. She looked quite sexy.

"Doesn't she look like a model, Mum?"

"Ooh, she does," agreed June, frantically dusting and arranging her commemorative plates in one of her glass-fronted cabinets. She'd bought the entire set off an infomercial a fortnight ago and had been beside herself with excitement when they'd arrived earlier. There were eight plates in total and each one depicted a different member of the royal family at various events. "Lovely color. I like you in brights."

"Thanks," said Jennifer, who was pleased with her new dress. She felt sexy in it. It was bright pink, quite fitted, and showed off her figure. Being with Steve these last couple of years had given her a newfound confidence in her body. He complimented her every day and always seemed to mean it sincerely. He always noticed when she'd had her hair done or when she was wearing something new, and he had an opinion on what he liked her in, which she found very sexy. Yes, it was important to dress for yourself, but it was an added bonus if how you looked made your boyfriend want to take your clothes off. He hadn't asked her yet, but one day Jennifer suspected that if they ever got that far, it might make shopping for a wedding dress far easier too, because he was even able to verbalize his idea of a beautiful bride (hair up, dress that wasn't too big). Though having said that, whenever he alluded to their future together, a few doubts had started to creep in. For a long time, it had felt like Steve just assumed they'd stay together forever but seemed to have forgotten along the way to ask her what she felt about this.

"Right, Mum. I'll see you soon. I'll be staying at Jen's for the next few nights or so," said Steve, grabbing his jacket.

"Oh, really? All right then, love," said June, looking downcast.

"What?"

"No, no, it's nothing," said June, rearranging Prince Andrew into a more prominent position and relegating Princess Anne firmly to the back. She had a most definite pecking order.

Jennifer tried to ignore the nugget of irritation building in her stomach. She hated it when people said "nothing" when clearly there was "something." With June, there was always "something."

"Come on," cajoled Steve, his voice laden with patience like he was talking to a small child. "Let's have it. There's obviously something on your mind and we're not leaving for this party till you spit it out."

Jennifer didn't necessarily agree with this last statement. If June took too long, she, for one, would be off.

"Honestly, it's nothing."

"Mum…"

"No, it's silly really," said June. "It's just I assumed you were coming back here, so I went and got everything to make a roast tomorrow."

Steve looked stricken. "Oh no, did you?"

Eager to leave, Jennifer quickly assessed the situation. "I tell you what," she chimed in. "Why don't we just crash at my place tonight as planned? That way we don't have to spend a fortune on a taxi or leave the party early, but then we could always come back here tomorrow for lunch."

"But what about you getting to work on Monday, babe?"

Damn. To be fair, Jennifer hadn't totally thought that one through, but she could hardly backtrack now. "Hmm, well…I guess I'll either have to go back home tomorrow night or I could just leave here very, very early on Monday morning."

She was rewarded for her peacekeeping efforts with a ridiculously grateful smile from Steve, who she knew hated upsetting his mother. The two of them were extremely close, and it was another aspect of Steve's comparative warmth she'd always appreciated and had been surprised by when they'd first gotten together. Tim had barely given his mother the time of day. He'd never been able to get her off the phone quick enough, always answering her questions with bullet points and hardly ever bothering to inquire after her. But Steve checked in with June daily and told her everything. They had an amazing relationship, although lately Jennifer had found herself wishing he'd stick up for himself a bit more when she was being bossy. Sometimes it seemed like she had her son wrapped around her acrylic-nailed little finger.

"Really?" asked June. "You'd come back tomorrow? It's just since Derek and I split up, Sundays can be so lonely. But only come if it's not a pain."

It would be a pain. A massive pain. Jennifer had been desperately excited about spending a rare day in bed doing nothing. Now they'd be trekking across town with hangovers, but to hell with it. At least she wouldn't have to cope with Steve feeling guilty and fretting about his mother all day. Plus they'd get fed.

"Course it isn't a pain," said Steve. "How could it be a pain when it involves having one of your roasts?"

Jennifer cringed.

"What roast is it, anyway?"

"Your favorite," said June. "Beef."

Steve made a face similar to the one he made during orgasm, sort of cross-eyed with bliss. He rubbed his hands together. "Nice one, Mum. Can't wait. Right, my gorgeous, shall we go?"

———

On the subway, Steve thanked Jennifer profusely. "I'm so sorry, babe. I know you were really looking forward to lying in bed all day. It's so kind, what you did, and so typical of you to be so unselfish."

"That's all right," said Jennifer. "As long as you promise me that next time you'll make it clear, days in advance, that we're not coming back. So she doesn't get all that bloody food."

"Hmm," said Steve, looking torn, clearly debating whether he should be divulging what he was about to tell her next. "Actually, I kind of did, but I think she just loves having us around so much, she chose to forget."

Jennifer wished Steve hadn't told her this. If June had in fact manipulated them into coming back to Leytonstone tomorrow, it was very irritating, especially since she was facing a horrible trek to work on Monday. Suddenly she felt far less inclined to be doing June the favor. Damn it.

Steve picked up her hand and gave it a little squeeze. "I'll make it up to you, babe."

Jennifer took a deep breath and tried not to let this ruin the night. She'd been looking forward to this party for ages. According to Esther, there was going to be an amazing DJ, loads of booze, plus all her best friends would be there. Toby, Esther's boyfriend, was a good laugh too, so his friends were bound to be up for fun.

"You know what my mum's like," Steve said. He could tell Jennifer was fed up. "Like I said, she loves our company and you know how lonely she gets."

"I know," said Jennifer, but she couldn't quite leave it at that. Usually she never dared criticize the mother ship, but today it felt warranted. "Only perhaps, just occasionally, you could try putting me first? After all, we do spend a lot of time bending over backward to make sure she's happy, and if I'd known she was being sneaky, I would never have offered to go back tomorrow. You always go on about how she wants to see both of us, but it's kind of annoying because she doesn't really. She wants to see you. Not me."

"That's not true, babe," said Steve, looking genuinely aghast. "She loves you. Just the other day, she was asking when she's going to be a grandma."

"And what did you say?" Jennifer asked slightly frostily.

"I said as soon as I could persuade you to have my babies."

"Well, you're going to have to wait a bit longer, I'm afraid."

"I know," said Steve. "One more year."

As the subway rattled through the tunnels, Jennifer despaired. Steve insisted on hanging on to that "one more year" for dear life. She'd only said it to shut him up. She definitely wanted to start a family at some point, but they weren't even engaged yet and she hated the pressure. She loved Steve very much, but his constant nagging to have a baby was starting to get on her nerves.

"And again, her becoming a grandma has got nothing to do with me. It's the baby she's after," she added through gritted teeth, her mood worsening by the second.

"All right," Steve warned. He was a softie, but not when it came to his mother, and Jennifer knew she was treading a fine line before he got annoyed, although given the mood she was in, she wasn't sure she cared.

"Look, I'm sorry, okay, and I know it's going to be a bit of a ball-ache tomorrow, but we can laze around until at least ten thirty and it's not *that* much of a big deal going back. At least we'll be getting Mum's roasties."

Jennifer battled with the urge to tell him she'd always found his mother's "roasties" a bit oily and that what she really fancied tomorrow was Chinese takeout.

"Oh shit, I forgot to tell you, babe," said Steve, wisely changing the subject. "You know Mum entered me in that competition with Price Smash, the shopping channel? The one looking for a DIY expert?"

"Yes…"

"They've been in touch. They want to get me in for a meeting or something. Or maybe even a, hang on, what did they call it? Oh yeah, a screen test."

Steve had chosen his timing well. This was an instant distraction.

"I can't believe you didn't tell me. That's hilarious!"

"I know, although I reckon they only looked at her entry because she keeps the entire company afloat with her spending habits."

Jennifer laughed. This was golden gossip. She couldn't believe Steve was only telling her now, and it certainly helped improve her mood.

"So are you going to go? When is it?"

"Nah," said Steve dismissively. "Can you imagine me fumbling my way through a screen test? I get embarrassed enough as it is just having my photo taken, let alone talking on camera."

"Still," said Jennifer, "can you imagine what a housewives' favorite you'd be? And besides, they've seen the tape your mum sent, so they must think there's some talent there."

Steve frowned, assuming she was having a laugh.

"I'm not joking. You've seen the usual cheese balls that work on those channels. I saw one the other day who had so much fake tan on he was pretty much orange, his suit was shiny, and his eyes were slightly too close together. You'd be the handsomest thing they'd ever clapped eyes on."

Steve rolled his eyes and shook his head.

"Seriously, babe, I reckon they'd love you. Plus there's nothing you don't know about DIY, so it's not like you wouldn't be in your comfort zone." Jennifer laughed, mainly at herself. "I can't believe I'm encouraging you, but you never know. You might find you're good, and I bet they'd pay well too."

"Well, you're very sweet, baby, but somehow being Price Smash's DIY expert isn't exactly a dream I'm up for pursuing. No matter how much Mum insists."

Jennifer felt a definite sense of satisfaction that for once it looked like he was going to defy mother dearest. Steve was right—if he were to work on one of her beloved shopping channels, she'd be the happiest woman ever. Still, in this instance, she was kind of on June's side. She couldn't see what he had to lose. He was a great plumber, but in terms of broadening his horizons, prospects, and earning power, this could be his big opportunity.

Jennifer tried another tactic. "She'll be devastated if you don't go. She'd never forgive you. I heard her telling Sue about it the other day. She was so pleased with what she'd sent in and to be fair, I was very cynical about it. I reckoned so many people would enter that you wouldn't stand a chance, so she's done well. I bet hundreds entered."

"Hmm," said Steve, still not looking wholly convinced. "Price Smash is hardly QVC, though, is it?"

"Oh, I don't know. I'd say it's definitely up there." Jennifer started chuckling. "Oh my God, listen to me. What have I become? I'd never so much as glimpsed a shopping channel before I met you. Now I'm a bloody connoisseur."

"I know." Steve laughed. "It sort of seeps in, doesn't it? Even I nearly got sucked in the other day. I sat down to have a beer, fully meaning to switch over and watch something proper. Next thing I knew, I'd watched ten minutes of someone talking about an air fryer and was on the verge of buying one."

Jennifer cackled wholeheartedly before eventually spluttering, "How much do you reckon she spent last month alone on crap from those channels?"

"Dread to think," said Steve drily. "I caught her buying a steam mop the other day, and I know for a fact that disgusting necklace she gave Sue for her birthday was bought from one or other of them. It might even have been Price Smash."

Their shared despair of both June's viewing and buying habits succeeded in defusing what otherwise could have become a fight, and for much of the remainder of the journey, they sat together in comfortable silence. As the train finally pulled into Hammersmith, however, Steve leaned in and whispered, "One day you're going to be the best mum in the world, you know, babe. Even better than mine."

Jennifer laughed.

"What?" asked Steve, looking a bit miffed that his stab at being romantic was being giggled at.

"Bloody hell, Steve," she exclaimed. "Until the day I give birth, you really are not going to let it lie, are you? You've got to change the record! You make me feel like a walking womb sometimes."

Steve shot her back a rueful grin. Then he shrugged.

"Honestly," said Jennifer, shaking her head and feeling really irritated. "You're a nightmare and I need you to give it a rest. I've told you, I don't know how many times, that at the moment, I need to concentrate on getting this promotion at work. After that, we'll see. In a year or so."

"Good," said Steve, grinning to the point of stupidity.

The Past

Steve

T he party was in full swing by the time they arrived. There were loads of familiar faces, and as soon as they'd set foot in the hallway, they were engulfed by friends. Drawn toward the music, Lucy enthusiastically pulling her by the hand, Jennifer had headed straight to the makeshift dance floor in the lounge, her free arm in the air, moving in time to the strains of the funk that was being played. Meanwhile, Steve had bumped into Pete and gone off to replace the warm beers he'd brought with him for cold ones. Pete had seemed genuinely pleased to see Steve, so Jennifer knew he'd be all right. All Jennifer's friends really liked him, but then he was easy to get along with, so becoming part of their group had been an easy transition.

"There she is," said Lucy, shoving Jennifer in Karen's direction. "She's been pining for you."

"Yeah!" screamed Karen upon realizing her friend had finally arrived. If the sweat patches under her arms were anything to go by, she'd been dancing energetically for a while.

"It's too loud for me here," yelled Lucy at the top of her lungs. "I'm going outside for a cigarette."

She left them to it, right by the speakers where the mixer was set up. She was right. The music was loud enough to make your ears bleed.

"You all right?" yelled Karen.

Jennifer took a deep breath in preparation to scream back her answer. "Yeah, good," she shouted. "Just glad to be here. It took ages."

"Oh well, you've done your stint at June Towers for the week. Now you can chill, babe."

Jennifer was about to fill her in and explain that she couldn't and that she'd be trekking back there tomorrow but decided it would only inflame her annoyance, which she was doing well to keep a lid on at the moment. Plus it would be too much effort to make herself understood over this racket.

"I haven't seen Esther," she yelled directly into Karen's ear instead, which was the only hope either of them had of hearing each other. The volume was ridiculous. The police would probably be by soon.

"Upstairs, I think," said Karen, making a face. "She and Toby were having a huge fight about something when Pete and I arrived."

"What about?"

"What?"

"I said what about?"

"I think he was eyeing up Rochelle. You know Rochelle? Silly cow with the big tits. The one Esther hates."

Jennifer couldn't make out what she'd said so she just nodded and smiled.

"How's Steve?"

"Good."

"No ring yet?" teased Karen.

"What?"

Karen tapped her ring finger.

"No, thank God." Jennifer laughed, only half joking. "He'd rather get me knocked up first anyway, I reckon." It had become a standing joke within the group that out of the two of them, it was Steve who was eager to settle down and have babies while Jennifer was doing her best to cling to her last vestiges of freedom.

Then the music changed and someone saw sense to reduce the volume to a less painful threshold. The funk came off and one of Jennifer's favorite house tracks came pouring out of the speakers, causing her to squeal with delight.

"Wooooh," yelled Karen, hands aloft.

Jennifer turned around to show her appreciation to the DJ, only to find that he'd gone and that someone else had taken his place. Someone who perhaps wasn't deaf? The guy behind the CD mixer had dark hair, an attractive, lopsided grin, and was wearing only a scruffy T-shirt and black jeans yet managed to look really good. He caught Jennifer's eye. She didn't need any more encouragement than that to go tell him how much she appreciated his choice of track. "Oh my God, this is such a good song," she squealed.

He nodded, smiling at her girlish enthusiasm. "Better get dancing then," he said, shooting her a grin.

Jennifer did as she was told and, for the next couple of minutes, danced with gusto to the tune that sent shivers down her spine whenever the chorus kicked in. At one point, she and Karen clutched onto each other and jumped around together. A far larger group had been attracted to the dance floor.

"Who's the DJ?" panted Jennifer after the fifth brilliant track in a row.

"Max Wright," said Karen. "He's cute, isn't he? He's a mate of Drifter's."

Jennifer looked blank.

"You know Drifter, don't you? Toby's cousin's ex."

Jennifer shook her head.

"Why do you want to know?"

"No reason. I just love the music he's playing. It's brilliant."

"Do you want a drink?" Karen asked. "I'm going to see if I can hunt down some vodka. If I can't, I'll probably go to the store. Do you want to come?"

"Do you mind if I stay here for now? I want to dance a bit more."

Karen nodded and disappeared off into the crowd. The party seemed to be filling up by the second.

Jennifer turned to see if anyone else she knew was around. As she did, her eyes met with the DJ's again. She'd sensed him watching her a few times when she'd been dancing, and now he was looking directly at her. He gave a small nod of his head. Jennifer smiled back and acknowledged to herself that if she wasn't attached, she'd probably be making a beeline for him right this second.

Right. Definitely time to find Steve.

It took her a while to locate him. By this point, the party had crossed the line from being pleasantly heaving to unpleasantly packed. The stairs were three people deep and not one inch of carpet could be seen. After a pretty unpleasant ten minutes of barging her way through small groups of people who were so engrossed in what they were doing that they were reluctant to move, she finally found her boyfriend in one of the bedrooms. Even then, it took her a while to detect him because the room was so full of smoke, she could hardly see into it. There were about eight lads in there doing shots of limoncello. Pete was one of them. In fact, it was obvious he was the main instigator and that when it came to the acrid yet sweet-smelling smoke that hung thick in the air, he was also the culprit. He had an enormous joint hanging from his lips, and Jennifer watched amazed as he offered it to Steve and he accepted. Steve wasn't a big drinker and certainly never normally smoked pot or went anywhere near drugs, which was probably why he was looking a bit green now.

"Hey, gorgeous," he said, looking up, finally realizing she was standing over him. It had taken two whole minutes for him to notice her. Oh God. He was wasted.

"Hey, you all right?" she inquired gently, aware that he wouldn't want her to make him look like a loser in front of the other guys by exposing how out of it he was.

"Yeah, good," said Steve, beckoning to her to sit next to him on the bed. His hand was all floppy and limp. She perched on the end of the bed, very conscious of the fact that she was the only female in what felt like a male dorm room. Steve tried to sit up more so he could give her a kiss. He missed her mouth a bit and ended up smooching her cheek. She had to resist the urge to wipe her face with her hand. She felt like she'd been kissed by a Labrador.

He reached over and rubbed her leg, which was fine. But then he sat up and started kissing her neck and stroking her hair, which was a bit weird given that there were seven other people in the room. She tried to pull away before Steve's actions drew too much attention, but she clearly hadn't done so fast enough.

"Oy oy," said one drunk-looking guy.

"Get a room, you two," said Pete, and Jennifer felt her face redden.

"If I want to kiss my beautiful girlfriend, then why shouldn't I?" proclaimed Steve.

Pete pretended to stick his fingers down his throat and replied, "Because you show us all up, mate, and I'll have Karen moaning at me later saying, 'You don't show me as much affection as Steve shows Jen,' blah blah blah."

"Er, I am in the room, you know," said Jennifer, firmly pulling away from Steve's hands, which were still trying to stroke her. He was getting on her nerves. How had he gotten so out of it so quickly?

While Pete turned around to concentrate on the serious business of doling out another round of shots to everybody, she took the opportunity to turn to face Steve properly. He looked stoned. His eyes were bloodshot and his expression was positively dopey.

"Babe, I hate to say it, but it's still pretty early, so don't get any more out of it, because we've got to get all the way back to Leytonstone tomorrow, remember?"

Steve's face instantly clouded over. "Ugh, you're not still going on about that, are you? I wish you'd give it a rest. Honestly, you're making such a big deal out of it," he slurred.

Jennifer was outraged. "Oh my God," she fumed in a seething whisper she hoped no one else could hear. "As if! I was hardly having a go. The opposite, in fact. I was trying to look out for you and was only saying that if you get too wrecked, you'll pay for it tomorrow. But if you want to be like that, then do what you want."

Steve sighed heavily and she could see him trying to come up with a good defense, but it was never going to happen. He was looking really peaky now. Pale and a bit sweaty. She gave up. She didn't care what he had to say anyway. He was being an idiot.

"I'm going back downstairs," she said, shaking off his right hand, which was trying to paw at her again. As she left the room, she heard Steve calling out, "Oh, babe, come on; come back a minute. I didn't mean it."

She cringed. Great. Well done, Steve. Now they'd all know they were arguing.

Back downstairs, the party was starting to lose its appeal. There were simply too many people, and many of them obviously hadn't been invited. No one dared go up to the group of unsavories who were loitering in the hall to ask what they were doing there, but their presence seemed to create an uneasy atmosphere.

Jennifer searched for Karen for ages, failing to find her anywhere, but she did bump into Esther and Lucy. "Hey," she said, delighted to see them, until she realized Esther's face was tearstained and that Lucy was leading her by the elbow like an old lady. Her mascara had clumped and she had rings of black eyeliner halfway down her face. "Oh my God, what's happened?"

"It's okay," Lucy said on Esther's behalf. "She just split up with Toby."

"Oh no! Why?" Jennifer asked.

"He's been a total prick."

Jennifer looked to Lucy, who shook her head and pulled a warning face, telling her not to inquire further. "Okay, so what are you both doing now?"

"I'm going to take Esther outside and make sure she gets in a cab. I'll either come back or I might just get in with her," Lucy replied.

"Okay," Jennifer said, feeling really sorry for Esther, who was clearly so drunk and upset that she couldn't even talk. Jennifer watched as she shuffled off, Lucy keeping a firm grip on her.

"You okay?" asked a voice.

Jennifer turned around and was pleasantly surprised to see the man she already knew was called Max standing there. "Oh, hello. It's the DJ who isn't deaf."

Max grinned. "It was a bit painful before, wasn't it? No doubt it will be again. Drifter's on for his next set. Do you fancy a drink?"

"What you got?"

"Rum," said Max, pulling a bottle out of the back pocket of his jeans.

"Don't mind if I do."

Max gestured to a small two-seater sofa that had been dragged up against the wall and had miraculously just become free. "Quick," he instructed. "Ah, bloody brilliant. I've been dying to sit down for ages," Max said once they'd successfully nabbed the seats. Jennifer had to admit it felt very good to sit. Her heels were starting to kill her. "So how come I haven't met you before then?" asked Max.

"Don't know." Jennifer shrugged, grasping the bottle he was handing her and taking an enormous swig.

"Because I've met Karen and Pete a few times now, but you've never been around."

"International woman of mystery, that's me," replied Jennifer.

"It's Jennifer, isn't it?"

"Yes, and you're Max?"

He nodded. "So, Jennifer, international woman of mystery, have you got a boyfriend?"

"Yes," she said, turning to look him straight in the eye. Her tone was almost defiant.

"And who is he?"

"Steve."

"Steve, eh? And what's Steve like?"

"He's lovely. Obviously. Or I wouldn't go out with him."

"Fair enough," said Max, grinning and taking the rum back from her.

"What about you? Are you single?"

"Yup."

Jennifer looked around the room. A couple was making out up against the opposite wall. They were both so drunk it was pretty off-putting and rather grim to watch. You could see their tongues rotating.

"Nice, eh?"

Jennifer made a face. "I hate public displays of affection like that."

Max laughed. "I'm not sure if that counts as affection. More like desperation."

They sat in silence for a while, Jennifer wondering if perhaps she shouldn't be going to find Steve. But she knew he was fine, and she and Max had found a pretty good spot. She was reluctant to give it up and return to stalking around the house, looking for something to do or someone to talk to.

"Great set earlier, by the way."

"Oh, good. Glad you liked it. To be honest, I haven't DJ'd since my university days, but Drifter was desperate for me to help him out so he didn't have to do it all night."

"Ah, well, that answers the next question I was going to ask, which was do you do it for a living? There's a girl at my work who's looking for someone good for her thirtieth."

Max regarded her in a way she liked. He was very sexy. She turned away. She didn't want to encourage him or give him the wrong impression.

"Well, you never know. If it was for a friend of yours, perhaps I could come out of retirement," said Max, which only confirmed what she'd thought.

"Okay, great. Are you expensive?"

"If it's her birthday, I'm sure I can come up with a reasonable rate."

"Ah, I like that," Jennifer said with a smile.

"What, that I'm cheap?"

"No, that you would be generous because it's her birthday."

"Well, they only happen once a year. Obviously."

"Which is exactly why I've never understood people who can't be bothered to celebrate. I always celebrate mine by doing something. In fact, my whole family makes a big deal out of everyone's birthday. Always have."

"Even as they get older?"

"*Especially* as they get older. I mean, a birthday isn't just about the day itself. It's about celebrating another whole year of living, isn't it?"

"Heaven forbid your boyfriend ever forgets yours. I can tell you feel quite strongly about this."

Jennifer grinned. "He wouldn't forget. Not if he knew what was good for him."

Her gaze drifted back to the couple really going at it across the room. His hands were everywhere, up her skirt, down her top. It was horrible.

"So where's Steve now?" Max inquired.

"Upstairs. He's a bit wrecked."

"Ooh, upchucking, is he? Last of the great romantics."

"Oy, you," said Jennifer, giving him a bit of a nudge. "I'll have you know Steve is ridiculously romantic."

"Is he, now? In what way? What's the most romantic thing he's done for you?"

She toyed with telling him to mind his own bloody business but in the end decided he was only having a bit of fun, so she went with it. "Okay, well, he's always telling me I'm beautiful."

Max nodded. "Well, he's got a point there. He's a lucky guy, your Steve, and I hope you know I'm only being like this because I'm disgustingly jealous of him and totally unable to get a lovely girlfriend like you myself."

Jennifer laughed. "You're terrible."

"Why? It's true. Now come on, I'm intrigued. What else does he do? You've got to tell me because maybe I can learn from this. Does he compile playlists of music that remind him of you?"

"No," admitted Jennifer, thinking that would be quite nice. Steve had never been into music, certainly not as much as she was.

"Really?" asked Max. "I'm surprised. I would have thought that would have been a definite. But the two of you have a song, obviously?"

Jennifer wrinkled her nose up. "Um, not really."

"Oh okay, maybe I'm thinking too inside the box," admitted Max. "It's just when I saw you dancing earlier, I assumed you loved music and that you'd be the sort of person who would always have a song for everything. You're a good dancer, by the way."

"Thanks," said Jennifer, blushing.

"So, what is your favorite tune?"

"Impossible to answer," she answered. "Totally absurd question, if you don't mind me saying, because it depends on the mood, doesn't it?"

"All right, Miss Pedantic, then how about if you could only ever hear one song for the rest of your life and you *had* to choose one or have your tits burnt off with a soldering iron. What would it be?"

"'Bittersweet Symphony' by the Verve then."

"Interesting," mused Max. "Rum?"

She took the bottle and swigged from it greedily. "We're like pirates," she said, gasping as the strong liquor trickled down her esophagus.

"Not really," said Max in a way that made her giggle. "I've got all my teeth, for starters. I haven't got scurvy, and I'm not wearing an earring. You look a bit like an addled old sea dog admittedly, but only a bit. Anyway, back to your romantic boyfriend. I want more details."

"Why are you so interested?"

Max shrugged. "Well, my options are to sit here and chat to you about life and the universe or get forced to DJ for another hour and a half, which I really can't be bothered to do. Besides, I've played all my best tunes already, trying and failing to impress you."

Jennifer was thoroughly enjoying herself.

"Right. Well, let's just sit and talk rubbish then, because the last thing this party needs is the scrapings of your DJ barrel."

"Pirate barrel," added Max. "Right, let's continue the interrogation then. What else does Steve do for you that's romantic?"

"Okay then," she began. "He cooks for me a lot."

"Nice. And of course he does. I can tell we're dealing with a proper twenty-first-century specimen of manhood here. What kind of thing does he cook?"

"All sorts," lied Jennifer. The fact was Steve did cook for her regularly but only ever a variation on one thing, breakfast, which always comprised of four of the following—sausage, bacon, beans, egg, grilled tomatoes, mushrooms, and toast. She'd probably had every possible combination and she loved his breakfasts, though she sometimes wondered if he'd ever experiment with anything else. When questioned, he always said there was no point learning to cook when his mother was so good.

"I've heard this before, you know," said Max. "That being a dab hand in the kitchen makes girls go weak at the knees. I'll have to brush up. I can pretty much only do roasts and curries."

"Well, that sounds pretty impressive," said Jennifer truthfully. "Chuck in a mean spaghetti Bolognese and I reckon any girl would be very happy with that."

"So what else?" persisted Max. "He cooks, he tells you you're beautiful, but what else? Has he ever whisked you away to Paris in the spring, bought you flowers for no reason, showered you with thoughtful gifts, written you poetry, or are these sorts of gestures all too trite and cliché for perfect Steve?"

"Aha," said Jennifer triumphantly, glad to have finally come up with something. She'd been starting to panic. "I tell you what he did that was very romantic. He bought me a piece of the moon for my birthday."

The expression on Max's face was not what she'd anticipated at all. Rather than impressed, he looked thoroughly offended.

"What?" asked Jennifer, feeling herself get embarrassed and faintly wishing she'd never mentioned it.

"You are kidding me," said Max. "You're not telling me you're the kind of girl who thinks that sort of thing is actually cool? You've suddenly gone right down in my estimation."

"Why?" she squealed, blushing furiously.

"You're telling me that your boyfriend handed over good money for some bullshit piece of paper that says you own however many square feet of the moon?"

Jennifer didn't say anything but gave him a look designed to warn him not to laugh at her *too* much.

Not that he took any notice.

Max laughed, holding his sides as the concept really took hold. "Let me guess. Did it come with a revolting teddy bear to go with it?"

"No, it did not," lied Jennifer, hating Max for being so spot-on but hating herself more for having given Steve's lunar purchase as an example of something romantic when at the time, she herself had thought it a truly senseless gift.

"But who did he think he was buying it off?" said Max, really enjoying himself. "No one owns the bloody moon, so no one has the right to sell it. I tell you what—if I go and make a nice certificate on the computer that says you own some of the sun, will you buy it off me for fifty quid?"

"Shut up, you," said Jennifer, though she couldn't help but smile a bit. It was pretty ridiculous when you thought about it.

"Is that really romantic or just gullible?"

"Well, if anyone were to colonize the moon, then at least I could claim my piece of it," she said lamely, remembering what Steve had tried to tell her as she'd looked blankly at her pointless "certificate," wishing it was a new shirt.

"Yeah, 'cause that's bloody likely, isn't it?" Max asked. "That's really likely to happen in our lifetime. Mmm, let's inhabit a freezing cold, oxygen-less satellite we can't breathe on."

"You're very sarcastic, aren't you?" Jennifer asked, turning away so he couldn't see how much she was starting to laugh.

"And of course, if anyone did decide to inhabit the moon and found a way to do that without dying, then traditionally, wouldn't it be the people who colonized it who'd be the ones staking their claim? Not numb nuts like you, all the way down here, waving your meaningless certificate around and berating them with your teddy bear."

Jennifer narrowed her eyes, but Max was laughing so hard it was becoming increasingly infectious, and eventually she was laughing as much as he was. The truth was she completely agreed. At the time, she'd told her friends how sweet and meaningful she'd found Steve's present, but deep down she had wondered how anybody over the age of nineteen could have fallen for such a load of garbage.

Still, he could tone it down a bit.

"Screw you," she said to Max, elbowing him in the stomach while he was bent double laughing.

———

A few hours later, it was definitely time to leave. The police had been around to warn them to turn the music down, people were starting to look like they needed to be horizontal, and Jennifer was concerned that Steve was going to vomit everywhere if she didn't get him back to her place soon.

"Come on," she urged, trying to heave him up from where he was slumped on the bottom stair, his head leaning against the wall for support.

"Coming," he slurred, just about managing to stagger to his feet.

"Where's your sweatshirt?" asked Jennifer, who'd really had enough.

"Shit. My sweatshirt. It's upstairs. Let me go and get it."

"For God's sake," she tutted.

"Why are they so annoying?" asked Karen, who was also in the hall, shivering with tiredness, waiting for Pete to stop male bonding with someone so they could leave.

"I'm starting to feel like a bloody sheepdog," Jennifer said with despair.

"Exactly. I'm dying to get this bra off too. It's really digging in now."

Rather than wait in the hall any longer, Jennifer decided to pop back into the lounge to say good-bye to Max, where he was back on the decks. They'd been keeping each other entertained most of the night and she'd found him to be great company. Steve had been unable to leave the bedroom, and although she'd sat with him for a while, stroking his brow and reassuring him he'd feel better tomorrow, after a while, his uselessness had started to bore her. As a result, she'd ended up hanging out with Max for the majority of the party. He was really bright and funny and challenged her more than Steve ever did. It was quite refreshing.

"Hey, you," she said, giving the back of his arm a little tap.

"All right? You off then?"

"Yeah, so I thought I'd come say bye."

"Bye," he said.

It was sharp and to the point. Jennifer felt a sharp little stab of disappointment at his lackluster farewell. However, just as she was about to walk back into the hall, the unmistakable sound of the sweeping strings from the beginning of "Bittersweet Symphony" filled the room.

Her automatic response was to turn and walk back in. She was so happy to hear it. Back in the room, she pointed at Max to acknowledge his gesture and, touched that he'd remembered her favorite song, blew him a kiss.

In return, Max did something tiny that felt so intimate it was even more romantic than all the compliments she'd ever received from Steve and definitely beat all the extravagant gifts she'd gotten from Tim. He raised his right hand up, made a little fist, and patted his chest right where his heart was and gave her a look that told her all she needed to know.

Her stomach whooped with real delight and with that fluttery feeling of butterflies. *Oh God, what is happening here?*

Having managed to stay in control all evening, convincing

herself they were just getting along well as friends, she suddenly didn't know what to do.

Sensing her quandary, Max left his post and came over. "Can I give you my number?" he asked over the sound of the tune's beautiful violin chorus. "Actually, scrap that because you'll never ring and I'll spend the rest of my life staring at my phone or getting all excited when it does ring only to discover it's my mum, so can I have yours?"

She was so confused.

She had a boyfriend. A boyfriend who wanted to her to have his babies.

A boyfriend who was sweet and lovely to her. A boyfriend who was currently upstairs, staggering around, trying to find his sweatshirt.

But she was attracted to Max on so many levels, and he wasn't the only one who had picked up on how well they got along. They'd connected in a way that seemed quite rare.

"I don't think I can," she said eventually. "I'm sorry."

She turned to go, but giving it one last shot, Max said, "Well, at least let me take it so I can talk to you about DJing at your friend's birthday. In other words, let me take it in a professional capacity."

Jennifer smiled, her mind racing, knowing that what he'd done was provide her with an excuse. "Bittersweet Symphony" was still playing. She was feeling quite tipsy and was annoyed enough with Steve to reason that giving out her number hardly equated to being unfaithful. It would almost be rude not to if all he wanted to do was talk about playing at Jackie's birthday party...

Present Day

Tunnel number three was beckoning to her. Its light entranced her, beguiled her, and promised something completely different from the painful experience she'd had in tunnel number two. This would be her life with Steve. With sweet, good-looking, gentle Steve. Surely this life would have been more straightforward? The first two tunnels were completely sealed off. The third was waiting and shining brighter than ever.

TUNNEL NUMBER THREE
What Could Have Been—Steve

As soon as she reached the end of the tunnel, everything froze for a second, like a film that had been paused. In that moment, Jennifer found herself circling her twenty-five-year-old self. And it was the strangest thing, because of course she knew precisely what was supposed to happen next. She knew that here, at the party, she simply hadn't been able to resist the pull of Max and that she'd had a feeling deep within her gut that she would be insane to let him slip through her fingers. Furthermore, she knew that any second now, she would get her favorite lipstick out of her pocket and write her number down Max's arm, ruining the lipstick in the process.

But as everything started moving again, none of the above was what she saw, and Jennifer understood that this was the point where "what could have been" was about to become apparent. She could practically feel her younger self's indecision, could see her conflicted mind swirling, and knew it was the exact point when things could have very easily gone the other way.

And in this version, she said, "I can't. I just can't give you my number. I'm really sorry." Then she tore out of the room and into the hall, where Steve had managed to return with his sweatshirt, and left before anything else could happen.

TUNNEL NUMBER THREE
What Could Have Been—Steve

Jennifer and Steve sat in the car, both gazing fixedly ahead at the windshield. The weather matched their mood. It was a gray, bleak, miserable day.

She was the one to break the protracted silence first by sniffing loudly before rummaging in her handbag for a tissue.

"We'd better get going, hadn't we?" she suggested, voice tight. "You don't want to be late."

Steve sighed heavily and turned the key in the ignition.

While he was putting his seat belt on, Jennifer asked, "Is there really no way you can get out of going in? Surely if you said you'd been violently sick, they'd have to cope without you somehow, wouldn't they?"

Steve shook his head, his face despairing. "I'm not lying. No point letting them down."

"Okay."

"What about you? Where do you want me to drop you off?"

"Um…" Jennifer's brain felt utterly blank. She decided then that there was no way she could put herself through going into work feeling like this. "If you've got time, just drop me at home. I'll phone and say I'm going to work from there."

"Fine."

Twenty minutes later, Jennifer waved good-bye to Steve and shut the door behind her. She had thought she'd prefer to be with him, but as it turned out, it was a relief to be alone. Besides, Steve was a big boy, and if he thought going in to work was the best thing to do, she wasn't going to stop him. Perhaps he needed the distraction. There was so much to say to each other. But not yet. They needed time to absorb. Time to digest.

Unsure what to do with herself, she pottered aimlessly about the kitchen for a while. It was already pretty tidy, but she still wiped all the surfaces and unloaded the dishwasher, drawing comfort from the mundane tasks. Once there was nothing left to clean, she made herself a huge sandwich stuffed with cheese, ham, and mayonnaise, which she chewed morosely at the table.

Once she'd finished, despite feeling full, she decided to have a piece of cake as well. It would be comfort eating, but frankly, it was comfort she was after. She could always put her yoga DVD on later and have a workout. Not that she really felt like it. She was dealing with so many different emotions at the moment: relief, horror, grief, pity, and above all a huge sense of injustice. Her stomach churned at the mere thought of how they were going to cope.

"Hello-o," came the familiar voice of her mother-in-law. She heard the front door slam, destroying her solitude. She felt like screaming. "You home, Jen?"

"In here," she called back, glancing at the clock. Damn. For once, she'd thought she'd have the house to herself. She could have sworn June had said she wouldn't be back until after six.

"What are you doing back so early?" she asked, trying but failing not to sound accusatory. Not that June noticed.

"Sue had to leave. We were at the café having a nice éclair and a cup of tea when she got a text. There was some emergency," she said, bustling in, arms laden with shopping bags. "So her daughter-in-law needed her to pick up the little one from day care. Sue was only too happy to help. That little girl is the love of her life."

Jennifer smiled a rueful smile, used to these kinds of veiled digs.

"Anyway, have you set the DVR? Stevie boy's on in a minute, isn't he?"

"He is indeed," Jennifer said. "I was going to watch him with a piece of cake and a cup of tea."

"Good idea. Get the kettle on then, love. Though I'm not sure you want to be having any cake. You'll lose your figure before you've even gotten preggers," the older woman cackled.

Jennifer's jaw dropped. What a bitch. She hated living with her mother-in-law sometimes. She could still hardly believe she'd allowed it to happen. Yet it made perfect financial sense. She and Steve were saving a fortune each month between the two of them and had already built up a pretty impressive nest egg. Their wedding had been stupidly expensive, and if they wanted a chance of buying a place of their own, this was the only way. Still, at moments like this, she'd rather rent for the rest of her life.

As Jennifer and June sank into the settee, Jennifer felt a dull ache in her lower abdomen.

"I'm just going to the bathroom," she said to her mother-in-law.

"Well, hurry up," June said. "He'll be on in a minute."

Jennifer thought she would probably get over it if she missed a few minutes but didn't say anything. In the privacy of the bathroom, however, once she'd seen the inevitable telltale sign that once again there would be no baby that month, she wept. She may have been far cooler about getting pregnant when she hadn't wanted to be, but the minute she'd decided it was time to go for it, it had become her be-all and end-all. She and Steve had been mutually upset every month when their attempts kept failing. In fact, more recently, she was probably the one who'd been most despondent as every period had arrived with sickening punctuality.

Right, she needed to be strong. First, because she was not ready to discuss anything with June yet, and second, for Steve. She fumbled under the sink for a tampon, washed her hands, splashed her face with cold water, and went to join June in the lounge just as the title music for the Price Smash DIY bonanza was about to begin.

"Good afternoon and welcome," said the heavily made-up blond who Jennifer had met a few times and quite liked. Her off-screen persona wasn't nearly as brassy as her on-screen one. "You're watching the Price Smash channel with me, Debbie Pierman, and Steve Barrett, our resident DIY expert. Hiya, Steve."

"Hiya, Debbie."

"Now, over the next two hours, we're going to be bringing you some incredible deals on big-name brands from the world of home improvement, aren't we, Steve?"

"That's right, Debbie. Not only have I got a leaf shredder coming up for you, but also a power drill from Black & Decker and a pressure washer from Kärcher that we're selling at the lowest price it's ever been."

"He's so slick," June said.

Jennifer nodded and was relieved to see that on screen at least, Steve appeared to be okay.

Later that night, Jennifer lay in bed watching a movie, passing the time as she waited for Steve to come in.

It was past midnight when the door finally opened, and Steve tentatively peered around it, trying to detect whether his wife was asleep.

"Hey, you."

"Hey," Steve said, coming in and going to hang up his suit jacket.

"How are you, babe? Are you okay? How was work?"

Steve took off his tie and sank down heavily onto the end of the bed, narrowly missing Jennifer's foot under the duvet. He hung his head and massaged his temples with his thumb and finger for a while but didn't say anything.

Jennifer crawled across to where he was and stroked his back, at which point her husband turned around. Her heart ached as she realized he was crying. Clearly the ordeal of having to go to work and not only appear normal but talk about power tools for two hours straight, while looking as if he actually gave a shit, had caught up with him. As sobs racked through his tired, stressed body, his shoulders shuddered. It was so sad. Jennifer's heart contracted with pain.

"Oh, Steve," she said soothingly, her own tears finally catching up with her properly.

A while later, having let it all out, they lay in bed, facing each other. Eventually Jennifer decided to ask the question that had been on her mind all day.

"So what are we going to do? Do we adopt?"

Steve sniffed and raised a hand to stroke her hair. "I don't know. I don't think I want to. I just don't think it would be the same."

"But you're not ruling it out?" Jennifer asked in a whisper. She also had no idea at this stage how she really felt about anything.

"No, I'm not ruling it out," Steve said.

Jennifer leaned in to kiss him on the mouth, but Steve pulled away. "I'm sorry. I can't. Not tonight."

"I'm not trying to have sex," she said. "Just a kiss."

He pulled her in close and kissed her on the top of her head. It would do. It was closeness Jennifer was after.

"Everyone's going to laugh," he mumbled into her hair.

"What?" asked Jennifer, bemused and by this point utterly exhausted too.

"When it happens this way. Guys get laughed at."

Jennifer was moved to sit up. "I'm sorry," she said softly, resting on one elbow, "but if anybody thought this was an appropriate thing to laugh at someone for, then frankly they're not worth knowing."

Steve shrugged and gave her a strange look that took her a while to decipher.

"Oh my God. You want to say it's me, don't you?"

Unable to say it, Steve shut his eyes and turned over.

Jennifer started to cry again. It was all so bloody unfair. Why them? Eighteen months they'd been trying for a baby. Eighteen months they'd endured shagging on cue, not drinking, peeing on sticks, and taking supplements, interspersed with bitter disappointment every four weeks or so. All of that time, money, energy, and effort had been used up, only for Jennifer to find out that her fit, seemingly virile husband, who had desperately wanted to be a father ever since she could remember, was firing blanks and had as much hope of conceiving as he did of becoming president of the United States.

Steve turned around, his face full of despair. "I'm so sorry, Jen, and I will completely understand if you want to leave me."

"Oh, you silly sod." She sniffed. "No, I'm just a bit flabbergasted that you care so much about what other people are going to think. Personally, I think we don't tell them anything. It's none of their business, and I for one will just say that we've had trouble and that it's not going to happen. End of story. I don't think either of us need to go around filling people in on the details."

"Okay," said Steve, looking sheepish. "But also...if you do want to leave me and find someone who can give you children, I'd understand."

"Are you kidding me?"

"Kidding me," said Steve, his eyes full of bitter disappointment and despair. "Good choice of word."

327

Jennifer laughed through her tears. "Oh, come here, you."

She held him tight and could feel some of the tension slowly starting to seep out of his body. They clung to each other for hours, united in their grief for the family they would never have.

"I love you so much," said Steve. "I can't believe you're not going to leave me."

"If you even so much as suggest that again, I'll be livid," said Jennifer firmly.

It was three a.m. by this point. The digital clock by their bed displayed it in green. Sleep for either of them seemed unlikely.

"But…"

"But what?" asked Steve, his expression one of pure panic.

"Please don't totally rule out adoption. There are lots of children out there with nobody to love them."

"I know," said Steve. "I know. I love you, Jen."

"I love you too. And, Steve?"

"What?"

"I'm so, so sorry."

J ennifer was getting used to finding out things she never could have predicted. Poor Steve. Of all the people to be infertile. Sometimes life played cruel tricks on people.

Jennifer pondered the lives she could have had and the children she'd borne in each of them. If she'd been with Aidan, she'd have had endearing, sweet Nathan who she knew she would have loved fiercely. Then there were the four children she'd shared with Tim, each one lovely but very much a product of their upbringing and ultimately all to be damaged by losing their mother at such tender ages. Then she thought of Polly and Eadie, and with a stab of potent, maternal love, her insides lurched with a sense of urgency, another sign that reality was slowly taking hold. She needed to return to them. She needed to feel their small bodies in her arms. Her little girls. Her real, living, breathing little girls who thrilled and drained her every day in equal measure.

Jennifer could sense that her experience was beginning to draw to a close. Something was either going to change or end soon. But first she had one more journey to make. She hoped, really hoped, that everything was going to be okay. Not perfect. She would probably never expect that ever again because she no longer believed it even existed, but okay would be just fine. Okay would be nice.

TUNNEL NUMBER THREE
What Could Have Been—Steve

Jennifer got out of the shower and wrapped herself in a towel before removing her shower cap. She'd been to the hairdresser earlier and hadn't wanted to ruin her hair before the party. She was very pleased when it tumbled out and didn't look frizzy.

"You all right, gorgeous?" called Steve from the bedroom where he was getting ready. "You excited?"

"Very," replied Jennifer, applying a generous portion of moisturizer to her face. As the steam started to clear from the mirror, she regarded her reflection. Her hairdresser had done a great job. All the gray was covered, and she'd started having a few lowlights put in, which helped soften everything up a bit. She was confident that once she had her makeup on and was wearing her new dress, she'd look really nice, elegant, "good for her age." Although when your age was sixty, you were never going to exude a youthful bloom or the kind of sex appeal you had in your thirties and, to an extent, your forties. Still, one of the few advantages of getting older was that you tended to care less about things that weren't really important. Walking past a building site and not being whistled at wasn't the end of the world. These days, Jennifer was happy to blend into the background and be a spectator rather than the main event. As time marched on, she had an increasing amount of life to look back on and less future to worry about, which enabled her to enjoy the present more.

Her patience levels had improved too. Take the arrangements for today, for instance. The person she'd been in her twenties would have spent the last few weeks panicking that it wouldn't be perfect, that people would be bored/not come/hate the food. As it was, she'd taken all the planning in her stride, knowing that of course her guests would have a lovely time, and that if the caterers she'd hired to do a barbecue weren't very good, it wouldn't be the end of the world. *Perhaps people should put off getting married till they were in their sixties*, she mused idly. For if she had her time again, she certainly wouldn't waste all that energy fretting over tiny details no one cared about.

"Who's dressing your mother?" she asked, poking her head out of the en suite as the thought occurred to her.

"I'll do her," replied Steve, bending down from where he was sitting on the edge of the bed, levering his shoes on with a shoe horn. When it had come to what suit he was going to wear, he'd been spoiled for choice. As one of Price Smash's highest sellers, he was provided with a new suit every quarter. Over the years, he'd accrued so many that he regularly sold them on eBay.

"Thanks, love," said Jennifer, glad he was happy to do it. She wanted to quickly paint her nails, and getting June dressed would have meant she couldn't.

Three hours later, glass of champagne in hand, Steve stood under the gazebo that they'd had erected on the patio the day before. He clinked his glass.

"Hi, everyone. Can I have your attention, please? And don't worry, I'm not going to try to sell you anything."

The forty or so assembled guests laughed with varying degrees of gusto determined largely by how much they'd had to drink. Jennifer experienced a huge pang of thankfulness as she surveyed the scene. So far, the day had been blissful. The garden and house looked fantastic, the weather had held, the food was delicious, and everyone seemed to be enjoying themselves. To be surrounded by all their friends and family was a wonderful thing and so rare too. She loved the mix of generations present, and it was great watching her parents, who were both still in good health, catching up with some of her friends. She could tell they were having a wonderful time, as was June who, despite driving Jennifer mad on a daily basis, had earned her respect over the years. She may have been in a wheelchair for the last five of them, but today she was sitting upright in it, surveying proceedings almost regally. Of course she loved the fact that so many of Price Smash's presenters were currently standing in her back garden.

"Come on, you rowdy lot, listen up now," bellowed Steve, a huge grin on his face.

Jennifer felt a swell of pride. Steve had aged very well and was still incredibly good-looking. He hadn't let himself develop a paunch, unlike so many of her friends' husbands. She glanced at Pete, who was still tucking into the remains of the buffet. That must be at least his third plate, and the way his shirt was straining to contain his belly suggested that one small portion would have been plenty. Some people mocked Steve for being groomed and taking care of his personal appearance, which he did because of his job, but she had no complaints and knew his fitness levels contributed to his still-healthy libido.

As Steve waited for quiet, some people persisted in carrying on chattering, forcing others in the crowd to eventually do some very loud shushing until those who weren't listening finally shut up.

"Thank you. Right," began Steve. "So, as you know, we're all here because, as hard as it is to believe, Jennifer, my beautiful wife, has turned sixty years old today."

A few people cheered and someone at the back did a wolf whistle that made everyone laugh.

"Jen, I don't want you to go anywhere near that man," joked Steve, pointing at the culprit. "He simply can't be trusted. Take it from me; I know," he added, winking at his work colleague. "Jen, actually, where are you, babe?" he asked, scouting the crowd, one hand up to shield his eyes from the sun. "I want you up here next to me where we can all see you."

"I'm here." She waved from where she'd been attempting to keep a low profile by the buffet table.

Lucy, who was standing next to her, gave her an encouraging shove.

"Well, get up here," Steve insisted.

There was another loud cheer, at which point Jennifer realized she should have served the food earlier than she had. They were all three sheets to the wind. Grinning madly, she went up to join her husband.

"Come here, beautiful," said Steve, waiting for the cheers to subside. "Now, I just want to say in front of all our friends and family that I feel like I owe you my life, for you, Jennifer, are the kindest, most unselfish, gorgeous woman ever to have walked this earth."

Jennifer could feel herself welling up. Steve had never been anything but lovely to her. Sometimes he drove her mad, like when he insisted on watching his Price Smash shows as soon as he got home or when he refused to go to the theater or watch anything that wasn't certified a blockbuster, but over the years, he'd almost drowned her in love, partly due to the guilt he felt over not being able to give her a child. Still, she'd always tried to reassure him that she was happy with her lot. Having their own family simply wasn't meant to be. It had taken a while for true acceptance to arrive, but she'd gotten there in the end. Strangely she'd been experiencing fresh pangs of grief recently as she'd contemplated not just never being a mother, but also never being a grandmother. But she refused to dwell on it for too long, knowing that in so many other ways, her life was very blessed. There had been some advantages to not having children, ones they reminded each other of regularly. Over the years, she'd witnessed how the very tiring years when children first arrived had damaged some of her friends' relationships, turned marriages stale, and left people with no energy for anything until they resembled empty, tired husks. Without anyone else to focus their time, energy, and money on, she and Steve had been able to concentrate on themselves and what they wanted to do. There had been periods when unlimited time for each other had felt like a luxury they didn't want, but she simply had to look at the upside or die bitter and full of sadness, which would never do. Determined never to lead a life that felt even remotely empty, she and Steve had made every effort to achieve the opposite. As a result, they were one of the most well-traveled couples she knew, having toured around the continents of Asia, Africa, and South America. They'd climbed the Himalayas, raised £110,000 for their charity, and, thanks to Steve's ever-increasing salary at Price Smash and not having to shell out on dependents, had never had to worry about money to fund all these ventures. They entertained constantly, played golf, did yoga, and took classes. Their lives were full to the brim—maybe different from the ones they perhaps would have had given the choice, but a perfect example of making the most of your lot.

"Not only does she look after me," continued Steve, "but she's always helped take care of my old mum, the duchess, June. All right, Mum! In fact, we should all raise a glass to my mum because without her, shopping channels would probably go bankrupt. If you don't believe me, take a look at how many figurines are crammed into our cabinets. And in case you were wondering, four combination ovens for a three-person household is three too many, but there's no telling her, is there, Jen?"

Laughing, Jennifer shook her head in agreement and gave June a little wink. June, in turn, cackled away, adoring being the center of attention.

"So here's to June," instructed Steve, and there was a long pause as everyone raised and then drank from their glasses. "To June."

"And watch out, Kevin Jameson," Steve said, pointing toward another long-serving Price Smash presenter. "She's got her eye on you." This got a raucous laugh from the crowd.

"Right, lastly I'd like to thank Jen's parents as well. Lesley and Nigel, you've been a constant support to us both over the years. Nigel, we still can't believe you ran a half marathon only twenty years ago for our charity. I'm not sure we'd want to see you attempt it now, but what an achievement that was, mate. I'll never forget it. And also, Jennifer's gang of friends. Where are you girls? That's Esther, Karen, and Lucy, who between them have given the two of us five godchildren in total. We may not have been blessed enough to have our own, but they've made sure that we've had lots of wonderful little people to spoil at Christmas. Of course they're all grown up now and it's so lovely that three out of the five could be here today. We really do love them as our own, don't we, Jen?"

She nodded, a huge lump in her throat and tears threatening to ruin her eye makeup.

"You've all enriched our lives. Well, apart from the time Suzy stayed over and wet the bed… Sorry, Suzy! You were only four. It's all right; we know you wouldn't do it now. Although the way I'm drinking today…I might."

Another huge laugh.

"Anyway, on a serious note, you've really all meant the world to us."

By this point, Jennifer had lost it. She frantically tried to stem her happy tears with a hanky.

Steve leaned in and gave his wife a kiss on the forehead. "My darling Jen, you're one in a million, and if we could please now all raise our glasses to my wonderful wife. To Jennifer. Happy birthday, babe."

"To Jennifer. Happy birthday," everyone said in unison.

———

Much later, Jennifer was slumped on the sofa with her best friend. The rest of the guests had left, either having been seen into cabs or, in a couple of cases, after having arguments about who'd drunk less and swerving off into the night. Jennifer hadn't wanted Karen to leave, so she and Pete and their daughter Suzy decided to stay over. Suzy, Pete, and June had all hit the sack, leaving Jennifer and Karen to have a good gossip and to laugh from time to time at Steve, who was snoring loudly, passed out in the armchair.

"Bless him, he's wiped out. Ah, you're a lucky girl, you know," said Karen, patting her friend's wrist.

"I do know," said Jennifer, and it was the greatest feeling in the world to really mean it.

"Not many people can say their husband adores them like he adores you."

"Pete adores you," said Jennifer.

Karen gave her an arch look and raised one eyebrow. "I'd say tolerates, more like."

"No. Don't be silly."

"Oh, we're all right," said Karen. "We're fine and I'm very fond of him, even though I do wish he'd take a leaf out of Steve's book and do a bit of bloody exercise. These days it's like going to bed with a big hairy buffalo."

Jennifer snorted.

"It is! When he rolls on top for a quickie, I feel like I'm getting crushed," she complained.

"Yeah, well, I think you two are great and you've got lovely Suzy," said Jennifer, the drink making her sound more wistful than she would ordinarily allow herself to be.

"I know, love," said Karen, "although you know she sees you as her second mum."

Jennifer squeezed her hand. "Right, you, come on. Time for bed. Now we're old crones and eligible for our senior discounts, we need all the sleep we can get."

"We do," said Karen, heaving herself reluctantly from the sofa. "Love you, Jen."

"Love you too," said Jennifer, going over to attempt to wake up Steve so she could get him up to bed, where they would both sleep very soundly.

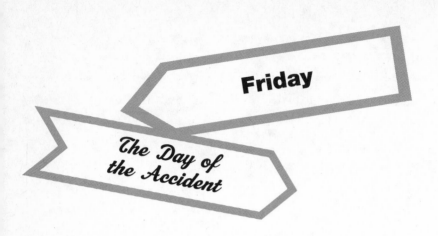

Friday

*The Day of
the Accident*

Jennifer was ready, which had taken a huge effort. Max had somehow managed to mess up the entire house during his day off. When Jennifer had returned home from her therapy session, she'd walked in to find the girls' bedrooms in a complete state. Every toy had been pulled out in the living room, and nothing had been cleared up from lunch. Still, she'd managed not to say anything. The kids were having a lovely time playing with their father, and despite her broken arm and how uncomfortable her cast was, Eadie was in good spirits, and that was the main thing.

Later, the minute Max left the house to go to the gym, it meant Jennifer only had a small window of time to get everything ready for her night of seduction. In order to have the children fed, bathed, and in bed, the house tidy, the dinner on, herself looking attractive and wearing sexy underwear underneath her clothes, she'd had to run around like a woman possessed.

She was finally ready but slightly concerned she'd be too exhausted for the sex she was making all this effort for.

Nevertheless, as she crept out of her bedroom, she felt a

flush of excitement as her satin G-string rode up her bum. How anyone could wear these for nonsexual pursuits, she had no idea, but she was happy to suffer it for tonight. She went to check on the girls. By some miracle, it seemed they were both actually asleep. Yes!

Then, just at that second, Eadie, who was still very much awake, rather ruined the moment by calling from her bed, "Muuuummy."

Damn, Jennifer cursed inwardly. She should have known it was too good to be true.

She tiptoed into her bedroom. "What is it?" she asked, slightly impatient. She and Max so desperately needed to have a good night together, she'd worked herself up into a bit of a state. "Come on now," she said to her daughter. "It's time to go to sleep."

"I'm not tired, though."

"Yes, you are," insisted Jennifer, halfway out the door again. She wanted to make a nice mushroom sauce to pour over the steak.

"What time is it?" asked Eadie, refusing to play ball and sitting up and looking around as perky as a meerkat, waving her plaster cast about.

"Ten o'clock," lied Jennifer.

"Ten o'clock?"

"Yes, it's very, very late."

Eadie didn't look convinced. She wasn't stupid. Apart from anything else, it didn't feel like ten o'clock, probably because it was only quarter to eight.

And then they both heard Max's key in the door.

"Daddy!"

"Okay, that is Dad and I'm sure he'll come up quickly to say night night, but then we're going to have some grown-up time, so I want you to go to bed like a good girl. If you go to sleep nice and quickly, I'll buy you some sweets tomorrow."

"Can I have a magazine too?" asked Eadie, spotting an opportunity.

"Eadie," hissed Jennifer, her patience starting to wear thin. "Don't you blackmail me. I'm getting cross now. Just *go to bed*."

Jennifer left the room and went downstairs to see Max.

"Hello," she said. "How are you?"

"Good. I really went hard today. Legs are going to kill tomorrow. I need a shower. Are the girls already in bed?"

"Yes, well, Polly is. Eadie's still awake. In fact, can you quickly say good night to her? Then, with a bit of luck, we can have our dinner in peace."

"Mmm, smells lovely. What are we having?"

"Steak, salad, baked potatoes with sour cream, and corn on the cob."

"Oh wow," said Max. "Fantastic. I could eat a horse."

"Well, you'll need to leave some room for me," said Jennifer in an attempt to get the whole sex thing rolling. Her comment was rather lost, however, because Max was looking straight past her.

"Hello, Eadie Beadie," he said, managing to ignore what Jennifer had said and gazing up at his daughter, who had appeared at the top of the stairs, arm aloft. She looked like a tiny angel.

"What are you doing?" spluttered Jennifer. "You promised Mummy you'd stay in bed."

"All right," said Max. "Calm down. She's not doing anything. It's not even eight yet anyway."

"See," said Eadie triumphantly.

Jennifer gave up. Leaving them to it, she took a deep breath and headed to the kitchen to make her sauce.

By the time Max finally appeared, showered and wearing a T-shirt and checked pajama bottoms, dinner was on the table.

"Ooh, this looks amazing," said Max appreciatively. "A bit of red meat's just what I fancy."

"Me too," joked Jennifer, injecting tons of innuendo into her voice and wondering if she should flash Max a bit of stocking so he'd get the hint. "Is Eadie asleep?"

"What do you think?"

Jennifer groaned. "Do you think she wants us to never have sex again for the rest of our lives or something? It's like she knows."

"It doesn't matter," said Max, tucking in. "She'll be asleep soon enough, so let's just enjoy our dinner, take our time, savor it, and by the time we're done and have had another glass of wine, she'll be out like a light and we can go upstairs and have sex."

"Okay," said Jennifer, feeling calmer. Once they'd gotten tonight out of the way, she was going to ensure they got back into a routine of having sex far more regularly. She was nervous, having left it this long. Not in an exciting, butterflies-in-the-stomach type of way either. Instead, it had reached the point where having sex with her husband felt like some sort of barrier she had to cross. She knew this was a slippery slope and was terrified of starting to view Max as her best friend or housemate. She needed him to want to be physically intimate with her and vice versa. Simply put, occasionally having your husband's penis inserted into you was what marked your relationship out as special and different from the ones you had with everyone else, wasn't it? She picked up her wineglass and drained it.

"So anyway, how was therapy?" inquired Max. "Helpful?"

Jennifer appreciated him making the effort to ask. She was well aware that he really thought it was a load of old hokum.

"It was fine," she said. "In fact, it was good."

"Good," said Max, as if that was all sorted.

"I mean, there's a long way to go but…you know…I felt like I really got something out of it today."

"Eadie, what are you doing down here, sweetheart?" asked Max when their daughter suddenly appeared at the door.

Jennifer glared at her daughter.

"I can't sleep. My arm's itchy."

Jennifer stopped glaring, felt guilty, and rearranged her face into one of concern instead. "Hang on. I'll go find the itch cream."

An hour later, Eadie was finally asleep, and Jennifer and Max were both stuffed with food and had polished off a bottle and a half of red wine between them. Jennifer's face was hot and she could feel her tongue furring up already.

None of this was particularly conducive to sex but she didn't care.

"Right, shall we go up then?" she suggested almost briskly. At that point, she'd have herded him up the stairs if that was what it took. Anything to get the deed bloody well done.

"Yes," said Max. "Let me check in with Judith first, though. Make sure everything was okay today, what with me being out of the office."

"Why don't you do that after?" asked Jennifer, trying not to sound intensely irritated.

"Because I'd rather get it out of the way," said Max, "and also because I don't want to disturb her too late."

Jennifer knew she was quite drunk, because she felt like sticking her tongue out and giving the whole notion of him calling Judith the finger. Still, she found some restraint from somewhere.

"Okay, well, be quick, won't you?" she said, walking as sexily as she could out of the room. "I'll be waiting upstairs for you…although, I need to take some water up. That wine's made my mouth so dry."

When did life get so unspontaneous? she thought, scuttling back to the tap.

Twenty minutes later, Jennifer was starting to get deeply pissed off. She'd been lying wantonly on the bed in her temptress underwear, waiting for Max for what felt like ages. As soon as she'd gotten upstairs, the first thing she'd done was to check that the girls were asleep. Upon finding out they were, she'd stripped out of her clothes, leaving on only her new bra, stockings, garter belt, and G-string. She'd put on her highest pair of stilettos, glugged down half a pint of water, brushed her teeth, and then arranged herself on the bed and waited, all the while thinking she was pretty sure that there had once been a time when she and Max had barely been able to make it up the stairs, so eager were they to have sex with each other. Making her wait like this was very depressing and didn't exactly make her feel attractive. It was almost like he'd be doing her a favor or something. As if having intercourse would be his final chore of the day. I mean, why of all times did he have to pick now to phone bloody Judith? He'd had all day to do it. If he'd been truly looking forward to a night of passion like she had, wouldn't he have called Judith earlier and gotten it out of the way?

From downstairs, the sound of Max's phone conversation floated upward to the landing. It was like pouring gas on the flames of her suspicion. He sounded so jovial, so alive, and like he was making every effort to be charming and engaging. This wasn't helping her mood at all, and if he laughed that nauseating laugh again, she'd be tempted to take off one of her shoes and stab him in the eye with the heel.

Another ten minutes and Jennifer was prickling with embarrassment. She felt so stupid. She felt unloved, unbelievably jealous, rejected, and because she was trying so hard not to cry, all these emotions were transforming into fury. How could he do this to her? She had given up sprawling on the bed and had camped out on the landing, where she was squatting on the floor, head stuck between the banisters. That way, she could hear exactly what was being said. Max and Judith's conversation was all fairly innocuous but also seemed largely unrelated to work. Instead, they were gossiping and sharing private jokes, which only confirmed that this was a chat that they definitely didn't need to be having now. The rawness of what she was feeling, combined with how much wine she'd drunk, meant that by the time he did finally terminate the call, the only thing she was ready for was a fight.

"How could you?" she asked a surprised Max as he finally rounded the top of the stairs to find her crouching on the landing, dressed like a prostitute.

"What are you doing? What are you wearing?"

"I'm wearing what I thought you might possibly find sexy

enough to want to fuck me in. Only clearly I was wrong. Why did you have to talk to that stupid cow for so long? You knew I was waiting for you up here. It's so rude," she cried, hot jealousy welling up inside her, like a volcano about to erupt.

"Calm down," said Max, only fueling the fire further. "I told you I had to phone her because I took the day off today to help you. I'm sorry it went on for a bit, but you know what Judith's like once she gets going."

"Oh, and I suppose you were physically unable to say something like 'I need to keep this quick because I'm in the middle of something.' Or, 'I'm sorry, Judith. I've got to go because I haven't had sex with my wife for so long she doesn't know if I even love her anymore.' Or 'I must dash. My wife's dressed like a slut, only I've gotten to the point in life where I don't even care because I'd rather be talking to you.'" Jennifer was so upset that she knew she was looking deranged but was unable to stop herself. She just needed to hear him say sorry.

"You're being ridiculous," Max thundered.

Jennifer recoiled because of course she *felt* ridiculous. There wasn't any part of her that wanted this to be happening. This was supposed to be their evening for a bit of love and romance. Instead, she was dressed in this getup that she'd hoped he'd find sexy but that was making her feel like a cheap hooker, and she felt totally embarrassed. Worse still, Judith had impinged on their lives once again. She couldn't stand it.

"You're so out of order," she cried.

"Oh, for fuck's sake, you're being so dramatic. Just because you've had a couple of glasses of wine, you act like an idiot."

"Fuck you," screamed Jennifer.

"Shh, keep your voice down. You'll wake the girls."

Jennifer was trembling with rage and hurt. She took a sharp inhalation of breath in an attempt to calm herself. Max had never taken kindly to histrionics. Plus she didn't want to wake the children.

"Look, I'm sorry I've gotten myself into this state," she said, happy to acknowledge that she was acting like a crazy woman but determined to make him understand why. "I just want you to try to get how I feel. I've made loads of effort for tonight and I had hoped you might like what I was wearing. I wanted you to fancy me and for us to feel like we used to when we had sex. I wanted us to be close."

"You look great," said Max unconvincingly.

"But instead," Jennifer continued, smearing mascara across her face, "it's just another time that has been dominated by Judith, who you know I feel insecure about as it is."

Max traipsed wearily from the landing into their room where he sunk onto their bed, shook his head, and rubbed his face with his hands. "I'm too tired for this, Jen. I just want to go to bed."

Following him in, she felt sick. His lack of effort to make things better made her stomach turn. She felt terrified, yet intuition was telling her to keep digging. Why should she let him get away with this shitty treatment? Why was she constantly apologizing? It wasn't fair. It wasn't *all* her fault and she was fed up with being made to feel like it was.

"I think you have feelings for her. Do you?"

"Oh, Christ," Max said angrily.

"I mean it, Max. I want to know. Do you have feelings for Judith? Because I think you might. I think that's why you hardly look at me these days. I know you think I'm a mad, crazy cow, but you're the one who keeps making me feel like that. You used to make me feel beautiful and loved and happy, and now I'm miserable all the time and feel like I'm constantly waiting for you to announce something."

Max looked pained and refused to even glance in her direction, staring into the distance instead.

"I don't have feelings for her," he said quietly.

"Swear on the girl's lives," said Jennifer so menacingly that Max actually gulped.

And then he did something that practically cracked her heart in two. He finally found it in himself to look at her briefly but then couldn't hold her gaze or say what she so desperately needed him to say. He looked away again and sighed. A heavy, sad, terrible sigh that felt like such a huge betrayal that Jennifer thought she might have a panic attack. Her whole body went cold and clammy. She wondered if she was going to be sick or faint.

"You'd better tell me everything," she said. "And I mean *everything*."

Even as she was saying this, she was wondering if this was the end of her marriage. It was so surreal. Could this be the end of life as she knew it? She willed Max with every cell in her body to make it all go away. To look at her in such a way that she would know he was playing with her, trying to be funny. Only that could make this all okay. But he didn't.

Instead, looking truly wretched, he said, "Jen, I swear, there's nothing to tell. Nothing has actually happened and that's the God's honest truth…"

"But…"

"But nothing," he repeated, getting up and coming over to her.

"Don't lie to me," she warned him, and as he reached over to touch her arm, her entire body flinched, a reflex action. *This* was harming her. The pain she was experiencing was on a physical level. Again she wished fervently she wasn't dressed as she was, and yet it hardly mattered.

"Tell me."

"There's nothing to tell."

"But you'd like there to be."

Max gazed at her, his expression bleak, his eyes searching hers as if he hoped to find an answer through her. And then he shrugged, almost imperceptibly, and that was all she needed to know.

"Have you had sex with her?"

"No…"

"But?"

"I haven't…actually slept with her."

Jennifer froze, and for a fraction of a second, time seemed to stand still.

"So what have you done?" she asked eventually.

Max shrugged again, clearly unable to speak the words.

"Tell me…now."

"It was a mistake. I don't know… I don't want to hurt you. It was nothing really."

"Nothing?" Jennifer was incredulous.

"Not nothing exactly, but it meant nothing and like I said, we didn't actually have sex."

She tried to absorb what he was saying, knowing the full impact would be hitting her any second. Did he expect her to be grateful that they hadn't gone the whole way? Because if so, she wasn't. It was almost worse. The longing he'd obviously been experiencing, the fumbling, the kissing. She could imagine it all and felt sick and cold with rage. For another second or two, she didn't know what to do.

And then she ran. Stopping only to discard her heels, she hurtled out of the room and practically threw herself down the stairs in a bid to flee. Downstairs in the hall, she desperately searched for something to put on her feet that didn't come with a six-inch heel. An old pair of disgusting gardening shoes her mother had left the last time she'd been around would do. They were far too big, but Jennifer didn't care; she just needed to be away, to escape from what was happening. She couldn't breathe. She'd go to Karen's. That's what she'd do. She wouldn't stop to think until she got there. Wouldn't stop to contemplate what this all meant until she was safe with her friend. Karen was only ten minutes away. That's where she'd go.

When Max came thundering down the stairs after her, she only increased her efforts to get away, but he tried to block her exit by standing in front of the door.

"What are you doing? You can't go out of the house dressed like that," he said, his face frantic. "Jen, stay so we can talk. You've got it all wrong anyway."

"Oh, I don't think so," she cried. "In fact, the only thing I've gotten wrong is putting up with your bullshit for this long. Now get out of my way."

"Look, calm down," tried Max again, using the same tone he often used on the kids. "You can't go out dressed like that."

"Fuck off," she spat, grabbing a coat from the hooks in the hall and shoving it on. She grabbed her phone from the hall stand so she could call Karen and then, with every bit of strength in her body, shoved Max out of the way so that she could wrench open the door. Once free, she sprinted down the road as fast as her oversize shoes would allow.

———

Max didn't know what to do. He suspected she'd be going to Karen's or to start a new job as a pole dancer. Either or. Part of him thought it was probably for the best that she took some time out to calm down. Another part of him wanted to run after her, grab her, hold her, and tell her it was all going to be okay. He was hit by a monumental urge to simply say sorry. How had they gotten here? How had he let things get to this point? She was right, of course. Over the last few months, she'd picked up on his absence. Not a physical absence, but his mind had been elsewhere, and rather than admit it, he'd let her think she was the one to blame. It was ridiculous, and in that second, Max was only grateful he hadn't gone the whole way with Judith. Though what he didn't want to examine too much was that this was more down to circumstances than his own restraint. Tonight he'd seen the hurt and grief an affair would have caused, and it had been the sharp reminder he'd needed that he didn't want to lose his wife. He loved her. He wanted to throttle her sometimes, and Judith's attentions had been flattering, but from this moment forward, he needed to sort himself out. It had all spun out of control.

He felt totally drained. Making sure the door was unlocked, he walked out and stood at the gate where he called down the road. "Jen, what the hell do you think you're doing? Come back. For goodness' sake, you've made your point."

She didn't so much as look back, and eventually she was a pinprick at the bottom of the road. The boring bloke from number forty-two who'd witnessed everything and been rubbernecking quite spectacularly gave him a judgmental look. Max returned it with a glowering frown.

Right, there was nothing he could do. He'd leave it for a bit, let her cool off, and then send her a text telling her he loved her and that he was the biggest idiot on the planet. With that thought, Max was just about to head back indoors when he heard the ungodly sound of screeching tires, a sickening crunch, and a scream. From what he could make out, the sound had come from the end of the street. His heart skipped a beat, and the fear Max experienced in that second was white and petrifying. And then he did something he hadn't done since he was in grade school. He prayed.

Present Day

One of Jennifer's eyes, her left one, slowly opened. She couldn't focus on anything specific. As light flooded in, it took a while for her retinas to adjust. They had become so accustomed to a vista of black. Everything was very hazy, very blurry, and before her vision had had a chance to fine-tune itself, the eye snapped shut again.

Half an hour later, the same eye opened once more and then the second one fluttered open as well. But this time Max was in the room, having just returned from the cafeteria, where he'd bought himself a doughnut and a cup of tea.

"Jen!" he cried. The sound of his voice penetrated through to Jennifer, who knew he was talking to her. She knew Max was there. Where was *there*, though? That bit was all a bit foggy, and she was pretty sure that although she'd like to ask him, she wouldn't be able to. Articulating anything would be impossible at the moment. She wouldn't know how to.

An hour or two later, and Jennifer's brain and body were making huge leaps back into the real world. The doctors had swarmed around her as soon as Max had raised the alarm. Blood had been taken to check levels of serum glucose, calcium, sodium, potassium, magnesium, phosphate, urea, and creatinine. Then, as Max had known they would, they'd wheeled his wife off to perform yet another MRI.

A while later, the results were in. As far as they could tell, her brain was showing no signs of permanent damage, although it would be a long time before they could confirm it. After five long weeks, Jennifer was coming out of her coma.

Max couldn't believe it. What he had prayed for each day was happening. It felt as close to a miracle as anything he'd ever experienced.

For the next couple of days, Jennifer woke up for short bursts and would sometimes be profoundly confused and at other times relatively lucid.

The moment when she recognized her husband and was finally able to speak was the best of all.

"Hey, you," he said, stroking her hand gently with one finger. She was looking right at him and not as though he was a stranger as she had been previously.

"Hey," she said. "What's happened?"

"You were in an accident, Jen. You got hit by a car. You've been asleep for weeks. We didn't know..." Max stopped, took a gulp, and composed himself.

"Eadie and Polly?"

At this, Max was almost overwhelmed by relief and happiness, and it took every bit of his willpower not to break down. "They're fine, Jen. They're absolutely fine. I don't think either of them ever doubted they'd be seeing you again. I think they reckon you're Sleeping Beauty."

That was more than enough for her first proper conversation, and as the doctor urged Max to let his wife rest, Jennifer fell into a deep sleep.

"Is she okay?" Max asked the doctor when he came for his rounds. "She hasn't gone into a coma again, has she?"

"No," the doctor replied. "Don't worry; your wife is doing phenomenally well. Recovery usually occurs very gradually, though, and Jennifer will take a while to acquire the ability to respond for any decent length of time. However, I think her outlook is extremely positive. But be prepared for your wife to still appear confused at times and try not to worry if she does. It's totally normal after somebody has been in such a deep coma."

It was a good thing the doctor had warned him about this, because in the early hours of the morning, Jennifer started muttering in her sleep. Max, who had been sleeping fitfully on the pullout bed (which by this point in time he officially hated and viewed as an instrument of torture), sat bolt upright. "Jen?" he whispered, but when it became clear that she was only sleep-talking, he got up and went over to see what she was saying…

The next day, Karen brought the girls to the hospital in the afternoon during visiting hours. They'd all decided that with so much less machinery around her, it was time for them to finally see their mother again.

It couldn't have gone better. The timing was great. Jennifer was awake and clearly aware of their presence. She was so happy to see them. Just the fact that she recognized them was another incredibly encouraging sign that she was on the road to a full recovery. Eadie and Polly had been lectured at length about not wearing their mother out and were rising to the occasion beautifully, being quiet and good as gold.

Until at one point they asked if they could sing a song to her. "What song?" asked Karen.

"'Gangnam Style'?" suggested Eadie.

"No, that's probably not the best idea," her godmother vetoed. "Why don't you sing Mummy a lovely lullaby instead? 'Rock-a-Bye Baby' or something?"

The girls obeyed, and as they started to sing, Karen took the opportunity to take Max to one side and ask, "How are you holding up?"

"Good," said Max, an emotional wreck. "I can't believe this is all going to end okay."

"I know. Thank God."

"Karen?"

"Yes?"

"I'm so sorry, you know. I never wanted this to happen, and I can tell you now that I will spend the rest of my life making sure she's happy."

"I know you will," said Karen sadly. "And it's fine. You really don't need to apologize to me. Besides, now you can apologize to Jen herself."

Max looked sheepish. It was obvious Jennifer had confided in her friend before the accident that things weren't great. Not that Karen would know the worst, of course. He had no idea how much Jennifer herself would remember either. The suspense was nothing short of horrendous.

"Listen," reassured Karen, "I understand and I don't judge

anyone else's relationships. After all, you get to our stage and learn that life isn't black and white like you think it is when you're young. It's bloody gray."

"Fifty shades?"

"Ha ha," said Karen. "And no, more like one thousand shades of gray, but it's all going to be fine. It'll all work itself out now that Jen's on the mend. I know it will."

"Thanks," said Max. "For everything. For all your help with the girls, everything."

"You're very welcome," said Karen.

"Oh, and by the way," said Max. "I was thinking of making a donation to the hospital."

"Oh, nice idea."

"I'm buying them a single bed with a really comfortable mattress so that the next poor bastard who ends up staying in here might have a chance of actually getting some sleep."

"Good one. Now, Max, do you think we should stop Eadie and Polly singing? Otherwise, I'm worried Jennifer might wish she was back in a coma."

"Oh God yes," agreed Max, jolting back to the present and realizing how right she was. The caterwauling was pretty terrible, and Jennifer was looking glassy-eyed, dazed, and a bit exhausted. "And excellent sick joke, by the way. Jen would approve."

"Thanks," said Karen.

Epilogue

Six Months Later

Karen, Pete, Suzy, and Jennifer's parents were on their way over for Sunday lunch. It was early December and the kind of day they wouldn't go out in unless they absolutely had to or unless someone was cooking a lovely leg of lamb and an apple crumble. The house was full of the smell of cooking, the girls were playing peacefully in the front room with their Play-Doh, and Max was working out what sort of wine they should have with lunch and generally pottering about the kitchen, pretending to be helpful. From the outside looking in, the scene was one of domestic bliss. Which is precisely why no one should ever make assumptions about what's going on in anyone's household other than their own.

Jennifer may have looked content, but as she peeled and chopped carrots, what she was wondering was whether anybody would be able to hear her if she were to turn the volume on her iPod right up, go into the utility room, and scream at the top of her lungs.

As she plunged the carrots into boiling water, Max came into the kitchen.

"Have you thought about what I said?"

"Yes." She sighed. "And I'm still thinking about it."

"What's there to think about?" Max snapped. "You're my wife and you need to come back into the marital bed and that's that. Enough is enough."

"I really don't think this is the right time to be discussing this," replied Jennifer, who didn't want to start fighting. She also didn't want to be bullied into doing anything she didn't feel ready for. Physical contact between them still made her feel tense, and the thought of sleeping in the marital bed repelled her. "Now let me get lunch on the table, will you?"

"Fine," said Max, looking fed up and worried. He bent down to open the oven to check on the meat.

"This needs to rest," she said, swatting away clouds of steam with a dish towel when the doorbell rang.

Max looked so worried and full of despair that, for a brief second, Jennifer thought about giving him a hug, telling him it would be okay, and promising that she would try sleeping in their bed soon. But then he said, "We'll talk about it later then, but I'm warning you that if we carry on at this rate, you might find that I'm the one packing a bag. My patience has pretty much run out with you being such a drama queen."

And just like that, they were back to square one. It was how it had been for months. Three steps forward, two steps back. The doorbell rang for the second time so the two of them had no choice but to rearrange their expressions so no one would have a clue what was really transpiring between them.

Lunch was a raucous, slightly chaotic affair. Jennifer had to eat her meal one-handed because Eadie insisted on sitting on her lap. Ever since the accident, she'd demanded constant affection. Not that Jennifer minded in the least. She couldn't get enough of her children either. Their physical presence was a comfort, especially as she was unable to shake off the feeling she'd had for months now that she was standing on the edge of a cliff, trying to decide whether to jump.

After the meal, people slunk away from the table to go sit in the living room until finally Karen and Jennifer were the only ones left. As they halfheartedly cleared the table and wholeheartedly picked at cheese and drank wine, Karen decided to tackle something she'd been meaning to bring up for ages.

"How much has Max told you about when you were in the coma?"

"Not a lot," said Jennifer, grabbing a clean dish towel from the drawer. "He's mainly filled me in on how uncomfortable his bed was. Why?"

"Okay," said Karen, idly wiping a drip of custard from the side of a jug with her finger before sucking it off. "It's just there was one night, you had a seizure. I was there."

"Oh God, you poor thing. I don't think I knew that. That must have been horrific."

"Wasn't the best night of my life," admitted Karen drily. "But anyway, the point is, you said a word out loud."

"Did I? Was it 'makeup bag'?"

"That's two." Karen snorted a laugh.

"'Vodka'?"

"No, you idiot. You said 'Joe.'"

Jennifer immediately stopped grinning. "Are you serious?"

"Yes. Jen, I've got to ask. Have you met someone? Because things between you and Max seem very strained."

"No," Jennifer said, her arms suddenly slack in the sink, which was full of dirty dishes and soapy suds. She turned to look at Karen, weighing whether to say anything. "Okay, I need to tell you something, but it's probably going to sound really odd…"

"Go on," said Karen, looking worried.

"Since the accident, I've had this strange feeling at times that my brain knows things but can't tell me what they are exactly."

"Like what?"

Jennifer struggled to put it into words. "I'm not sure. Just this feeling that I'm really lucky to have you in my life, for instance, and like…I don't know…like I've lost things. Sometimes when I look at the kids, I get this huge pang of emotion, and then the other day, Max told me I'd said the name Joe and it was the strangest feeling. I wanted to burst into tears with frustration because I couldn't grasp what my brain was trying to tell me. I don't know. I'm probably going crazy."

She looked so unsettled that Karen got up to give her a hug. "Come here, you."

Jennifer dried her hands and took her up on her offer, at which point she started to sob quietly into her friend's shoulder.

After a time, Karen held her at arm's length. "Jen, what the hell is going on? Tell me."

"I need to know I can trust you," said Jennifer, wiping away her tears.

"Of course you can. Where are you going?" asked Karen, utterly bemused.

A minute or so later, Jennifer returned with her laptop. Making sure the kitchen door was firmly shut, she placed it on the island.

"Here," she said, and her expression was so odd Karen couldn't for the life of her imagine what she was about to be shown.

It was a page from reUNIon. Staring back at her was a picture of a man she didn't recognize. A man named Joe. His name was listed alongside his photo in the usual reUNIon format, and at the top of the page, it said that he was a "friend" of Tim Purcell's.

"Since when are you friends with Tim Purcell on reUNIon?" asked Karen, astounded.

"Since the other week when I sent him a request," replied Jennifer. "So I could look at his contacts. Look at the name."

"I know," she replied. "Joe. But who is he?"

Jennifer shrugged. "I don't know."

Karen was so confused.

"I know this probably sounds mad, but I think I once knew this man, or that I'm supposed to. I don't know. Maybe I'm even supposed to find him. Maybe the accident happened for a reason."

"Jen, listen to me. You've had a terrible, terrible time of it, but I'm not going to patronize you by pretending any of this makes sense. It's crazy talk, no doubt brought on by the extreme bump to the head you suffered. So you said the name Joe? Big deal. That doesn't mean to say that just because someone you once knew knows a Joe that he's got anything to do with you."

Jennifer wasn't convinced. Why had she felt such a strong compulsion to reach out to people from her past in order to search for someone or something? And if this man was nothing to her, then why did her whole body react so strongly every time she looked at that picture? It was a face she didn't know, yet it was so familiar. Of course, she was aware that none of this made any sense. It was why she'd avoided telling anyone. Maybe she was going mad. If she didn't understand what was happening to her, how could she expect anyone else to?

"Jen, if you want to save your marriage, you need to be concentrating on Max. Not some man you've never even met."

"But I don't think I can forgive him," said Jennifer, eyes full of tears. "I wish I could, because I look at the girls and this house... Then I think about the life we have, the friends, and how this is my family. But I'm just not sure I can do it anymore. Part of me hates him. I nearly died, Karen."

"I know, but you didn't. You're here."

"Exactly, so I'm determined to make the absolute most of whatever I have left. I don't want to do anything because I think I should or because it's perceived as the right thing to do if it doesn't feel right. One day, the girls will be grown up and have lives of their own, and I know it would be really hard in many ways, but if I was on my own, I would cope. I would find a way to make it work."

Karen spoke firmly. "Max is sorry, isn't he? And I'm sure he'll never look at another woman as long as he lives. Isn't he entitled to one mistake? He didn't even sleep with her."

"So he keeps saying." She sighed, her expression anguished. "But that's not the point. And besides, I don't really think he is sorry. One minute he says he'll do anything to save our marriage, but the next he's talking like he despises me. He's said some awful things lately, and you have to remember that for months I was torturing myself while he was busy fantasizing about being with that awful woman. I'm so angry with him, Karen, and it's not going away. I want it to. I can't tell you how much I want it to because I don't want to lose my lovely life because of his stupidity. I was happy for a long time. But if I can't love him anymore..." She trailed off. "Do you think I should just settle for the children's sakes?"

"I'd hardly describe what you've got as settling. You've got a lovely family and a great life. Plus, no matter how determined you are, I don't know if you *would* cope if you left. It's hard out there these days," whispered Karen urgently, conscious that the kids had thundered down the stairs and were in the hall. "You'd have to sell the house, the girls would suffer, and, I hate to say it, but between the two of you, there wouldn't be enough money to run two households. Being on your own would be a nightmare."

But what if she didn't have to be on her own? Jennifer decided not to voice this thought. She also decided in that moment not to tell Karen something else. That she'd spent most of last night on reUNIon, composing one of the hardest messages she'd ever written in her life. And that this morning, after hours of indecision, she had finally pressed Send. She hadn't been able to reason that she had nothing to lose because the opposite was true, but she couldn't carry on as she was. So she'd reached out, fully expecting not to hear back, figuring that even a lack of reply might help her find the answer she so needed.

It was all a mess. She was terrified by the thoughts and feelings she was having. Everything Karen had said was true. Yet, for whatever reason, all she'd been able to see for the last few months was her life stretched out before her and that there were two directions she could go in. Two tunnels almost, only one was a far easier route to take. She could continue as she was, in what felt like a damaged relationship, full of resentment. And who could tell? Perhaps with a lot of hard work and effort, they would get back on track.

But there was another way. There always was. But when she tried to look in that direction, she had no idea what its future held. All she could be sure of was that it was full of uncertainty and difficulty but also of hope, excitement, and change. This route thrilled her as much as it terrified her. The familiar versus the unknown. Safety versus risk. Head versus heart.

"But listen," added Karen. "At the end of the day, I can't tell you what to do because only you know how you feel, so whatever you decide, know that I am here for you. One hundred percent. Always."

It was exactly what Jennifer needed to hear.

Later that night, after everyone had gone, Max put the girls to bed. As soon as they were settled, he came to join Jennifer on the sofa where she was watching the news.

After a few minutes, he took the remote control from her and turned the TV off.

"What are you doing?"

"I need to know, Jen. I can't go around pretending that everything's okay anymore, because we both know it isn't, and it seems the harder I try, the more detached you become. So are you in or out? Because if you're in, you have to forgive me. You have to find a way to forget and to let me in or we don't stand a chance. But if you think you can't do that, then I need to know, once and for all."

Jennifer stared at her husband, wondering why she had to do anything.

"The thing I'm most upset about," she said eventually, hoping desperately that what she was about to say would make him understand, "is that you forgot."

"What do you mean?"

"You forgot what we were about. How good we used to be. How in love we were. Because we were, you know. We were best friends, but you risked all of that for some pathetic thing, whatever the hell it was, with Judith. And the thing is, I get that after years of being together, things can feel stale or boring. But isn't the romance in trying? Isn't that the point? All I wanted for so long was for you to notice me again. I was desperate to get your attention, to feel close to you, because I didn't forget."

"Oh, for God's sake. I'm getting sick of this."

Jennifer gulped. It wasn't the reaction she'd been expecting.

"You act like I'm the only villain in this piece. Well, maybe you should look at yourself and work out why my attention wandered in the first place."

"Wow." Jennifer gulped, stung beyond belief. She blinked back tears, refusing to cry no matter how much she wanted to.

Max sighed. "Look," he said, his voice full of frustration and more than a hint of anger. Jennifer hated how hard he'd become. "I'm sorry, all right, but I'm just getting a bit fed up with being made to feel like some lowlife when thousands of men do far worse than I did."

"So I should be grateful?" asked Jennifer incredulously.

"Not grateful, but more understanding perhaps, yes. I mean, you go on about how you wanted my attention. Well, you've got it."

"Yes, but look what it took. And how aggressive you're being now. You're hardly acting like someone who loves his wife and wants to make amends. You're hardly treating me like your girl in the pink dress."

"This is the problem with you," said Max. "You're a ridiculous romantic. God knows what you expect from me—hearts and flowers and romance probably. It's not enough that I just love you."

"This doesn't feel like love," said Jennifer grimly, sad that he was making the situation so impossible to heal. "And yes, Max, I don't think a bit of romance would go amiss. And why should I? Why shouldn't I occasionally want to feel loved and cherished by my husband? In between loading the dishwasher and taking the car to the shop, of course. And no, you're right, a bunch of flowers wouldn't be the worst thing in the world either."

"So what are you saying?"

"I'm saying that I've had enough. We owe it to the girls to at least try to work things out. But if I'm being honest, Max, I have no idea if we can be fixed. Or if I even want us to be. My head's all over the place. I'm sorry. I know it's not what you want to hear, but I don't know what else to say."

Max nodded sadly. "Fine. I don't know how much longer I want to continue like this myself."

"Fine," said Jennifer, who no longer cared what he thought or felt anyway.

Her phone flashed. It was a message notification from reUNIon. Her heart felt like it had plummeted into her stomach.

Ignoring Max, she grabbed her phone and headed upstairs to the spare room. After reading the message, she stared out of the window and knew life wasn't about to get any less complicated.

She was in control now. She needed to make a decision. Perhaps she already had.

Reading Group Guide

1. Is there such a thing as "the one"? Or is it more likely that we could potentially have a great connection with many people, most of whom we won't ever meet?

2. In the book, Jennifer is able to see how her life could have been if she had made different decisions. In reality, would the ability to relive your life be a gift or a terrible burden?

3. We meet three men from Jennifer's past—Aidan, Tim, and Steve. She split up with each of them for good enough reasons at the time, but perhaps she also wasn't ready to settle down. Are you more likely to marry someone partly because you have met them at the right time in your life?

4. Jennifer is suffering from a midlife crisis. This is a stage that the book takes very seriously and chooses not to laugh at. But what do you think a midlife crisis is by definition? What causes it? And is it an inevitable phase that most of us will

go through, or have gone through, upon hitting the halfway point of our lives?

5. Jennifer's therapist suggests during their session that if she were to change her life partner, she may only be "swapping one set of problems for another." Does this idea resonate with you?

6. Max was unfaithful to Jennifer emotionally and physically. However, he didn't actually have sex with Judith. Should this make his behavior easier to forgive?

7. *If You're Not the One* explores how the partner we choose to share our lives with greatly affects our circumstances. The choice of a spouse or partner governs who our in-laws are, where we live, what we do, even our finances. Are the full consequences of this one decision something you have ever stopped to think about, and would any of the above criteria prevent you from being with someone? For instance, if you had a mother-in-law, or potential mother-in-law, you despised, how much would that affect your relationship and govern whether you stayed? Or are all external factors irrelevant in terms of how happy someone makes you?

8. All of the men Jennifer has been with are very different. Does what we look for in a life partner change as we get older, or do we just learn more about what we want and need in a partner as we gain more experience?

9. When we first meet Jennifer, she is thinking a lot about her life and about her past. Is there someone you think of from time to time and wonder how life would be if you'd stayed with them? Or do you prefer to never look back?

10. Jennifer's friendship with Karen suffers while Jennifer dates Tim because of Karen's and Tim's dislike for each other. In Tunnel Two, it becomes clear that had she stayed with Tim, her relationship with Karen would have deteriorated further. Are female relationships often affected by who friends are married to or are dating? If so, is this right?

11. Divorce is very common, although Jennifer really struggles with the idea of leaving her husband. Do people in our generation give up too easily? Or are we just benefiting from living in a time when people aren't condemned if a marriage fails?

12. Jennifer has two children. Some may argue she should stay with Max for her daughters' sakes, but if she is unhappy, is that really the best option?

13. Should Jennifer stay with Max, or should she leave and pursue another path?

**Do you have a favorite character in *If You're Not the One*? Why,
and what inspired you to write him or her?**

Jennifer is my favorite character in the book. She's by no
means perfect (who is?), but I really like her and can relate to her
enormously. The idea for her story came to me during a period
in my life when, like Jennifer, I was trying to figure a few things
out. On paper, she *should* be happy. But she's not and is hurtling
toward a midlife crisis, unsure of what she wants. We meet her at
a time when she's wondering if there should be more to life and
is asking herself, "Is this it?" I would imagine she's not alone. We
live in confusing times, encouraged to reach for the stars, to have
the best career, the best relationship, and not to settle. Of course,
there's a lot to be said for safe and steady and secure, but only
as long as it doesn't trickle into dull, unfulfilling, and suffocat-
ing. Previous generations were programmed just to get on with
things, and people's reluctance to "put up or shut up" these days
is often labeled as selfishness. Is it, though? I'm not sure. This is
why I found Jennifer's character so interesting to write, because

she doesn't have all the answers, and I truly believe that, like her, most of us aren't completely happy all of the time or completely miserable. Instead, most of us have good days and bad. Life can be beautiful and also sad. As a result, she feels very real to me, and I loved exploring how all the different relationships she experiences make her feel and, to a degree, act in a different way. She's also funny. All the best people are.

Which man do you think Jennifer would be happiest with and why?

I think the man who was her real soul mate and with whom she had the most passionate connection was Joe. Of course, their feelings were dramatically heightened by the situation they were in, but I like to think that, given the chance, they would have made each other very happy.

With the book as a whole, I wanted to demonstrate that most of the time, when we break up with someone, it's for a very good reason. More often than not, our instincts are correct. Therefore, it was important to me to show that had she stayed with Aidan or Tim, she would have been fairly miserable. However, I was also determined to show that had she stayed with Steve, she could have been quite content, thus destroying the romantic notion that there's only one person out there for each of us.

Would you like to be able to see what "could have been" like Jennifer does?

I'm not sure! I think it's something we all wonder about and not just in terms of relationships. I often ponder what might have been had I chosen a slightly more standard career path, for example. I think perhaps it's better we can't and that we just live in the moment and try to have faith in our own decisions and not too many regrets.

If there's one thing you'd like readers to take away from *If You're Not the One*, what would it be?

That our lives are all made up of a series of small and large decisions that determine everything. Who you choose to share your life with is the most far-reaching, for it affects not just your emotional needs, but also where you live, your financial status, your friends, extended family, etc. I wanted readers to be able to form their own opinions about Max and Jennifer. They've got a lot going for them but stopped putting much effort into their relationship. I don't think the book necessarily provides any concrete answers, but I do believe it asks lots of questions, and I hope this makes it an interesting and thought-provoking read. I also set out to try to demonstrate that from the outside looking in, it can be easy to imagine we know how people feel or what it's like to be them, and yet no one really does unless they are in those four walls or in that person's brain. Most of all, however, I simply hope that it's an enjoyable read with some sad parts and some funny parts that passes the time enjoyably and makes people want to tell their friends about it.

Where do you write? Are you a paper-and-pen girl or a coffee-shop-with-a-laptop sort?

Laptop all the way. It's terrible to confess, but my seven-year-old son and nine-year-old daughter have far better handwriting than me these days. When I write a card or something, it's like I've forgotten how to write with a pen. Forgotten how to *hold* a pen even. To be honest, I don't know how anyone could bear to write anything in longhand. What happens if you want to edit a chunk or move things around? This would not be at all practical if using a pen. My next deadline would probably need to be about 2038. And half of that would be taken up just looking for a pen, as in my house, they disappear as soon as they're bought. Full respect to pen wielders. I don't know how you do it.

What do you love most about being a writer?

The satisfaction of creating an entire world and the people who inhabit it. It's the best job in the world and the only really hard aspect of it is coming up with what your next idea is going to be. Once you've cracked that, though, there's nothing better than a day when it's all flowing and at times you've made yourself chuckle or (and this has been known to happen) cry at what you're writing. Those are the moments when you know you're onto something good. The absolute best thing about being a writer, though, is that your only commute is to the kitchen to get caffeinated drinks, you can wear your most comfy (revolting) loungewear, and no one knows if your hair's greasy and you look awful.

What piece of advice would you give to aspiring writers?

Have a good osteopath on speed dial. (Being on a laptop all day is terrible for your back!) When you start to hate your manuscript (about fifty thousand words in), take a break for a few weeks in order to get back some objectivity. Don't write with your audience in mind; otherwise, you'll start fretting about whether your mom will approve and end up restricting what you want to say. Know where you're trying to get to. It's an obvious point, but every story needs a beginning, a middle, and an end, and it helps enormously if that has been thought out before you begin. Also, don't forget to read other people's books! Reading keeps you inspired and keeps you tuned in to what will make your writing interesting and good. Try to think about what the point of the book is. To my mind, there isn't any point if there isn't a point. And lastly, don't give up. Rejection is par for the course, but if you love writing, you should continue anyway. Do it for the love of it, and with a bit of luck, one day your perseverance will pay off.

When you're not writing, what else do you do?

I have plenty to keep me busy. I have two children, and I work in television. I act in commercials and also do TV hosting.

Where does the inspiration for your novels come from?

From this crazy thing we call life. Sometimes I get inspiration from films, conversations, my personal life experiences, or just from musings and imaginings. And sometimes I can be inspired by the smallest idea that sort of catches fire and spreads into an entire story. I usually find that the best ideas are the ones that almost take you by surprise. That only happens about once every three years, during a full moon, though.

Acknowledgments

Writing a book is a solitary activity. Getting it on the shelves, however, is a hugely collaborative effort, so I have a lot of people to thank. Enormous thanks must go to my publisher, Sourcebooks, in particular to Shana Drehs and Anna Michels. For an English gal, being published in the US of A is particularly thrilling, so thank you for giving me something to boast about. I'm very proud to be "coming out" across the pond. Many thanks must go to my brilliant agent, Madeleine Milburn, and to her lovely sidekick, Cara Lee Simpson.

Thanks too to my wonderful family. I wrote this book during a fairly turbulent period in my life, and there are times when that "blood is thicker than water" business really rings true. Times when your family members are the only ones who will put up with you; not that they have any choice, of course! Dad, Sally, Mum, Mauro, Jessica, Isabel, Paddy, Jim, Harry, Imogen, and Georgie, you're all the best. Thanks to my beautiful, funny, bright, kind children, Lily and Freddie, the best kids in the world. I look forward to embarrassing you for many more years to come. Lastly, thanks to Ross.

Not a day goes by when I don't think, "Gosh, you're tall." Then, after that, I ponder how lucky I am to have you in my life and to have your friendship. I love you more than pasta and don't know what I'd do without you.

About the Author

Jemma Forte was a Disney Channel host in the UK for five years and has gone on to host shows for ITV, BBC1, BBC2, and other channels in the UK. *If You're Not the One* was first published in February 2014 by Harlequin MIRA in the UK. She lives in London with her children, Lily and Freddie.

Photo by Natasha Merchant